CW00798345

Trouble in College

A group of undergraduates form a club for the purpose of committing crimes which cause no permanent harm to persons or property; but when an unexplained robbery is followed by a sudden death, they feel they are getting more than they bargained for.

You are invited to spend a week at St. Chad's, Cambridge, and meet an amusing yet typical group of dons and junior members who become involved in a succession of baffling mysteries.

Other Cambridge Crime Titles

R E Swartwout: *The Boat Race Murder*
ISBN 9781906288 006

Aceituna Griffin: *The Punt Murder*
ISBN 9781906288 013

Douglas G Browne: *The May Week Murder*
ISBN 9781906288 020

V C Clinton-Baddeley: *Death's Bright Dart*
ISBN 9781906288 037

V C Clinton-Baddeley: *My Foe Outstretch'd Beneath the Tree*
ISBN 9781906288044

V C Clinton-Baddeley: *To Study a Long Silence*
ISBN 9781906288 198

V C Clinton-Baddeley: *Only a Matter of Time*
ISBN 9781906288 204

V C Clinton-Baddeley: *No Case For the Police*
ISBN 9781906288 211

Christine Poulson: *Murder is Academic*
ISBN 9781906288396

Michelle Spring: *Nights in White Satin*
ISBN 9781906288495

T H White: *Darkness at Pemberley*
ISBN 9781906288532

All titles available from
Heffers
20 Trinity Street Cambridge CB2 3NG
Telephone 01223 463222
Email literature@heffers.co.uk

Trouble in College

by

F. J. WHALEY

Author of
"Reduction of Staff"

Ostara Publishing

First published in Great Britain 1936

A catalogue record for this book is available from the British
Library

Every reasonable effort has been made by the Publisher to establish
whether any person or institution holds the copyright for this work.
The Publisher invites any persons or institutions that believe
themselves to be in possession of any such copyright to contact them
at the address below.

Some of the words used and views expressed in this text, in common
usage when originally published, could be considered offensive today.
The Publishers have reproduced the text as published but would wish
to emphasise that such words and terms in no way represent the
views and opinions of the Publisher.

ISBN 9781906288730

Printed and Bound in the United Kingdom

Ostara Publishing
13 King Coel Road
Colchester
CO3 9AG
www.ostarapublishing.co.uk

CHAPTER I

In the College Hall the members of St. Chad's sat at evening dinner, a meal and function known throughout Cambridge by the name of the place where it is held, that is to say "Hall". It is a duty and function inasmuch as, with very rare exceptions, it is the one daily occasion on which a college, as a corporate whole, meets together.

And here, at the very outset, the author is brought to a pause. Many of his readers will have at one time or another enjoyed the asset of three or four years at Cambridge or, as the next best thing, Oxford. To such fortunate people digressions from the narrative to explain technical points of manner, custom, and vocabulary will be superfluous, or even tedious. But what of those many others who, as they turn these pages, will be for the first time transported to the bustle of Trinity Street, the scholastic calm of the lecture room, the sluggish, willow-fringed waters of the Cam (not mentioned, I fancy), and the trim, grass-covered courts of St. Chad's? Must they gaze upon these scenes as through a glass darkly, and depart like fleeting American tourists with but an imperfect understanding of all they have seen and heard?

A possible solution is to give them some instructional footnotes or a glossary which the *cognoscenti* can skip without further delay. But in the realms of the light mystery story such things as footnotes and lengthy family trees strike a false note. Readers jib at them. They regard such appendages and their study as "too much like hard work". Even the sketch-map, marking with a cross the spot where the body was found, can produce a feeling of irritation. So there must be a compromise. Into this chronicle of events, moving sometimes quickly and sometimes slowly, must be inserted sparsely and unobtrusively a few details of interest and information which, it is hoped, may enable the most unacademic reader to follow every turn of events with the knowledge and self-assurance of an undergraduate of three weeks' standing.

The Hall and its occupants were typical of any Cambridge college. Suspended from the lofty, shadowy roof, where the carved-oak beams curved upwards to meet in points, clusters of lights partially illuminated the panelled walls, spaced at intervals with gilt-framed portraits of past Heads of the college, some sharply defined by a direct ray of light, others reduced to a mere blur of oils, or shrouded in a

5

patch of shadow. Night had robbed the Hall of the beauty of its high mullioned windows centred with coats-of-arms fashioned in coloured glass. Now the only spot of bright colour came from the red robes worn by some of the painted forefathers as they looked placidly down from their frames on the busy scene below.

The body of the Hall was filled by the undergraduate members of St. Chad's, accommodated at three long tables according to their years of residence and numbering about a hundred and fifty. Thus Chad's, though it had grown since the war, could still be reckoned as one of the half-dozen or so smaller colleges, and, unlike some others, could accommodate all its number in Hall at one sitting. At a smaller table, near the top end of the main hall, sat a dozen young men of slightly older and more sedate appearance than the rest and wearing somewhat longer and tidier gowns. This was the graduates' table, occupied by those few who had already taken their B.A. degrees and were up for a fourth year of extra study or research.

The general flow of conversation on all tables swelled to a kind of low, steady roar punctuated by occasional bursts of laughter, together with the clatter made by the arrival and departure of hundreds of plates on the serving-table at the far end of the room, which was partly obscured by wreaths of steam rising like incense from several tureens of soup. The volume of sound was least intense and the general standard of decorum most admirable on the tables occupied respectively by the B.A.s and the freshmen. The former had determined, in the novelty of their promotion, to put childish things behind them, whilst the latter, in the first half-term of their lives in college, had not, for the most part, had time to contract that close state of friendship which makes for hilarity at meals.

At the second and third-year tables a less satisfactory tone was in evidence, especially among two or three little groups where certain tough and athletic elements were concentrated—possible danger zones easily to be recognized by such experts as the head steward, who, from a vantage point on the platform, kept a watchful eye both on the service of dinner and the behaviour of the diners. In these areas, where also tankards and other vessels of supplementary drink were more in evidence than elsewhere, the talk and laughter were at times distinctly raucous, and imperfect table manners were brought to a head by the outbreak of a bombardment with bread pellets. But the steward made no sign. Taking it all round, it was a quiet evening.

Finally, at the end of the hall, on a raised platform, sat some representatives of the senior membership of St. Chad's at what is known as the High Table. Of the ten resident fellows, or senior members of the college, five only were present. It was not a guest night and, since celibacy is no longer enforced upon university dons, some of the married fellows had gone home to dine with their wives and families. The Master was over at the Lodge, presiding at a private party, and his place in Hall at the head of the table was taken by his immediate deputy, the Senior Tutor, a thick-set, efficient-looking man in the middle fifties, having a good crop of dark hair turning grey and curving moustaches after the fashion of a senior cavalry officer. The Tutor of a college performs much the same function as that of an adjutant towards his colonel. Whilst nominally head of his college, the Master, especially if elderly, is apt to become a figurehead and distinctly in the background of daily affairs. Much of the routine and organization, more especially the control of the undergraduates, is thus delegated to the Tutor.

On his right sat the Dean, a clean-shaven, distinguished-looking gentleman in the middle thirties, dressed unusually well for a don in a blue double-breasted pin-stripe of Savile Row cut and with a monocle screwed firmly into one of his shrewd blue eyes. Here, once more, a word of explanation is necessary. The surprisingly unclerical appearance of the Dean is very simply accounted for by the fact that he was not a cleric. The term Dean is used to denote the Dean of College as distinct from the Dean of Chapel. The latter official, an elderly, white-bearded gentleman of most benevolent appearance, was seated opposite, on the Tutor's left, and, as can be easily surmised, was mainly concerned with the organization of the chapel services.

Gale, the Dean of College, hereinafter known as the Dean, was, in an even more direct manner than that of the Tutor, concerned with undergraduate discipline. In his hands lay the business of granting or refusing leaves of absence, or exeats, as they are called, and of checking irregularities, great or small, on the part of junior members of the college.

In dealing with such little difficulties as nocturnal outbursts of riotous conduct, unbridled merriment, or discordant outpouring of music, Deans are wont to enlist the services, as a go-between or emissary, of the one person of whom undergraduates stand in awe— namely, the Head Porter. Head Porters, like rare vintage wines, are the product of careful initial selection followed by years of expert handling and preservation. Outwardly they are generally elderly men of most distinguished appearance, being a blend of an archbishop and a sergeant-major. They are seldom seen in public without the clothing of a frock-coat and top-hat. Like the best butlers, they can be courtly and urbane, paternal and, at times, mildly jocular, or frigid and speechless with outraged propriety, according to circumstance. They are utterly incorruptible and possess an uncanny knack of remembering names and faces even after their owners have left the College for many years. Small wonder, then, that nocturnal roisterers seldom fail to be quelled by the appearance in their midst of the Head Porter uttering dispassionately the time-honoured formula:

"The Dean's compliments, gentlemen, and will you kindly refrain from further noise and disperse quietly to your rooms."

In his office as Dean, Gale was quite a success. Easygoing and with a sense of humour, he never antagonized the undergraduate element by unnecessary interference with harmless rags and noise, but, when required, he had a sharp tongue and a firm will which effectively curbed most offenders without the threat or application of academic penalties. Nominally a university lecturer in modern history, he was an inveterate dabbler in new ideas and crazes, which were at times a source of amusement to his juniors whilst arousing apprehensions and misgivings in the minds of the more orthodox of his colleagues; the more so, in each case, since many of his frequent and changing ventures had a curious repercussion on his outward appearance and costume.

In the long vacation of 1932, for instance, he had returned from a holiday in Brittany with a professed admiration for all things French and, after assuming on all possible occasions a beret worn at a most rakish angle, he had proceeded to grow an imperial beard. In this unusual state of body and mind he had remained until a fortunate chance at Christmas took him into a circle of artists in Chelsea, whence he returned in a velveteen jacket and flowing cravat, and redecorated his room with the most futuristic of pictures. Worse still, the beard was allowed to extend in all directions, but was sacrificed in the spring owing to a sudden and fanatic hatred of Bolshevism contracted at the time, and following an unfortunate mistake on the part of a myopic Trinity don, who mistook Gale for a prominent Soviet official at that time visiting Cambridge. His present smart appearance was due to his having being lately fired with political ambitions. He was seriously hoping to be adopted as one of the university Conservative candidates at the next election, and his present turn-out, the monocle in particular, was intended to further a fancied resemblance to Sir Austen Chamberlain.

The Dean of Chapel, who in particular was accustomed to display anxiety and concern about his colleague's vagaries, was well content at the present state of Gale's mind and wardrobe, though his complacency was on one occasion badly shaken by the Bursar, a dangerous type of quiet humorist, who pointed out that it must be only a matter of time before Gale became converted to rabid Socialism and appeared in a flaring red tie, a thought most odious to the true-blue Tory mind of his clerical friend.

Coupled with his excursion into party politics Gale had shown great interest in the science of amateur detection and had become an omnivorous reader of fiction dealing with that subject; but up to the present he had not been presented with any opportunity of showing his deductive abilities, whilst the impossibility of combining the dressing-gown, carpet slippers, and hypodermic syringe of a Sherlock Holmes with the correct attire of a cabinet minister had prevented him dressing for this part.

The Bursar was, at this moment, seated next to the immaculate Gale. His name was Waddington and he was a plump, rosy-cheeked, cheerful man of indeterminate middle age. Possessed normally of two chins, he was now in the act of displaying a third as he sat comfortably back in his chair waiting for meat to succeed fish, his head sunk forward on his chest and his hands clasped across his ample stomach. He was an incurable optimist, loved to make quiet fun of other people and things, and never allowed himself to become surprised or rattled. Opposite to him sat a young mathematical don from whom little in the way of general or interesting table talk was ever expected or received. Conversation having flagged, the Bursar decided to tease his neighbour, the Dean of Chapel, by crossing swords with the eccentric Gale.

"One reads in the papers," he observed blandly, "what an increase there has been recently in the cult of nudism. There certainly seems to be some sense in the idea. You, for instance, Gale, in that expensive but tight-fitting new suit and stiff high collar, have undoubtedly strayed further from nature than in your eminently simple outfit as an artist or a Breton peasant."

The Dean of Chapel stirred uneasily in his seat and swallowed the bait wholesale.

"Good heavens, Waddington!" he exclaimed. "Don't, I pray you, incite Gale to start going about with nothing on!"

Gale, as has been stated, was no fool, and he at once divined the Bursar's intention, which he proceeded to frustrate.

"I'm afraid, my dear Waddington," he remarked sadly, "that in the extremely chilly and damp climate of Cambridge in November I cannot undertake to go to such lengths to satisfy your rather debased desires, or vulgar curiosity, to study life in the raw. Besides, the movement has no political backing on the part of the Government, or the Opposition for that matter. I fear it would produce alarm and despondency among my constituents."

"Perhaps you are right," agreed the Bursar, changing the subject adroitly. "And how are your studies in crime progressing? It seems a pity you cannot help the authorities over these harmless yet unsolved pranks which have been happening just lately."

At this the Tutor, who had hitherto said little, began to sit up and take notice.

"I'm inclined," he remarked, "to take rather a serious view of these recent happenings. It seems to me that somewhere, in some college, there is a dangerous young man loose. Up to now, I admit, his actions have been comparatively harmless, but I should like to know where it will all end."

"What is all this about?" inquired the Dean of Chapel plaintively. He was a man who lived much in a world of his own and frequently displayed ignorance of the most current topics.

"We were referring," explained the Bursar, "to the series of escapades in which some person, or persons, has committed criminal actions which can hardly be classed as crimes since, in nearly every case, some form of restitution or compensation has been accorded to the injured party. I thought everyone was aware of these little mysteries."

"Oh! Yes, to be sure," murmured the Dean of Chapel. "You are speaking of the loss of the Florentine manuscripts from the college library at the end of last term. But I thought they were soon found again. I suppose Henderson had mislaid them somehow. He is very unmethodical."

"There was no question of their being mislaid," interrupted the Dean of College, considering that, as a student of crime, it was his duty to clarify the position. "It is true that Henderson is absent-minded, but there is no shadow of doubt that the manuscripts were abstracted feloniously from the library. As you know, they are kept in a glass case which, rightly or wrongly in the case of such valuable exhibits, is not locked or secured in any way. In summer, as you know, there are sometimes as many as half a dozen tourist visitors a day who are allowed to wander round inspecting the collection. On one particular day Henderson remembers the presence of a black-bearded man wearing blue spectacles. On the day following this man's visit Henderson noticed, to his consternation, that the case containing the manuscripts was empty, and an exhaustive search of the library failed to bring them to light. On the next day Henderson received the manuscripts in a registered parcel from Bedford. On inquiry the sender was said to be a clean-shaven young man giving his name as Smith."

"Really?" exclaimed the Dean of Chapel. "Well, I had no idea the facts were so conclusive. And you tell me there have been other outrages of a similar nature?"

"I should hardly class them as outrages," said the Bursar. "The temporary removal of Pogson's car was a very ordinary kind of affair."

Pogson was the young mathematical don at the end of the table, and he broke silence to take exception to the Bursar's airy view of the matter.

"I must say, Waddington, I fail to agree with you. This lawless disregard for private property on the part of undergraduates is getting beyond all bounds. I consider the whole thing most reprehensible!"

"Come, my dear fellow," rejoined the Bursar, happy to find a fresh leg to pull, "after all, it was a four-year-old car of doubtful vintage and none the worse for its little outing."

"Perhaps if it had been your own Lagonda," replied Pogson, "you would have been less amused. Not all being bursars, we can't all run to Lagondas."

Indignation had certainly sharpened the mathematician's powers of repartee.

"Being aware of the local custom of borrowing bicycles and other vehicles," answered Waddington, "I have taken simple precautions to prevent my car being started in the absence of its owner. Personally, I think the thief paid your car a great compliment by troubling to drive it away."

Pogson subsided, mumbling indignantly. The Dean of Chapel eased the situation by remarking:

"Now you mention it, Pogson, I remember your telling us about the unfortunate loss of your car, though I understood you recovered it almost at once."

"Then, of course," continued the Tutor, "there was the most singular incident of the abduction—I cannot think of a better term by which to describe it—the abduction of Withers."

"Withers, the Egyptian pottery expert, of Trinity?" inquired the Dean of Chapel in bewilderment. "I never knew he had been abducted. What were the exact circumstances?"

The Tutor gave a slight frown of annoyance. He did not wish to interrupt a serious discussion by going over old ground for the benefit of his uninformed and unworldly colleague. He glanced down the body of the Hall.

"I fancy the regrettable incident was rather hushed up," he replied, "and, meantime, I think everyone has finished, so we had better adjourn."

So saying he struck a small handbell at his elbow, whereupon with a noise like a dull rumble of thunder the whole student body of St. Chad's rose to its feet and the Tutor rattled off a lengthy Latin grace.

Whilst the undergraduates crowded out at the far end of the Hall the five senior members passed through a door at one end of the platform and entered an ornate antechamber also with panelled walls and a gilded ceiling. This was the Senior Combination Room, and at its long table the dons were wont to round off their dinner with dessert and port wine. When the decanter had made its first circuit of the table the matter under discussion was reopened by the Dean of College.

"So it is your opinion," said Gale to the Tutor, "that these three escapades are the work of one adventurous undergraduate?"

"It would seem so," agreed the Tutor, "and it would also seem that he is a member of this college, since two out of the victims are also of our number."

"I'm inclined to agree with you," said the Bursar. "But I should have thought that our budding criminologist would have had something to tell us by now. Come, Gale, have you no opinion on the subject?"

Thus addressed the Dean turned a languid eye on his interrogator, removed his monocle, polished it, reset it deliberately in one eye, and prepared to make the most of a big moment.

"Why, yes, my dear Waddington," he observed, "I have made certain investigations and conclusions, but I hesitated to bother you with them until I had completed my case. However, since the matter has cropped up, I may say that you are right in one particular and wrong in another. I am fairly certain that these three offences are not the work of one and the same man. On the other hand, one case, that of Pogson's car, is the work of a Chad's undergraduate whose identity is known to me."

Whereupon Gale leaned back and took a sip of port, enjoying the sensation he had produced. The Tutor was the first to adjust his mind to sensible comment.

"But surely, Gale, if you know who is responsible it would have been your duty to take action against him. And, anyway, how can you be certain that this youth is not guilty of the other and more serious offences?"

"Suppose you tell us what you think you know, and how you found it out," suggested the more practical Waddington.

"Certainly," said the Dean. "You may remember that Pogson's car was reported missing at about six in the evening during the first fortnight of term, just as it was getting dark. Pogson had left it outside the college at tea-time. That's right, isn't it, Pogson."

The mathematical don corroborated this.

"The loss was reported by telephone to the police, who were unable to discover anything until twenty-four hours later the car was discovered some four miles away, in a lane near the village of Shelford, undamaged and none the worse for its temporary absence. Now, let us ask ourselves what is the significance, first of the times of theft and discovery, in each case about six in the evening, and secondly the locality of Shelford."

Gale had the undivided attention of his audience. Even the sceptical Bursar looked impressed.

"At six o'clock it is just dark enough to carry out the taking and return of the car without incurring the risks of daylight. As regards Shelford, it is the nearest station with a fairly frequent service of main-line trains which would enable the culprit to be back in Hall by seven-thirty. Also, just outside Shelford is the recently acquired residence of one Patterson, lately a member of this college and now a gentleman farmer. Thus it seems probable that one of Patterson's old friends who is still in college prevailed upon Patterson to give shelter to the stolen car for one night until the time came for it to be left for the police to find and restore it to its owner. The whole thing was probably the result of some foolish wager."

"That seems most ingenious and convincing," commented the Tutor. "But how, with a hundred and fifty to choose from, could you pin the thing down to a certain one of the undergrads?"

"In the first place," explained Gale, "one could safely exclude a third of that number, namely the freshers, for none of them were up with Patterson. Patterson, moreover, moved in a certain athletic set containing various likely customers. I therefore took the trouble to conduct a small matter of routine investigation which, as it happened, proved entirely successful. I noted that between six and seven there were two trains from Shelford to Cambridge. I travelled to Shelford, taking with me some athletic groups of our various teams which I had borrowed from the photographers. Arrived at Shelford I interviewed the two station officials present, and asked them if they could recollect a young man having travelled to Cambridge once or twice during the week on either of these two trains. The number of passengers at Shelford is seldom excessive, and thus one of them was able to recall such a young man who had left Shelford on the evening of the theft, and on the following night had arrived by train half an hour previously from Cambridge, returning as on the preceding night.

"There could be no possible doubt that this was my man. I therefore produced my photographs and, posing as a plain-clothes policeman, requested the official to try and pick out the passenger, which he was duly able to do."

"But why on earth," cried the usually placid Tutor, "did you take no action in the matter? Surely, in your position, it was your duty either to deal with him yourself as Dean or else report him to me. It's most irregular of you!"

"Yes," added the aggrieved car owner, "I should like to have given him a piece of my mind myself."

"I don't see why I should," replied Gale. "For one thing, it was a matter outside the college itself, and goodness knows I have enough disciplinary action to take within these walls without going outside them. I consider it a matter for the proctors, not for me. I had the satisfaction of solving my case. That was all that mattered to me. And besides, the youth in question is a very decent young man and a great asset to the—well, I should say a good athlete. We don't want our good athletes gated or sent down."

"All the same," grumbled Pogson, "he deserves to be punished."

"I don't agree," answered Gale, who seldom agreed with Pogson if he could help it. "I consider, rather, that the thief should be commended."

Pogson rather heatedly asked why.

"There are far too many motorcars in this country, and especially in Cambridge," explained the Dean. "With our narrow streets they make life a perfect curse. To use a prevalent expression, Cambridge is awash with cars. Anyone who reduces their number by even a single unit has acquired merit. My only criticism is that the thief should have painlessly destroyed the vehicle instead of tamely allowing it to retake its place as a danger and burden to the public."

His companions received this surprising outburst in silence. The Bursar was slightly amused at the discomfiture of Pogson, who was now inarticulate with annoyance, but, as the somewhat reckless driver of a fast sports car, he felt hardly in a position to subscribe to the Dean's point of view. The Tutor, who was still pondering over the hidden identity of the criminal, was the first to break the long pause.

"You have certainly given us a most clever and convincing piece of reasoning," he observed, "and I must congratulate you on it. All the same, I confess I'm rather surprised at your attitude in wishing to shield the culprit."

Gale ignored the rebuke and went on to develop his theme on the modern traffic problem.

"The whole question calls for parliamentary action," he continued. "I really feel inclined to devote my attention to transport reform if or when I am elected to the House. The only thing is that, with this alarming spread of Soviet influence in Central Europe, it seems my hands will be full with foreign affairs."

It was left to the practical Waddington to steer the conversation back into more topical channels.

"It seems a harmless enough show, whoever brought it off," he observed. "But you were saying that this fellow could not have been responsible for the other more serious affairs, notably the trick played on Withers. How do you make that out?"

"The abduction of Withers," explained the crime expert, "occupied the whole afternoon of a day last month, and on that particular afternoon the young man in the Shelford case was representing his college in a certain branch of athletics, and, I may add, representing it with considerable distinction."

There seemed no way of gainsaying this, and the company digested the information in silence. The Tutor looked thoughtful. He was curious about the identity of Gale's suspect, and made a mental note to find out what teams or boats were representing the college on the day of the Withers case. Another weighty silence was broken unexpectedly by the Dean of Chapel, who had become more and more fogged by the trend of the talk.

"But I don't understand," he said querulously. "Withers can't have been abducted. I saw him myself, only yesterday, walking down Sidney Street. I know him quite well by sight, and I'm perfectly certain it was he."

"Oh yes!" answered the Tutor testily. "He is no longer in a state of abduction, even if he ever were abducted, which I'm beginning to doubt. I think he's in his dotage and imagined part of what happened."

"But he's a most able man," objected the Dean of Chapel. "His book on the Hargai excavations was most scholarly."

His audience reflected to a man that antiquarian ability and modern common sense do not always go hand in hand, in which respect Withers might well be classed with the last speaker; but they were too polite to say so.

"What is all this, anyway," persisted the Dean of Chapel, "about Withers being abducted?"

"I'm afraid I haven't time to tell you the whole story now," said the Tutor impatiently, pushing back his chair and rising to his feet. "Perhaps one of the others will oblige, for I should think it's common knowledge to the rest of the university." And so saying the Tutor bade his colleagues good night and walked out of the Senior Combination Room.

CHAPTER II

At the moment when the Tutor had intoned the Latin grace and turned away to the Senior Combination Room the two courts of St. Chad's stood deserted. In the larger of the two a trim grass lawn was surrounded on four sides by grey, creeper-clad buildings, students' sets of rooms for the most part. On one side lay the higher, buttressed walls of the chapel, and on the opposite side the Hall, built on similar lines. On the south side, surmounted by a tower, was the arched portal of the main gateway. Another smaller archway, in a corner near the chapel, gave access to the smaller court.

A moment later, the large court, lately so cold and silent under the November moon, was filled with a tidal wave of undergraduates and the chatter and laughter of many voices, as the members of St. Chad's surged out from the big double doors of the Hall and began slowly to disperse to their various places and pursuits. A number, mostly freshmen who lived out, made for the main gate en route for their lodgings; some others also left the college for less obvious reasons— the last house at the cinema possibly, or a visit to some other college; single members, mostly of the more studious type, made a bee-line for their rooms and their work; others, in groups, made off with more social intentions, whilst a few more groups lingered on the gravel path as though uncertain how to round off the labours or pleasures of the day. The flashing of matches showed that a number of less law-abiding young men were impatient enough to take advantage of the darkness by breaking one rule, if not two, namely smoking in the court and smoking in academical dress.

An impartial Cambridge man, if asked to pass a verdict, would probably say, "a small college, but quite a decent one", or words to that effect, in reply to an inquiry about St. Chad's. To the casual visitor the colleges of Oxford and Cambridge, like the clubs of Pall Mall and Piccadilly, externally of great similarity yet in neither case bearing any title or distinguishing mark of identity—if we exclude coats-of-arms— must present something of a puzzle. How, they may ask, do these colleges differ one from another, if at all? Are some reckoned good and others bad? What are the criteria of excellence? Success in the field or on the river? Or the percentage of first-class honours degrees?

These are hard questions and are best answered by stating that in these days there is little invidious distinction between best and worst.

15

The main distinction lies in the fact that certain colleges tend to cater for, and thus to assimilate, certain types of undergraduates; or, to put it conversely, there are certain sorts and conditions of student which one could usually be safe in guessing as members of one or perhaps two particular colleges. The Eton or Westminster man who is a keen oar; the medical student who, in view of hospital days to come, is great on rags and rugger; the worker with a close scholarship from a northern grammar school; the horsy gentleman who is a member of the Pitt; the rowing man from the colonies; the dusky student "not of European extraction", and the latter-day aesthete with side-whiskers, a broad-brimmed black hat, and socialistic ideas—all these types tend to group themselves in one or more of the various college foundations.

Oxford, unlike Cambridge, possesses one college peopled with a confusing number of Evanses, Davises, and Williamses, a kind of ghetto, in fact, almost invariably patronized by the Welsh. Whether these concentration tactics on the part of Oxford are preferable to the Cambridge practice of disseminating Celtic manners and culture as widely as possible is a question which, again, must be left unanswered.

It has also been asserted that one or two colleges at each university, wishing to make a special reputation on river or playing-field, were once wont to admit promising athletes without reference to the fact that such entrants were incapable of passing the simplest examination; nay, more, that they even competed for the presence of such athletes by the bait of awarding exhibitions. I am, however, assured that such practices are now a thing of the past, if indeed they ever existed.

But to return to St. Chad's. It may be classed as an average college specializing in none of those types which have previously been mentioned. The college had a sufficiently full waiting list to enable it to fill its ranks from the better known schools, whilst making a careful choice of deserving scholars and athletes from schools of minor repute. Though a small college, they had a boat in the first division of both the Lent and May races and a second boat lower down. The branch of sport on which Chad's prided itself most greatly was, however, Rugby football.

A group of some half-dozen undergraduates which lingered in the court that night was mostly composed of rugger players. Most prominent amongst the little group of second- and third-year men, whose ages averaged twenty, was the hefty figure of Peter Duncan, second row forward in the varsity fifteen and a trial cap for Scotland, thus a big man in Chad society. In contrast to the big Scotsman stood the stocky little Davies, who was a very efficient college scrum half.

The slim, fair-haired, athletic-looking figure in the middle of the group was that of Martin Trevor. By virtue of being a third-year man as against Duncan's second year in residence, Trevor, though a less finished player, was captain of the Chad's fifteen. Next to him and again in contrast was a lanky, untidily dressed youth in spectacles and with a shock of unruly black hair tumbling over his forehead. Though no good at any game, Tom Tanner was the firm and particular friend of Martin Trevor, and varsity friendships are generally of stronger and more lasting stuff than those of the schoolboy. It was an instance of where there was a mutual admiration of opposite qualities. In the case of Trevor there was physical fitness, athletic ability, and a smart and popular personality set off by a certain measure of impatience, intolerance, and a slack attitude towards the sterner realities of life.

Tanner, an ungainly and less sociable figure, bore with patient resignation uncertain health and inability to achieve a secret ambition of shining at some single branch of sport. He owed to Trevor his social position in the best athletic circles in the college, but for which he would probably have remained an obscure recluse. In return he gave the influence of a steadying, philosophic wisdom worthy of one beyond his years. His admiration for Trevor was very obvious and a matter for good-natured comment in the college. He never failed to watch his friend take the field at cricket or football, sometimes travelling long distances to away matches. Thus Tom Tanner had come to be an accepted person among the rugger set, and was humorously regarded as a kind of team mascot.

A moment later the party of four was joined by two more arrivals from the Hall, one a thick-set fellow of medium height and the other built on smaller lines. The former came to a halt directly under one of the lamps which stood at each corner of the court where the grass was flanked by a gravel path. The light illuminated a somewhat scowling and heavy countenance rendered the more pale by reason of the thick, black hair above it. The face belonged to one John Starbright, who was somewhat of a puzzle to his immediate associates. Sometimes witty and amusing, he was now more often morose or quarrelsome. He played a fair though uncertain game of rugger on the right wing, and was thus an accepted member of the footballing fraternity. But he could hardly be termed a popular member, and he had other sporting interests which threatened to displace his interest in rugger and were not shared by many of the others. For one thing he professed great enthusiasm for the Turf, alternately boasting of big wins and lamenting unforeseen losses. At times he donned loud clothes and draped himself with binoculars, departing forthwith to Newmarket or some other racing centre. He was also fond of a gamble at cards, and here, again, his uncertain temper made him a noisy winner and a grumbling loser. He was, as the wise Tanner put it, an anachronism: one of the type nearly extinct in varsity circles of today.

Between Tanner and Starbright there was no love lost, but the latter went out of his way to cultivate the acquaintance of Trevor, who could not make up his mind whether the moody three-quarter, at his best and worst, was a likable person or not.

John Starbright, like Martin Trevor, had a non-athlete as boon companion. Raymond Baxter-Smith, who now stood at his elbow, was a slender, rather dandified youth with superficial good looks and affable manners. He was regarded as a harmless satellite of Starbright's. But for this latter circumstance it was doubtful if he would have had anything in common with the group he had just joined.

The first four members of the party had been talking rugger shop when Starbright and Baxter-Smith strolled up; whereupon there was a pause in the conversation. It required to be seen whether Starbright's present mood was friendly or quarrelsome. He then showed himself affably disposed.

"Well, well," he remarked. "What's to do?" And receiving no immediate reply he continued: "What about a little flutter?"

"I don't see why not,' agreed Duncan, rightly interpreting the suggestion as meaning a party of poker or some similar round game. Davies agreed, and so, after a moment's hesitation, did Trevor.

"Remember you've an essay to do for Bright by tomorrow evening, Martin," came a warning from the faithful Tanner.

"Oh, to hell with Bright's essays!" was the characteristic reply. "Come on, old man, you never know your luck."

A momentary frown crossed Starbright's face. He had not intended the invitation to be extended to Tanner. However, that was what might have been expected. Trevor seemed unable to go anywhere without him.

"Right you are, then," said Tanner, rather reluctantly. "I'll be with you in five minutes. I must go to my rooms and get a pipe. Coming, Martin?"

"By the way," Starbright called to them as they were moving off, "it won't be in my rooms. Colley asked me to bring a gang round to his rooms, so I'll see you there. Don't be long."

Trevor acknowledged these directions carelessly, but Tanner, in his turn, frowned into the darkness and, when they were out of earshot, gave voice to his thoughts.

"That's typical of Starbright," he observed.

"What's typical, old man? I don't quite get you."

"Why to drag in a youngster like Colley, fresh from school, into his poker parties. A pigeon for the plucking."

"Colley?" inquired Trevor absently. "I don't think I know him. How is it he's in coll., anyway, if he's a fresher? At least, I hope he's in coll. I don't want to sweat out to digs half-way to Trumpington or somewhere."

"He's a fresher of the freshest," Tanner informed him, "and has rooms in coll. because he's an exhibitioner of sorts. Which being so, he ought to be doing a spot of work instead of gambling with his elders and betters."

"He ought to be honoured to be in the same galley with the likes of us," commented Trevor.

"That's just his trouble," answered his friend cryptically. "He probably is."

By this time they had reached Tanner's rooms, where their owner selected and filled a pipe. Five minutes later, having inquired the locality, they found themselves in the rooms of Colley, which were situated in the far court.

The remainder of the party was already present. Starbright was seated with a proprietorial air at the table impatiently flicking a pack of cards. Their host was bustling about with coffee, beer, and cigarettes. The number and importance of his guests had also induced him, rather unnecessarily, to add a bottle of whisky to the refreshments, and this was nearly wholly accounted for, in the course of the session, by Starbright and Baxter-Smith. The others drank comparatively little, since Peter Duncan, on his day a good hand at beer, was in training for the varsity match, whilst most of the others were observing the less exacting duty of keeping fit for their college matches. There was also present a friend of Colley's, a freshman who played full back for the college, and this provided a kind of connecting link between Colley and his distinguished company.

The poker game, like so many of its kind, progressed quietly enough for some time, but ultimately tended to rise to high stakes. Nothing extreme had occurred in the way of wins and losses, though Starbright had been winning fairly consistently, and was consequently in a good humour and anxious to raise the limit.

Tanner, playing carefully and well, glanced across the table at his host and frowned thoughtfully. There was certainly no mistaking Colley as the freshman of the party. Though in actual fact nearly as old as the rest, he might have passed as being quite three years younger, the more so as he craned eagerly over the table engrossed in the play. His round, boyish face was a trifle flushed. Feeling it his duty to live up to the standard of these big men of the college, and being hampered by no training restrictions, he had conceived it his duty to emulate the Starbright consumption of drink, though fortunately he had elected to stick to beer. Still, four glasses, even of beer, were sufficient to make his game a trifle reckless.

Shortly before midnight his freshman friend, who lived out in lodgings, was obliged by the rules of the college to take his departure, and this caused Duncan and Tanner to move the closure of play. Trevor and Davies, however, supported Starbright and his friend in wishing to continue, and, as their host was equally insistent, it was agreed to play a few more rounds. Starbright succeeded in enforcing another raise of stakes.

Presently a bout of high bidding left the field between Starbright and Colley. Both considered, with a fair amount of justification, that they held pretty good cards. Starbright made a substantial raise, whereupon Colley paused irresolutely.

"I don't like to chuck in on this lot," he complained, "it's a damn' good hand. But I've been losing a bit and can't manage much more."

"Must take a risk sometimes, old boy," said Starbright cheerfully.

"Why not reckon how you stand?" suggested the practical Tanner. "Then you'll know how much further to go, if at all."

Starbright gave him a disapproving look, but complied with the idea. They had been using counters, and the details of considerable borrowings and lending had been noted on paper. Against Colley's name was quite a long list of borrowings from more fortunate players. Starbright made a rapid addition, frowned, and pushed the list to Trevor.

"Check it up, will you, old man? Addition's not my strong point."

Trevor ran a pencil along the lines and then looked rather awkward.

"I make it three quid, four and fivepence. I say, that's tough! I'd no idea you were so much down. Bad luck!"

Starbright, glad to have been relieved of breaking the bad news himself, added words of sympathy. He felt a little concerned. It was a nuisance the kid losing a packet the first time of asking. Fellows who were keen without being too good were scarce, and young Colley might have proved a source of gradual profit if induced to become a regular player.

Colley himself was even more surprised than the others at the extent of his losses, but strove desperately to conceal his dismay. To one fresh from school three pounds seemed a vast sum. Luckily he had three pounds and a bit over, but he had meant it to last several weeks.

"Oh, thanks," he said, with a brave effort at unconcern; "well, I— I'm afraid I can't back my hand any more. I'm sorry."

Starbright, searching his mind for some solution which would ease the situation and prevent the resignation of this promising recruit, now came forward with a suggestion.

"Look here, old boy, it's tough to drop out of a good hand just for a temporary shortage of the needful; and I feel a bit sore about it, having won a packet myself." He once more consulted the reckoning. "Good lord! I'm up thirty-seven bob. I'd no idea. I don't like winning that much in a friendly game. Now look here. I've an idea. Have you got anything worth a quid or two you don't want, or want to get rid of? If so, never mind about money, but put it up against my winnings for a show-down on this hand."

"But, I say," exclaimed Colley, "that seems almost too decent of you! You shouldn't do that. Besides, I don't know if I've got anything you'd fancy."

The others were also thinking it was very decent of Starbright, quite unlike him, in fact; all except Tanner, who was aware of the science of playing fish or nursing poor bowlers.

"Perhaps you've a hockey stick or something you don't want," suggested Starbright. "I rather covet that pair of hunting prints on the wall, but perhaps you don't want to part with them."

"As a matter of fact," said Colley awkwardly, "I rather value them. They were given to me by a favourite uncle. I'd rather owe money than part with them. ... But I say! I wonder ... would you fancy a revolver?"

"A revolver!" exclaimed Starbright, in a surprise which was echoed by all those present. "That's a queer thing to keep in college. Let's have a look at it, anyway."

"I didn't really want the thing," explained Colley. "As a matter of fact I bought it off Sergeant Stumpy for two quid."

There was a general laugh at this. Sergeant Stumpy was an odd-job man in college, an old soldier with a stiff leg and a heavy thirst which had turned him into an inveterate cadger, borrower, seeker after tips, and spinner of hard-luck yarns.

Colley's purchase was passed round and inspected. Starbright looked it over critically, broke it open to see it wasn't loaded, and clicked the trigger once or twice.

"H'm ... a Smith and Weston," he observed. "It seems O.K."

"Let's hope so," said Peter Duncan, "but if it came from that old scrounger Stumpy I should expect it to burst or something."

"Yes," agreed Starbright, "if it's on a par with some of his racing tips it's damn' sure to come unstuck. However, I'll wager my winnings for it. By the way, have you any bullets for it?"

"Oh yes, a packet of twenty or so. But, I say, this is very decent of you, Starbright. Are you really sure you want it?"

"Yes, that's all right. Besides, I haven't won it yet. Let's have a straight show-down of hands."

"One moment," said Tanner. "I don't quite get this. What happens exactly if you win?"

"If I win," explained Starbright, "I get the gun and the thirty or so bob debt is washed out. If I lose, the thirty bob is still a wash-out and Colley keeps his gun."

Tanner considered this. It seemed a suspiciously generous offer on the part of Starbright. Still, Tanner supposed he was anxious not to choke Colley off poker at the outset. The others appeared to think it a fair bargain.

"Well, then," said Starbright briskly, "let's see what you've got."

"A full house," exclaimed Colley eagerly, "aces and tens," and he put down three aces and a pair of tens.

"Good thing you didn't put any more cash on it," was Starbright's comment, as he threw down three eights and the two of spades. The two of spades counted as a joker, so he had won on four eights. This brought the game to a conclusion and the players most likely would have dispersed there and then but for a chance remark by Duncan.

"Late hours!" he observed. "You should get your team to bed earlier, Martin, with the All Saints match so near."

All Saints were St. Chad's great rivals in all fields of sport, and this naturally led to a renewal of rugger talk. Starbright said little at first, and it might have been noticed that his recent affability had given place to a frown of displeasure. A remark by Davies on the merits of the Chad's three-quarter line finally caused him to break silence. It will be remembered that he played on the right wing.

"Good three-quarter line my foot!" said Starbright. "How can we score tries with that blighter King in the centre?"

King was a promising fresher who played inside to Starbright. In the previous season this place had been filled by a very good centre, a varsity trial player, by means of whose clever feeding Starbright had been enabled to score a large number of tries, but with regard to his successor Starbright had already expressed his dissatisfaction.

"What's wrong with King?" inquired Duncan amiably. "His defence is good, and that was a nice cut-through when he scored against Clare."

"Nice cut-through!" echoed Starbright bitterly. "That's just the trouble. He's so damned selfish. Never lets the ball out to his wing. Scores one try himself and loses another three or so by hanging on instead of passing it out."

"As for the Clare try," replied the blue, "if he had passed, it wouldn't have been a try at all. The Clare wing and full back were both covering you. You'd never have got through."

"I don't see how you can criticize the backs," grumbled Starbright; "you can't see much with your head in the scrum half the time."

At this there was a chilly silence. Most of the others were thinking that such a remark to one of the varsity team from a player of Starbright's class was not in the best of taste. Trevor, as captain of the fifteen under discussion, thought it time to put in a word. It was perhaps to his credit that his tone was quite amicable in asking:

"Well, if you're so fed up with King, whom do you suggest we put in? Suggestions welcomed, you know. Personally, I can't think of any other possibilities."

"There aren't," agreed Starbright, "but the obvious thing is to shove King out on the wing and let me go centre. Let him hang about waiting for passes and see how he likes it!"

"Frankly," answered Trevor, "I think you're more use on the wing than in the middle. What do you think of the idea, Peter?"

"Lousy," said Duncan laconically.

This short comment, given in perfect good nature, served to bring Starbright to a state of extreme ill-temper, and with Starbright in a temper anything might happen. Recklessly he plunged further towards bitter dissension.

"I'm sick of this stupid arrangement. If I've got to go on playing outside to King I'd as soon not play at all. As it happens, I'd wanted to go to Newmarket on Thursday, but you must needs arrange the Saints match that very day."

It was then that Tom Tanner, the most level-headed person in the room, gave way to pent-up annoyance and spoke incautiously. To hear his idol, Martin Trevor, submitting to the rudeness of one whom he detested was more than he could stand.

"I should have thought," said Tanner, "you'd have thought twice before trying to teach rugger to people who are a jolly sight better at it than you."

"And who the hell," shouted Starbright, "are you to talk about rugger? You! Why, you couldn't tackle a baby in arms!"

This bitter attack on one who, as they knew, had been sadly disappointed of athletic distinction by injury and ill-health at school had the unfortunate effect of angering Martin Trevor, who, up to then, had kept his temper commendably.

"For God's sake, Starbright, chuck telling me my business," he cried, "and try to think of the team instead of yourself. You're in the team and have got your colours, so it's up to you to play where you're put and not grouse."

"Is it?" answered Starbright truculently. "I'm not all that keen on you and your team. If you don't arrange things better, and also show a bit of civility, you can look for someone else. I'm through with it."

An angry retort trembled on Trevor's lips. Then, realizing that the conversation was one which both parties might later regret, he adopted what was meant to be a more conciliatory tone.

"Dash it all, you can't let us down like that. I'm sorry if you don't like the arrangements, but I'm doing my best and it's up to you to back me up."

Starbright refused this attempt to restore harmony. "I can't help that. Either I play in the centre on Thursday or I don't play at all."

The tension was partially relieved by Peter Duncan. When disturbed in mind he was apt to relapse into his native idiom, as on this occasion.

"Away and boil your head, Starbright!" he exclaimed. "Or cool it, I should say. You've had a drop too much of Highland dew."

Starbright was already half-way to the door. At the threshold he recollected his manners as a guest.

"Well, so long, Colley, and thanks for the game. Sorry you didn't have better cards."

And to Martin Trevor he added darkly: "I mean that, mind. Centre or nothing as far as I'm concerned."

Duncan sought to alleviate the heavy silence that followed the departure of the disgruntled wing three-quarter.

"Too full of himself, that lad," he commented cheerfully. "But don't worry, Martin. He'll have forgotten all about it by tomorrow and probably he'll play quite a stout game on Thursday. Well ... good night, all."

The others followed him out, leaving a rather dazed Colley in a room full of empty bottles and glasses and heavy with the stale fumes of tobacco. What with the lateness of the hour, the unusual amount of beer he had taken, and the hectic nature of the closing conversation, he was at a loss to make up his mind whether his entertainment of the Chad's aristocracy had been a success or a failure.

CHAPTER III

Aᴛ a few minutes to ten the following morning, King's Parade, the broadest and most picturesque thoroughfare in Cambridge, presented that aspect of crowd and bustle usual at the hours when hundreds of undergraduates were hurrying from one lecture to another. Martin Trevor, with a torn gown over one arm and a pile of notebooks under the other, turned at a smart pace off the parade into the narrower length of Bene't Street on his way to attend a lecture in the Art Schools on the subject of eighteenth-century poetry and drama.

A close observer conversant with the habits and character of Martin Trevor—Tom Tanner, for instance—would possibly have been struck with something a little unusual in his general manner and bearing. The fact that he was wearing a new and carefully creased pair of flannel trousers, or that his hair was more carefully oiled and brushed than usual, might in itself have called for no comment. But the haste with which he moved, the eager anticipation stamped on his face, and the fact that he was fully three minutes ahead of time, all these things would have given the observer furiously to think. They would suggest on the part of Trevor a glowing lust and enthusiasm for the poetry and drama of the eighteenth century. Yet every friend of Trevor's knew perfectly well, and Trevor himself had been frequently the first to admit, that the poetry and drama of the eighteenth century, especially as presented to the public by M. H. Pringle-Perkins, M.A., of All Saints College, was a weary burden to the flesh, a tiresome formality in the process of becoming a bachelor of arts, a thing to be approached unwillingly at the last possible moment and quitted with joy—in short the hell of a bore.

The lectures of Mr. Pringle-Perkins, being university as opposed to college ones, were open to students from every college, including those two which were founded and set apart for the higher education of the fair sex. With the giving of this significant piece of information Martin Trevor's curious condition should at once become clear. To put it bluntly, he was the victim of that actual or imaginary benefaction or affliction, Love at First Sight.

The growth and emancipation of women students have not been without their influence on the general life of Oxford and Cambridge. From small beginnings in a subordinate and detached capacity, the ladies have gradually come to take a prominent and equal share in

24

most university activities and privileges, though, it is true, they do
not yet pack in the same scrums or pull in the same boats as their co-
students of the male sex. Opinion, both inside and outside the two
universities, is divided as to the effect and desirability of this female
emancipation.

Certain writers of fiction have portrayed the mingling of the sexes
in somewhat alarming colours. Influenced, possibly, by films of student
life in America, they present a picture of undergraduates and
undergraduettes gathered together in aesthetic little groups lounging
on silk cushions to discuss such profound subjects as cubist art,
birth control, the theories of Freud, free verse, and free love, being
sustained the while by a diet of Russian cigarettes and vodka.

On the other hand the average undergraduate, when sounded on
the subject, will affirm a very opposite state of affairs. Though admitting
that lady students might at times make agreeable dancing partners or
furnish an ornamental addition to a river picnic, he will assert that
the field of choice is very limited, and he prefers to amuse himself
with his own sex. If pressed to be more explicit, he will tell you that
nine out of ten of them are a set of ugly, spectacled bookworms, saps,
and frumps not worth serious consideration; in short, that there is
very little doing.

This dictum, though a trifle callous and unkind, is nearer the truth
than that given by the new school of fiction. Unlike many of her
brothers, the average woman student comes up with the serious and
exclusive idea of working hard, and has already set her heart on
being a spinster wage-earner. She does not encourage advances from
the male sex and, more often than not, studiously avoids the cultivation
of any form of sex-appeal. Thus, to the undergraduate mind, it is
neither fashionable nor dashing to seek conquests in the ranks of
the ladies' colleges. He will be more of a gay dog in the eyes of his
companions if he can establish familiar contact with a chorus-girl, a
barmaid, or the inevitably attractive tobacconist's daughter.

Martin Trevor, being, as the conventional novelist would say, an
example of clean-cut British manhood, had avoided these latter
distractions only to fall for a girl in his own station of life, to wit, a
fellow attendant of Mr. Pringle-Perkins' lectures on the poetry and
drama of the eighteenth century.

At Cambridge there are two women's colleges—Newnham and Girton.
Lest the ensuing revelations contained in this narrative should tend
to throw any discredit upon the morals and discipline of these
institutions, it must be stated forthwith that the lady in question was
a member, not of the irreproachable Girton College, but of the hardly
less respectable foundation of Newnham. And that was why Martin
Trevor, eager, spruce, and with head held high, was hurrying to the
Arts School that morning in November.

Up to now he had but viewed his divinity from a distance, twice a
week for five weeks, at an average range of five yards. The problem

was how to convert this tantalizing state of affairs into terms of introduction and speech, or, as they say, to get off. In courtships of the baser sort the conditions are elementary. The deserted interior of the tobacconist's shop, the emptiness of Sidney Street on a foggy evening, or the ample elbow-room outside the stage door of a provincial theatre present few difficulties in the process of scraping acquaintances. But to establish contact with a girl who attends lectures surrounded by a bodyguard of earnest seekers after knowledge, and departs under strong escort of the same type, is a problem which might well baffle the gayest Lothario. Such thoughts as these brought a passing cloud to Trevor's brow as he entered the gates of the Arts School.

To appreciate the difficulties of the situation it is necessary to have a mental picture of the lecture-room itself, and an understanding of the usual disposition of the audience. The room was a large one, entered by two doors in the south-east and south-west corners. Immediately inside these doors lay an expanse of floor occupied only, in its centre, by a kind of lectern behind which Mr. Pringle-Perkins took his stand. Beyond the lectern the floor rose in a series of tiers, as in an amphitheatre, each having rows of desks and benches. There were three distinct blocks of desks which were reached by two central aisles up which one could ascend a step at a time right up to the highest tier.

Though these particular lectures were well attended by members of Newnham and Girton, their numbers were generally less than a quarter of those from the men's colleges, and it was the custom for the former to segregate themselves, leaving the greater part of the room at the disposal of the menfolk; and whereas the ladies, for the most part eager seekers after wisdom, chose front seats as near as possible at the feet of Gamaliel, the undergraduates presented an actual or assumed indifference to the proceedings by tending to occupy the highest and most remote areas.

Thus a casual spectator or inspector, entering the room any time between ten and eleven on Tuesdays and Thursdays, would have noted the following disposition of students. In the left-hand block of seats, mostly near the front, some thirty lady students clustered together; across the aisle in the centre block and again in the right-hand block nearly a hundred male students, mostly in the middle and back seats save for a few of studious appearance who occupied front seats parallel with the ranks of Newnham and Girton. During the past month there had been two striking exceptions to the usual procedure. In one spot, on the extreme left of the male sector, a brother and sister, both very plain, flaxen-haired and bespectacled, sat defiantly side by side, establishing an unusual unity of the sexes, whilst two girls of certain physical attraction and of the brazen hussy type were wont to sweep right to the very back of the room and join two tough and athletic-looking undergraduates with whom they spent most of the time whispering, fidgeting, or playing noughts and crosses.

On the day when Trevor had first seen and fallen for the young student of Newnham he had been sitting fairly far back. Having observed that she was invariably one of a row of girls occupying the second row from the front in the female sector, he had since made it his practice to take the end seat at the nearest extremity of the men's third row. From this position he could obtain an uninterrupted view of her profile without himself being observed by her in the process of so doing. Thus she was just across the aisle; but, alas, between the two there were always three or four Newnhamians of forbidding aspect.

A fortnight previously he had made one great step forward. He had, by a stratagem, discovered her name, and in so doing experienced an additional thrill. Esmeralda Fairfax! What a charming name and how suitable! In attempting shortly to describe the lady one cannot perhaps do better than quote a short account given later by Peter Duncan when asked by a friend in Chad's what manner of female had captured the heart of their football captain.

"Medium-sized blonde; quite trim figure and good legs; nice complexion and face, especially when she smiles; slight turn-up nose; looks quite a sporty bit, and Martin's picked a winner."

The method by which Trevor had obtained the name of his Esmeralda was by no means an original one. It is the custom, at most lectures, to check the attendance of students by passing round a sheet of paper on which all present write their names. It is, of course, a defective system, in that there is nothing to prevent anybody to present adding to his own name that of an absent friend, and this indeed is frequently done by undergraduates. It later transpired that this practice was not limited to the male attenders of lectures. Thus Trevor, following the list in its course, was able to see his chosen one inscribe her name. The list then passed through the hands of the other three girls in the row, was handed across to the solitary occupant of the men's second row, and then back to Trevor. Trevor, casting his eye up the list past the one undergraduate and the names of three girls, was thus able to come upon the name he sought—Esmeralda Fairfax. Since then he had striven, without success, to find any undergraduate member of the university who was a friend or relation of the said Miss Fairfax. Fortunately, as it afterwards proved, he had not met with success.

Entering the lecture hall that morning he was relieved to find his new seat, in fact the whole row, conveniently empty. Then he cast a loving eye downwards and sideways to the row already filled with keen young women. His anxious gaze travelled along the row and back again. His heart missed a beat and he experienced a feeling of sick disappointment. She was not there! Carefully he scanned the other rows. No, she was absolutely and indubitably elsewhere.

Distant clocks were striking the hour of time. A last spate of undergraduates swept in through both doors bearing in their midst the two brazen hussies, who swept up the aisle past Trevor with a swish of skirts, a generous exposure of leg, and a fleeting whiff of face-powder. Mr. Pringle-Perkins made a dignified entry, laid some notes on the rostrum, adjusted his spectacles, gazed round the room in a suspicious manner, frowned slightly in the direction of the brazen hussies and their escort, who were sharing some eatable out of a paper bag, shuffled his notes, cleared his throat, and began:

"Last week we were considering together the early career and work of Alexander Pope. The immature nature of his work in the Pastorals called for little notice. We dealt at some length, however, with his Essay in Criticism. ..."

The members of Newnham and Girton, as was their custom, began to scribble furiously, filling pages with notes. The rest of the audience listened with various degrees of interest and boredom. Here and there an undergraduate jotted down some point of interest. Martin Trevor was not listening. He felt forlorn and miserable. Mr. Pringle-Perkins droned through the opening three minutes of his lecture to be then interrupted by the simultaneous arrival of two late-comers through the two doors immediately behind him.

By a strange coincidence the doors, at opposite extremities of the south wall, opened almost simultaneously to admit two figures in approximately the same state of confusion. Through the south-east door came a shock-haired, untidy undergraduate with the face of a country bumpkin and very large spectacles through which he peered round in a nervously short-sighted manner. Through the south-west door came a figure which caused Trevor's heart to leap and bound. It was Esmeralda. She also seemed confused at making such a late and conspicuous entry. She paused uncertainly on the threshold.

"Let us pause for a moment," continued Mr. Pringle-Perkins, resuming his discourse, "to consider Pope's next important work— the Elegy to the Memory of an Unfortunate Lady——" and then broke off, his voice unexpectedly drowned by a sudden outburst of sound closely resembling the roll of thunder.

It is the playful habit of undergraduates in lectures, if anything excites their amusement, to stamp and drum their feet on the floor, a frequent occurrence received with resignation by all but the sternest of lecturers. Late arrivals generally earn a round of stamping.

The present incident of an usually attractive Newnhamian arriving at the same moment as a particularly comic representative of the opposite sex, coupled with an unconsciously apposite piece of lecturing, went down as an extremely good turn and earned a most hearty round of applause. The hollow wooden tiers made splendid conductors of sound. The noise swelled to deafening proportions, and the effect on the two new-comers, as yet unaccustomed to such surprises, was to reduce each to a state of bewilderment and panic. Again their reactions were similar and simultaneous. Both stood for a moment rooted to their respective spots, and then both plunged towards the left-hand aisle, seeking the sanctuary of a front seat.

As they converged on the aisle and did the last lap shoulder to shoulder, a gentleman having the peculiar gift of being able to whistle through his teeth overcame the tumult and made himself audible in rendering the opening bars of the wedding march. The short-sighted undergraduate, completely unnerved, made a dive for the front row, and in so doing gave a sharp bump to Esmeralda, who was vainly seeking a seat in her usual second row. Thus impelled from behind, the unfortunate Newnhamian appeared likely to trip headlong up the step leading to the third row, and it was here that Trevor had his golden opportunity and took it. Leaning out and extending a saving arm he steadied the girl, and in a second had drawn her into the seat by her side where she sat scarlet-faced and panting.

"Don't worry!" he whispered. "It doesn't matter a bit really."

"I'm quite all right now," came her reply, "and thanks awfully."

"A pleasure," declared Trevor fervently, "Rotten position to be in. I felt awfully sorry for you."

"Hush," admonished the lady, glancing nervously round. "People are staring at us."

Following her gaze Trevor was bound to admit to himself that such was the case. To one flank two undergraduates were grinning with a mixture of envy and amusement, whilst from across the aisle a severe and spectacled member of Girton directed a disapproving eye at her rival collegian. The latter edged a trifle away from Trevor and began furiously to take down notes. Trevor felt nervous and at a loss. At all costs he must not allow this lucky and dramatic meeting to be the beginning and end of their acquaintance. At length, seized with an inspiration, he detached a page from his notebook, wrote a few words, and pushed the piece of paper gently along the desk.

His neighbour, who was thinking less of the words uttered by Mr. Pringle-Perkins than of the pleasing manners and exterior of the young man next to her, became presently aware of the paper sliding mysteriously into her field of vision and bearing this message:

I say, would you care to come and have some coffee at eleven? If you prefer, I'll wait for you outside. I say, do come.

Squinting anxiously out of the corner of his eye the writer saw her frown slightly, smile faintly, make a very brief annotation which, at a distance, looked fatally and suspiciously like the word "No", and finally give the sheet a faint return push. Retrieving it with trembling fingers Trevor uttered a silent prayer before reading the brief but entirely satisfactory reply, which was in the form of the two letters— "O.K."

At the conclusion of the lecture she gave him a quick glance and a half-smile before making a quick exit from the room. Two minutes later they stood together on the pavement of Bene't Street and Trevor was proposing an adjournment to a small but comfortable coffee-house near the market-place. Whilst praising the quality of its coffee he thought better than to add that he had chosen it in preference to the larger establishments mainly owing to the spacious and secluded nature of its seating arrangements. It was then that a thought occurred to him, smiting his conscience. His roving eye caught sight of the freshman, Colley, strolling away from some other lecture.

"Excuse me just a moment," he begged, and hurried across the street. "I say, Colley. I wonder if you could do something for me, if you haven't got another lecture at once?"

"Oh yes, rather," said Colley, glad to oblige a football captain and member of the Hawks.

"Well, look. I'm supposed to be meeting Tom Tanner at Matthews' just now. I wonder if you could go down there and tell him I'm frightfully sorry, but I can't turn up this morning. I'd be most awfully obliged."

"Oh yes, rather," said Colley. "Matthews'. Right-ho! I'll pop down there right away."

Thereupon with an easier mind Trevor piloted the lady of his choice down Bene't Street and across the marketplace.

"I'm afraid this is rather, er ... un ... unconventional of me," he stammered. "I don't often do this—er ... sort of thing, you know."

The lady said no, she supposed not.

"Still," argued Trevor, "we're not exactly strangers. I've noticed you since the very first day of lectures and I know your name. Esmeralda Fairfax. What a topping name! Esmeralda!"

Its alleged owner began unexpectedly to laugh.

"You like the name?" she inquired sweetly.

"I should say so!" declared Trevor fervently.

"What a pity!" murmured his companion. "Because it's not my name at all."

"Not Esmeralda! But I'm sure. ... Well, I must apologize."

"Not at all. You got it off the attendance sheet, I suppose. That's an old dodge. But I'm afraid you miscounted."

"I'm pretty sure I didn't. I took great care over it."

"Oh! I think I see how it happened. A fortnight ago Esmeralda cut the lecture and I put her name down after mine. That must have been how the mistake occurred. So it really wasn't your fault after all. But I'm afraid it will be a bitter disappointment for you when you do find it out. It's so very plain and ordinary, nothing so grand as Esmeralda Fairfax."

Trevor asked if he might be permitted to know the truth.

"Just plain Jane Brent," was the reply.

"Certainly not plain!" exclaimed Trevor, now beginning to get into his conversational stride. "And I think it's a very nice name. If you come to think of it, Esmeralda and Fairfax sound a bit high-falutin. Rather er ... stagy and theatrical, don't you think? Now Jane is nice and simple and genuine."

"Still," said Miss Brent mischievously, "if you still fancy the name I dare say I could introduce you to Miss Fairfax. She's very plain and has no boy friends, so she would probably be rather bucked. By the way, it might be as well if I knew your name. I don't want to press the matter, but if some of Newnham want to know who I've been out with, it would sound better if I was able to tell them."

With fresh apologies Martin Trevor hastened to declare himself as such, and by this time they were safely seated at coffee. Their ensuing conversation was as banal and commonplace as most talks between two well-bred young people of the opposite sex who have met for the first time, and may safely be taken as read.

Meanwhile, the faithful Colley, hurrying in the opposite direction, presently passed up Trinity Street and entered the busy interior of Matthews' Café, where he soon located Tom Tanner seated alone at a table. Having attended a lecture just over the road, in Trinity, he was an easy first at the rendezvous, and had already ordered and obtained two cups of steaming coffee. He looked slightly surprised to see Colley approaching his table.

"I say, Tanner," said Colley, "Trevor asked me to look in and tell you he's frightfully sorry but he can't join you at coffee this morning."

Tanner looked up without speaking. Four days a week for nearly a year the two had never failed to meet at that spot for their morning coffee. There was something quite unexpected in this absence of Martin Trevor. Colley felt bound to volunteer some explanation.

"As a matter of fact," he said, "Trevor was with a girl, a Newnhamian, I fancy."

"Oh! ... Ah! I see," answered Tanner slowly. "Well, thanks very much for telling me."

He sat frowning thoughtfully into space. He had heard, without paying much serious attention, Trevor's admiring descriptions of the fair disciple of Mr. Pringle-Perkins. No doubt unlooked-for developments had taken place in this direction. He tried mentally to share in the pleasure of his friend's good fortune, but it was difficult. He foresaw the break-up of an inseparable friendship. No longer could he count on Martin as a certain companion in feeding, working, and the many recreations of Cambridge life; and he realized sadly that he had no other real friend in St. Chad's.

Colley paused awkwardly in front of the table. He felt that in some way he had been a bearer of bad news. Then Tanner seemed to recollect himself. Brushing his usual drooping black curl from his forehead he looked up, and his frown gave place to a smile. "Well, it seems a pity to waste a good cup of coffee. Won't you stay and join me?"

"Thanks awfully," said Colley.

CHAPTER IV

At the same hour on the following day Martin Trevor felt at peace with all the world as he made his way to another lecture, this time held in another college and dealing with the history of literary criticism. It was true that this lecture lacked the patronage of Jane Brent, but the latter had consented to take tea with him that afternoon in the same secluded café. In recent years the rules governing the conduct of the fair sex had become so relaxed that the old system of chaperonage had died out, and it would have been quite in order for Jane to have taken tea in his college rooms, and indeed to have remained there until a late hour of the evening. However, she had agreed with him in preferring not to make such a public parade of their friendship in its initial stages. Besides, he had hopes that she would afterwards accompany him to the cinema.

One load off his mind had been the cheerful acquiescence of Tom Tanner in this novel state of affairs. He had been conscious of the fact that his friend might resent the intrusion of romance into the even tenor of their life together, and his rather shamefaced explanations and apologies had been very genuinely meant. To his great relief Tanner had received them cheerfully and in a spirit of banter. It did not occur to him that Tom Tanner might be concealing his true feelings. Of the only other speck on the horizon, the quarrel with Starbright, he thought curiously little. He had half hoped that the situation would by now have been cleared up by an apology on the part of the surly wing three-quarter, who, after all, was a friend of sorts. But Starbright had made no sign. Trevor supposed that with the coming of the morrow and the All Saints match the affair would straighten itself out as the optimistic Peter Duncan had suggested. The great thing was to win this important match, for in the ensuing jubilation all petty grievances would surely be forgotten.

The afternoon's programme was duly and pleasantly carried out. In view of the morrow's match the Chad's football team was inoperative, so Trevor's tea-party was able to start in good time and be followed by a visit to one of the latest and most successful films. The undergraduate audience, true to its type, received the most supposedly humorous episodes in stony silence, whilst scenes of drama and pathos which, as intended by the producers, were wont to tug at the heart-strings of provincial audiences, drew laughter and mockery from the youth of Cambridge.

Martin Trevor was back in college in time for Hall since he had remembered Tanner's parting reminder:

"Don't forget there's an Amal. meeting at eight-thirty."

It is usual for all branches of sport in every Cambridge college to be combined under one management, that of the Amalgamated Club, of which all undergraduates, whether or not of athletic bent, are expected to be members. A small sum debited on the terminal bills supplies the funds on which the various branches subsist, from which the costs of equipment, refreshments, and possibly the rent of grounds or boat-houses are defrayed. The Amalgamated Club has its committee of athletic undergraduates, and from time to time holds general meetings under the chairmanship of one of the senior members of the college.

The presidency of St. Chad's Amalgamated Club was vested in the person of Mr. Waddington, the Bursar. Though of no consequence as an athlete, Mr. Waddington was gifted with two valuable attributes in the fulfilling of this office—a knowledge of the purchasing power of pounds, shillings and pence and a sense of humour and proportion. The former quality was useful, since the deliberations of the meeting were often of a financial nature, whilst tolerance and a sense of proportion were essential in handling the usual clash between the boat club and the other clubs.

This latter difficulty is one which frequently arises in all save the ultra-rowing colleges. In Chad's, like other ordinary colleges, there were only some twenty members whose interests lay on the river, whereas more than double that number were devotees of rugger, soccer, cricket, or tennis. It is, however, an unfortunate fact that rowing, by reason of the preliminary expense and subsequent wear and tear of its equipment, is usually of preponderating cost in the accounts of most Amalgamated Clubs, a fact which causes frequent friction when it comes to a discussion on ways and means.

At half past eight, then, that Wednesday night, nearly half the undergraduates of Chad's were assembled in the Junior Combination Room, a somewhat comfortless apartment furnished with tables, wooden chairs, and daily newspapers, and, in the ordinary way, not extensively patronized by its present occupants. In the middle of the top table Mr. Waddington spread his ample proportions; on his right sat the secretary, a fourth-year B.A. tennis blue, who, as the president fondly hoped, would preserve a balance in any passage of arms between the boat club and the rugger faction. Round them were grouped the committee, which included Martin Trevor and Peter Duncan.

After the reading of previous minutes and other preliminaries the captain of boats moved the absolute necessity for the provision of a new set of oars for the first eight, but before this proposition could be further discussed, the truculent-looking secretary of the rugger team stood up to say that the prime matter of the moment was the repairing of the sports ground pavilion together with the addition of some toilet conveniences. This was at once seconded by the secretary of soccer, with the secretary of cricket a close third and the secretary of tennis also running.

"Order, please, gentlemen," said the Bursar patiently. "Don't all speak at once. I think we had better consider these two motions under one head. I have already had notice of these matters and I am advised that the first eight, in order to work to the best advantage, do, in fact, require a new set of oars, and that the roof of the pavilion is in bad repair and does, in fact, leak. Whether or not we are justified in spending money over increased interior amenities is another question."

"We ought to have hot and cold water," urged the rugger secretary. "The place isn't fit to entertain visiting club sides."

"It seems a desirable addition," agreed the Bursar, "but you must bear in mind that our present balance allows for little more than the usual current expenses of the term. In other words, we can barely afford absolute necessities, let alone luxuries."

"I don't see," said the rugger secretary fiercely," that the boat club ought to ask for new oars. Only two years ago they had a new boat and cleaned us out of all our savings. They spend all our money and the other clubs get none."

This unpalatable argument was greeted with the murmur of dissent and approval which had long since become familiar to the president.

"Order, please," he said once more. "Mr. Marlow, the question you raise is an important one and of long standing. You argue, from the point of view of the game in which you yourself are most interested, that our funds should be spread evenly over the various clubs. I suggest, on the other hand, that our funds be devoted to the most necessary purposes irrespective of exact calculations. I am the first to admit that the necessary expenses of the boat club exceed those of the field games. If you wish to abolish that state of affairs there is only one course open to you. You must formally move and carry a motion for the abolition of official rowing at St. Chad's. We have had a long and distinguished career on the river, and whether posterity would honour your name for having brought that career to an end it is not for me to say."

The Bursar sat back with a sigh of relief as he observed the deflation of Mr. Marlow. He had employed this little speech in so many words about once in three years for twelve years, and it had never yet failed. He then returned to the pith of the matter. "I have taken the trouble to ascertain the exact amount necessary both to renew the oars and to repair and bring the pavilion to the desired state of luxury and comfort. I propose to submit to you the gross figure for all these items under one head, thus avoiding invidious comparisons of the expenses of our different branches, which we should properly consider as one."

The B.A. secretary smiled at his president's ingenuity.

"The total," proceeded Mr. Waddington, "is just one hundred pounds, and from our present balance I can authorize an expenditure of thirty pounds. Thus it is necessary for the club to raise, by some means or other, the sum of seventy pounds odd."

The meeting received this intelligence in perplexed silence. At length the captain of hockey had a brainwave.

"Couldn't we have an addition to the Amal. sub. put on our college bills?" he inquired.

"Ingenious!" commented the president. "Make the parents pay, as usual. But it can't be done. In these hard times nothing extra can be tacked on college bills without the sanction of the authorities, and that we should never get away with. No, but if I may make a suggestion it is this: The seventy pounds we need represents roughly ten shillings a head. It seems likely that if we appoint a body of official canvassers representing every branch of sport there will be few members of the college who will be unwilling to part with a ten-shilling note. Supporters of rowing will feel that they are buying new oars, whilst players of field games will be glad to convert our pavilion into a species of palace. What will be the reactions of cross-country runners, if any, I confess I do not know.

"So there is a suggestion, if you care to put it to the vote. I shall naturally assume that those signifying their approval will be equally agreeable to parting with ten shillings, and should we have a unanimous vote from the present company, which numbers at least half the college, I think we may take it that the other half will be equally generous."

The meeting unanimously voted it a good idea, whereupon the Bursar clinched the matter by concluding:

"Then I will call upon the secretary to appoint a body of, say, six collectors of prominence in our various sports. They will endeavour to cover the necessary ground as soon as possible. I believe we have great hopes of beating our rivals, the Saints, tomorrow, in which case I should think tomorrow evening would produce a fruitful harvest in the first flush of victory. Shall we say, then, that the collectors will try and bring me their sheaves of ten-shilling notes not later than Friday night? Of course I should add they need not insist on subscribers limiting themselves to ten shillings."

A ticklish question having thus been settled, the lesser business of the meeting was soon carried through and the attendance dispersed quite content, with the exception of the secretary of rugger, who had arrived with the firm intention of having a bang at the rowing crowd, and had, through circumstances beyond his comprehension, ended by voting them a new set of oars.

It was after ten o'clock when Martin Trevor and Tom Tanner left the Junior Combination Room and came to a halt on the gravel path bordering the main court. In view of the morrow's match most of the players were in favour of an early bed.

"There's one thing you must do before you turn in, Martin," Tanner reminded him. "You've not put up the team for tomorrow, have you? Just a small point, but the chaps will want to know."

"Good lord! Nor I have. Lucky I've a thoughtful fellow like you handy !"

He paused irresolutely. Both were meditating on similar lines.

"About that Starbright business," said Trevor at length. "You are a pretty good judge of the side, old man. Do you reckon I'm right in leaving the three line as it is and hang Starbright's grousing?"

"In my opinion, absolutely, Martin. King in the centre and him on the wing. A damn bad show, anyway Starbright having the nerve to say anything about it to you or to anyone else."

"I agree with you. I think I'll just stick up the usual side right away. A nuisance, though, having ill-feeling in the side. I half thought Starbright would have come round and apologized, or else had the whole thing out."

"Yes," agreed Tanner thoughtfully, "it would have cleared the air. But I didn't think he would, somehow. He's an obstinate devil, Starbright."

"Do you think I ought to go round and see him about it? We don't want any trouble just before the match. Of course, he'll turn out. He wouldn't let us down over a match like the Saints, not even Starbright. Would he?"

Tanner looked very thoughtful.

"I don't see why you should cheapen yourself by going to reason with him about it. You just post him to play and leave it at that. ... All the same, I wonder. His last words were that he wouldn't play outside King and, as I said before, he's an obstinate cuss."

"Well," said Trevor uncomfortably, "perhaps I ought to try and see him and put things right. But I'm not going to give way to him; don't think that for a minute."

"No," agreed his friend, "don't do that. Far better leave him out altogether. Still, perhaps there would be no harm in seeing him. I expect the fact is he knows he's made a fool of himself and is sorry he spoke; at the same time he's too proud to come and admit it. Probably he'd be relieved to see you."

"Very possibly," replied Trevor without enthusiasm. He hated rows, drudgery, or, indeed, trouble of any kind, being a disciple of the line of least resistance. "Perhaps you'd come and back me up. You're good at that sort of thing, you know."

"Good lord, no! I'm not a rugger man and have no standing whatever. It's up to you. Besides, I've some work to do and I've wasted enough time already tonight listening to the usual business of the boat club *contra mundum*. Good night, old man, and good luck."

Left alone in the empty court Trevor felt a little forlorn and unhappy for the first time in two happy days. Then he braced himself for the work in hand. He was in doubt which item to tackle first. Almost at once he settled this problem by returning to his room, writing out the usual team on a crested card, and returning with it to the notice boards which hung in the porch at the front gate. Then he went back to the smaller or Craven Court, in which were situated both his own rooms and those of Starbright, only to find that those of the latter were empty. The rooms of Baxter-Smith were likewise deserted. On returning to his own rooms he was shortly enabled to come to the conclusion that both these two men were likely to be out of college until an hour up to which it would not be worth his while to sit up; so he went rather unhappily to bed. Being, however, of a sanguine and easy-minded temperament he did not lose much sleep on this account.

CHAPTER V

There is probably no type of rugby football more purely enjoyable than that played by the first fifteens of Oxford and Cambridge colleges. The standard is, of course, lower, yet the conditions less exacting, than in international and first-class matches, but the average college team is as good as the "A" side of a crack club or the best of the public school fifteens. But whereas the London club player has generally to contend with a hectic rush from the office to the suburbs or further in the midst of Saturday midday thousands, and the public school season is a deadly serious battle of odds waged, as a rule, against heavier and more experienced forwards, the college player can find a plentiful variety of level opposition two or three times a week at the trouble of a mile or so on a push-bike to the environs of his university.

As a rule the games are pleasant without being lackadaisical. During the winter term they are confined to inter-college "friendlies" which do not usually belie their name, whilst after Christmas, when the blues are at the disposal of their various colleges, a more serious competition takes place in the shape of the Oxford "Cuppers" and the Cambridge "Knock-outs". A too liberal interpretation of the latter expression led to the suspension of these matches in the latter university for a few seasons after the Great War, but they have since been renewed.

To the usual run of "friendlies" there are, however, a few exceptions to be found in the cases of certain colleges between which exist feuds, often of long-standing and obscure character, and here the rivalry and robust nature of the play equals or even exceeds the average standard of knock-outs. Such was always the case in the annual winter term encounter between the fifteens of St. Chad's and All Saints. There appears, some time in the 'eighties, to have been bad blood between the two colleges, culminating in destructive raids one on the other. Time has healed any scars born by St. Chad's, but in the case of their opponents, the rambler round Cambridge, in crossing the beautiful All Saints bridge which spans the Backs or upper reaches of the Cam, will notice the absence of one of several large stone balls which decorate its parapet. One day long ago, during a raid made by the men of Chad's, these stone balls were dislodged from their cement moorings and precipitated into the water below. All were recovered and replaced save one, which remained for ever buried in the primeval ooze of the Cam.

Thus, in contrast to the usual inter-college friendlies, the All Saints versus St. Chad's encounter was always a strenuous and earnest battle between sides which were generally well-matched, and was quite the most important fixture on the cards of either college. As a rule there are few spectators at college matches, but at two-thirty that Thursday afternoon both touch-lines were filled with representatives from both colleges concerned, some drawn by the hopes of a good display of rugger, others expecting a kind of gladiatorial exhibition, and others dutifully attending an annual function at which the traditions of their college required them to be present. For once in a way the members of the boat clubs had forsaken the river to lend their support. Probably many of them were secretly glad of a solitary holiday from a pursuit which took them on an average of six days a week for three terms of the year to the willow-fringed waters of the Cam.

The proceedings before and during the match were enlivened by the presence of a barrel-organ which, for the sum of two half-crowns subscribed by the teams of each college, had been present on this occasion for many years. On the stroke of zero hour it concluded a rendition of "A Bicycle made for Two", and began its latest and most up-to-date number—"Alexander's Rag-time Band".

"Your fellows all ready?" inquired the referee of Martin Trevor. This somewhat unenviable position was held, in this important instance, by a youngish, competent-looking individual who was, in fact, a don of Pembroke and an ex-rugger blue, two attributes which were likely to stand him in good stead in the handling of a "needle" match.

"Yes, I think so," answered Trevor. Nearly all the side had been kicking about for the last ten minutes.

"Then let's get on with it," said the referee. "It's gone half-past."

As the teams trooped to midfield, a forward hurried up to Trevor.

"I say. Starbright's not here yet."

"Oh hell!" muttered the captain. "Just like him to be late! We shall have to start without him. Here, half a minute, chaps; we must pull someone out of the pack to take his place."

The All Saints captain, overhearing the difficulty, offered to delay the start for a few minutes, but Trevor said they would go straight on. He did not want to ask any favours from the Saints. Besides, an unpleasant thought had struck him. Possibly Starbright would be as good as his word and not turn up at all. Apparently the same thought had occurred to Tom Tanner, for the latter left his place on the touch-line and hurried across the field.

"I say, old man, it's my belief Starbright has let us down altogether. Hadn't I better try to get another man?"

The difficulty was, however, to get another man. Unfortunately the Chad's second fifteen was playing in another ground and beyond them there were few if any reserves. Tanner, as usual, had an idea.

"Look here. Liddell is on the touch-line. I'll get Tony Smith to run him back to college on his motor-bike to change and come back. Then he can play if Starbright hasn't turned up by then. It'll take a good half-hour though."

Liddell had played for the first during the previous season, but owing to an injury and the fact that, as a medical student, he had frequently to work in the afternoon, he had stood out of the side during that term. Trevor gave a hurried assent and went to take his place for the kick-off, having pulled the most suitable forward out of the pack to play wing three-quarter and told the remaining seven to pack three and four in the scrums.

Amidst a roar from both touch-lines the Saints kicked off, and King, the freshman centre, fielding the ball, made a good return into touch.

It was soon apparent, however, that the loss of a player was likely to handicap St. Chad's severely. Being a forward short they were pushed in the scrums and failed to heel the ball, whilst the deputy wing three-quarter had not the pace to be very effective either in attack or defence. For all his faults and grumbling, Starbright was an asset to the side. Though not exceptionally fast, he was a dangerous attacking player who took a lot of stopping anywhere near the line, whilst his tackling was deadly. The King-Starbright wing, had been, in fact, the strongest scoring factor in the side.

For a time the game proceeded on equal terms. The two sets of forwards played well and fiercely, the red and green of the Saints mingled with Chad's in black and pink, and a welter of legs showing the stockings of many prominent rugger schools, including the red from North of the border. The Saints were heeling from the set scrums, but their backs were not making the best of numerous opportunities. Trevor, at fly-half, and the centres were lying well up on their opposite numbers, tackling quickly and surely before the game could be opened up. The Saints backs seemed a little rattled by this solid defence. Passes flew astray and attacking movements broke down at the outset. Still, they were having most of the game and keeping Chad's round their own twenty-five. A Saints centre, tackled by his opposite number, was further molested by two forwards who seized him by the waist and neck respectively and hurled him to the ground. For the next few minutes he was limping badly and messed up two good openings.

It was soon evident, however, that the Saints left wing, who should have been left to the tender mercies of Starbright, was a speedy runner with a good swerve. Having at length been given an opening in which to exploit these assets, he took a pass at top speed, ran round Starbright's deputy, and scored a try which was converted. It seemed highly probable to those who knew, that Starbright would have saved this try, and those of St. Chad's who were versed in the difficult accomplishment of grinding their teeth did so to a man.

Spurred by this reverse Chad's made renewed efforts, and a mistake by their opponents gave them a sudden opening. King broke away and at the right moment gave to the deputy wing. But whereas with Starbright it would have been all over bar the place-kick, his substitute lacked the necessary speed. The Saints full-back tore across and floored him a yard from the line. The game was pushed slowly back to midfield.

On the touch-line Tanner glanced anxiously at his watch. The game had been in progress half an hour already, yet there was no sign of the fifteenth man. Then, as once more he took his eye off the game to gaze towards the main road, he saw Tony Smith's bike, with a pillion passenger, come bumping in at the field gate. At this precise moment the second tragedy occurred. Once more the Chad's right-wing, though a trier, proved too slow for his place and the Saints were now ten points up.

As Trevor prepared to kick off, Liddell came running on. Trevor paused and then approached the Saints captain.

"I say, old man, our missing man has just turned up. I suppose you don't mind him coming in now?"

"Not a bit; of course not. Very glad he's got here," was the reply. The Saints captain was feeling affable and magnanimous, as well he might.

"You don't need to ask permission, anyway," the referee told Trevor rather drily. "You're entitled to field a fifteenth man. He can come on a minute from time if he likes."

There were now only five minutes left till half-time, and this period passed without incident. When the game was resumed it became clear that the advent of Liddell would make a considerable difference. With a full pack St. Chad's began to get more than their full share of the ball, and in some attacking movements set up by the outsides it was seen that Liddell still maintained some of the form which had earned him a cap in the previous season. The game swept into the Saints' twenty-five and the Chad's supporters set up a roar of encouragement. Trevor received a quick pass from Davies and missed a dropped goal by a few inches.

For the next twenty minutes the Saints kept their line intact, and then King, going through on his own in the manner disparaged by Starbright, dived over the line for Trevor to convert, bringing the score to ten-five. Then came a Saints counter-attack which carried the game into the last ten minutes of its duration. With a supreme effort the Chad's forwards rushed the ball back towards their opponents' line, where there ensued a fierce mêlée almost under the posts. The ball having been buried under a heap of struggling forwards, the referee blew his whistle and ordered a scrum, waiting grimly whilst one forward after another sorted himself out and rose from the mire. As the scrum packed down, Davies, at scrum-half, glanced back and noted Trevor standing stationary straight behind the scrum. It was clear that he was waiting for a second and easier chance to drop a goal, if only his forwards would manage a quick heel. But the Saints scrum-half, to whom it fell to put in the ball, had seen this as well. At all costs Chad's must not get it.

As he stooped to put it in, he glanced quickly at the referee, who appeared to be watching a Saints three-quarter attempt to rush off-side the moment the ball was in. This the referee was doing, but he also had the scrum-half in mind. The referee did not like the scrum-half. The latter's rather strident voice had annoyed him, especially the manner in which its owner employed it in the exhortation of his forwards. Also, when cautioned for obstructing his opposite number, the scrum-half had given him what the referee considered a nasty look. Lulled into a sense of false security, the scrum-half made it as sure as possible that Chad's would not heel the ball from that particular scrum by putting that essential article well under the feet of his own hooker. As he did so, the referee whipped round very sharply and blew a long blast on his whistle.

"Ball in crooked," he snapped. "Free kick to Chad's."

This decision was received by the crowd with cheers and groans. Inter-college matches were as a rule singularly free from penalties. They were seldom essential, and most games were allowed to run without much check on minor infringements. At this stage in such a match the incident was most sensational.

With the time and state of the game as it was, Trevor made haste to take the kick, but not so hastily as to fail with it. Thus, with the addition of three points St. Chad's were being led by ten points to eight. Another score of any description would give them the victory.

For the last five minutes all previous records of hard play were eclipsed. The Saints leader of forwards, a truculent individual with legs like tree-trunks encased in red stockings and wearing a war-like scrum-cap, urged his men to a supreme effort.

"Kill these blighters," he remarked earnestly. "Use your boots."

To which a Chad's opponent responded: "Crash 'em; smash 'em up. We must score again."

A foreigner, unused to rugger, and college rugger in particular, would have been surprised to see the two players in question walking off the field arm in arm five minutes later.

From the kick-off the Saints went off with a rush. King got the ball only to be taken by the neck and borne heavily to the ground, together with his tackler. The latter, wishing to make the best of a good job and finding himself on top of King, proceeded to throttle him at leisure. A rush of forwards added themselves to the duel headed by a Chad's player who, observing the plight of King, drew back his foot and aimed a kick at the Saints man's head. At the moment of imminent impact, however, a spasm of better feeling prevailed, and with a skilful change of target he gave his opponent a sharp hack on the elbow, causing him to relinquish the throttling operations with a cry of pain, at the same time rolling an eye up at his assailant. But his expression as he did so bore no malice. He quite understood. Next moment all three were buried beneath another tidal wave of players.

The referee watched them for a few moments in a detached manner and then, despairing of any reappearance on the part of the ball, blew his whistle and ordered a scrum. Once more, in the last two minutes, Chad's had an opening which might just have been a Starbright try. Liddell came very near it, but a minute later the Saints were leaving the field with a two-point win to their credit.

Trevor walked slowly off the field and joined Tom Tanner. Neither had much to say and both were thinking the same thing, It was not the fact of losing the match which weighed on their minds so much as their conviction that with Starbright on the field or even Liddell for the full time they would certainly have won. At the pavilion they were met by Peter Duncan, still in football clothes. After finishing his scrum practice he had hurried down to see the end of the match. With him was no less a person than Mayfield, the varsity rugger captain, who frequently put in a visit to a college match in search of new talent.

"Tough luck!" said Duncan cheerfully. "I believe with another five minutes or so we'd have pulled it off."

"You were certainly the better side all the time I was watching," commented Mayfield, "but you were short of a man in the first half, I understand."

"Yes, that's right," Trevor replied. "Some misunderstanding. He didn't turn up till just on half-time."

He did not go into further details, not wishing to wash dirty linen in the presence of another college. Instead he changed the subject.

"I don't know if you noticed our right centre, a fresher called King. I was wondering what you thought of him."

"Yes, I did," answered the varsity captain. "Played quite a good game, what I saw of him. Useful fellow. Of course I shouldn't put him as quite up to varsity standard."

"Oh no! I wasn't thinking of that," explained Trevor. "Only it was suggested that he wasn't a good enough centre for our college side, and I wanted an unbiassed opinion about it."

"Well, all I can say is, some people in your college expect the hell of a lot! In Pemmer we should probably be glad enough to have him and we've a fair sprinkling of outsiders to pick from."

"Thanks," said Trevor as they reached the parting of their ways, "that's about what I thought."

As the three Chad's men wheeled their cycles out of the ground Peter Duncan remarked:

"A bad show about Starbright, Martin. I'm thinking people will have something to say about it."

"It seems to me," said Trevor unhappily, "that I'm the fellow who will have to do the saying. I suppose I shall have to sack him from the side and tell him the reason. It's a pity, though. He's a useful player. But what else can I do?"

"Nothing else," said Duncan, "as far as I can see. But I'm thinking possibly there was some reason he couldn't help. Perhaps he had an accident on the way or something."

"I don't think so," commented Tanner. "He's a man of his word. He said he wouldn't show up, and I'm convinced he never meant to play."

"But the Saints match!" exclaimed the simple-minded blue. "Well, if it is so, I'm thinking there's lots of the fellows will have something to say to Mr. Starbright tonight. I shouldn't care to be in his shoes."

"Beat him up, you mean?" inquired Trevor. "Well, personally, I'm rather opposed to that sort of thing. After all, it's really my job to deal with him and I suppose I shall have to get on with it. I don't see that people in general need butt in."

"What do you propose to do, anyway?" inquired the practical Tanner.

"I'm damned if I quite know, old man. I'm hoping he'll climb down and apologize, or something; then we might let him into the side again."

"I don't think he'll do that for a minute," said Tanner.

"I'd rather like to be handling him myself," said Duncan. "Just the two of us, with or without gloves."

They were now pedalling back towards home, and as they approached more crowded thoroughfares it became difficult to keep up this serious discussion. When they had reached the college and were putting their machines in the shed Peter Duncan said:

"Come and have some tea in my rooms when you've changed, Martin, and you, Tom. Then we might get some ideas about this blasted affair."

"Sorry, I can't," replied Trevor rather awkwardly. "I've a date to be out to tea as soon as poss."

"Oh! Ah! Quite, old man," said Duncan, making a somewhat clumsy attempt at being extremely tactful. "I quite get you." He was well aware of the romance which had begun in the lecture room of Mr. Pringle-Perkins, and his surmise was quite correct. Trevor had arranged to do a late tea and film with Jane Brent. He was, however, meaning to be back for Hall in order afterwards to take part in collecting the subscriptions for the expenses voted at the Amalgamated Club meeting. So far he had done nothing about it, and the money was due to be paid in to the Bursar on the following evening.

He hurried through a quick bath and change, reflecting, almost with a feeling of guilt, that the excitement of the match and the subsequent worry over Starbright had very nearly made him forget all about Jane. Soon, however, over tea and crumpets, his feelings were reversed. Chad's and all its works seemed quite remote. So remote, in fact, that at the end of the big picture he realized with slight dismay that it wanted exactly three minutes to the start of Hall. Wherever else he was to dine, it would certainly not be there. The Newnham evening meal was luckily timed to start fifteen minutes later, and Jane, hopping nimbly on an opportune bus, departed in haste with a good chance of being punctual.

Left to himself, Trevor hesitated what to do next. He was uncommonly hungry and had nearly an hour to fill in before Hall would end and it would be worth while returning to start his round of collecting money, and, more important still, try to come to some understanding with the defaulting wing three-quarter. He decided to walk to a snack bar in Trinity Street where it was possible to satisfy the inner-man at reasonable expense, and having ample time, he sauntered gently in that direction and in due course reached his destination.

It is sometimes the case that when one has more than sufficient time to carry out a certain programme, time on one's hands in fact, one takes longer than the ample time allowed and ends up by being late. The initial lack of necessity for considering time leads to its being finally and fatally overlooked. In this way Trevor was late for the second time that evening. It was his intention to consume at leisure a large portion of bread and cheese, together with a pint of beer. This he had almost finished, when he was joined at the bar by two old schoolfellows from Trinity whom he had not seen for some weeks. As a result of this meeting he remained to consume two more half-pints and talk at length about the past and the present. In a conversational lull he was surprised to find it was nearly nine o'clock. Hall would have finished half an hour by the time he was back in college, and much valuable collecting time had already elapsed. He excused himself and hurried back to college.

He had decided first to seek out Starbright and thus tackle the most unpleasant job to start with. What he was going to say he had no exact idea. That would appear largely to depend on Starbright. Entering Craven Court he passed through the ground entrance to the staircase on the first floor, of which Starbright's rooms were situated. As he climbed the stairs he heard a confused noise of voices from above. Apparently there was company already present. That would be rather a nuisance. He paused at the half-way level where there was a turn in the stairs, a wise move as it turned out a moment later.

As he stood thus, wondering whether to advance or retreat, he was startled by a loud and sudden bang, as of a gun being fired from the top of the stairs. The next moment there was a wild rush of footsteps and about ten young men tumbled downstairs in the greatest haste and disorder. Trevor was almost swept off his feet by the rush, but managed to flatten himself against the angle of the wall, leaving a gangway for the runners, who tore past without seeming to notice him. In the confused moment of their passing he noticed they were mostly members of the fifteen, including Davies, the scrum-half. If, as he could hardly believe, somebody up above was indulging in a little shooting practice, it seemed prudent to Trevor in some measure to follow their example. He turned and hurried, though with less precipitation, to the court doorway whence he took a couple of uncertain steps out on to the gravel. Looking up towards the floor above he could see some wisps of smoke dispersing in the moonlight.

In the distance came a patter of footsteps from the others, who were dispersing like rabbits bolting to their holes.

Almost immediately the forces of authority took the place of the vanishing party of undergraduates. Alarmed by the noise the Tutor and the Dean made a hurried appearance from the side door of the Senior Combination Room, whilst, from the opposite direction, the impressive figure of the Head Porter approached with considerably more dignity. Trevor, lingering in astonishment, was spotted by the two dons. He meditated flight, but then thought better of it. It would suggest a guilt which certainly did not apply to him.

"What is this, Mr. Trevor?" said the Tutor rather breathlessly. "Are you responsible for this—er—uproar?"

"I'm afraid I can't tell you, sir," answered Trevor quite truthfully. "I heard a kind of bang quite close, but I've no idea what it was."

"H'm ..." said the Tutor doubtfully. "You seem to be the only person on the spot. It seems curious you know nothing of it. You cannot tell us what is the meaning of it? It sounded distinctly like an explosion."

"That's what I thought, too," agreed Trevor amiably, but unhelpfully, and then relapsed into silence. The Tutor paused, at a loss how to proceed. The Dean, his detective instincts aroused, now took up the running. During the Tutor's unproductive inquiry he had been looking up at the windows and sniffing the air.

"It would seem to me," he observed, "that some kind of firearm has lately been discharged. You do not appear to be armed, Mr. Trevor, and I take it you do not plead guilty to having been doing any shooting. May I ask if you have been shot at, or seen any evidence of shooting?"

"No, sir. I saw nothing. I just heard a bang."

"May I ask what you were doing here at the precise moment?" pursued Gale. "This does not appear to be where you yourself reside."

"No, sir," agreed Trevor. "I have only just come into college and was just going upstairs to call on a man on this staircase, when I heard the bang and came down to investigate."

"You've only just come into college?" repeated the Dean. "Then it seems you have been breaking regulations, for you don't appear to have a cap and gown with you."

Members of the university are obliged to wear academical dress in the street at night.

"However," continued the Dean, "that is neither here nor there. If you have succeeded in eluding the proctors I can only congratulate you."

"I was out earlier in the evening and by mistake didn't get back in time for Hall," explained Trevor, who was beginning to feel a criminal in spite of himself. "That's why I hadn't a gown. I had to stay out and get some supper."

"Well, never mind," said the Dean more amiably. "If you don't know anything, you don't, and if you do, I suppose you will hold your tongue. That's only to be expected." He turned to the Tutor. "I suggest we inquire in some of these rooms. I notice curious faces at most of the windows, but in one, Mr. Starbright's, I think, there is no face. That room will probably bear investigation."

"Yes, a good idea," agreed the Tutor quite impressed by his colleague's handling of the situation. He turned to the Head Porter, who had been standing silently in the background.

"Can you throw any light on this, Meadows?"

"I regret, sir, no. I heard an explosive sound and came out of the Lodge to investigate. As I did so I was conscious that some gentlemen were running away from the spot, but I saw or recognized nobody."

At this moment a figure, unseen by the little group on the gravel, detached itself from the shadow of a neighbouring doorway and walked slowly into the little circle. Trevor saw it was a rather amusing Irishman called Sullivan, a member of his forward line.

"Excuse me, sir," said Sullivan, addressing the Tutor as senior member present.

The Tutor and the Dean, both a little startled by his unexpected and unheard approach, asked rather sharply what he wanted.

"I was afraid you might have been disturbed by that bang just now and had possibly come to see what was the cause of it."

"We most certainly were disturbed," answered the Tutor with asperity, "and we wish to know the cause. May I ask what you have to say about it, Mr. Sullivan?"

"Rather a foolish little mishap," explained Sullivan airily. "It happened that some of us had come across a firework apparently left over from the fifth of November. We made the mistake of believing it to be a comparatively silent article producing gold and silver rain—a very pretty effect. Unfortunately it proved to be some type of squib or cracker and exploded with a single, loud report. We were most startled. I hope it has caused no serious inconvenience, sir."

The Tutor gave a kind of snort.

"Really, Mr. Sullivan! Stupid, senseless thing to do! ... Disturbing the whole college. You know fireworks are forbidden in college. It is most irregular. I suppose nobody was hurt."

"Oh no, sir! A very stupid thing, I agree, sir."

"Of course you were not the person who let it off," observed the Dean rather acidly. He was becoming tired of the Tutor's methods of procedure.

"Me? Oh no, sir!"

"A very curious firework," was the Dean's summing up. "Both in sound and smell it produces a remarkably good imitation of a revolver. Well, I don't think we need detain either of you any longer. And you might tell your friends who are peering round the corner of that doorway that there is nothing further for them to wait for; or there had better not be, I should say."

Sullivan acknowledged with a grin a brain and wit the equal of his own, bade the company good night, and went away to his rooms.

As the dons moved off to finish their interrupted glasses of port, Martin Trevor was left wondering what to do next. He shared the Dean's doubts as to the accuracy of the statement just made by the affable Sullivan. His best plan was to try and find out what had happened. With this object in view he set off to find Tom Tanner, and failing him, the scrum-half, Davies.

Whilst Martin Trevor and Jane Brent had been improving their acquaintance, events concerning the conduct of Starbright had gradually been moving towards a crisis. The bulk of the Chad's supporters were unaware of the quarrel which he had originated, and at first busied themselves by inquiries about his absence made to other members of the team. The latter, most of whom were very angry and disappointed, made no secret of what had really happened, and in the interval between tea and Hall the college buzzed with growing indignation.

Among the members of the team Starbright had few friends and one or two definite enemies, of whom one of the chief was Davies, a leader of thought and action in his own circle. Thus it was a matter of no surprise to Tom Tanner, as he sat as a somewhat unusual guest at the tea-table of Peter Duncan, when there was a loud knock at the door and some half-dozen footballers, headed by the scrum-half, trooped into the room. Their general air was one of gloom.

"Do you know where Martin is?" asked Davies. "We thought he might be here."

"He's out and won't be back till Hall," replied Duncan. "Any of you chaps want some tea? I don't know if there are enough cups and things, but still ..."

"We've had it, thanks," said Davies rather shortly. "Damn it, though! It's a nuisance Martin being out just now. It's about this blasted Starbright. Something must be done about him. The whole college is furious. We can't take a thing like that lying down!"

"I suppose there's no question of his having had an accident on the way or anything," suggested Tanner. "Has anyone seen him or spoken to him? One wants to be sure before thinking the worst."

"It's the worst right enough," exclaimed Davies angrily. "Just as we'd finished changing we saw him in the court. I was going to tackle him about it, and he damn' well walked off out of college without a word and hasn't come back since."

"I think Martin means to see him and ask for an explanation when he gets back," said Peter Duncan. "So I suppose we must wait and see what comes of that."

"All that will come of it, I should think, would be that Martin will get a sock on the jaw," commented Davies.

"Just as likely Starbright will," retorted Tanner, quick to stand up for his friend.

"It's not good enough," went on Davies. "Starbright can't get away

with it like that. We must do something about it. The rest of the
college will expect it. They're furious."

"Well, what do you propose we do?" asked the practical Duncan.

"Something damned unpleasant," answered Davies. "The thing is,
though, to find him at home."

"Beat him up," suggested a wing forward.

"De-bag him," said an advocate of less painful methods.

Duncan considered these proposals. Although on the football field
he did not err on the side of humane considerations, he was not an
exponent of violence in everyday affairs. Least of all did he derive
any amusement from seeing a single person set on by a mob. "I rather
think," he said, "that Martin would rather you waited till he has
decided what's best to be done. After all, it's really his job to decide
what's best."

"Well, he should be here to decide it. Meantime the rest of the
college expects action to be taken. Let's take it, I say."

There was a murmur of approval from the Davies contingent.

"I agree with Peter Duncan," said Tanner, whose opinion had not
been asked.

"Then you won't join in with us?" asked Davies. "You don't sympathize
with the blighter, surely?"

"Not in the least," replied Tanner, "but I'm not a member of the
team, worse luck, so I've no right to interfere with anyone who is.
Also, I think you should wait for Martin's opinion."

"That's so," said Davies thoughtfully. Like others he had a kind of
respect for the words of this unkempt, spectacled non-athlete; and
then he was Trevor's best friend. "What do you think, Peter?"

"Martin will be back for Hall," he reminded them. "Why not leave it
a bit and hear what he has to say? Personally, I'm for doing whatever
he thinks. In a way I don't count in this, as I wasn't playing, and I
never did think much of these beat-ups. Now if I could have had the
gloves on for a few minutes with Mr. Starbright ..."

This compromise had the effect of postponing any immediate action,
and the punitive expedition withdrew to await the return of the football
captain. Unfortunately for Starbright the hour of Hall found Trevor
still out of college.

Five minutes before that time the unfortunate cause of all this trouble
walked grimly into college and up to his rooms. He had half thought
of remaining out in the hopes that the storm might then have time to
abate, but this plan he quickly dismissed from his mind. By his own
reckless conduct he had got himself into a mess which no temporizing
would diminish. He must at least meet the trouble half-way. Already
he had thought out the probable turn of events and had set out
methodically to cope with them. Under his arm he was carrying a
large paper bag which he had just brought from a grocer's shop.

He entered his room half expecting to find it a desolation of
destruction, for such was one method by which undergraduates were

wont to signify disapproval of one of their number. However, all was in order. His room had not been ragged. Doubtless, he reflected grimly, any callers would wait until the owner was at home. The bell was now ringing, so he made his way across the court and into Hall.

As he sat down and began on a plate of soup he was at once conscious of tension in the air. He was the recipient of many glances, some curious and others openly hostile. His neighbours seemed to draw away a little, and carried on conversations in low-toned groups. Baxter-Smith, sitting next to him as usual, appeared acutely uncomfortable. Having made some futile remarks about the weather, he confined himself strictly to a contemplation of his own plate.

Starbright's thoughts, as he ploughed grimly through his meal, were as gloomy as could be. What a fool he had been to antagonize everyone in such a purposeless manner! How different things would have been that night had he played a good game and his side had won! Then everything would have been joyful and hilarious. His own previous bad temper would doubtless have been forgotten and forgiven. As it was, he had rendered himself a social outcast and had gone too far for his pride to admit of any climbing down. Nor was that all. Another and even more serious crisis in his affairs was impending, and that very night might hold more momentous consequences than even the wrath of all St. Chad's could bring forth. What a fool he had been to let himself in for this trumpery football row at such a time as this! Still, Starbright had brains of a sort coupled with obstinacy and strong resolution. He set himself grimly to compete with both his immediate problems.

The head steward, looking down on the assembly, reflected how strangely quiet they all were that night, even for the occasion of a notable defeat. There had been some muddle over the full side turning up punctually, he understood. The assistant chef, a keen follower of the game, had been present and reported something of the kind, though he had not been clear about the precise facts. Queer what a difference winning or losing a match made to these young men! They were really just like so many children.

When the Latin grace had been said and the diners surged out of the hall, Starbright strode quickly away with never a glance to right or left. A crowd of freshers fell nervously apart to make way for him as though afraid of being defiled by contact with him. He overtook his friend.

"Coming up for some coffee, Baxter?"

Baxter-Smith started and gave a nervous glance round.

"Er—not tonight, old man. I've—er—spot of work I simply must finish."

"I thought you would have," answered Starbright, with a grim smile, and made off to his rooms without another word or a glance.

Baxter-Smith uncomfortably followed his example. That weak, foppish young man was fully conscious that he had failed his friend when, for once in a way, he might have been some use. After some ten minutes' pondering his better and sterner feeling at last prevailed. He would go across and join Starbright. As he entered Craven Court he observed, on the opposite path, a party about a dozen strong, mostly rugger players and led by Davies, which seemed to be heading for the same destination as himself. He paused uncertainly in the shadow of a buttress and then slunk back to his own rooms.

At the conclusion of Hall the anti-Starbright footballers had gathered in the rooms of Davies, who had sought to stimulate the unanimity and resolution of the party by broaching a full bottle of whisky.

"Well," he said, "you see how it is. Trevor hasn't turned up at all, so we're no further on in this business. The fact is, it seems to me he's a little gutless over this business. He was too easy with Starbright on Tuesday night when the row occurred. Damned offensive the man was, and Trevor, look you, taking it all lying down."

Whisky and a grievance were making Davies unusually Celtic.

"It's no good mucking about any longer," declared another of the Council of Action. "Let's go and have it out with the fellow."

"What's the plan exactly?" asked a forward.

"It seems to me," said Sullivan, who liked to see fair play, "that we ought to see first if he has anything to say for himself. He may have some reason or other."

"Oh, quite," agreed Davies. "We'll hold a trial and then decide what the punishment will be."

"A pity there's no pond or fountain in college," said a forward regretfully. "Still, I expect we shall be able to think out something as we go along."

"Well, finish up those drinks and let's get a move on," exclaimed Davies.

"Isn't Peter Duncan in this act?" asked Sullivan. He somehow felt that the presence of the blue would have made the whole thing more satisfactory.

"I don't know," answered Davies, rather untruthfully. "He knows all about it, so I expect he'll roll up sometime. Come on, chaps, and let's go quietly. If there's going to be a rough house, we don't want to attract attention before we need."

The party moved in purposeful silence across Craven Court.

"He's in," whispered the full back. "There's a light in his room."

The party quietly climbed the stairs and the vanguard came to a halt outside Starbright's door.

"And his oak isn't sported."

Varsity slang is tending to decrease in these days, but a locked door is still a sported oak. Nearly all sets of rooms in college have two doors, one with an ordinary handle and an outer door with a lock. The latter is nearly always found to stand permanently open save on the rare occasions when its owner wishes to seclude himself for hard work or other reasons. Starbright's outer door was, as usual, open.

"Too easy," commented Sullivan. "Do we knock or walk right in?"

Davies answered this question without speaking by striking the door a thump with his fist and walking straight in. The three or four immediately behind him also entered the room, and then all stopped short in surprise at what they saw.

In the far corner of his room, next to the window, Starbright sat in a little triangular space against the wall. Between him and his visitors lay an effective barricade in the shape of a large table dragged up to the corner with its edges touching the two walls and further strengthened by the flanking protection of two arm-chairs. He sat watching them in silence with one arm resting on the table and holding in his other hand an egg. On the table was a large plate of eggs, also a revolver and a small packet of cartridges.

The head of the advancing column halted in momentary astonishment and then gave a lurch forward, impelled against its will by the pressure of those behind.

"Hullo!" said the owner of the room inhospitably. "What can I do for you, Davies?"

"Hullo!" echoed the gentleman thus addressed. He was considerably taken aback. "What's the idea of all this?"

"I should have thought that would be obvious, even to you. And just keep where you are, will you?"

Davies, who had begun to edge forward, stepped back again, for Starbright had half risen in his chair and was drawing back the hand containing the egg.

"I don't know how many of you there are," continued Starbright, "but two at a time will be enough to go on with. The rest of you keep out. Suppose I take in you and Trevor for a start. Where is your captain, by the way?"

"He's not here at the moment," said Davies irritably, "but I expect he will be along any minute. And look here: you might as well cut out this funny business. We've all come to have a word with you and we're damn' well going to have it."

Protesting voices from outside the door were heard requesting those in front to move along and asking what the hell the delay was about. Davies decided that action must take the place of words.

"Come on, chaps!" he cried, and stepped quickly forward. As he did so, an egg flew very close past his left ear and burst in the face of the full back, who uttered a cry of anguish and jumped sharply back. His jump landed him on the toes of a forward who carried on the retirement, and sent back a bump which travelled back amongst the others, as when a line of trucks is being shunted. The last man of all lost his balance and fell downstairs.

Sullivan, fourth man from the front and not far from being the recipient of the egg, chuckled in ungrudging admiration of the defence tactics. Davies returned to verbal parley.

"Look here, Starbright," he said, "you might as well give in. You'll only get hell if you don't. You can't keep this up for ever, you know.

The longer you muck about, the worse it will be for you."

"I can keep it up a good time yet," retorted Starbright. "And, anyway, what do you want? I'll talk with any two of you, but not with a whole mob."

"We were going to ask for an explanation of your rotten conduct today. But as it is, all I'm going to do is to get my hands on you and half kill you."

"You'll have your work cut out," commented Starbright. "As a last line of defence I have this gun, as you see."

Davies was no coward, nor was he a fool. He dismissed the threat with a short laugh.

"Don't be an ass. You know damn' well you daren't shoot at us. You'd better put it away before there's an accident."

"No. I shouldn't be such a fool as to shoot at you. But if I'm rushed, I'll shoot out of the window. That'll bring the dons out pretty quick and the explanations will be up to you. Meantime I shall go quietly to bed."

"There's something in that," murmured Sullivan to his neighbour.

Davies, however, did not mean to retreat without a fight. He withdrew his vanguard to the doorway and conferred with them in low tones. Starbright picked up another egg and shifted his revolver nearer. He also put a heavy book within easy reach. Davies, followed by his vanguard, began to edge back into the room. Outside, the main body could be heard shuffling forward.

"Stay where you are !" cried Starbright sharply.

Davies paused for a moment, gave a quick look round, suddenly shouted "Go!" and leaped forward with one arm curved to shield his face against eggs. Six of his followers, also with bent arms, rushed after him. The rearguard became temporarily jammed in the doorway.

Letting fly two eggs with good effect, Starbright saw, nevertheless, that he would soon be overpowered. Already three of the enemy were dragging at the table, whilst the astute Sullivan, attacking in flank, had slung aside one of the protecting arm-chairs. However, he had still one more shot in his locker before the literal one which should be his S O S to the forces of law and order. Grabbing the large book, he flung it accurately at the single light which hung in the middle of the room.

There was a pop and a tinkle of broken glass. The room was plunged in total darkness. Starbright hurled four more eggs to the front and flanks. There was the sound of a heavy impact followed by cries and curses. The rearguard, coming up in haste, had become entangled with their forerunners. But the respite was only temporary. The table was jerked violently forward and a clutching hand seized Starbright's coat. Starbright clenched his fist and aimed a blow above and beyond the hand. He felt his fist land on something hard and bony, and the grip on his coat relaxed. Snatching up the revolver he leaned out of the window, took an aim at the grass in the middle of the court, and pulled the trigger.

There was a red spurt of flame and a deafening explosion. The attackers stood rooted in their places, except three, who continued the process of sorting themselves out and rising from the floor.

Davies swore roundly.

Sullivan, taking a quick appreciation of the situation, issued the next order.

"It's no go, chaps," he shouted. "Beat it, everybody!"

In a little over five seconds the room was empty and still. Starbright took a quick look out of the window. There was a stir and sound of voices in the distance and other windows were being opened. Thereupon he set quickly to work. Hurrying into his bedroom he thrust the revolver into a drawer. Then he took the electric light bulb and rapidly transferred it to the sitting-room. Light having been restored, he mopped up a welter of egg as best he could, together with most of the broken bulb, pushed back the table and chairs, and surveyed the room to see if it appeared reasonably normal. Returning to the window he listened without looking too far out. Immediately below him was a small group in earnest conversation, but what they were saying or who they were he could not tell without revealing himself. Presently the group dispersed and it seemed that the incident was closed. The clocks of Cambridge began to strike nine, recalling to Starbright that the night held for him matters of even greater importance.

Meantime the repulsed attackers were dispersing as inconspicuously as possible to forgather once more in the rooms of their leader, who was in extreme ill-humour. In addition to the yolk of an egg, he had collected a bruise in the back, inflicted by the head of a blundering member of his own side. His joy was in no way restored by the entry of Sullivan, Duncan, Tanner, and Trevor. The latter had already been apprised of events by Sullivan, who bore no ill will in the matter and had given an amusing and impartial account of the unsuccessful assault. Peter Duncan affected to be less well-informed and amused himself by remarking to Davies: "Well, what happened to your raid? I hear you came away without doing much. I thought you were going to beat him up."

"Rotten swine!" exclaimed Davies. "Going and shooting off a gun like that! Might just as well go and sneak to the dons and have done with it!"

"Well, he warned us he'd do it," remarked Sullivan. "If a dozen toughs were going to beat you up, I bet you'd take any way out that offered, dons or no dons. In any case it seems to have blown over."

"Let him just wait!" said Davies. "I'll get him yet."

"That seems to be rather a point," said Duncan. "What exactly do you propose to do now? Go on and on at the wretched fellow till all his eggs and ammunition are used up?"

"Personally," said Trevor, having been primed by Tom Tanner, "I think you might have waited for me to decide about this. After all, I have some say in the matter, I think."

"Quite, old man," agreed Davies, rather uncomfortably, "but you were nowhere to be found, and the general opinion seemed to be that something must be done for the credit of the college."

"I intended to see him myself before anything was done," added Trevor, "and, anyway, I don't think much of this mobbing business."

"Nor do I," said Peter Duncan, "and I must say, Davies, you seem to have balled it up rather."

"That may be," said the Welshman doggedly, "but I'm all out to make another shot at it if the rest are agreeable."

The rest, however, were inclined not to agree. They were impressed by the fact that their action had apparently not been approved by Trevor and Duncan, the two men in college whose opinion, with them, counted most. They also felt that, as a strategist and tactician, Davies was hardly an unqualified success. Sullivan summed up the general opinion and added one of his own. "Personally," he said, "though I dislike Starbright and think he behaved abominably over the match, I rather admire the show he put up tonight and I don't propose to be one of another crowd to try physical violence on him. Of course, if Davies wants to fight a duel with him, that's no concern of mine."

"I think, if you don't mind," added Trevor, "I'll try and see him before anything else is done. If I could get some sort of an apology out of him, it would clear things up. Of course we can't have him in the side again. Not at once, anyway."

This reasonable proposition met with general approval, though Davies said nothing for or against. Trevor then departed on his difficult errand.

As he approached Starbright's room, which was lit up and occupied, he wondered rather uncomfortably whether he would be greeted by an egg or a bullet before having time, so to speak, to show a flag of truce. He knocked and waited for the word to come in before making his entry. There seemed to be no defensive measures in force, for Starbright, with a shrewd insight into human nature, had reasoned that there would be no more hostilities that night. He was, however, slightly surprised when he saw the identity of his caller. Trevor found him sitting quietly at a table, apparently calculating some figures in a small notebook.

"Sorry if I'm disturbing you," said Trevor, trying to speak politely yet coldly and succeeding tolerably well. "I'd rather like a word with you."

"You don't disturb me," replied Starbright ambiguously. "I see you've apparently come without a bodyguard this time."

Trevor frowned for a moment and then took his meaning.

"Oh! I see. Look here, Starbright, I'd like to say, in the first place, that I've only just heard about your previous callers and that it was no affair of mine. As it happens I've only been back in college a short time, and what took place was against my wishes. I wanted first to hear whether you had any explanation to offer about this afternoon."

Starbright did not pretend to misunderstand him.

"I should hardly think any explanation is necessary. I told you clearly two nights ago that I did not intend to play under the present arrangement of the side. I thought I made it quite clear. You wrote up the same side and said nothing further to me, so I kept my word. That's all there is to it. As regards the little party that called, I'm obliged to you for having nothing to do with it. I'm sorry to have supposed you had, only Davies gave me to understand you were following on in the rear."

"Did he?" said Trevor grimly. "That's very interesting. Well, I hope you'll take my word for it that he was wrong. You say you're sorry for the mistake. Have you nothing else to be sorry for?"

Once again Starbright did not bother to fence with words.

"In some ways I'll admit I'm sorry for not having turned up, but I told you that was my intention and I stuck to my word. I'm not going back on that and I'm not going to apologize. You forced my hand and I had to play it."

"Don't you think," continued Trevor, "that, if you dispute my ruling as captain and then let us down for our most important match, it's a pretty bad show on your part?"

"I don't know about that," said Starbright. "I disagreed with you over the whole business and told you so clearly. It was up to you to consider my point of view, or else dispense with me and play someone else."

"I don't agree," persisted Trevor, "and, as you have no apology to offer, it's my painful duty to tell you I think you're a damned swine."

As he got this difficult summing-up off his chest, he drew back, fully expecting an explosion of wrath on the part of his listener coupled with some violent physical outburst. He was quite surprised when Starbright considered his words for some seconds and then answered in a curiously dull, flat tone:

"Well, in a way, I can't say I'm surprised at your thinking that. It's just a difference in outlook. I rather admire you for having the guts to come here alone and tell me so. A much better show than your friends put up. ... Still, what's done is done. It's no good harping on it. What do you propose to do about it? That's the main point."

"Well," said Trevor, disarmed and rather confused by this strangely reasonable mood on the part of his truculent opponent, "as you suggest, there's not much can be done. Personally, I wish the whole thing could be washed out and forgotten. But since you won't give any explanation or apology, I shall have to drop you permanently from the side."

"Oh, naturally! Of course," said Starbright, showing signs of irritation for the first time. "That's obvious."

"I don't mind admitting we shall miss you, and if the present feeling dies down I shall be the first to agree to your being reinstated, provided you would agree to play when required and where required."

"I don't think you need worry about that," said Starbright. "I told you my objection to playing, and as long as that holds good, there's no question of my wanting to play, even if asked."

It was Trevor's turn to express annoyance.

"Well, as regards King, it might interest you to know that the varsity captain saw part of the game today and told me he thought King was a very good college centre. I'll take his opinion before yours any day."

"Quite," said Starbright amiably. "I don't blame you, my dear chap."

"Well, there it is," concluded Trevor, once more mollified by Starbright's attitude. "I've more or less said what I came to say, so now I'll push off. I don't mind adding that, from the general point of view, I'm damned fed up with you and the whole business, but as far as I'm concerned it's finished with."

"Thanks," said Starbright awkwardly. "So it seems I shall merely have to contend with Davies and his crew till further notice."

"I don't know what you've done to deserve my telling you," was Trevor's reply to this, "but I very much doubt whether you will hear any more from that quarter. I'm not in with them over this business and neither is Peter Duncan. I shall say I've settled the matter with you, and turned you out of the side, and that, I should think, will be the end of it. Your name will be rather mud for a bit, I think, but that's your own doing."

"Quite," said Starbright once more. "Well, I must say you've behaved as well as you possibly could over this, and I'm duly obliged. I'll go as far as to say I regret my part in the show. Still, I've made my bed and I must lie on it. I'm glad you came. Good night."

A kind of surprise at the way the interview had gone prevented Trevor from doing more than returning Starbright's parting words. As he turned back in the doorway, he saw the ex-three-quarter's head sunk once more over his pencilled calculations. His lips were moving and his brows were knitted. In a moment of time he seemed to have dismissed the day's misfortunes from his mind.

A queer fellow, thought Trevor, as he crossed the court to his own rooms; touchy and unreasonable when no excuse existed, yet cool and unmoved in the face of blame and recrimination. A pacifist in everyday affairs, Trevor was glad his mission had ended on a note of compromise and goodwill. It was not long before he was to feel even more glad of this circumstance.

Meantime Starbright was looking at his watch. It was five minutes to ten, and at ten o'clock the college gates were closed. From that hour until midnight undergraduates were admitted into college on the debit of a small gate fine, and those living out were allowed to depart to their lodgings. But after ten a dweller in college could not pass out through the gates.

Starbright snatched up his gown and a battered, pulpy mortar-board. He slipped quickly past the lighted doorway of the porter's lodge, for he was anxious that his departure should not be noted. The porter was busy inside, so Starbright passed unnoticed into the night.

CHAPTER VI

As Martin Trevor passed through Craven Court next morning on his way to a lecture, he felt once more that it was a very good world. The troublesome events of the previous day seemed now to have straightened themselves out. After breakfast he had been able to tell Peter Duncan and others that he had carried out his intention of interviewing Starbright, conveying the displeasure of himself and the rest of the team, and informing the wing three-quarter that his services would no longer be required. It had, therefore, been the opinion of Sullivan and other members of last night's punitive expedition that the incident might now be considered closed, particularly as Starbright, whilst not actually apologizing, had treated his captain with a measure of courtesy and regret. Whether or not Davies intended to carry on a vendetta on his own account remained to be seen, though it appeared that the fiery Welshman had lost most, if not all, of his backing.

Martin Trevor would have been even more cheerful had the morning been an occasion for one of Mr. Pringle-Perkins' lectures. Unhappily this was not the case, and he was in consequence rather late. Nearly everyone else had already departed to lectures or other pursuits, and the college appeared deserted save for the presence of the Dean of College. Exercising his privilege as a don, Mr. Gale was pacing slowly up and down the middle of the grass-plot, a form of exercise often indulged in by the senior members, though unsuitable, as it seemed to Trevor, for such a morning in November when the turf was soft and wet underfoot. The Dean's head was bent towards the ground as though its owner was in a profound and scholarly reverie. Reflecting what a pity it was that Gale, of all people, appeared to be showing early signs of donnish senility, Trevor left the court and hurried out of college.

As it happened, Gale was devoting his saunter to plans of a definite purpose. On leaving his rooms, which were in Craven Court and on the same staircase as Trevor's, he had stood for some moments gazing absently across to the window of Starbright's room. Then he had walked slowly along the opposite side of the court gazing idly at the walls and windows of the various sets of rooms. Seeming to find nothing unusual in this inspection, he had commenced his slow pacing up and down the grass in tracks which never took him twice over the same ground. In point of fact the eyes in his lowered head were very definitely functioning.

At length he stopped short, and a sharp look round served to inform him that he was apparently alone and unobserved. He bent his gaze closer to the ground. At this particular spot the trim, carefully mown stretch of grass was marred by a little groove scored in the turf and terminated by a little round hole, as though someone had poked the ground with a small, round stick from a very acute angle. The Dean felt in his pocket and produced a penknife. Then, grunting slightly at a twinge of rheumatism, he squatted down and began to dig into the hole. Presently his efforts were rewarded by his being able to prise out a small object which he had no difficulty in identifying as a revolver bullet of medium calibre. He took a brief look at his find, slipped it in his pocket, carefully eliminated traces of the excavation by treading down the turf, took another look round the empty court, and returned to his rooms.

The early part of the evening was fully occupied by Trevor in making up lost time collecting donations for the Amal. Club fund. The personnel of the contributors had been divided amongst five collectors representing the boats and various games. Trevor was fortunate in having few freshers on his list, for these latter were likely to prove elusive. Living mostly out in lodgings, they could seldom be run to earth in college except at the hour of evening Hall. Trevor was accompanied on his rounds by the faithful Tanner, who kept a check on the names and amounts subscribed. For the most part the donors parted cheerfully enough with the ten shillings suggested, though the rueful chaff about the extravagance of the club and the poverty of its members tended to become monotonous.

"This should be easy meat, anyway," said Tanner, as they arrived at a staircase bearing, among others, the painted name and title of "Prince Samadan".

The owner of these rooms was an Ethiopian potentate in the very early twenties who, though a freshman, had, by virtue of rank, been allotted spacious rooms in college. He was no sort of athlete and, since he had started his life in newer continents by a visit to the United States and later indulged a liking for American talking films, his employment of the English tongue, besides being limited in knowledge and vocabulary, was at times somewhat peculiar. Still, owing to his good nature and to the lavish nature of his hospitality, which was frequently rather exotic, he was quite a popular member of the college.

The collectors received a cordial welcome from their royal host.

"Welcome, folks," said the Prince, showing an excellent set of teeth in an expansive grin. "Please park yourselves. Take a park, do." Whereupon he produced some large but valuable glasses together with a bottle of Green Chartreuse, which he was mistaken in thinking a customary and suitable apéritif. Anyway, it had appeared to be the most highly priced drink in the list, so he supposed it must be the right thing.

His guests, however, refused this refreshment, Tom Tanner reflecting to himself with some inward amusement the likely result if they were to be offered and accept a glass of this particular fluid at every port of call that evening. Remembering, however, that a refusal of Oriental hospitality may hurt the feelings, he asked if there was any sherry, and three glasses of the latter were speedily filled, what time Trevor attempted somewhat inadequately to explain the cause of their visit. The Prince waved his hand airily and dismissed the topic.

"Sure thing, friend. That's OK, quite OK."

Rummaging in a side-pocket the Prince produced a crumpled collection of papers in which a number of bank and treasury notes were carelessly muddled with theatre-ticket counterfoils and letters, together with a very ornate feminine garter.

"Most of the fellows are giving ten bob," Trevor told him.

"A tenner. Sure thing!" proclaimed Prince Samadan, rummaging amongst the exhibits. English money was to him a tiresome mystery. He mistrusted cheques as some form of Occidental post-war credit not worthy of consideration by an honourable payer of money. He was consequently kept supplied by a bank with paper money of high valuation. Pound and ten-shilling notes he regarded as two grades of tips suitable for head-waiters or underlings respectively. For his own purchases he generally offered a five or ten-pound note. The subsequent production of coin of the realm in change he regarded as a burdensome nuisance.

He rooted amongst the paper money with exclamations of annoyance. Some one and five-pound notes fluttered to the ground.

"No tenners!" he remarked. "Only small stuff. But two fivers is one tenner, yes?"

Trevor pondered for a moment and then, overcome by scruples of honesty, pushed back one of the five-pound notes and picked up the other.

"One's quite enough, old man."

"Only one fiver!" exclaimed the Prince, rather scandalized. However, supposing that the collectors knew best, and having learned that, at Cambridge, one did not parade wealth ostentatiously, he did not pursue the matter. Instead he decided to take advantage of the occasion to acquire a little local knowledge.

"Say, folks," he inquired earnestly, "you know that fair girl, what you call Ethel, yes?"

"Ethel?" repeated Trevor. "You mean the Master's daughter?"

"Sure that's right. Nice bit, what? You think she come to Savoy with me. What?"

"Savoy?" said Trevor, puzzled. "But that's in Italy. It's the hell of a way. Whatever for, anyway?"

"I think you mean the Savoy Hotel in London," explained Tanner. He had heard that the Prince patronized that hostelry.

"Sure. Come with me for jazz and whoopee."

Trevor appeared so bewildered by the suggestion that his friend helped him out by answering the question.

"I'm afraid she wouldn't go dancing with you without an introduction," he explained. "Those kind of girls are rather particular about proper introductions."

"So?" said the Prince, rather surprised. "Well, you think the Master present her to me if I ask him, no?"

"I should say definitely no, old chap. He's a bit old-fashioned about dancing and so on. I'm afraid it's no go."

"Tough cheese," commented the Prince sadly, having comprehended the gist if not the precise details of Tanner's remarks. "Well, maybe you two come to Savoy one time. Bring your women or else my agent in London he fix up the women for all."

"Very good of you," murmured Trevor, with an attempt at enthusiasm. "But we're pretty well booked up just now. Thanks all the same."

"Oh, well!" said Prince Samadan philosophically. "Maybe later on you can do. And anyhow, the agent send not too good woman to dance last time. Lousy, I tell you, sirs. Bum show! Why, she ..."

At this point the two friends managed to plead shortage of time and pressure of business, so took their leave in a parting atmosphere of bows and smiling white teeth.

The remainder of their round produced no further events of interest and they finished just in time to present themselves and their proceeds to Mr. Waddington.

The plump, cheerful Bursar had just received piles of notes from the captains of boats and hockey. He checked over Trevor's amount very hastily and, as the first notes of the Hall bell sounded through the open door, he gathered up the whole harvest into a bundle, and thrusting it into an open drawer hurried out on the heels of the three collectors.

Shortly after Hall was over, Martin Trevor and Tom Tanner fell in with Peter Duncan as the three made their way towards a staircase in one corner of the main court. Duncan appeared to know the destination of the others, for he joined them without a word and the three passed through the doorway and upstairs.

The room in which they presently found themselves was owned by a prominent member of the college called Winterton. Though not a great athlete—he rowed in the second boat—Winterton had gained prominence since his early days as a freshman as an author or abettor of various spectacular rags, and his name was well known in this connection far beyond the bounds of St. Chad's. In his first year he had organized the famous motor-cycle picnic which had completely disorganized the traffic of Cambridge for over an hour, and in his second year planned the scheme by which a monster fifth of November bonfire was held in spite of careful arrangements to the contrary. The strategy by which the bulk of the police was drawn away to a false rendezvous whilst the real fire blazed suddenly to the skies was grudgingly praised by the authorities themselves. Recently he had emulated Mr. Gale by becoming an addict to criminal fiction. In spite of a reputation amongst undergraduates, Winterton had a clean sheet with both the university and civil authorities.

As the three newcomers knocked and entered, they found a party of five seated rather formally at a big table in the centre of the room. Their host, a big, sandy-haired, snub-nosed, and freckled young man, sat at the head of the table in front of a large notebook and some papers. Amongst those present were Davies and Sullivan. Drinks and sandwiches stood on a side table.

"That makes us all present," said Winterton, when he had greeted the latest arrivals. "Will you sport the oak, Davies?"

A casual observer might have supposed that he was seeing the start of some college club or society meeting, and in this instance he would have been correct. At both Cambridge and Oxford there exist clubs of all kinds and for all purposes. Best known at Cambridge are the Union, primarily a debating society, the Hawks, and the Pitt, for which athletic and social status is required as a qualification, and for dramatic productions the Amateur Dramatic Club together with the less formal "Footlights". All these have their own premises and their membership extends over the whole university.

Smaller and more numerous are the many college clubs whose meetings are generally held in the private rooms of individual members. Some are of a purely social and possibly bibulous character or have old and respected traditions which make their membership a coveted honour, like the Eton Society; others are for the mutual study of literature, drama, science, or religion. Some flourish openly and their club ties are known outside their own colleges, whilst others are of a secret nature and meet behind closed doors, thereby affording the sensational novelist or journalist the opportunity of assuring us that black magic and other vices form the spare-time recreation of numerous undergraduates. In point of fact such clubs often owe their existence to a survival in the minds of the members of that childish love of secret societies which they felt as young schoolboys and rejected in their years as prefects.

When Davies had returned to his seat, Winterton cleared his throat and began to address the meeting in very formal tones:

"Our first business tonight is concerned with the fact that we have with us a new member, Mr. Carter."

The eyes of most people present were here turned upon a gentleman of slightly younger appearance than themselves who sat with rather a self-conscious expression on his face.

"His election has been duly approved by you all and, according to the rules, I have given him a very general idea of the nature and objects of the club, in order that he might decide whether or not he wished to accept the offer of membership. This he has accepted without reservation and, therefore, I propose, as we go along, to explain our rules and procedure as best I can. It is, then, open to him to accept the full rules and responsibilities, or else he has the option of withdrawing from the club on the solemn promise of divulging nothing about the club or its activities. You understand that, Carter, don't you?"

The novice, swallowing nervously, replied that he quite understood.

"Right, then," said the chairman, becoming less formal. "Well, first of all I'd like to remind the existing members that it was my own idea to have a fresher added to the club. Most of us have only a year to go, and it seemed to me that, if we don't have some fresh blood, the club might die out. That would be a pity."

There was a murmur of approval from the meeting.

"And, as I said last time, I think Mr. Carter should make a very able recruit. He did very stout work in the recent fifth of November doings, as some of you know."

Being favoured with some glances and murmurs of approbation, Mr. Carter blushed becomingly.

"So for his benefit I propose to run quickly over the rules and objects of the club, and then discuss the latest business for the benefit of the rest. Prompt me, you chaps, if I forget anything important.

"First of all, we have no minutes of previous meetings to read, as the secret nature of our proceedings makes it risky to put things on paper. Whenever anything is written down, no names are included, only numbers. We all have a number, and yours will be eight. There are no officers in the club, which was founded last term, and up to now the members have insisted that I, as its inventor and founder, shall fulfil the offices of president, secretary, treasurer, and anything else necessary. At the moment there are no subscriptions and expenses, and the meetings take place here."

"There ought to be some expenses," interrupted Sullivan. "I don't see why you should stand the drinks and grub at every meeting."

"President's privilege," explained Winterton. "Any way, we'll not bother about that now. Now this club is called the Chad's Crime Club and its objects are the study and actual carrying-out of criminal enterprises. In the past we have heard of various clubs which aim at the breaking of rules, such as roof-climbing and breaking out of college clubs. This club has higher aims than that. It exists definitely to break the law of the land."

Pleased with this climax in his oration, the speaker made an effective pause, which was rather spoilt by Sullivan remarking conversationally:

"That's damned well put, eh, you chaps?"

"Order, please," said the chairman. "In committing crimes, however, our aim is to bring no permanent loss or misfortune on anyone or do anything permanently harmful, but to break the law in such a way that any loss or damage can be made up to the injured party. To quote a simple example, if the crime is theft, then the member takes steps to return what he has stolen. It thus stands to reason that certain serious crimes, such as murder or serious assault, are definitely barred."

"Have we a definite list of barred crimes?" inquired a member.

"No, I don't think so," said Winterton. "One must rather leave it to individual common sense. Arson, for instance, would appear out of the question, unless someone was prepared, say, to burn down the pavilion one night and then build another one the next."

"What about de-bagging a don?" asked Sullivan. "It seems questionable whether one could leave things as one found them."

"Order, please," said Winterton once more. "That seems a frivolous observation, Mr. Sullivan. Well, to continue. The object of every member is to commit a definite crime, if possible of a risky and spectacular nature but which can finally be put right. Having done so, he gives a full account, with proofs if possible, at our next meeting, and a summary of the case is recorded by myself in this book, which I keep in the strictest confidence and which contains no names, only numbers, of members.

"Now I come to the main feature of our intentions. At our first meeting, early last term, we decided to hold a competition for the most brilliant crime committed by a member between then and the end of the present term. I am keeping a record of all crimes committed and, when the time comes, it is proposed to review all the crimes in turn and decide by vote which crime is the best. All members will contribute a pound apiece, and the sum total will then be handed to the winning member. That's the main outline. I don't think I've forgotten anything."

"No," agreed Peter Duncan. "I think you've explained things very fully, old man."

"We have already discussed, from time to time, the various points which should count most in judging the merits of our crimes. For one thing, it is a definite disadvantage to cause any undue worry or fright to women or children, even of a temporary nature. The value of a crime should depend definitely on the risks it involves to the member concerned and the possible penalty if discovered. For instance, to steal a fresher's cap and gown would acquire little merit, since the thief, if caught, would run little risk of exposure. Obviously crimes committed against people of importance, especially outside the university, are the riskiest and should count highest. On the other hand skill in technique, rendering detection unlikely, would score marks. At the same time crimes producing publicity, though without pain or distress, should count more than those which are either undiscovered or cause little or no public stir.

"At the moment we have not fully decided the final conditions of judging the various crimes. That we shall decide nearer the time, allotting some proportion of marks for the various features of a successful crime so that you will all have something definite to work on in making your final choice. For the present our meetings are chiefly concerned with recording any new effort in crime on the part of members. Having committed a crime, the member supplies me with the details which I record. The record is then discussed at the next meeting.

"Going over old ground for a moment, we have already dealt with two crimes. Carter probably knows something about them already, since they gave rise to much public gossip and surmise. I won't waste the time of the meeting by repeating them fully, and Carter can read the official accounts later, if he likes. The two crimes were, firstly, the theft from the college library of the valuable Florentine manuscripts by our respected fellow-member, Mr. Clark, and the theft of a car belonging to Poggers—I should say Mr. Pogson—a fellow of this college—by Mr. Trevor. In each case there was a hue and cry, involving the presence of the police, which gave ample proof that the said crimes had, in fact, been committed as subsequently declared, and in each case restitution was made without loss or inconvenience to the injured parties." Winterton made another pause. He was reading for the Bar, and no doubt his director of legal studies would have been highly pleased with his display of forensic ability.

"It is not for me, at the present stage, to attempt any assessment as to the comparative value of these crimes, but I must say I consider them pretty hot—er, that is to say of considerable merit and excellence. In the first place, both victims were members of the college, which gave the criminals additional risk of being recognized. The manuscripts are of great value, and the thief operated boldly in the light of day. On the other hand, Trevor's exploit with the car deserves special praise as one which the police are at special pains to combat. You will remember, however, that he was forced to employ a confederate for the secretion of the car. This I regard as a definite minus point and one which, if extensively employed, might lead to the unmasking of our activities.

"Tonight I am happy to bring to your notice two new crimes, one which I submit with modesty, being myself the author."

There was some mild applause at this, and the meeting, which had become rather tired of stale repetition, roused itself to greater attention.

"In introducing the matter of the first crime I confess I cannot regard it with much enthusiasm, much as I respect its author, Mr. Strangeways. In fact, I'm not clear that he has broken the law at all."

The gentleman mentioned, a useful tennis player, stirred in his seat and began a protest. He was silenced by the chairman.

"Furthermore," pursued the chairman, "the victim himself was apparently unaware of any felonious intent, for, after guarded inquiries, we cannot find that he made any complaint to the proper authorities or, indeed, even mentioned the affair as a bare matter of fact. However, we will let the facts speak for themselves.

"It appears that on the morning of November the second Mr.

Strangeways posted on the college screens a notice purporting to be written and signed by the Dean of Chapel and extending a general invitation to all undergraduate members of the college to attend a bottle party in the said Dean of Chapel's rooms at six-forty-five that evening. As a result of this notice, which gave rise to many curious conjectures, between fifty and sixty members of the college sought and mostly gained admittance to the Dean's rooms.

"Mr. Strangeways was amongst the first to enter the room, being anxious to observe and report on his crime. He states that, owing to an intended ambiguity in the invitation, some came with bottles whilst others relied on the hospitality of the reverend gentleman. Some few believed that they were expected guests, whilst the majority, having some inkling of the truth, arrived merely to see the outcome of the affair. These latter, to their surprise, were cordially received and offered what sitting space was available, though it was clear their host was somewhat bewildered by the number of people who had apparently chosen that evening to pay him a social call. After some forty persons had with difficulty found sitting or standing room, the Dean of Chapel was regretfully obliged to turn away a number of late arrivals, requesting them to call another night.

"The party seems to have conducted itself with fair decorum, being impressed by the polite way in which their invasion had been received. In some quarters conversation was a little noisy, especially in areas where the bringers of bottles had been induced to open them, but in the neighbourhood of the Dean a decorous discussion was held in which their host took a full part. The guests finally drifted away, with the exception of two earnest theological students who remained to finish a technical discussion. The only regrettable feature, from the point of view of the Dean of Chapel, was that he forgot to go and take evening service, at which the Master was forced to deputize at short notice. However, it being not the first time he had thus failed, the matter called for little or no comment among his fellow dons. It does not seem that he made any mention to them at all regarding his unexpected guests and, beyond a certain amount of merriment in other quarters of the college, the incident was closed."

A chilly silence greeted Winterton's lucid exposition.

"Is that all?" inquired Davies at length.

Strangeways, conscious that his *magnum opus* of crime had fallen flat, hastened to make an extra contribution to the story.

"As regards reparations," he explained, "the Dean of Chapel didn't put up any drinks himself, but he passed round some cigarettes and cigars and they vanished pretty quick. So next day I went round to the tobacconist and had some more sent up to his rooms."

"Well, I don't see much in that," continued Davies.

"What I'm not quite clear about," said Winterton, bringing his legal mind to bear on the subject, "is exactly what crime you claim to have committed. I don't see where you have broken the law of the land."

"Why, forgery, of course," explained the criminal.

"H'm ... yes, I see," said Winterton, silencing with a glance the caustic comments which were shaping on the lips of certain members. "Well, I'll pass on to my own little effort—the abduction of Dr. T. H. Withers, D.Litt., of Trinity College."

Once more the meeting was stirred to interest and undivided attention. The Withers affair had been freely discussed in all colleges and a garbled account had appeared in the press. But even those then present were as yet unaware of the exact facts. But everything pointed to the fact that their founder had set an example by bringing off a coup of the first magnitude.

"Yes, let's hear all about that," said Duncan, in keen anticipation.

"It's rather a long story," said Winterton. "I think we might relax a little. What about some beer? It's thirsty work doing all the talking."

When the members had helped themselves from the side table the president filled a pipe and settled down to tell the story of his crime.

"In order that you should understand how I came to figure out the whole thing I must tell you first of all that I have known of Dr. T. H. Withers for some time and do not approve of him. He once behaved somewhat rudely to some relations of mine, and, though I had never met him, I considered that I should be doing a good thing by putting it across him in any way I could. I tell you this in case you may think I treated him rather badly without any particular reason.

"You doubtless know that distinguished antiquarians, such as Withers, are greatly interested in discoveries or relics in the possession of others in the same line of life. Recently I stayed with some friends who have a place in the county of Midshire. I shall mention no names or localities nearer than that, and amongst their acquaintances was another Egyptologist who, as I casually ascertained, knew Withers by reputation, but had never met him. To simplify the story I will call this antiquarian by the name of Brown. Whilst in the district I met an eccentric and rather peppery retired colonel by the name—shall we say—of Smith, who was not popular with my friends. This Colonel Smith was somewhat of a recluse, and lived in a very isolated house about five miles from anywhere and about ten miles from that of the antiquarian Brown.

"The outline of my plan was to lure the objectionable Withers away from Cambridge by a false invitation to view certain rare discoveries from Egypt in the possession of Brown, and cause him to be marooned in the desolate abode of Colonel Smith. The actual details took a lot of working out.

"In the first place I had to put in some hours of research at the University Library, priming myself with the details of recent excavations in Egypt. At length I had the necessary data to write a letter worthy of an expert. The next thing was to compose my faked invitation.

"It happens that, owing to my father being a member, I belong to the somewhat exclusive Rare Arts Club in London, of which Withers might well be a member but, as it happens, is not. Running up to Town for half a day I drafted on the stationery of the Arts Club a letter purporting to come from Professor Brown. It stated that the writer had just become possessed of some rare Egyptian finds, of which I gave technical details, and was returning in three days' time to his home in Midshire to examine the stuff in the presence of experts. The professor would greatly value the opinion of such an expert as Dr. Withers. Would the latter, therefore, like to make the journey to Midshire and stay the night? If so, a car would meet him at the nearest main-line junction at a certain hour in the late afternoon of the following Saturday. The correct home address of the professor was given, together with the right junction and time of train, and Dr. Withers was asked to reply direct to the Rare Arts Club, since the writer would be staying there up to the Saturday morning. Thus I had taken every precaution to see that the letter appeared thoroughly authentic.

"At this point I enlisted the services of my only confederate, the head porter of the Rare Arts Club. I informed him that I expected a letter to be addressed to me at the club under the name of Professor Brown. Since there was no member of that name, he made no bones about sending me a wire as soon as such a letter should arrive. The next day I heard that the letter had arrived and had it forwarded on. It contained a short acceptance of the invitation couched in the rather terse style which one would have expected from Withers. The way was now clear for the final touches to my scheme.

"You may know that, owing to varsity restrictions, I keep a car out at Trumpington which is not registered on the proctor's list as required by the rules. The distance from Cambridge to the Midshire junction is nearly a hundred miles, and the train taken by Withers was due to arrive there at six in the evening. I had chosen an hour of darkness to avoid the possibility of recognition, and I had further arranged to assume a small false moustache, which I have employed on certain occasions to cover my resemblance to an average undergraduate. Driving easily through the afternoon I reached the junction in plenty of time to meet the train, keeping my car well in the shadows to avoid any possible recognition of its number. Withers came off the train and I introduced myself as Professor Brown's secretary, saying that the drive was of about six miles. Brown's house was, in fact, six miles away, but the direction I now took was six miles in the opposite direction towards the house of Colonel Smith.

"I was anxious that Withers' absence should, if possible, be the subject of immediate inquiry. I had, therefore, stopped on my way an hour previously and dispatched to Professor Brown a wire from a town half-way to Cambridge. This was said to come from Withers of Trinity to say he would be arriving at the junction by the quarter to seven train and would like to be met. I judged that when Withers failed to appear on that train the professor would start inquiries which might end in telephone messages to Trinity.

"Meantime we had driven through the deserted moorland to the house of Colonel Smith. I have seldom seen or known a more desolate spot. There was not a village or post-office for four or five miles. Last vac., when I first had my plan in mind, I had explored the surroundings and knew that the house had a telephone with a wire running down to the poles on the main road. There was also a long drive running through a shrubbery from the road to the front door. Withers, as I had supposed, was a morose and uncongenial companion. Finding that I had little expert knowledge of Egyptology, he ignored my presence, and any scruples I might have had about landing him in a mess were soon laid to rest.

"When we reached the front gate I stopped the car and explained that I could not take it up the drive since new drain-pipes were being laid. Perhaps he would not mind walking to the front door whilst I took the car down the road to the village garage. In point of fact there was no garage and no village. Withers grumbled a bit, but climbed out and asked me rather shortly to carry his bag up when I returned. This made me smile, as I thought that, by his rudeness, he would be deprived of its contents for that night.

"As soon as Withers had vanished round the bend of the drive I set quickly to work. By the gate was a low pole carrying the house telephone to the main road. I shinned up the post, which nearly broke under my weight, and cut the wire with a pair of cutters I'd nearly—but not quite—forgotten. Then I hopped into the car and got back to Cambridge in time to walk into college between eleven and twelve and say what a good film I'd seen.

"On my way I remembered his wretched bag. My route lay through Peterborough, and I went into the station and got a platform ticket. I had written 'Trinity, Cambridge' in large letters on the label of the bag and, when nobody was looking, I left it with a pile of luggage stacked up for a south-bound train and then went back to the car.

"I had figured it out that Withers must unavoidably be marooned with the colonel till a late hour the following morning. The house was five miles from anywhere, the telephone was cut, and I knew that the colonel, who detested modern contraptions, refused to keep a car— hiring one on the rare occasions when he left home. Peppery or not, he could hardly turn Withers out into the night. What they said to each other I should dearly like to know, but I suppose I never shall.

"Meantime, as it afterwards transpired, Brown was greatly puzzled by the telegram, and further by the non-arrival of Withers. The latter was known to him by repute, and he had rung up the junction garage to have him met. It appears he later rang up Trinity and the local police, and much perplexity ensued until a late hour the following morning, when the colonel's butler was able to reach the nearest town on a bike and charter a car to remove the angry Withers.

"Withers had discovered that Brown lived quite close, so he drove there in a towering rage and demanded an explanation from the professor. It sounds rather rough on the poor old prof., I know, but he was really rather a nasty old blighter and had behaved badly to my pals there over a little matter of the children wandering in his meadow. Brown swore black and blue, no doubt, that he had never written to Withers nor heard from him. It also appeared, from what Brown told friends in the district, that Withers couldn't produce the alleged invitation, so neither of them would accept the other's explanation and they parted brass rags. When Withers got back to Trinity he found several people, including the police and the press, anxious to know what had happened about his proposed antiquarian jaunt, which he had talked a lot about before starting. Of course, he was furious, and talked about bringing an action against the professor, so the affair got as much publicity as I could have wished, or even a bit more.

"The only danger I could see was that inquiries might lead to the Rare Arts Club, and so they did. However, I had with difficulty squared the porter with a pound-note to swear he knew nothing about a letter coming for Professor Brown, which, to save his own skin, he was quite ready to do, though those sort of chaps are hard to bribe as a rule about things of that kind.

"My last action was to send from London a pound-note to Withers in a plain envelope to cover his fare back and a possible couple of motor drives, though as a matter of fact the business had cost me considerably more than it had him. That's about all there is to say about it, and I claim it as a criminal piece of abduction. I could, of course, equally well have taken him to a lonely barn and left him to starve to death without likelihood of discovery, so I think the crime should rank as a potential murder."

During his discourse the audience had with difficulty suppressed exclamations of wonder and admiration. At the conclusion there was an outburst of congratulations.

"By Jove, old man," said Strangeways, "that's pretty hot, upon my soul it is!"

"It'll certainly take some beating," agreed Davies.

"What organization!" said the simple-minded Duncan. "I could never have thought out all that."

"Well, it'll give some of you others a lead anyway," said the hero of these exploits. "There's only a few more weeks left before the entries close, and I'd like to see everyone have a shot by then."

"Well, look you!" exclaimed Davies, fired with excitement by his leader's example, "maybe you'll be hearing something from me any day now. I'm nearly all set for something."

"Same here," said Peter Duncan. "But I don't know that I can turn out anything to equal tonight's show. What about you, Tom?"

Tanner shook his untidy head dismally.

"Nothing doing yet," he admitted.

"Now then," said Winterton resuming his formal manner, "I don't think there's much more to do, except refresh ourselves and also ask our new member whether he thinks he'd like to stick in with us."

"Oh, rather," cried Carter at once, "I'm frightfully——"

But what he was exactly will never be known, for at that moment there was an urgent knocking on the locked door. The members looked uneasily at their leader. Carter quite expected to hear a demand to open in the name of the law.

"Might as well see who it is and let them in," said Winterton. "We've finished, anyway. Gentlemen, the meeting stands adjourned."

So saying he crossed the room and opened the door to reveal the unexpected presence of Mr. Waddington, the Bursar. That affable and unruffled individual looked a shade less benign than usual. He appeared as near as possible to being worried about something. "I'm very sorry to disturb you, Winterton; I seem to have interrupted some sort of a meeting. Most improper of me! The fact is I've been quite a time looking for Trevor, and at last someone said they thought they saw him coming over here. ... Ah! There you are Trevor. I wonder if you would mind coming over with me. The matter is um ... ah ... urgent. There are few urgent things in this world, my dear fellow, but this really seems to be one of them."

"Certainly, sir," said Trevor, rather surprised. "I'll come at once."

"I am summoning you in your capacity of rugger captain," explained the Bursar. He paused and took stock of the others.

"H'm ..." he observed, "I perceive a fair sample of the athletic and social bloods of the college here present. Perhaps it would be as well if I acquainted you all with the present pother. You will all have to know sooner or later." The Bursar paused awkwardly and then resumed: "No doubt most of you are anxiously awaiting the pavilion improvements or alternately the new oars which will carry you to a bump this Lent."

Several persons present signified their assent. The Bursar sighed sadly before continuing:

"I feared as much. It seems now likely that there may be a vexatious delay before the work can be put in hand. I blame myself and crave your indulgence. Tonight I lingered long in the Senior Combination Room discussing the affairs of the nation."

Sullivan became strengthened in a suspicion that the Bursar was the worse for drink. Next moment these thoughts were swept aside by the shock of the Bursar's next words:

"As most of you know, the money collected for the Amal. Club was handed to me before Hall tonight and put in a drawer. When I returned to my rooms a short time ago the money had unfortunately vanished."

There were gasps of amazement, whilst the Bursar went on:

"I thought it best to summon the police at once, and an inspector is impatiently awaiting the collectors, who, with myself, were the last to see the money. So come along, Trevor, and you too, Tanner, if you wish."

As the three people concerned left the room, the rest of the Crime Club gazed at one another with a wild surmise. Winterton closed the door. The prevalent thought was voiced by Peter Duncan.

"Another of our shows?" he hazarded. "Can we congratulate you, Davies?"

Davies appeared much upset by the suggestion.

"Good lord, no! I don't know a thing about it."

"Well, it's to be hoped one of us has done it," observed Sullivan philosophically, "and then we shall get the money back in due course. Otherwise, it looks as if we shan't."

"In any case," said Winterton judicially, "it's not in order for us to ask any member to account for a crime until the whole thing has been carried through according to plan and the necessary restitution made."

There was an uneasy silence, broken at length by Strangeways, who remarked nervously:

"It seems funny Waddington coming straight here and catching us at the meeting. It looks as if he suspected somebody."

"Nonsense," replied the president. "He wanted Trevor, that was all."

"Perhaps we'd better disperse, all the same," persisted Strangeways. "It's getting late, anyway."

Following his example the members took their leave of Winterton and dispersed rather thoughtfully. Meantime the Bursar and Trevor had returned to the rooms of the former, whilst Tanner, considering that he had no status amongst the athletic collectors, had asked to be excused and had then retired to his own abode.

Trevor felt mildy excited at the prospect of an official meeting with the forces of the law. The upshot was, however, lacking in much dramatic excitement. Inspector Norman, of the Cambridge Constabulary, was exactly what Trevor had pictured him as being; his questions were of the dullest routine nature, and the answers did not serve to throw the faintest light on the robbery. "It seems, then," said the Inspector, at length, "that these five gentlemen brought you the various sums of money shortly before seven-thirty. You put the money in this drawer, shutting but not locking it, and then left the room together with these gentlemen?"

The Bursar said that was so.

"As a matter of form," pursued the Inspector, smiling slightly to indicate he was not intending to accuse those present, "I must ask if everybody left the room at the same moment or, in other words, whether it would have been possible for any of these gentlemen to have lingered behind a moment and put the money in his pocket?"

The Bursar said no, certainly not. They had all walked out ahead of him.

"Quite so," said the Inspector. "Just a routine inquiry, of course. So it appears the money must have been taken between the time dinner ended and the time when you returned here, which you say is nearly an hour. It might have gone during dinner, of course, but then I understand that all the students and most of the college servants are in the Hall all that time."

"That's so," agreed Mr. Waddington. "Undergraduates can sign off Hall, but that generally means they are feeding outside the college. Then there's actually no check on those who don't sign off. They may be there or not, but as they are charged for Hall if they don't sign off, it stands to reason they are mostly there."

"We can try and check that, of course," said the Inspector rather doubtfully, "but you think it would have been just as easy for an intruder to come in after dinner as during the meal?"

"Easier, I should say," corrected the Bursar. "There are four other sets of rooms on this staircase, and, in the general moving about after Hall, anyone walking up here would attract less attention than if he were noticed during the time dinner was on."

The Inspector grunted sadly. Of all places in the world which could be burgled with impunity there appeared to him to be nowhere to equal a set of rooms in college. One might as well look for a needle in a haystack. He then addressed himself to the five athletic representatives:

"I take it all you gentlemen went straight in to dinner after you left this room?"

All five admitted that this was the case.

"Now I want you to think carefully. Did any of you refer to this matter in the hearing of other students? More particularly, did you mention the fact that the money had been put in an unlocked drawer? This is important."

The five undergraduates looked troubled. One looked at another, waiting for someone except himself to make the first statement.

"I was talking at table about all the money having been given in, but I didn't say where it was put," said the captain of boats at length.

"I said something about it too," admitted the captain of hockey. "A lot of fellows were keen to know how much we had collected. But I don't think I said anything about its being in a drawer. I think I said we'd given it in to the Bursar."

The captain of cricket shuffled his feet and grew red in the face.

"I'm afraid I said at table that Mr. Waddington had left the money in an unlocked drawer," he muttered awkwardly.

The Inspector at last showed signs of animation.

"Ah! Did you, sir? Now, that's interesting. Can you remember exactly what you said?"

The captain of cricket looked even more uncomfortable. He could and did remember exactly what he had said, which was:

"I had the hell of a rush to get the stuff in by Hall time and the others were late too. Old Wadders just had time to shovel the whole lot in a drawer and then buzz off to Hall. Didn't even lock it up! Just like him! Casual old blighter."

He decided to repeat a very amended version.

"I think I said we were all rather rushed to hand in our money in time, so that Mr. Waddington had to put it in a drawer and then had to hurry into Hall without having time to lock it up."

"Ah!" said the Inspector, "then students sitting round would have become aware that the money could easily be got at. I wonder how many others heard you, and whether you could remember, if needed, who was or wasn't within earshot."

"I'm afraid that's difficult to say, sir, except they would only be third-year people. I dare say ten or a dozen might have heard. But it's hard to say, with a lot of talk going on all round. We don't always sit in the same places, either, so I can't remember everyone within earshot."

The Inspector sighed again and his brow became puckered, giving him the appearance of a little boy about to burst into tears. He continued, still in a gloomy tone and addressing the Bursar: "You say the money was all in pound or ten-shilling notes, plus a little silver? Of course treasury notes will be impossible to trace."

"Yes, nearly all ten-shilling notes," agreed the Bursar. "A pity, as you say."

"But there was a fiver among them," interrupted Trevor. "I took it in myself."

The Inspector beamed at Trevor. At last the case was going to offer something tangible.

"And did you note its number, sir? Or you, Mr. Waddington?"

Trevor said he had not done so, and the Bursar added, somewhat untruthfully:

"I'm afraid, owing to pressure of time, I put it away without doing so. Of course, I should have noted it down as soon as I had a moment to spare."

"A pity," commented the Inspector. "There's no time like the present. Still, it's most likely the previous owner may know. One should always keep the numbers of bank-notes. Of course, you know who gave it you, Mr. Trevor?"

Trevor told him. He did not add that he thought it extremely unlikely that Prince Samadan would have any idea of its number.

"Then we must see this—er—Prince at once. Perhaps you will come along too, Mr. Trevor, and you, Mr. Waddington. I don't think I need keep you other gentlemen."

Thus, for the second time that night, Trevor found himself in the presence of the potentate, who was delighted to receive another batch of distinguished visitors. Mr. Waddington did the honours.

"Good evening, Prince. I must apologize for disturbing you so late. It's rather a pressing matter, though. You know Trevor, I think."

"Sure, that's oke," said the Prince hospitably. "Good night, Sir Waddington. Good evening, Mr. Trevor."

"And this is Inspector Norman of our local police."

To Prince Samadan, unfortunately, all grades and ranks of police meant much the same thing. He thus meant no offence by greeting the Inspector by the title conferred by undergraduates on most members of the Cambridge Constabulary.

"How do, Robert? You like vermouth, yes?"

The Inspector was considerably startled. In the first place the Prince's form of address sounded like a piece of impertinence. As regards vermouth, the Inspector was vaguely familiar with it as a rare type of liquid occasionally mixed with gin. He mistook the invitation to a drink for a kind of general question, as though the Prince had said, "Do you like mixed bathing?" or "Do you like Mae West films?" He opened his mouth to administer an official rebuke. Prince or no Prince, he had not come here to be made a fool of.

"He doesn't understand English properly," interposed the Bursar, "and I think he's trying to offer you a drink."

The latter explanation did more than anything else could have done to mollify Inspector Norman. He managed to say a word of thanks and refusal, mumbling something about taking nothing when on duty. Noting his confusion, the Bursar decided to take upon himself the task of interrogation.

"What we are wanting to know, Prince Samadan, is this: You will remember that Trevor came to see you tonight and you kindly gave him a five-pound note. An unfortunate difficulty has arisen about it."

"But so I tell 'im," cried the Prince in triumph. "He say a tenner first. Then, when I give him two fivers—which is one tenner, is it not?—he say no I take one only. I tell him then he was wrong. But don't worry. I give you another fiver now, then you will be O.K. Yes?"

"No," said the Bursar, getting a little fogged himself. "That's not it. It was very good of you to give five pounds. More than enough. The point is, unfortunately, that we have lost the five pounds."

"Oh!" remarked the Prince, as though it were a piece of good and reassuring news. "Is that all? But don't worry yourself, Sir Waddington. I think I have some more here. I give you another, yes?"

Whereupon he scrabbled among a heap of papers on the table. A theatre programme, a copy of La Vie Parisienne, and some assorted bank-notes slid to the floor. The Inspector followed their fall with bulging eyes. With great patience the Bursar declined a further donation and gradually conveyed to the intelligence of the Prince their desire to know the number of the missing note. It all seemed very childish and unnecessary to the Prince, who could not for the life of him make out why they could not accept another note, or half a dozen, and call it a day.

At length, the Bursar established the fact beyond dispute that the Prince did not know the number of the note or of any notes; and furthermore, that he was unaware that bank-notes had numbers, and that, granted they had, he could see no reason for the fact. Noting the fact that his visitors seemed, for some reason, disappointed and depressed, the Prince hastened to suggest his sovereign remedy. The fact of an initial repulse did not deter him.

"You take some spots, friends? Vermouth? French, Italiano, or mingled?"

So saying he displayed the contents of a well-stocked cupboard. The Bursar, whose habitual cheerfulness had evaporated, was about to give a mechanical refusal when his eye was caught by one of the bottles. He craned forward to obtain a closer view, and his face brightened, as though he had conducted a tiring inspection of a cloud and finally discovered its silver lining.

"Well, thank you, my dear fellow, no vermouth, I think. But I observe you have a certain kind of liqueur brandy which——"

"Licker brandy?" cried the Prince. "Sure thing! And also for you, Sir Robert? And Trevor?"

The Inspector shook his head in dumb misery, whereupon the Bursar murmured:

"Better accept, Inspector. It's an extremely rare and expensive brand. You shouldn't miss such an offer. Besides, it'll do you good. You've had a tiring and disappointing evening, I fear."

"Very well," said the Inspector obediently.

As the four savoured and sipped their drinks, which filled the greater parts of four champagne glasses, and as the expressions of three grew cheerful under the influence of the mellow liquid, there was a knock at the door and Tom Tanner entered. He bowed politely to the Prince and then addressed himself impartially to Mr. Waddington and Inspector Norman.

"You'll excuse me interrupting," he said, "but I saw you coming in here and it occurred to me I might be of some assistance."

The Inspector lowered his glass and eyed him blankly, whilst Mr. Waddington observed:

"If you are an expert interpreter we should have welcomed your presence, but now, I fear, the hour and the need are past."

"It occurred to me," explained Tanner, "that you might be wanting to know the number of the five-pound note."

The Inspector gave vent to a gasp of sudden hope and the Bursar beamed.

"You ... you took the number?" cried the Inspector.

"Oh yes!" replied Tanner, producing a slip of paper. "When I was collecting the money. Here it is."

The chorus of thanks and congratulations was interrupted by the voice of their host.

"You take a spot of brandy, Tanner? Yes?"

"Yes," said the Bursar, answering for the undergraduate in question, "he most certainly does. Give him a double. He deserves it."

CHAPTER VII

"I STILL think," said the Tutor, stroking his moustache, "that this is another escapade on the part of this mysterious practical joker, if indeed one can describe his behaviour as a joke."

"I'm inclined to disagree with you over that," observed Mr. Gale, the Dean of College. "For one thing, as I proved to you the other night, the affairs you mean were not the work of one man. Also they had certain touches of humour which could make them pass as jokes. There is nothing funny about this. It's just common or garden theft."

"There's one thing," said the Bursar, anxious to look on the bright side. "If it is the work of our tame humorist, we ought to get the money back in a plain van any time now. In these other cases the loss has always been made good. I understand even Withers received a pound-note anonymously."

"How much money was there, then?" inquired the Dean of Chapel, in tones of surprise. "Surely not enough to fill a van?"

Nobody replied to this earnest inquiry. Contrary to custom, the little group of dons was holding a morning session in the Senior Combination Room, though it was little past breakfast time. It had started as an official meeting, at which the Master had been present and at which nothing in particular had been decided beyond the measure of calling together the undergraduates at lunch-time that day. What he could say beyond the fact that the subscription money had been stolen the Master was not at all clear. What was clear, however, was that the news of the theft was already known to everyone in college. Still, it seemed to the Master that he ought to make some official announcement on the subject. Having stated these views he went back to the Lodge to resume work on his *Life and Works of the Prophet Nahum*.

"What I do think most strongly," resumed the Tutor, "is that, in view of the present development, you have no right to go on shielding the man who took Pogson's car, Gale. As I said before, I think you acted improperly in not following up the matter at the time. Now that things are going from bad to worse, we have a right to know the name of this potential thief."

"The affair of Pogson's car," replied Gale, "I regard as done with. We cannot take any disciplinary action after all this time. I myself think there is no possible connection between it and the present case, and I should not like to bring Pogson's assailant into suspicion of something which I'm convinced he knows nothing about. I regard this as a real theft, and that particular fellow is, in my opinion, the last person to descend to common stealing. After all, the thing was discussed in Hall and overheard by the waiters. It's more likely to have been a servant than an undergrad."

"I don't agree with your point of view at all," persisted the Tutor. "At such a time as this we should leave no avenue unexplored. If you know of a lawless member of the college, it is your clear duty to inform us, and leave us to judge whether or not he is likely to have committed this more serious crime."

The Dean looked uncomfortable. He wished he had never mentioned anything about his solution of the Pogson case. Had he visualized the present state of affairs he would certainly have kept it to himself.

"I don't know what the rest of you think," he observed, playing for time. "Pogson, of course, is prejudiced, but I should think some of you will agree with me that it is rather unsporting to bring up a trivial thing like his car at a time like this. In any case, the money may be returned by the next post."

In saying this he hoped to enlist the support of Waddington, who usually took a tolerant view of things in general. On this occasion, however, the Bursar's charitable instincts were overcome by the trouble to which he had been put and also the wish to set right, at all costs, the fruits of his own negligence.

"The main thing is to get the money back," he said, "and it's my belief it won't walk back. That being so, we must employ any information we can get. We might as well know who this fellow is. After all, it doesn't mean we've got to go and accuse him of taking the money just because of the car incident. At the same time it might give us a lead in the right direction. Unless you propose to go ahead and solve the whole thing yourself, Gale. Meantime we shall have to whistle for our oars and pavilion lavatories."

"Quite so," said the Tutor, "I'm glad to see you taking such a proper view of the matter." (And surprised too, thought Gale.) "So you see, Gale, we all think you ought not to keep this a secret any longer."

"I still don't think it's quite fair to mention his name in this connection," maintained the Dean. "Why not wait a day and see if the money comes back?"

"Even if it does come back," objected the Bursar, "I should very much like to know who took it, and have a few words with him. Look at the worry he's caused me. That awful cross-talk act I had with Samadan! I felt like Alexander or Mose. No! I want the fellow's blood as well as the Amal. Club's money."

"You don't seem to find it so amusing as the loss of my car," said Pogson acidly.

"Come, gentlemen," said the Tutor. "You have heard our views, Gale. Do you still persist in this attitude of subverting the discipline of the college? Who is this person?"

"You describe my conduct rather strongly, I think," said Gale dispassionately. "Still, I will bow to the opinion of the meeting on two conditions, namely that no action is taken with regard to the car incident and that the matter is not mentioned to the police. They are apt to jump to conclusions and take hasty action."

"It seems reasonable to forget the car incident," the Tutor concurred, "but I think we ought to give the police every fact of significance that we know."

"If you tell them about Pogson's car," the Dean reminded him, "the police will want to know why they weren't informed sooner. You will remember the theft was referred to them at the time."

"H'm. ... Yes ... Quite," said the Tutor. "Very well, then. We must agree to store the information for future reference."

"But what about my car?" bleated Pogson. "The thief should be punished."

This time it was the Bursar who surprised everyone, and especially Pogson, by a show of irritation.

"Oh! Forget your car! It's finished with. You've heard what's been said, and no action is to be taken against whoever is supposed to have removed it. Anyway, we've only got Gale's theories to go on."

"Quite so," said Gale; "then let us say that I don't pretend to know who took the car, but that I do know who travelled to and from Shelford on those two days, and who has a friend with a car there, but who I don't believe for a moment stole the Amal. money. Now, are you all listening?"

"What was the Amal. money for, exactly?" asked the Dean of Chapel, emerging from a kind of trance.

"Oh, don't keep interrupting!" cried the Tutor, bouncing in his chair with a mixture of excitement and irritation. "Go on, Gale."

"It was the captain of rugby football, Trevor," said the Dean.

There was a moment's silence and then the Tutor burst out:

"But ... but he was one of the very fellows who collected the money and saw where Waddington put it! He had the best chance to take it!"

"No better than four others," said Gale.

"I shouldn't have thought Trevor a likely fellow," remarked the Bursar thoughtfully. "I've met him a few times, and I should consider him rather simple and straightforward. Not the sort to steal money. In fact he doesn't seem the kind of person to have taken Pogson's car. Are you sure of your facts about that, Gale?"

"I've told you all I know about Pogson's car," answered the Dean. "And you must judge for yourselves. In any case we've agreed that the car incident is closed. As regards the money, I told you before that I consider Trevor the last person to have taken it, whether for a rag or not."

"Certainly he has a very good record here," admitted the Tutor. "His name has never come up, even over harmless rags; which is more than one can say of certain other young men of the athletic set."

"Well, there you are," said Gale. "You've forced me to drag up his name in a very unpleasant connection, and where are we as the result of it? Precisely nowhere. There's nothing more to be done in that line."

"We might question Trevor as to his movements," said the Tutor.

"I don't see what further questions we could put to him," objected the Bursar. "After all, he was one of the first people to make a statement to the Inspector last night, and all the ground was covered then. Besides that, Trevor and his friend Tanner were most helpful over tracing that five-pound note, which was really the only good clue we have. If the thief tries to pass it, we are bound to get him."

"As regards the possibility of the money having been taken during Hall," said Gale, "I've looked at the signing-off book. Three men signed out of Hall last night—Gorton, Robinson, and Campbell, all third-year men, but harmless enough fellows I should think."

At that moment they were interrupted by the respectful entry of the Head Porter, who had a message for the Tutor. It occurred to the latter that, of all persons best informed about what goes on in colleges, there are few to surpass Head Porters. He decided to explore this avenue.

"Thank you, Meadows. Er—one moment, Meadows. I suppose you have heard a certain amount of talk about the regrettable affair last night?"

"If you are referring to the theft of money from Mr. Waddington's rooms, yes, sir. I learnt of the matter fairly soon, since the Inspector in charge of the case had a few words with me on the subject prior to his departure last night."

"Ah! Good," said the Tutor, reflecting that the Inspector, like himself, seemed to appreciate the omniscience of Head Porters. "And were you able to throw any light on the subject, may I ask?"

"I think not, sir. Had I known anything of significance I should of course have communicated my knowledge to yourself or the Master. The Inspector asked me whether I had seen any gentlemen moving about the college whilst Hall was in progress. As a rule it is unlikely that any member of the college would be about at that particular time, but it so happened that last night I chanced to see an undergraduate moving about the college whilst the rest were in Hall."

All the dons looked interested to hear this information. The Tutor pressed for more details.

"The gentleman was Mr. Davies. I was going into Craven Court to assure myself that the museum was properly locked. I saw Mr. Davies a little way ahead of me. He entered the door leading to Q staircase, and I did not see him again, though I was in the court for three or four minutes."

As regards furnishing a clue, this news was slightly disappointing, since the Bursar's rooms were not in Craven Court at all. The Porter added that he had seen nobody else.

"Do you know who keeps in Q staircase?" inquired the Dean, meaning who had rooms there.

The Head Porter ignored the implication of this question. That he, as Head Porter, should fail to know the exact location, status, appearance, and general moral character of every member of college was quite unthinkable. He replied without hesitation:

"Mr. Gorton, Mr. Manders, Mr. Gore-Thomson, Mr. Starbright, Mr. Peploe, and Mr. Smith, J. C. B."

"Ha! Mr. Starbright," murmured the Dean half to himself.

"If it would be of any interest to you to know," said Meadows casually, "I think I can inform you as to the probable destination of Mr. Davies on this occasion."

"Well, it might be worth knowing," observed the Tutor. "It's a curious thing that an undergraduate should not come into Hall and yet be in college. He hadn't signed off, either. What is your theory, Meadows?"

"I think, sir, that Mr. Davies went to the rooms of Mr. Starbright, but that Mr. Starbright was not there at the time. He was in Hall, I fancy."

"How did you reach that conclusion, may I ask?" inquired Gale, displaying the interest of one trained investigator towards another.

"When I entered the court first of all, sir, there were no lights showing in any room on Q staircase. When I was leaving the court a few minutes later, there was a light in Mr. Starbright's front room."

"That seems conclusive," agreed the Tutor. "Would you say Mr. Davies was a friend of Mr. Starbright? It seems curious, going into his rooms like that."

"At the moment, sir," replied the Head Porter, "I fancy the two gentlemen are the reverse of friendly, though I cannot tell you the full and exact reasons. That is to say, sir, I don't know the exact reason except that Mr. Starbright is generally unpopular just at the moment."

"Quite," said the Tutor, wondering whether to pursue this topic any further. "I heard something about that myself, but it seems to have no bearing on the theft we are investigating."

"It would seem not, sir."

"Very well, Meadows. Then I take it you cannot help us any further. Oh, by the way. There were three gentlemen who actually did sign off last night. Let's see, I forget. ..."

"Mr. Gorton, Mr. Robinson, and Mr. Campbell, sir. They were intending to go to a reunion dinner of their old school; at the 'Red Lion', sir. I fancy they carried out their intention."

"Oh! And ... er ... on what do you base that conclusion, Meadows?"

"The three gentlemen in question left the college shortly after seven o'clock wearing evening chess. At eleven-thirty, just as I myself was about to leave the college, having handed over to my subordinate, they returned in a cheerful condition and singing snatches from the theme song of a recent talking picture. Not," added the Head Porter hastily, "that their conduct was noisy or disorderly; they were merely, shall I say, sir, merry."

"Quite," said the Tutor once more. The inquiry seemed to have been switched away from the real matter in hand. "Well, thank you again, Meadows. We must not detain you any longer."

"Well," concluded the Tutor, "I'm afraid we have not made much real progress. But, by Jove, it's after half past ten. I'm lecturing at eleven and have lots to do. We must hope the meeting of the whole college will produce something."

At this point the Dean of Chapel came to life again. He had been roused by the pushing back of chairs and had caught the Tutor's reference to the time.

"Half past ten!" he exclaimed. "But that's absurd, my dear fellow! It can't be half past ten."

The remainder looked at him in surprise, but nobody seemed to pluck up courage to ask why. At length the Bursar said:

"Well, I'll buy it. Why can't it be half past ten?"

"Why," cried the Dean of Chapel, "I'm lecturing myself on the Epistle to the Ephesians at ten o'clock, and I've never been late for a lecture in my life."

The Bursar answered not a word, but deliberately took out a large gold watch and extended the dial for his colleague's inspection. Then he pocketed the watch and followed the Tutor out of the room.

Having worked for the next hour on various college accounts, the Bursar filled a pipe and began to think over the events of the previous night. His habitual cheerfulness had undergone a temporary eclipse. He could not disguise from himself the fact that the loss of the money, willingly subscribed by many who could ill afford it, was mainly due to his own carelessness. Until it had been restored, his conscience could not be set at rest. Of course he might offer to make good the loss, but this he was unwilling to do, not through care of his own pocket, but because it would signify a public avowal of his own blame in the matter, and this he did not wish to admit. He racked his brains for some course of action which might lead to the solution of the mystery. He had little faith in the ability of the police to solve the problem, not because he distrusted their efficiency, but because they were operating in surroundings to which they were unaccustomed.

Thinking things over he was forced to the conclusion that the best brains on the spot lay in the head of his colleague Gale, the Dean. In spite of his eccentricities, there was no doubt that Gale had a flair for detection. His handling of the Pogson car case was a proof of his ability in this direction. At the time the Bursar had affected to make light of it, though in reality he had been impressed in spite of himself. Weary of inaction, Waddington decided to seek out the Dean and discuss his view of the case. In the common room, what with the tedious methods of the Tutor and the occasional inanities of the Dean of Chapel, it had been impossible to concentrate on essentials.

Passing into Craven Court he ascended to the first floor of Gale's staircase, noting subconsciously that the opposite set of rooms, across the passage, were the property of the recently discussed captain of rugger. Being himself keen on games, the Bursar was sympathetically disposed towards athletes of the Trevor type. He did not think Trevor the kind of fellow who would steal money, least of all games fund money.

An answer to his knock told him that Gale was at home. He entered the room and then stopped short in amazement. The Dean was standing in front of his mantelpiece-mirror apparently in the act of trying on a hat—a new hat seemingly—for a cardboard hat-box festooned with tissue paper was lying in the middle of the floor. The Bursar's eyes became riveted on the hat. It was of hard black felt and appeared to be a cross between a top hat and a bowler; that is to say it started from the brim as a bowler and its medium-sized crown ended in a round, flat top. The Bursar had never seen anything quite like it, except that it reminded him vaguely of the type of head-gear affected by old-fashioned farmers at horse-shows and funerals. He stood speechless.

"How do you like it?" inquired the Dean.

"I'm sorry, my dear fellow. It gave me rather a shock for the moment, but I feel better now, Well, since you ask me, I don't like it at all. Might one ask what it is for? What are you meant to be disguised as?"

"To make one's mark in politics," explained the Dean, "I'm convinced one needs some idiosyncrasy or feature of distinction which keeps one before the public eye. A noted statesman must be the subject of frequent and recognizable caricature. If he possesses no natural features of abnormality, he must assist the caricaturist by providing some easily recognizable mark by which he can be portrayed and identified. Take the Prime Minister's pipes as a case in point. Disraeli achieved the same effect by the unusual nature of his clothing."

"Yes, but a hat like that. ... Well, dash it all!"

"The hat, I admit, is by way of being a piece of plagiarism. My idea was to emulate Winston Churchill, who, as you know, built up a great political reputation by the originality of his various hats. I have myself been seeking an entirely new and revolutionary hat as my badge and passport to political fame. Unfortunately, I am not satisfied as to the originality of the pattern. It has a resemblance to one worn by Churchill himself shortly before the war. I'm not sure he didn't wear it at the siege of Sidney Street. Anyway, it's only on approval."

"But nobody could approve of it," affirmed the Bursar. "Anyway, put it away for the moment. It distracts me, and I've come to talk seriously."

"I regard this hat as a serious matter," answered the Dean. "In a parliamentary career much depends on first impressions. However, as your own sartorial taste is deplorable, you cannot be expected to help much. For the moment I will shelve the matter."

He placed the hat reverently back in its wrappings, noted that it was midday, and having an old friend's knowledge of his colleague's likes and customs, filled two glasses of light sherry without inquiry and passed one over to Waddington.

"You are worried," he said. "You are worried because you realize the loss of the money is due to your casual methods. You are seeking a solution of your trouble and you have thought of me as the cleverest and most suitable person to consult."

The plump face of the Bursar expanded in a slow grin of admiration. "I hate to admit it, you old swanker, but that just about hits it off."

"Well, frankly, I think there's a very poor chance of bringing the thief to book unless he tries to pass the five-pound note. Our main hope is that it is one of those freak escapades which will end up by the money being returned. But, as I said in the common room, I don't think for a moment that it comes under that category. It's the wrong type of crime. There are some things I might solve, but I haven't much hope of this."

"That's not encouraging," said the Bursar gloomily. "Haven't you any line to suggest?"

"You must appreciate the difficulties. In the case of petty crime, especially theft, there is no easier place to operate and no harder place to find the culprit than a college. The same applies to a school or a regiment. In the first place it is so easy. A hundred or more people, all superficially alike, living a common life together with their rooms and possessions easily accessible to one and all; all theoretically honest and respectable, hence difficult to treat as suspects for investigation, and at the same time, frequently bothered with debts and shortage of money, hence liable to sudden temptation. Suppose, for instance, that we had actually found finger-prints, I hardly see how we could have taken the prints of everyone in college.

"However, let us see what few facts we have to go on. In the first place the unfortunate fact sticks out that the whole college, at any rate all those present at the Amal. meeting, knew that you would receive into your room a large sum of money immediately before Hall on a certain day. It would follow as inevitable that the money must remain in your room during Hall. It is also well known that you remain in the Senior Combination Room for some time after Hall, thus leaving the coast clear."

"Rather risky, all the same," commented Waddington. "Having all that money on hand, I might have come straight back and caught him in the act, unless he did it during Hall."

"That is so, but perhaps the thief was someone who knew his man. I, for instance, knowing you as I do, would feel certain that even the presence of the crown jewels in your drawer would not cause you sufficient anxiety to miss your port. After all, old man, you have purposely made a parade of telling the world that, in your opinion, nothing really matters very much. I suppose we all advertise our opinions. I dare say I do."

The Bursar smiled rather ruefully. He did not see his way to a contradiction.

"Then, if you had come in before he had actually pocketed the money, he could easily have made up some excuse for having called to see you. He could have said, for instance, that he had come to give an extra ten shillings before it was too late. That would certainly have disarmed your suspicions.

"That brings us to the question of whether the money was taken during or after Hall. There again we have no means of deciding. As you say, after Hall there was the risk of your returning prematurely. On the other hand the thief ran a risk of being identified by being one of the few not in Hall. Also the chance of his being seen going to your room during Hall, though remote, would be far more likely to excite suspicion than if he walked into your staircase amongst the crowds dispersing after Hall. After all, there are five other sets of rooms on your staircase. You can see that for yourself from the fact of Meadows spotting Davies, though that has nothing to do with the case as far as we can see. The fact remains, though, that there was a man about who did not hesitate to enter the rooms of a potential enemy when the owner was away. I'll come back to that later. Of course there's one thing that might possibly be done. I doubt if the Inspector has thought of it."

"What's that?" asked the Bursar eagerly. He felt in the mood to clutch at straws.

"One might interview the other five men on your staircase and make a note of any visitors they received in the hour after Hall. Then, if we hear of anyone else who was seen going in at that time, it will bear looking into. If it is to be done, I should think you would be the best person to conduct the inquiry. It seems very reasonable, and they could hardly resent being asked under the circumstances. After all, most of the college, especially the athletes, must be dead keen to get the money back."

"By Jove!" said the Bursar, "that's a good idea. I'll ask them all." Which, it may be stated, he afterwards did, with negative results.

"As regards Davies," continued the Dean, "there seems nothing to show that he had anything to do with the business, except that he was acting suspiciously elsewhere. But then, if he were going to do anything as risky as robbing your room, he would scarcely risk attracting attention by showing himself in other parts of the college. I think that's a strong point in his favour. As regards Trevor, there's nothing at all to connect him with the case. Of course, if he were asked, he could probably account for the whole of his time after Hall. I expect he was with other fellows after Hall, and we know he dined there."

"That's rather a curious thing," said the Bursar slowly.

"What is?" asked the Dean, and, remembering the best detective manner, added, "tell me every detail of the case, however unimportant it may seem."

"Well," explained Waddington. "When I had discovered what had happened and had decided to call in the police, this Inspector Norman wanted to see the five men who had collected the money and seen me put it away. So I went round to find them, and had the deuce of a job to find Trevor. In the end I found him in a set of rooms with the door locked. It took them half a minute or so to decide on letting me in."

"A sported oak, eh?" commented Gale. "That's all right when a fellow wants to work by himself, but I don't like to hear of a number of fellows shutting themselves in together. Some of these prayer-meeting societies do it, of course, but so do other little groups very much less harmless. Tell me, whose were the rooms and what did you make of the people inside? You got in, I suppose?"

"Yes," said Waddington. "They weren't that sort of crowd at all, and there was nothing at all suspicious. A group of athletes mostly, with a couple of jugs of beer between them. I couldn't understand it."

"Well, who were they exactly?"

"It was Winterton's room. He was there with some of the rugger crowd: Sullivan, Davies, Duncan the blue, Trevor and his friend Tanner, and two or three whose names I forget. Rowing men, I fancy. They seemed rather confused at my entry, though what about I don't know. They were all sober, and I saw no partially concealed chorus girls or opium pipes or anything."

"That's very interesting," said Gale thoughtfully. "At first sight they appear the pick of our most respected and respectable athletes. At the same time they're rather an interesting collection. Trevor, Tanner, and Duncan I regard as harmless, Davies I'm doubtful about. As regards Winterton and Sullivan—if there are two fellows going about who have joined in more rags and got away with less trouble than anyone in college, I should say it was those two. There's little or nothing officially against them, but I regard them as clever, tough customers. But there again, I don't class them as likely thieves."

"I told them all what had happened," said the Bursar, "and asked Trevor to come with me, which he at once did."

"Did they seem surprised at the news of the theft?"

"Very surprised. Even more surprised, in fact, than one might have expected such fellows to be. Almost horrified, you might say."

"You didn't notice if Starbright was one of the party, did you?" inquired the Dean after a thoughtful pause.

"Starbright?" said the Bursar in surprise. "No. I know him, and I'm sure he wasn't. Why should he have been?"

The Dean made a long pause, as though uncertain how to express his thoughts.

"There's something rather curious going on in college at the moment," he said at length. "Most likely it has nothing whatever to do with our theft. At the same time, when two mysterious things occur at much the same time, it may happen there is a connection which at first is quite invisible. What has struck me is the fact of seeing two or three people in close proximity in certain curious and different circumstances. It makes one think."

"I don't follow you," said Waddington.

"I'm thinking of four people—Starbright, Davies, Trevor, and Sullivan, none of whom are usually in each other's company. Now you probably know something about the unpopularity of Starbright over the All Saints match. I don't know the precise facts and I haven't been meaning to inquire further. Sufficient to say that, for some obscure reason, Starbright let them down and failed to turn up to the match. Quite rightly there was indignation in the college, and I quite expected some trouble to ensue.

"That night, as you may remember, there was an explosion which was said to be a firework. Having come to the spot we find Trevor, who professes to know nothing about it, and Sullivan, who, when questions are taking an awkward turn, makes a convenient entry from an adjacent place of concealment and explains it away as a firework in his usual plausible manner. Having observed smoke and smelt cordite, I was of the opinion that a firearm had been discharged in one of the upper rooms of which the most likely belonged to Starbright. To have gone up and tried to find a firearm or asked questions would have been so much waste of time. If a live round had actually been fired there would be traces in the room or else it must have found a billet somewhere in the court. A word to the bed-maker produced a report in the morning that there was no sign of a bullet mark in Starbright's room. I therefore looked round outside, with the result that I was able to dig out a bullet from the middle of the court."

The Bursar remarked in a surprised way that he was damned.

"Then tonight we hear of Davies making a surprise visit to Starbright's rooms. Later on we see the same three, Davies, Trevor, and Sullivan, closeted together with certain other leading lights in college athletics. Starbright, so you say, was not present. I should have been surprised if he had been."

"Then what do you suppose they were up to?" asked the Bursar.

"I think that this group has been devising some rag or punishment against Starbright over this football business. The night before last, I believe, some trouble took place between them during which a revolver was fired."

"But, hang it," objected the Bursar, "this isn't Chicago. Even if a man does let his side down, the rest don't start shooting him up."

"No," admitted the Dean. "I don't know what really can have taken place, but I'm not easy in my mind about it. I never did like these semi-serious rags against individuals. They generally end in someone getting hurt. And if people are going to start using firearms. ..."

"I think you've a bee in your bonnet over it," remarked the Bursar, restored to his habitual optimism.

"I'm not so sure. After all, Trevor is captain of football, and therefore the most likely man to take action against a defaulter; Duncan is a big man in football circles, and we have it from Meadows that Davies is on bad terms with Starbright. What should he be doing in Starbright's rooms?"

"Goodness knows!" said the Bursar. "Putting a time-bomb there perhaps, but then it ought to have gone off by now. I'm glad I live in the other court!"

"Then there's Winterton and Sullivan," continued the Dean, ignoring his colleague's suggestion. "They're both budding gangsters in my opinion, though they manage to keep within the law. The only thing is, I'm surprised at Trevor being mixed up in any rough stuff. I've always looked upon him as an easy-going, good-natured fellow."

"Very probably," grunted the Bursar absently, for he was growing tired of the topic. "Meantime we seem to have got away from the pressing question of the Amal. money. I take it you've nothing more to suggest?"

"Nothing at the moment, I fear, beyond suggesting you tactfully question the people on your staircase."

."Oh yes!" said the Bursar, who had forgotten all about it. "I shall most certainly do so."

Left to himself the Dean continued to meditate on the revolver episode. As the guardian of discipline in the college he was worried by the chain of circumstances surrounding it. As he had said to the Bursar, he did not credit Trevor with reckless or vindictive behaviour, and he had more than a passing acquaintance with the captain of rugger. As a freshman Trevor had read history, and once a week had presented himself to the Dean for the supervision of his studies. This entailed the reading aloud of his weekly essay, a few minutes' talk on work, and latterly a few more minutes' social conversation. Of all his pupils Gale had found Trevor if not the most intelligent at least the most pleasant and willing. Now that Trevor had come to live in the rooms opposite, he was an occasional guest of Gale's for tea or a glass of wine. This being the case, Gale felt that Trevor, if tactfully approached, might be willing to give some helpful information without having to tread on dangerous ground. The sound of ascending footsteps on the stairs suggested that the lodger opposite was returning from his midday lecture. This helped Gale to make up his mind. He crossed the passage and knocked at the door.

Trevor received him affably, but with a feeling of slight surprise. Though frequent guests in the rooms of dons, undergraduates are seldom used to receiving or entertaining the senior members. Trevor never remembered being visited by a don before. He wondered if Gale had come on business or for a social call, and whether he ought to offer him a drink. He compromised by handing a box of cigarettes.

The Dean chatted rather absently about football and the weather before broaching the subject of his call.

"There's a small matter I thought you might be able to help me over. As you know, I try not to take my duties as Dean too much to heart, and I seldom try to seek information about things that are not meant for my ears. So I haven't come to try and pump you. Still, it seems possible that without betraying any confidences or giving any other person away, you might, so to speak, be able to ease my mind on certain points."

Trevor looked frankly puzzled, but he answered readily:

"Anything I can tell you, sir, I'll gladly let you know; that is, I suppose, within limits."

"Quite," smiled the Dean. "I follow you exactly. What is worrying me at the moment is the question of any serious trouble arising over Starbright and the football club?"

As an experienced detector of crime Gale eyed his companion keenly in order to note his reactions to this reference. A look of comprehension crossed Trevor's face, as if to show he now grasped the purport of the inquiry, but he showed no signs of confusion or guilty conscience.

"I'm not fully aware of what the trouble was originally about and I don't want information on that point. I think, especially over games, it's best for you fellows to run your own show without any interference from above. I understand also that, quite naturally, there has been a certain amount of ill-feeling in college against Starbright, though I'm not wanting to know the details of that either."

"We were all rather annoyed with him," admitted Trevor, "but nothing much came of it and the matter is more or less closed."

"That's the very point I want to get at, if I can," said the Dean. "One is always rather nervous over feuds and rags which arise in cases of this kind. They so often lead to injuries and incidents which are afterwards regretted. Do you really think that this ill-feeling has died down, or must we expect any further outbreak of trouble in that direction? But perhaps that is hardly a fair question. Don't answer it unless you like."

"That's all right, sir. I'd like to answer it because I can tell you that, as far as I and my own circle of friends are concerned, we have fully decided to treat the thing as finished; in fact to discourage any reopening of it."

"I'm more than glad to hear it," said the Dean. "I'm most grateful to you for having taken this line."

"Of course," added Trevor, thinking of Davies, "there may still be one or two sort of private cases of ill-feeling which might lead to trouble, but that's nothing to do with most of us."

"Quite," said the Dean, also thinking of Davies.

Here the matter would probably have ended but for the fact that Trevor, wishing to be as frank as possible, thought fit to refer to the abortive attack led by Davies. He was about to declare his own absence from and disapproval of this affray, when it occurred to him that to do so might sound priggish and not very convincing. He therefore made what afterwards turned out a somewhat unfortunate alteration in his next remark.

"Of course," he said, "I admit some of us tried to make it rather hot for Starbright the night before last, but it rather fizzled out and no harm was done. That was really what caused the thing to be dropped."

The Dean thanked Trevor once more and rather abruptly took his leave, Up to the moment of Trevor's parting piece of information he had been extremely pleased by the turn things had taken, and was reassured of the speaker's sincerity. But by his final statement Trevor had unwittingly struck a false note. Back in his own room the Dean pondered over the inconsistency of statement and fact. Trevor had just admitted being in a rag which had come to a sudden end and had deterred the participants from any repetition. This could only mean the untimely resort to firearms. On the night in question Trevor had been found alone and nearest to the spot where the shooting had taken place, yet he had flatly denied any knowledge whatever of the affair, and had pretended to have only just come from the college.

In affairs of this kind the Dean could expect and excuse a certain amount of mild falsehood, such as the statement of the specious Sullivan, for instance. His story was an obvious excuse, made up on the spur of the moment and containing just sufficient lies to tide over an awkward situation. Probably not even the author supposed it would really be believed. But the lies told by Trevor seemed of a more serious nature by reason of the downright way in which they were uttered, and the conviction he had managed to put into his words seemed to suggest that he was well versed in the arts of deception. Gale felt puzzled and disappointed. He had always regarded Trevor as straightforward and harmless. It would appear that he had made a mistake. Could it be that Trevor was really a very clever fellow? For the height of cleverness was, in the Dean's opinion, to pass as a simpleton. He decided to keep an eye on Trevor. Possibly he had misjudged the rugger captain, but, then, one never knew.

Looking at his watch he found that it was nearly time for the meeting of the whole college ordered by the Master for one o'clock. He hoped that the Master would come primed with the necessary details and that he would confine his remarks to the matter in hand. The Master had ceased to take a very active part in the everyday affairs of the college and had lately begun to display some of the absentminded tendencies already so highly developed in his Dean of Chapel. In due course the Hall was filled with senior and junior members, and the Dean settled himself to hear the worst.

On the whole it was much as he had anticipated. In a somewhat rambling discourse their elderly and clerical Master gave a more or less accurate description of what was already known to the last detail by everybody in the room. He then dwelt at some length on his surprise and grief at the fact of such an event having taken place in a community of such fame and reputation as St. Chad's. Finally he adjured anyone having any information on the subject to communicate the same to himself or the Tutor without delay.

Gale had supposed that this would be the beginning and end of the morning's oratory. However, when the Master had sat down, the Bursar said a few brisk words. He profoundly regretted having been in some slight measure to blame for having made this mischance possible. He sincerely hoped that in the course of a few hours or days it might be possible to trace the thief and recover the money. Should nothing have been accomplished in reasonable time, there would be a meeting of the Amalgamated Clubs to decide what was best to be done. Then the meeting came to an end, having, as the Dean had supposed, accomplished precisely nothing.

CHAPTER VIII

THE latter half of that Saturday in November seemed to pass by without event. A proportion of the men of Chad's disported themselves on field and river, and then returned to spend the last evening of the week in relaxation from toil. In every class of society there is a special atmosphere about Saturday night, more especially amongst those who have done a hard week's work. It would be idle to assert that every member of Cambridge University works hard throughout the length and breadth of every week. Many, in fact, do more private reading in the vacation than in the term. Even so, Saturday night has its significance in the life of the average undergraduate. Many who, on five nights of the week, conscientiously withdraw to their own rooms after Hall to do a spot of work, make Saturday night a time of social enjoyment and rest from labour. Little groups forgather for rubbers of bridge or tables of vingt-et-un, or make up parties for the cinema. Three out of four rooms are empty, but from the fourth comes the sound of talk and laughter and perhaps the pop of a cork or the hiss of a siphon.

Most Saturday nights would have found Martin Trevor and Tom Tanner in some little gathering of which Peter Duncan, Sullivan, and possibly Davies would be among those present. This Saturday was to prove an exception to the usual rule. At different times and in different places certain peculiar things were destined to take place.

At two minutes past seven Martin Trevor looked at his watch for the fourth time in twenty minutes. He appeared to be in a state of impatience and suppressed excitement. He was in his bedroom, and had just finished brushing his hair with unusual care. The grey flannel trousers and check sports coat which he generally wore all day were now lying unfolded on the bed. He patted his pockets, took a last look round, and then passed into the sitting-room.

This was an old-fashioned and spacious room with windows facing in two directions. Large double windows looked down on Craven Court, and at the opposite end of the room was a smaller bow window shaded by dark curtains and having a single iron bar in the middle. Had it been daylight, an observer could have seen that this window overlooked a small plot of ground ornamented by shrubs and flower-beds. This was the fellows' garden and was very seldom used by the dons owing to difficulty of access. There was a gate leading into it through the high boundary wall flanking a side street outside the college, whilst from the interior of the college it could be reached by going through the college museum, which occupied the ground floor space below the rooms of Trevor and Mr. Gale. Occasionally in summer the Dean took a deck-chair and a book there on Sunday afternoons, but his colleagues generally accepted the more spacious hospitality of the Master's garden at the back of the main court.

In this window recess was a writing-table containing the usual furniture, including a small diary. Trevor moved over to this table and, picking up the diary, studied its interior for a few moments with a puzzled frown. Then he made an entry in pencil. Had an observer once more been present he would have said that if Trevor had been recording the day's events he must have had an extremely uneventful day, so soon was his writing finished. Then he crossed to a large cupboard which he opened. Five minutes later he left the room and made his way to the main gate. He had an overcoat and soft hat, but no cap and gown. As he passed the lighted door of the porter's lodge he observed with satisfaction that Meadows was engaged in handing letters to two freshmen who were just arriving for Hall from their lodgings. He thus left the college without being seen.

Ten minutes after Hall had ended, Peter Duncan stood in a bored way on the path of the main court. He had been talking to Sullivan, but the latter was going out to coffee in Clare and had just left him. He was at a loose end and did not know what to do next. For some reason or other there seemed to be nobody about and nothing doing. Trevor had not been in Hall, Tanner had spoken rather shortly about doing a spell of work, and Davies had pleaded an unspecified engagement. Tanner had seemed irritable and depressed, so Duncan thought. As for work, Duncan drew the line at that on a Saturday night. Perhaps there was a game of poker or vingty on somewhere. He began to stroll round the court and thence to Craven Court, looking at any windows of rooms whose occupants he knew. Perhaps Starbright would have a party. Should he look in on Starbright? After all the Saints affair was over, and there was no reason for not burying the hatchet. Starbright was a blighter in some ways, but then he had often cut Starbright's cards and drunk Starbright's beer in the past. It might be a good thing to show he bore no malice. But Starbright's room seemed empty; no light showed through the thin curtains. Perhaps he was over with his pansy friend, Baxter-Smith. No, there was no light in Smith's place, nor in Davies's rooms.

What a night! Well, he had a standing invitation from some rugger-playing Scots in Pemmer. That was an idea! There'd be no shortage of beer in that galley. Having gone to his rooms for a cap and gown, for his national upbringing had taught him never to run the unnecessary risk of a fine, he made his way to Pembroke.

Tom Tanner set out an array of text-books and notebooks and settled down to a good night's work. He wished to occupy his mind, since he was feeling depressed and his thoughts were not cheerful ones. His schooldays had not been altogether happy. Of a sociable disposition, he had been starved of the company of congenial friends. Deprived of an athletic career and devoid of much physical attraction, he had been passed over in the formation of groups and cliques in his house. Coming to Cambridge and meeting Martin Trevor he had, under the wing of his new friend, gained a passport to the most desirable circles that St. Chad's could afford. The pleasure of the last two terms had made him realize the more vividly all that he had missed in the past. The Saturday social evenings had been especially pleasant. The rounding-off of many enjoyable weeks. Now it seemed that there would be an end to all that. Martin Trevor had excused his absence without giving any reason, but Tanner had little doubt that Jane Brent was the cause of his friend's absence that night. He tried hard not to dislike Jane Brent, whom he had never met. Doubtless she was a very nice girl, but the fact remained that she had come between him and his best friend. It was an unusual inversion of the eternal triangle.

Tom Tanner switched his thoughts from these topics and became absorbed in Motley's *History of the Dutch Republic.* He read on until his thoughts were once more diverted by the sound of the midnight chimes. At this moment the last reveller should be safely back in college and, theoretically, none could enter college without exposure and severe penalties. Still, that was only theoretical. There were ways and means. He wondered if Trevor was back and whether all in Chad's save himself were safely tucked up in bed. Well, Trevor had chosen to go away without giving a reason. It was not for him to butt in where he was not asked. He forced himself back to Motley. ...

The clocks were striking one in the morning, and he had meant to run through a chapter on the special period, so as to have the detail up to date for Monday's lecture. It was no good listening to a lecture without first reading up the facts, and tomorrow night Trevor might be at liberty to make up for his present desertion. He hunted round for the appropriate book without being able to find it. Then he gave an exclamation of annoyance, for he remembered where the book was. Two days ago he had gone over to read in Trevor's rooms. Of course he must have left it there. Most people, at ten past one in the morning, would have called it a day and gone to bed, but Tanner, besides being methodical, had a streak of obstinacy. If he set out to do a thing he did it. He had decided to read that chapter before turning in, and read it he would. He went downstairs, passed into Craven Court, and climbed the stairs to Trevor's rooms.

At the moment when Tom Tanner was crossing Craven Court, a solitary car was standing silently under the shadow of a high wall bordering a residential road on the outskirts of Cambridge. Its side and tail lights burned dimly. From the far side of the wall the head and shoulders of a man came suddenly into view and their owner peered cautiously up and down the road. Satisfied that there was nobody in sight in either direction, he swung himself over and dropped lightly down on the pavement. Next moment he had started the engine and was driving slowly away.

In a short time his route took him along the even more deserted piece of road running between open stretches of grass and bounded on one side by the Backs and open spaces behind King's and Clare and on the other by tree-fringed playing fields and the newly built extension of Clare. Here the street lamps were few and far between, and in the winter moonlight he might have fancied himself on a country road. The driver sighed with relief, for his journey was nearly over, and in a very few minutes he should have returned the car to its garage up beyond Magdalene.

Suddenly he stiffened to attention and his foot came sharply off the accelerator. He had once more switched on his headlights and their beam showed a dark, confused shape in the middle of the road some little distance ahead. As the car drifted slowly towards the spot, the shape resolved itself into a bicycle lying flat in the middle of the road and crouched over it the figure of a man holding his head, apparently dazed or in pain. Clearly there had been some kind of an accident.

Seeming to become aware of the car's approach, the man in the road raised himself slightly and lifted a shaky hand in an appeal for assistance. Then he slumped forward again, with his face turned to the ground. Stopping a few yards short and jumping out of the car, the motorist went forward and put a hand on the cyclist's shoulder with an inquiry of what had happened. What had happened was not stated, but what did happen next was most surprising.

With an apparent access of strength, the cyclist straightened up abruptly, wheeled round upon the motorist, thrust something with a hard, circular end into his chest, and said:

"Keep absolutely still and put your hands up!"

The motorist gave a start of astonishment and his hands flickered uncertainly half-way to his face.

"Right up, or I'll shoot!" said the voice. It was a high, unnatural, snarling voice, obviously disguised. "I want your money and your driving licence, that's all. Hand 'em over quick, and I'll let you get away. Quick, now!"

The motorist gaped in astonishment. He perceived a man slightly smaller than himself muffled in a raincoat and with a hat pulled forward over his eyes. Identification was further made difficult by the fact that the eyes were surrounded by a cloth mask. The cyclist, too, could see little of his intended victim, for the latter also seemed to be using a broad-brimmed hat to conceal his features and was further obscured by the glaring headlights behind him.

The mind of the motorist worked with lightning rapidity. He was in a clever hold-up and about to lose his money unless he acted at once. Would the gunman dare to shoot? That was the question. More often than not a gun was bluff. Besides, there were college buildings within earshot. The fellow would never get away with it. He could ill afford to lose his money, whilst he could not enlist the help of the police in its recovery since his own presence must not be known. He decided to risk it.

Mumbling some words meant to be indicative of blue funk, he cautiously lowered one hand towards his breast pocket and fumbled with the buttons of his overcoat. The hand hovered above the muzzle of his assailant's pistol for a moment, then with a clenching of the fist it suddenly struck the muzzle sharply downwards, whilst its owner brought his other hand into play by aiming a blow at the cyclist's head. He braced himself for the sound or feel of a bullet, but none came, and the weapon clattered on the ground.

The next few seconds were crammed with incident. The cyclist, if a muddler with a revolver, made up for this by his skill in a hand-to-hand encounter. The motorist took a blow in the eye which brought him a vision of newer and nearer stars. Then he closed with his opponent and the two reeled across the road and rolled over and over on the grass bank.

The motorist came uppermost, and he had a grip on the cyclist's throat. This temporary triumph caused him to break silence for the first time.

"I'll damn' well teach you to try tricks like that!"

The cyclist appeared astonished at these words. His own grip suddenly relaxed and he made muffled sounds indicative of surrender. With a grunt of triumph the motorist tore off his assailant's mask, whereupon the grunt of triumph was changed to a gasp of astonishment.

"You!" he exclaimed, his hands dropping weakly to his sides.

"You!" echoed the cyclist, staring in astonishment.

Keeping in the shadows of less frequented streets, Baxter-Smith moved slowly in the direction of St. Chad's. It was well past midnight, so the time of his entry was of no great consequence. If admitted by the porter his offence would vary little whether his arrival was reported as one or two o'clock. As it happened, he was not worrying about that. All the same he was uneasy in his mind. He had not enjoyed the last three hours, and he had a premonition of coming trouble. As he turned down the narrow lane which runs by the back of St. Chad's, the clocks of Cambridge were striking the hour of one.

At half past ten Mr. Gale walked up to the first floor of his staircase and entered his rooms. He noted with relief that a good fire was still burning in the sitting-room. He had done well to warn the bedmaker to keep it going in case of his early return. He had just come from dinner at the Master's Lodge. The dinner, as a meal, had been good enough, but as usual the company had been elderly and largely clerical, and the conversation had given him little scope for indulging his favourite topics, for the moment, of politics or detection. As members of other colleges had been present, the subject of the theft had been studiously avoided.

Another disadvantage of dinner at the Lodge was, in the Dean's opinion, the fact that the evening petered out at an hour too late to embark on any other programme of social amusement and too early to retire tamely to bed, especially on Saturday night, for the Dean, perhaps subconsciously influenced by his surroundings, still retained the Saturday night complex of his juniors. He repaired a deficiency in the Master's ménage by mixing himself a whisky-and-soda, and then began to consider the best way of passing the final hour of the day.

Glancing at his table he was reminded of the fact that he had that afternoon brought back a book of crime fiction from the circulating library. It was his custom to draw one specially for Sunday, and his liking for the science of detection had given him a taste for thrillers. He decided to anticipate his Sunday reading by dipping into his latest choice, though he had forgotten for the moment which particular item on his list had been issued to him that day.

He picked up the volume and glanced at the title. He did not seem to recall the author as a famous writer of thrillers. Then he recollected that Anderson, the Dean of All Saints, had strongly recommended the novel in question. It was a public-school crime story, Anderson had said, and in parts quite humorous. Anything to do with education appealed to Gale, so he had put it on his list. He decided to spend an hour reading the first portion of the story and reserve the climax, if any, to the next day. He settled down in a deep arm-chair, lit a pipe, and began to read.

The clock ticked on, and there was no other sound except the steady rustle of turned pages. On two isolated occasions, at ten minutes to eleven and twenty past that hour, the Dean was moved to a slight chuckle, an unusual reaction in his study of crime. At a quarter to twelve he finished a chapter and paused with a feeling of perplexity and slight irritation. He had read over a quarter of a book which gave rather an amusing account of a school, but there was a conspicuous absence of shooting, stabbing, or any customary form of crime. The Dean wondered if Anderson had misunderstood him. Perhaps it wasn't a detective novel at all. That would be most annoying, since at that particular time the Dean regarded the reading of any fiction not dealing with crime or politics as a waste of time. He resolved to sample one more chapter before discarding the book for good and all. Tomorrow he would have to borrow a volume from the Edgar Wallace collection owned by the Bursar in order to supply his Sabbath reading.

He resumed his reading and, turning another page, stumbled, so to speak, over a corpse. His interest quickened, and he finished the chapter. At a quarter past twelve he paused once more. The murder, if murder there was, did not seem to produce much dramatic excitement. Perhaps he had better go to bed after all. Well, he would give, it until half-past to liven up. At half past twelve corpse number two was on the mat and things were warming up.

Here the Dean broke off and began to reason out the solution. He always tried to match his wits against those of the author and spot the villain, sometimes with success. On this occasion he was baffled but intrigued. Perhaps there were still some essential clues to come, so he hurried into the concluding stages of the book. The clock struck one. Goodness! How late it was! He had meant to turn in an hour and a half ago. There seemed only another twenty pages to go, and he was still in the dark. He could not rest without knowing the solution. He would sit back and make one more effort on his own, then see for himself. He mixed a fresh drink and sat down again by the dying fire. The clock struck half past one. With a sigh Gale gave it up, and turned to the last chapter but one.

The silence was broken by the shutting of a door and the sound of footsteps outside. Gale knew it for Trevor's door across the passage. His problematical neighbour had been keeping late hours also, it seemed. The footsteps of two persons could be heard descending the stairs. They seemed heavy, slow steps, as though the walkers were steering an uncertain course with difficulty. One of the walkers made a slight bump in an apparent collision with the staircase wall. The trained mind of the Dean registered the sounds, and he deduced that the two walkers might not be quite sober. He had half a mind to cross to the window and look out in order to satisfy his curiosity as to their identity. He was, however, sunk very deeply into a comfortable chair, and it would probably mean opening a window, thereby letting in cold air. Besides, it was Saturday night, and he was not one who went looking for petty trouble. If they had been having a thick night, good luck to them, and good heads in the morning!

Five minutes later the Dean had finished his book. He sat for another five minutes in deliberation, then he crossed to his desk and opened a note-book. In this he was accustomed to keep a record of all the detective fiction he had read, and he entered up each novel under the heading of A, B, or C according to merit. Noting once more the title and author of the book in his hand, he made an entry under section A and then went to bed.

At a quarter to two all was silent and no lights showed in the length and breadth of St. Chad's. All were abed, and all should have been asleep. As it happened, three of its members slept ill or not at all. But the sleep of a fourth might be said to have more than counterbalanced the insomnia of his fellows.

The dawn of a Sunday broke over the college, a day of late rising for all save those who attended the early service in chapel. As late as seven o'clock no footfall had sounded in Craven Court, but, as the clock was striking, the hour, the figure of the handy man, Sergeant Stumpy, might have been seen making for the south-east corner, where lay the college baths and a furnace of which the stoking was his first daily care.

As late as the commencement of the present century few colleges could provide anything much beyond individual hip-baths for their members. Gradually, in some spare corner or other, modern sets were installed to keep tardy pace with the march of culture and civilization. The baths of St. Chad's had been built in a little annexe at the back of Craven Court, adjoining the museum and the fellows' garden. They were reached by a small archway in one corner of the court, which passed under an upper set of rooms and terminated in a large, iron-spiked back gate which was seldom unlocked, except for the occasional delivery of coal for the furnace. The arch, or more properly tunnel—for it was between five and ten yards long—was furnished with an old-fashioned lamp carried by a short wrought-iron support which jutted out from one wall about ten feet from the ground. Builders had been engaged in refacing walls at that end of the court, and some of their gear, including mortar and barrels of cement, had been placed under the arch for the week-end.

As he approached his morning's work, Sergeant Stumpy's thoughts were distinctly unsabbatical, in fact almost unprintable. As an old soldier he might have been expected to possess that *esprit de corps* and willingness for work typical of many ex-service men. Alas, Sergeant Stumpy was an old soldier in the less admirable sense of the word. As a grouser, a scrounger, and lead-swinger he had been in a class—or more properly squad or platoon—by himself. Since leaving the army it had been his firm opinion that he had been consistently overworked and underpaid. He had now exchanged his red coat for the red flag, and had strong views on the rights of the worker and the wrongs of capitalism, though he was careful not to advertise his theories too strongly in the reactionary stronghold where his work lay.

At the moment he was thinking very unkindly of his immediate overlord, the Bursar. When the revolution came he placed that plump official—bloated on the sweat of the poor, in his opinion—in the first rank of victims. He had lately seen a film in which French aristocrats had gone in large numbers to the guillotine. Whilst admitting that the guillotine was somewhat complicated and out of date for present needs, Sergeant Stumpy had wished a similar fate for certain of the Cambridge aristocracy, notably the Bursar, besides some of the more arrogant undergraduates. He remembered that others in the film had been strung up from street lamps. That was certainly more practicable. The Bursar would look well as a decoration in the King's Parade system of lighting.

With such gloomy thoughts Sergeant Stumpy turned under the archway and then stopped short with a gasp of amazement and dismay. Many of us at different times utter prayers for this and that, yet, if or when such prayers are unexpectedly answered, we are disconcerted, or even dismayed, by the results. True, the Sergeant's wish had not been granted in the highest degree, but granted it had been.

His eyes were fixed wildly on the old-fashioned lamp with its iron bracket, from which was hanging the dead body of an undergraduate.

CHAPTER IX

AMONG the few early risers that Sunday morning was Mr. Gale, who purposed attending the chapel communion service. Awakened by an unexpected and unusual spell of morning sunshine, he was astir even earlier than necessary, and no later than seven-thirty was dressed and about to take a walk round the court before going into chapel.

Leaving his room he paused on the landing outside, his eye being caught by a stray object on the mat at his feet. Gale was a habitual picker-up of unconsidered trifles, besides being an unconscious pocketer of other people's matchboxes. He stooped down and pocketed the article without thinking much about it. Passing into the court, which he had expected to find deserted, he was surprised to see, besides the normal sight of two elderly and bonneted bedmakers entering a distant staircase, two unexpected and intriguing figures vanishing under the arch in his own corner of the court. He had time to observe that one was a middle-aged man in dark clothes and with a black bag, and the other no less a person than Inspector Norman.

With quickened interest yet unhurried pace Gale bent his steps in the same direction. The presence of the Inspector at such an early hour on a Sunday morning suggested some startling development in the Amalgamated Club robbery case. Gale wondered if it had been solved. He could hope so, for the Bursar's sake. At the same time it would be annoying for such an affair to come tamely to an end before he had a chance to exercise his own powers of detection in the matter. He approached the arch, trying not to hurry, and turned the corner as casually as possible.

Besides the two new arrivals the Dean found a small group, which included the Tutor, the head and under porters, Sergeant Stumpy, and a constable. The latter stood stolidly apart from the others and eyed Gale's approach with suspicion, as though about to tell him to move on, whilst the members of college present were gathered with white faces and amazed expressions round the figure which was still hanging at the end of a rope. The Inspector and the police surgeon were inspecting the body.

"You were quite right, sir," the Inspector was saying to the Tutor, "to leave everything just as it was found. It's always best, even in the simplest cases, if it's certain that Life is extinct."

"No doubt about that," the police surgeon remarked. "He's been dead for several hours." He began to handle the corpse gently.

The Tutor swallowed convulsively and turned away, looking rather unwell.

"This is a terrible thing!" he muttered, "and I don't like to see him left like that ... hanging all that time."

"That's all right, sir. Now you haven't yet told me: who was this unfortunate gentleman? I shall want to know all you can tell me about him."

"Starbright," answered the Tutor, pulling himself together with an effort. "John Starbright, a third-year man. But I cannot understand what could have induced him ... I mean, I suppose it must be suicide. It couldn't be anything else."

"Everything points to it," agreed Inspector Norman, "but we can be more certain when the doctor has had his say."

"Death was due to hanging right enough," said the police surgeon. "There seems no possible doubt of that. There's no sign to the contrary and every sign that he made a remarkably thorough job of it. I've never seen a better job, in fact," he added, with a kind of grudging admiration which the Tutor thought to be in very bad taste under the circumstances. "Of course, I shall make a more detailed examination later. Meantime, let's get the body down and decently covered until it can be moved."

"Yes, indeed," exclaimed the Tutor. "Why, Gale, I didn't see you. This is a terrible affair! Terrible! I don't know what to expect next. First a robbery, then a suicide."

"I wonder if there's any connection," was Gale's comment. This remark brought him to the attention of the Inspector.

"That's an interesting speculation, sir. By the way, I didn't see you join us. You'll be a fellow of the college, I take it?"

"I am already a fellow of the college," answered the Dean, who could never resist correcting other people's slips in grammar or diction. "I am also a student of crime and mystery."

The Inspector looked at him doubtfully. His acquaintance with amateur detectives was limited to the realms of fiction. He had never met one in the flesh and did not much want to. He returned to the matter in hand.

"If you've finished, Doctor, we might as well get the body down and decently covered before crowds begin to collect."

"One moment," said the police surgeon. "I've just noticed something. The deceased seems to have had a pretty hard knock on the back of the head. I hadn't seen it at first owing to hair. H'm ... that's rather funny."

"Possibly he had a blow at football which had not had time to heal," suggested the Tutor. "He was a prominent member of our rugger side, poor fellow!"

"I happen to know he hasn't played since last Monday," said Gale.

"Then it can't be that," said the doctor. "It's too recent an injury; very much too recent." He paused and regarded the corpse with a puzzled frown.

"It seems clear enough to me," said the Inspector. "The knots are normal; rather good for an amateur. And it's clear he stood on this upright barrel, which is close by, and jumped off. That would give him a drop of about two feet and I suppose would make death nearly instantaneous, wouldn't it?"

"From the state of the spinal cord I should say quite instantaneous," agreed the police surgeon. "I'm a trifle surprised to find it as it is. He certainly made a good job of it. Lift him up, Inspector, whilst I loosen the cord and let him down."

During this operation the Tutor and the Dean turned away, both feeling a little unwell.

"We'd better leave him covered up here for the moment and phone for an ambulance. Then get him away as quietly as possible," said the Inspector.

Meadows, who had remained an impassive spectator in the background, now came forward.

"I have brought over a blanket and sheet for that purpose," he said, "and the back gate, at the end of the passage here, gives access to River Lane. That is certainly the best route for the unobtrusive removal of the body."

The Inspector regarded him with a measure of respect and admiration. The Head Porter spoke as though the removal of corpses was a piece of everyday routine.

"If you will give me the number," continued Meadows, at the same time producing his blanket and sheet, "I will telephone the necessary instructions to the station."

As the Inspector and the doctor drew the sheet over the head, which lolled at a drunken angle, and were beginning to cover the body, Gale forced himself to take a last look at it. His final inspection suggested a curious circumstance which he then put into words.

"It seems strange," he observed, "that Starbright should have troubled to put on a raincoat to come here and hang himself."

The Inspector looked at him in surprise. He was not looking for amateur suggestions in a case that seemed so straightforward. However, he asked Gale what was strange about it.

"Well," explained Gale, "I suppose he died some time late last night, otherwise the fatality must have been discovered sooner, and presumably he came straight from his rooms to do it. His rooms are only twenty yards away on the other side of the court, and there wasn't even any rain last night, not up to one in the morning, anyway."

"Yes," admitted the Inspector, "that's certainly queer. What time would you say death took place, Doctor?"

"That's difficult to say. Roughly six to eight hours ago. I can't tell you nearer than that. It's not easy after this lapse of time."

"Well, then, it was probably after midnight," commented the Inspector, "so one would suppose he came straight from his room. He couldn't come into college without being admitted and having his name taken, if it was after ten o'clock. I believe that's the rule, isn't it, sir?"

"That's quite correct," agreed Gale. "We can easily check whether he came in after ten. Of course one believes that undergraduates have ways and means of making unlawful entry into colleges after hours, but how they do it here, if they do it at all, I really don't know. If I did, they would, of course, speedily cease to do so. In any case, it seems hardly likely that Starbright would make a difficult and dangerous entry into college at that hour simply to hang himself at once."

"Quite so, sir," said the Inspector thoughtfully. This budding detective certainly had some ideas, though in this case such reasoning seemed so much waste of time.

"If the deceased had rooms quite close," he remarked, "it would seem that he chose the nearest convenient place, seeing that it's secluded and has this lamp handy. And," he added, peering behind two more barrels further under the arch, "here's some more cord identical, I think, with the piece used. You have workmen here, I suppose?"

"Yes," answered the Tutor, reasserting himself. "They were using it to mark straight lines for relaying some flagstones, I think. Anyone in this court would have noticed it during the last two days."

"Quite," said the Inspector; "then it all seems very simple. The deceased, for reasons we must try to discover, made up his mind to take his own life. He noted that this spot provided everything necessary for hanging. He waited till late at night, when all was quiet, and then came and made away with himself. I think everything will be absolutely straightforward at the inquest, sir. The only thing is, can anyone give a reason for the young fellow doing such a thing? I'll have to talk it over with you later, but if you can suggest any motive now it would save a lot of trouble later on perhaps."

"I cannot imagine," said the Tutor. "Goodness knows, we are a happy enough little community as a rule."

"He looked a strong, fit young fellow," commented the Inspector. "A footballer, I understand. Now if he'd been one of the delicate, nervy kind ... We had a case last year, you may remember. A young fellow did away with himself seemingly because he'd failed in some examination."

"If all the failures did that," said Gale, "you'd have your hands full, Inspector."

The Tutor frowned. It appeared to him rather a frivolous and ill-timed remark. The Inspector continued without noticing the interruption.

"Would you say Mr. Starbright was popular? Most of these good games players are well liked, I take it?"

At the mention of popularity coupled with rugby football, the Tutor started nervously. The two things suggested sudden and unpleasant possibilities.

"Well ... er ... I did hear something to the effect that Starbright had had some trouble or ... er ... row with some of the others, but I don't really know. ... Perhaps you could tell the Inspector, Gale. I fancy it was you who mentioned the matter casually, though I did not pay much attention at the time."

This Mr. Gale seemed to know a lot about everything, thought the Inspector, as he turned an inquiring eye on Gale.

"There was some trouble last week over Starbright failing to turn up at a match and probably causing his side to lose. Consequently there was ill-feeling against him. But I understand it came to nothing serious and has now died down. I can hardly think that Mr. Starbright could have let it weigh on his mind to that extent."

The Inspector considered this. He could appreciate the enormity of failing to play when needed, and he knew something of undergraduates and their habits. There might be more in this than met the eye. "Do you know," he inquired, "if this trouble led to any threats or actual physical violence against the deceased gentleman?"

"I'm fairly certain there was no violence," said Gale. "As regards threats, I'm not so sure. But I was given clearly to understand that, for the last day or two, the matter was over. I cannot believe that it can have anything to do with this tragedy."

"I sincerely hope that no such suggestion will be made," exclaimed the Tutor. "It would be bad for our reputation and very painful for any of those who may have indulged in some harmless ragging of Starbright."

"Quite so, sir," agreed the Inspector. "We must hope that some better explanation will turn up. It will simplify things at the inquest if we can supply the motive. Mind you, we've had unfortunate cases before now where ragging and horseplay has got on a young man's mind. Still, possibly there are other reasons."

"Possibly they are connected with the theft of the money," suggested the Dean, with a view to steering the inquiry off an unwelcome topic. "What if Starbright were the thief?"

"It's possible," agreed Inspector Norman, "but having got away with a neat crime and being in no immediate danger of discovery, as I'm bound to admit, it doesn't seem logical to kill oneself." Here they were interrupted by the police surgeon.

"If there's nothing more for me to do, I'll be pushing off. I want my breakfast."

"Right, sir," said the Inspector. "I'll be having your report later. Meantime I must search the body as a matter of form and then his rooms. As a matter of fact, it's more than likely he's left some letter or statement which will save us wondering about the motive. It's the usual thing with suicides, and a very convenient thing, too."

The doctor lingered a moment.

"Half a moment, Norman. I'd like a word with you." He jerked his head slightly, and the Inspector, interpreting the gesture, stepped across out of earshot of the others, who waited apprehensively whilst the police surgeon spoke a few hurried words in an undertone. The Inspector looked very serious and finally nodded, whereupon the police surgeon walked away. The Inspector still looked thoughtful as he rejoined the group under the arch, but he made no comment as he once more knelt down beside the body and drew back the sheet, leaving only the face covered.

"I don't think I need keep you others any longer," he said rather pointedly, "except if you'd stay, sir." This to the Tutor.

"I reckon I must get on with my furnace," agreed Sergeant Stumpy gloomily.

"If there's no objection, I would like to remain," said Gale. "It is possible I might be of some use."

The Inspector was considering whether or not it would be polite or expedient to suggest to Gale that he could now manage by himself, when voices were heard in argument. The constable on guard outside could be heard discussing with somebody the impracticability of taking a bath at that moment.

"I'm afraid some of the undergraduates are turning up for their morning baths," explained the Tutor. "What is to be done?"

"Tell them the baths won't be available for half an hour and we don't want them hanging round," grunted the Inspector.

The unexpected appearance of the Tutor had the effect of clearing the scene. Further along the court, however, voices could be heard speculating what was in the wind. Meantime, the Inspector was unbuttoning the raincoat in which Starbright had gone to his death.

"A button missing," he remarked absently. "Torn off, too."

The Dean gazed down with a show of interest. There was certainly a button missing, and the waterproof cloth was slightly torn in token of a violent wrench, a circumstance quickly forgotten by the surprising nature of the next discovery. Feeling something heavy in the deep pocket of the raincoat the Inspector dipped into it, and, with a grunt of surprise, brought out a revolver. Handling his find with care, he opened the breech to disclose a full complement of cartridges. He emptied the six cases into the palm of his hand and it was seen that none had been fired.

"Now that's very odd," said the Inspector slowly.

"Odd!" repeated the Tutor. "It's most irregular! Firearms are strictly forbidden. Really, I don't know what's coming over the college."

"Suppose," said the Inspector, "that you wished to commit suicide, and you had a loaded revolver in your pocket, would you shoot yourself, or would you go through the difficult job of hanging yourself?"

The Tutor replied rather stiffly that he couldn't say. He'd never considered hanging himself and he hoped he never would. Gale, however, was quick to take the Inspector's point.

"It's certainly odd, as you say," he murmured. "Nobody would go out and hang themselves if they had a perfectly good loaded revolver. It doesn't make sense."

"Well," said the Inspector, "I'd better finish the job in hand." The search of Starbright's pockets revealed nothing else of a startling nature. There were keys, a watch, the programme of a varsity football match, some odd letters, which were mostly unpaid bills, and twopence-halfpenny.

"He wasn't carrying much money," was the Inspector's only comment. The time taken over the search had been sufficient to give Gale a fresh idea, which he now put to the Inspector.

"I can think of one reason, Inspector, why he might have a gun and yet hang himself."

The Inspector regarded him doubtfully. He was not yet clear whether to regard the Dean as the purveyor of wild theories or a shrewd detector of fact. He decided to hear what Gale had to say.

"The logical explanation is that there is something wrong with the revolver, since it seems, undoubtedly, to have been fully loaded with live cartridges. I was a musketry instructor during my temporary service in the war. Possibly I could give you an opinion on that point."

The Inspector massaged his chin for a moment, a favourite gesture of his when in doubt. Then he unloaded the revolver once more, held the butt covered with a handkerchief, cocked the trigger and pressed. The hammer fell with a smart click.

"Not much wrong with this gun, I fancy," he said, with a faint smile. But Gale was not to be put off so easily.

"It's possible that the hammer is broken or blunted," he remarked, "so as not to explode the cap."

The Inspector handed over the weapon in silence. Gale examined it carefully, pulled the trigger himself and looked crestfallen. "No," he confessed. "It seems I'm wrong. The gun appears in perfect order."

The Inspector smiled again and was about to say something, when he was interrupted by the reappearance of the Head Porter bearing the rarely used key of the back gate and the news that the ambulance might be expected any minute. The Inspector turned to the Tutor. "Well, sir, there's nothing more to be done at the moment. The constable will stay and see to the removal of the body. Meantime, I'll take a look at the deceased's rooms, if you'll kindly show them to me. Perhaps we shall find some farewell message there, since we've drawn a blank up to now. Later, when I've had some breakfast and seen to any business at the station, I'd be obliged if you could give me a few minutes in your room. By the way, I suppose you will notify the next-of-kin as soon as possible? You have the particulars, no doubt."

"Yes, yes," said the Tutor. "I must do that, of course. Dear me! It's nearly half past eight. I had intended going to the early service, but it must be nearly over by now. Yes, I will be at your service any time this morning; and the Master will have to be informed at once. Dear me!"

"Then perhaps you will kindly show me Mr. Starbright's rooms," prompted the Inspector, trying to curb his impatience. The Tutor began to lead the way, and the Inspector followed with a glance of farewell at the Dean.

"Ah! One moment, Inspector," murmured Gale.

Smothering his impatience once more, the Inspector halted and eyed the Dean with slight disfavour.

"Well, sir. What is it this time?"

"You noticed that a button was missing from the raincoat?"

"Yes, sir. What about it?"

There was a silence whilst the Dean slowly fumbled in his pocket and produced a button. It was a large brown button, and adhering to it were some strands of some waterproof material.

"It occurred to me," said Gale, handing the button to the Inspector, "that it might be the one missing from Mr. Starbright's coat."

The Inspector pounced on the button like a terrier on a rat. The sheeted body was once more unveiled. In a moment the Inspector had stood upright once again and was regarding the Dean with a new interest coupled with something amounting almost to suspicion.

"It is the missing button. May I ask how it came into your possession?"

"You may," answered the Dean, enjoying the sensation he had created. "I picked it up off a floor a few minutes ago."

"Whereabouts was this?" inquired the Inspector.

"Immediately outside the door of my rooms."

The Inspector digested this surprising information for a moment. He reflected that the Dean was a most annoying person. He seemed a voluble supplier of unsolicited information, yet in answering questions he required a great deal of pumping.

"Have you any idea how it came there? Did you see the deceased last night?"

"I have no idea how it came there. I have not spoken to Mr. Starbright for some weeks. He called on me about a month ago to obtain an exeat for an away match. I have not seen him since, except at a distance."

The Inspector gave his chin an intensive course of massage and gave Gale another doubtful look.

"You have rooms in college, Mr. Gale?"

The Dean admitted this and added that they were only a few yards away.

"I think I should like a few words with you later in the morning. You will be in, I take it?"

"Certainly," assented the Dean, "and, if you wish, I will forgo my attendance at the eleven o'clock service so as not to miss you. I shall look forward to further collaboration with you."

Inspector Norman did not appear fully to reciprocate this wish; however, he thanked Gale stiffly and departed with the Tutor in the direction of the dead undergraduate's rooms.

The Dean walked slowly back to his own staircase. The faint smile with which he had watched the Inspector's departure had given place to a thoughtful frown. At the foot of the staircase he stood for a short time considering his next move; then, having made up his mind, he went upstairs and knocked at the door of his undergraduate neighbour. Receiving no immediate reply he opened the door and walked into the sitting-room. At the same moment the inner or bedroom door opened to disclose a face smothered in shaving soap. It wore a puzzled expression, and at sight of the visitor its owner appeared startled and apprehensive, or so it seemed to the Dean, who was carefully noting the effect of his entry.

"I must apologize for disturbing you at this unearthly hour, and on Sunday, too," began the Dean pleasantly. "Please finish your toilet, and I will sit down and wait, if I may."

Martin Trevor replied that that was quite all right and that he wouldn't be a minute. The Dean employed the minute by gazing casually round the room. He crossed to the back window and stood for a moment looking down at the fellows' garden. At the same time his eye travelled over the writing-table and idly noted the diary. Old-fashioned things, diaries, he reflected. In these days of rush few young men bothered to keep them, he supposed.

At that moment the owner of the room appeared, clad in a silk dressing-gown over pyjamas and with hair brushed tidily. He begged his visitor to be seated.

"As you've only just got up I suppose you haven't heard the news," said the Dean.

Trevor looked puzzled, and asked what news.

"Tragic news, I fear," said the Dean, and watched closely to see how Trevor was taking it. Trevor still looked puzzled, yet somehow more relieved than when Gale had first entered. The Dean decided to spring the news at one fell swoop.

"An undergraduate has hanged himself under the arch just outside," the Dean told him.

"Good heavens, sir! But who is it?"

"John Starbright," said the Dean.

There seemed nothing suspicious about Trevor's reception of the news. He was genuinely shocked, so it appeared, and displayed the right amount of surprise and grief.

"Starbright. ... Good God! But ... why, why did he do it?"

"We don't know, Trevor."

"You don't think ... surely ... that ... well ..."

Trevor's words tailed away into silence and he looked very distressed and uncomfortable.

"You are trying to say, because of any ragging or ill-feeling over this wretched rugger business? I sincerely hope and believe not. You yourself gave me to understand that all that was over and done with. I only hope that was the truth; but you should know better than I, Trevor."

"I certainly thought it was, really, sir."

"The point seems to be whether anything happened last night in the way of fresh trouble against Starbright. Have you anything to tell me about that?"

The Dean observed that Trevor appeared discomfited and confused by this question.

"... I can't tell you, sir. I know nothing whatever about anything having happened. I never thought anything would, but I don't know."

"I don't want to seem inquisitive, Trevor, and it's not really my business at all. It's a police matter now, I'm afraid. But if we could be sure it had nothing to do with the rugger business or the rugger people themselves, it would save a great deal of trouble and lift a load off the minds of a number of people. Now you probably were with some of your rugger friends last night and could make a statement which would clear some of them, at any rate, of being in any way the indirect cause of this shocking tragedy."

The Dean supposed that Trevor, if he were being quite straightforward, would welcome this chance of clearing himself and his friends. Trevor, however, looked just as uncomfortable as before, and hesitated badly before replying:

"The rotten thing is, I can't speak for any of the others. I didn't see any of them at all last night."

"Oh, really? I thought you young fellows generally forgathered on Saturday evenings. Would it be ... er ... indiscreet to ask what you were doing all the time?"

"I ... er ... had a bit of a head and turned in quite early ... soon after nine."

If anybody ever gave the appearance of telling a clumsy falsehood, Trevor did so on this occasion, so the Dean thought.

"But you'd signed off Hall, hadn't you?"

"Yes. I ... I had a snack in a bar and came back early and turned in. I didn't feel too fit."

The Dean decided not to push this line of inquiry any further. His companion seemed rattled about something, but there did not appear to be a probability of finding out what, not at the moment anyway. He tried a new angle.

"I see. So of course you couldn't possibly know if anything took place with reference to Starbright. I quite see your point. And you honestly had no idea that any plot or plan against him was intended or carried out?"

"Absolutely no idea, sir. I honestly thought the whole thing had blown over. I say, I hope to God there's some other explanation of this awful affair. Otherwise I and some of the others will feel pretty rotten over it. Not that I ever wished Starbright any harm."

There was a ring of truth and conviction in these words. The Dean continued his examination as casually as he could.

"I suppose you didn't see Starbright at all last night?"

"No. I certainly didn't."

"Did you happen to have any other callers?"

"No; none at all." A little doubtful, that answer.

"When ... er ... did you last speak to Starbright?"

"Three nights ago, sir. The night of ... of ..."

"The night the firework went off," prompted the Dean drily and tried not to frown. So he had been right in his supposition. Trevor had actually been with Starbright when the revolver-shot had been fired, yet he had glibly asserted that he had that moment entered the college. Again, he had, according to his own account, been alone and in bed from nine o'clock the previous night. Yet at one in the morning two persons had made an unsteady descent from his room. It might be argued that they had come up, found him asleep, and gone away without disturbing him. Yet Gale felt certain that after his return from the Master's Lodge at ten-thirty only one person had walked up past his door. It would appear that the two mysterious individuals had been in Trevor's rooms for at least three hours without the owner's knowledge. There was something wrong somewhere, and the simplest explanation was that Trevor was not telling the truth.

As the Dean was wondering what to say next, a very awkward pause was filled by another knock on the door, followed by the entry of Tom Tanner. He registered surprise at the sight of the Dean.

"I'm sorry, sir. I didn't know you were here. Shall I come back later, old man? I came to look for a book I left two days ago. By the way, I suppose you've heard ..."

"That's all right, Tanner. I'm just off myself, so don't go. ... Yes, we both know about the tragedy. I suppose you can't, by any chance, throw any light on the reason why this poor fellow did such a terrible thing?"

"No, sir, I can't," answered Tanner, looking the Dean very straight in the face. "I suppose you've heard he was unpopular with many of us over the Saints match, but I can't believe it can be anything to do with that. If anything, he was let down lightly over it, as far as I know."

"I'm very glad to hear you say so," was the Dean's comment. "It agrees with what your friend here has been saying."

"Did you come over last night, old man, when I was in bed asleep?" asked Trevor suddenly, and when Tanner replied in the affirmative, he added: "What time would that be? I woke up once and thought I heard someone."

"Pretty late," Tanner told him. "One o'clock or so. I didn't want to disturb you, of course."

These remarks, which sounded harmless enough, nevertheless gave the Dean food for suspicion. It sounded almost as though Trevor was prompting his friend to support him in his sick-bed alibi. Trevor and Tanner were generally inseparable during their leisure hours, and it seemed remarkable that the latter had not known overnight about his friend's indisposition. The Dean thought he would very much like a few words alone with Tanner before the two young men had time for a solitary comparison of ideas. For the moment, however, that was impossible, and the main thing seemed to be to spin out his interview with Trevor until such time as Tanner should tire of waiting and take his departure, though what further questions it would be diplomatic to put Gale had no idea.

However, this problem was soon solved by Tom Tanner, who had been prowling round the room turning over books and searching the shelves. He now announced that he had found his missing book and would, therefore, be off. Gale had time to see that the volume in question was of the subject and period which Tanner was then studying; it seemed probable, therefore, that it was really his book and that the two visits in search of it were quite genuine. All the same, it was curious that Tanner had not been able to find it during his previous search in the early hours of that morning; unless there were two books in question, which, after all, was quite likely in the case of a friendly couple who often did their reading together.

The Dean very soon followed Tanner's example and, having thanked Trevor for his helpful information and added a few more words of sorrow and regret, he made for the door. In crossing the room he subconsciously noted some little detail which seemed to have altered since the time he came in, and a second later he was able to identify this little discrepancy. The diary, which had lain on the writing-table, was no longer there.

Without showing any sign of surprise or pausing in his departure, Gale crossed to his own rooms and sat down for a moment to consider this trifling yet curious circumstance. He recollected that Trevor, on coming out of his bedroom, had taken a seat near the fire and remained there for the duration of the interview. He had not been near the writing-table. It was clear that Tanner, under cover of looking for his history book, had slipped the diary in his pocket. The Dean felt an increased urge for a few words with Master Tanner, though on what grounds to base an inquiry he could not for the moment think. He could hardly ask to see the diary. He had no just cause whatever for making such a request and, besides, diaries are by way of being confidential documents. He decided, however, that Tanner, as a friend of the rugger players, could reasonably be approached on the subject of their recent attitude towards Starbright. From such a beginning he might succeed in gleaning some other significant information.

As he passed out of Craven Court and entered the main court, he was disappointed to see Tanner emerge from the staircase on which he lived and make briskly for the main gate. The Dean thought of shouting to him, but refrained. Tanner hurried away without a glance. It rather looked as though he wished to avoid the Dean. With his heart beating a shade faster at the prospect of doing something rather irregular in his work of detection, the Dean made his way swiftly to the staircase and entered the room just vacated by its owner. A quick look round the tables and chairs did not reward him with any sign of the diary, but, attracted by the brightness of the fire, he observed that the flames had very lately been fed with loose paper, of which a charred fragment had fallen into the grate. Gale could see at a glance that it was the greater portion of a page from a pocket diary. Without waiting to examine his find more closely, he assured himself that no other portion had escaped the flames and then made a rapid retreat to his own quarters.

It looked at first glance as though fortune had smiled very broadly in sparing this particular page from the flames. Each sheet would appear to contain spaces for three days, since two-thirds of the page had survived and showed two days on each side. On one side were the dates of Monday, November 18, and Tuesday, November 19, and on the reverse side Friday, November 15, and Saturday, November 16. This particular Sunday of ominous memory in the chronicles of St. Chad's happened to be November 17. Of the four spaces representing these four days all were blank save one—that of the previous day, Saturday, November 16, in which some isolated words had been written one under the other and then crossed out, rendering them almost wholly illegible. Furthermore, each of the four erased words was followed by a tick such as a schoolmaster might put against correct answers written and submitted by his pupils. Gale set himself to analyse his find.

In the first place it was apparent that the ticks were not all in the same handwriting, in fact each betrayed traces of a different author. In the case of the four smudged words the varying breadth of the pencilled cancellations suggested the same thing. The top word, which was longer than the rest, was entirely obliterated and so was the second. The third had been crossed through the middle, leaving the tops and bottoms of the letters just visible. It was probable that the Dean would never have been able to decipher the entry but for the fact that he knew the origin of the paper. As it was, he was suddenly confronted with the most obvious and likely solution. It was the name Trevor!

Gale's eye travelled hastily to the last word. It had been more roughly erased than the others, but its censor had been careless over the first two letters. They were far from obvious, but they suggested more than anything else a capital S followed by the small letter T. Assuming this to be another proper name connected with the college, the Dean picked up a nominal roll to check any possible mistake. He had been right, he discovered, in his supposition. Only one member of the college began his name with those letters, and that member was now dead.

Presumably, then, the entry consisted of four names put down, ticked off, and crossed out. Gale began to consider the possible significance of such entries. On first consideration they were exactly like those in his own pocket-book, in which he put down the names of his visiting pupils under the dates of their appointed times. However, that wouldn't do. Allowing for the fact that Trevor, though having no clients or pupils, might put down the names of invited guests, it would be absurd for him to write down his own name. It might be the composition of a bridge four, in which case he might conceivably complete the entry by adding his own name. But, then, there were the ticks in different hands and the suggestion that the names were all in different writing. So that wouldn't do.

As it stood, it was more suggestive of a book kept in some tennis or squash club in which different members enter their names under the days they wish to play. But then there should have been the addition of set times, which were lacking, at any rate opposite Trevor's name. In any case, there seemed no possible reason for the presence of such a book in the private rooms of an undergraduate. And why should Tanner have thought fit to remove and destroy it by stealth? Surely, if it had contained anything incriminating, its owner would not have let it lie in full view of any visitor. As he puzzled over these points, Gale felt that, in some connection, he had seen some book put to such uses as this one, but he could not remember what chord in his memory had been stirred. He put the scrap of paper carefully away for further consideration and sat down to review the general aspects of the case.

His two interviews with Trevor had left him in a puzzled and vaguely irritable frame of mind. In his position as Dean, with special duties connected with college discipline, it was inevitable that his dealings with undergraduates should frequently resemble those of a housemaster towards his boys. In his official dealings with them he must expect to be told a few untruths if, in the discharge of his official duties, he asked awkward questions. That he was quite prepared for. In the present instance, however, something more than mere college discipline was at stake. Unless involved in some terrible culpability, nobody ought now to conceal any truth concerning the suicide of Starbright, and of all the young men in Chad's, Trevor had hitherto appealed to him as one least likely to practise any mean deception, or, indeed, to have any reason for so doing.

Still, the fact remained that he had apparently lied badly about his connection with the Starbright shooting affair, and therefore his assurance that the matter was closed could not be taken as reliable. Moreover, it occurred to the Dean that the place outside Starbright's rooms, where Trevor had been found standing in apparent bewilderment, could not be far from the track of the bullet in its course from Starbright's window to the grass plot. What if it had been aimed at Trevor? It certainly seemed likely. Such a thought opened up a number of alarming possibilities. It further went to show that, as demonstrated an hour previously, there was nothing much wrong with Starbright's revolver.

Then the Dean had come to the fixed conclusion that, however and wherever Trevor had spent the hours between nine and two a.m. last night and that morning, it was certainly not asleep in his rooms. That was the most unsatisfactory feature of all.

On the other hand, his surprise and horror at the news of the tragedy had appeared genuine and spontaneous, whilst whatever part, if any, the mysterious diary played in the case, Trevor was apparently quite unaware of its significance.

He began to debate whether he should communicate any of his vaguely formed theories to Inspector Norman, and came to the conclusion that it would be best, at that stage, to say as little as possible. For one thing, if there was any mystery to disclose, he wished to have the opportunity of producing the grand solution off his own bat; for another thing, he had nothing solid to offer the Inspector beyond the button which he had already contributed, and he resented a certain indifference towards his help which had been displayed by the forces of the law. Besides, he did not wish to focus the attention of the police on the unfortunate Trevor, who might, as he still hoped, be perfectly innocent of any serious connection with the tragedy. In any case, the Inspector should investigate Trevor for himself, since the trail of the button, if properly followed up, would be found to lead to Trevor's door as well as his own.

Meantime, there was one other question he would have liked to have put to Trevor. At six o'clock the previous evening, when they had passed on the staircase, Trevor's outward appearance had been in every way normal. According to his own account the young man had retired to bed at nine. Yet at half past eight the next morning he had exhibited a perfectly good black eye.

The Dean spent the morning in his rooms for the purpose of being available to give Inspector Norman any assistance which that painstaking officer might desire, and he felt a little slighted when lunch-time came without any sign of his return to college. After lunch he settled down to an Edgar Wallace kindly loaned by the Bursar. At three o'clock in the afternoon he was roused by the appearance of the under porter.

"Begging your pardon," said the under porter, "but a message has come through from the police-station. The compliments of the Chief Constable, and would you be good enough to go down and see him as soon as convenient?"

The Chief Constable! It looked as if some startling development must have occurred to demand the presence of such an official on a Sunday afternoon.

CHAPTER X

"I'VE been on the 'phone to the Chief," said Superintendent Beecham, "and he's coming down. He should be here as near after two as doesn't matter."

"I'm glad of that," replied Inspector Norman. "Seems to me there's more in this case than what meets the eye."

"You've said it," agreed the Superintendent. "You've got all the dope for him, I take it? Full particulars of deceased, including next-of-kin, statement re finding of body, report on examination of body, locality and effects, statement of Tutor re possible motive, statement of police-surgeon, exhibits, viz., length of cord, revolver, bullets from revolver, and packet of bullets found in room of deceased, and, last but not least, appointment for Dr. Frank Summers to attend here at two-fifteen pip emma?"

Without waiting for the Inspector's affirmative answer the Superintendent sighed deeply, leaned back in the office chair which stood in front of his desk, folded his hands across his ample stomach, allowed his three chins to sag forward on his chest and appeared to compose himself to slumber. Actually he was thinking over the case in hand.

Superintendent Beecham was a plump, massive, red-cheeked, amiable man who looked like a prosperous farmer or publican. Seated at his desk or stationed in the forefront at some municipal ceremony he cut an impressive figure, but one could not have pictured him chasing a runaway undergraduate in a fifth of November rag. However, his duties were now mainly clerical, and beneath a sleepy and rather bovine exterior he hid a shrewd brain and a quick wit. In all kinds of conversation he was fond of using proverbial expressions and colloquialisms which were known by himself and others as "figures of speech".

Very soon after two o'clock a car could be heard pulling up sharply outside, and next moment the Chief Constable entered briskly. Inspector Norman rose to help him off with his overcoat, and the Superintendent shuddered, opened his eyes, and lumbered to his feet.

"'Afternoon, Beecham; 'afternoon, Norman. Sit down, do," said the Chief Constable, doing so himself. "The varsity seems to be keeping us busy just now. First a burglary, now a suicide, I understand."

116

"It never rains but it pours, sir," observed the Superintendent.

"Oh! We've had no rain out at Trumpington," said the Chief Constable. "Eh! What? Oh! ... er ... yes, I see. Well, let's see what you've got for me."

His eye travelled rapidly over the Inspector's report.

"Well, that seems fairly well cut and dried. Motive seems uncertain, though. No letter or anything, eh? Have the relatives turned up yet? Perhaps they may be able to throw some light on things."

"The nearest relative," explained the Inspector, "is an uncle, a Major Starbright, of London, S.W.4. He was telephoned for, but it seems, unfortunately, that he's been shooting in Scotland and is motoring back by stages. He's expected home tomorrow night or Tuesday, and meantime he can't be got at. We can't very well put out an S O S, can we, sir?"

"No," agreed the Chief Constable. "It's a pity. Still, perhaps the absence of sorrowing parents is a good thing."

"Might account for the young fellow doing what he did," grunted the Superintendent.

The Chief Constable asked why.

"No parents; harsh upbringing by wicked uncle," explained Beecham. "Strict military old bachelor; begging your pardon, of course, sir."

"Possibly," said the Chief Constable with a smile. "Still, it seems fairly straightforward. Was it really necessary, Beecham, to drag me out here on Sunday afternoon to see to this personally? You know I'd turn out any time for anything that matters, but I'm just asking you."

"There's a nigger in the wood-pile, sir," said the Superintendent.

"A nigger!" cried the Chief Constable. "I didn't see any mention of that. Has he registered properly as an alien, or is he one of the British subject kind? These foreign students are the devil."

"There's no nigger, sir," explained the Inspector hastily; "it's a figure of speech."

"Oh!" said the Chief Constable, recognizing the explanation from previous experience. "Yes, I've heard that one somewhere. But for God's sake talk English, Beecham! What's fishy about it?"

"In the first place, sir, it's a queer thing for a man to walk out of doors with a fully loaded revolver and then hang himself. It's contrary to human nature, sir."

"Yes, by Jove, that is queer! Is it his gun, do you know? Or do you suppose he didn't know how to fire it? Though I should think anyone could do that."

"Here it is, sir. It was in the deceased's pocket. It has no prints except a number of his own all over it. One round has been recently fired from it and the barrel was badly cleaned, if at all. A packet of similar ammunition was in an unlocked drawer in his rooms."

"That seems conclusive," agreed the Chief Constable. "Anything else, Norman?"

"There was a head wound, sir, that the police-surgeon seemed doubtful about. In fact he seemed doubtful about one or two points, and he has been getting an expert opinion."

"I don't follow this," said the Chief Constable, reading the medical section of the report. "If we cut out the technical points, he says here quite clearly that death was due to hanging and to no other cause. You don't suggest he was lynched or something, do you? In the middle of a college court with rooms all round?"

Inspector Norman made no reply. He was equally ignorant as to the latest developments of the case. The Superintendent took up the running.

"I'm not suggesting anything at the moment, sir; but from what the police surgeon told me on the 'phone an hour ago I think there's more in this than meets the eye. He'd had his expert give the corpse a 'dekko' ... an examination, I should say. Acting on his information, I requested the two of them to come round and meet you here. They should be here," pulling out a massive watch, "in one and a half minutes from now."

"Who is this fellow?" asked the Chief Constable.

The Superintendent, wheezing slightly, leaned over the desk, picked up a paper, and read out:

"Frank Summers, Esquire, M.D., F.R.C.S., Walker Professor of Pathology at the University of Cambridge."

As the Chief Constable was digesting this information, the police surgeon entered with a companion who turned out to be the learned gentleman just named.

"Ah! Good afternoon, Dr. Summers," said the Chief Constable cheerfully. "Good of you to come. Sit down, won't you? 'Afternoon, Purvis."

"Professor Summers," corrected the professor of pathology austerely, dusting a hard chair and seating himself.

"Yes ... ah! Yes," amended the Chief Constable, who did not quite get this distinction. "Now, I understand you have been good enough to give Purvis your opinion over this suicide business. According to the report we have had, everything was quite in order, and there was no question but that the deceased met his death by being hanged; that is, presumably, he hanged himself. May I ask if you agree with that finding?"

Dr. Summers was a thin, dry, expressionless man, and he answered in slow, rather metallic tones:

"I examined the body, and furthermore I examined the place where the body was found, and a piece of cord stated to be similar to or part of that which was found on the body: As a result of my labours I have not the least hesitation in saying that the sole cause of death was a dislocation of the vertebral column due to hanging."

"Well, then," said the Chief Constable, having paused to see any possible catch in this and having found none. "It seems a perfectly

obvious case. I'm afraid we've wasted your time, Dr.—er—Professor
Summers. I'm sorry."

Here he shot baleful glances first at the Superintendent and then
at the police surgeon.

"On the contrary," affirmed Dr. Summers amiably, "I count it as
time well spent. Certain aspects of the case interested me profoundly.
I fancy you will be interested as well."

The Chief Constable seemed anxious to hear more, and said as
much.

"There was a very curious feature about the whole thing, and it was
this. That the young man had been hanged there was no possible
doubt. But what is extremely doubtful is whether he was hanged at
the place and in the manner in which your men found him, and
what is quite impossible is that he was hanged with the kind of rope
which you say was round his neck when you took him down."

The Chief Constable was too astonished to speak. Inspector Norman
felt much the same, but being absolved from the necessity of saying
anything, he was able to conceal his emotions. The Superintendent,
who had been partially warned of what to expect, betrayed no sign of
discomposure.

"But ... but, I don't quite follow what you're suggesting."

"It's your job rather than mine to draw the necessary inferences,"
the anatomical expert reminded him rather acidly, "but I quite see
that the news has taken you somewhat by surprise. To me it suggests
that the dead man hanged himself or was hanged elsewhere, and by
other means, and his body was subsequently moved and a faked
hanging planted for you to find. And, mind you, it was well done. I
don't think you can blame Purvis for not having spotted it at once. In
fact he did well even to have sufficient doubts to request my assistance."

Dr. Summers grew quite genial in tone as he reached the concluding
stages of his explanation. He seemed to have an admiration for the
supposed faker of suicide. The Chief Constable had now recovered
his poise sufficiently to deal with this startling development in his
usual efficient way.

"This is certainly very astonishing; in fact almost incredible," he
said. "But I'm not doubting your opinion for a moment. What I should
like to know, though, and get down on paper, is exactly how you
arrived at this conclusion. Nothing too technical, you know, but
enough to convince a coroner's jury. Can you explain to me how these
things can be proved?"

"I'll try," said Dr. Summers obligingly, as though he were confronted
with the task of simplifying some difficult problem to suit the mind of
a small child. "Now you will know, of course, that there is a very
great difference between a judicial hanging, where the drop is
calculated in relation to the victim's weight and an instantaneous
death assured, and the most amateur efforts of those who hang
themselves in cupboards by their braces with no real drop at all. In

the latter case death is by no means instantaneous, but is by gradual suffocation. The victim of such a death displays such prominent after-effects as blueness and puffiness of the face, together with a swollen and protruding tongue. But in the case of the judicial, or what one might call long-drop hanging, death is instantaneous, and, in the first case, there are no after-signs of suffocation. Instantaneous death, in this case, is caused by a definite dislocation of the vertebral column. Such dislocation should occur only from a drop of several feet, or, conversely, from some tremendous upward jerk. The latter possibility is, of course, most unlikely, since it would appear to require the use of some kind of mechanical engine.

"In the present instance I was first struck by the fact, as also was Dr. Purvis, that the corpse presented every appearance of having been hanged from a considerable height and having had a long drop. There were no signs of gradual suffocation, whilst a careful examination served to show that the vertebral column was actually dislocated. This led me to inspect the actual scene and *modus operandi* of the hanging, from which it seemed to me doubtful to the point of impossible for the deceased to have met his end by jumping off an ordinary barrel. The degree of improbability would depend to a certain extent on whether or not the deceased was an exceptionally light or heavy man, and in this case his weight, just about eleven stone, was average for his age."

Dr. Summers paused and, without being asked, lit a cigarette. The three representatives of the law watched him in respectful silence.

"As things stood," resumed the expert, "I was morally convinced that the alleged place and manner of death was a fake, but with regard to the strict and searching requirements of expert evidence I should have hesitated to make a definite testimony to that effect in a court of law. Thus it was fortunate that I was able to make a fresh discovery which renders my opinion irrefutable, and when carefully pointed out, would be clear to most medical men. I examined the cord which was taken from the dead man's neck, and proceeded to satisfy myself whether or not it was that precise cord which had caused his death. I was very soon able to say for certain that such was definitely not the case. The cord in question had, of course, cut deeply into the neck, and produced the most obvious marks, but underneath these obvious cord marks were others, less clearly defined, which showed indubitably that the deceased had been previously suspended from a rope of a much thicker type. The strands of this rope have left clearly defined marks, and the mark of the knot, under one ear, is quite unmistakable.

"It is outside my province, but I should say that, if a thick kind of rope turns up in the vicinity of St. Chad's, your own medical experts should be able to tell you whether or not it may be the one actually used for the real hanging; and, as I said before, it is for you and not for me to draw what conclusions you like from this very peculiar state of affairs.

"Well, gentlemen, I don't think I can help you any more. Meanwhile,

I shall watch any possible developments with interest. And now I'll wish you good afternoon."

"Here, I say," interrupted the Chief Constable, who had been growing more and more astonished. "Hold on a minute. You know, this is a most extraordinary thing!"

Even Superintendent Beecham's eyes had opened wider than usual, and he had murmured to himself something about truth being stranger than fiction. Dr. Summers displayed signs of impatience.

"I know it's extraordinary," he said rather acidly. "You don't have to tell me that. Still, there it is, and as I've nothing to add to or subtract from what I've told you, I might as well return to more pressing affairs."

"Quite, quite," said the Chief Constable soothingly. "Only I should like to have got this down on paper and seen exactly what your evidence will amount to."

"Then may I suggest," prompted Dr. Summers, "that you prepare a digest of what you suppose me to have stated? Then, if you let me have it later today, I will either pass it as true and correct, or else make the proper emendations. That, I suppose, will be all that is necessary."

"Except for the inquest," said the Chief Constable.

"Inquest?" inquired Dr. Summers distastefully. "Surely my written statement will suffice without the reinforcement of the spoken word!"

The Chief Constable paused awkwardly, and then decided to apply some soft soap.

"In the ordinary way, yes, Professor Summers. But you must see that this seems a most unusual case and the facts you have just disclosed are most remarkable. The coroner and his jury would most certainly wish to hear these astonishing discoveries from your own lips, particularly since you will be speaking with greater authority than anyone else in Cambridge."

Since he had not previously heard of Dr. Summers amongst the galaxy of talent in the medical and scientific circles of the University, the Chief Constable gave a furtive glance towards the police surgeon to see if the latter appeared to endorse these sentiments. He hoped Purvis had raked in a really good man. Purvis gave no sign of disputing the merits of Dr. Summers.

"Very well," said the latter wearily. "I will attend your inquest if needs be. But I hope you will try and prevent them asking a number of difficult or unanswerable questions, such as exactly how far the body did drop; because that cannot be answered with any certitude."

"Certainly we shall try and keep to essentials," the Chief Constable assured him, "and I'm more than obliged to you for what you've told us. Though, for the moment, it's so surprising that I don't in the least know what to make of it. Meantime, I'll have the Superintendent make a draft of your statement and send it along later in the afternoon. Let me see. I forget your college for the moment. Er ... stupid of me ... Beecham?"

Dr. Summers relieved the anxiety of Superintendent Beecham, who had failed to verify this particular, by remarking shortly:

"Trinity. But that won't help you much."

"No, quite," agreed the Chief Constable, and then, not seeing why it didn't help, he added lamely:

"Er ... why not, exactly?"

"Because I shall be at my private address for the rest of the day, unless I decide to attend evening chapel, this being, in theory at any rate, my day of rest. Thirty, Barton Avenue. Good afternoon."

As Dr. Summers coupled his farewell with a stiff bow, and turned to leave the room, the Superintendent stirred uneasily and grunted to the Chief Constable:

"Head wound, sir."

"What's that?" cried the Chief Constable. "Oh! Yes, of course. Here, I say, just one moment, please. Oh! Thanks, Purvis!"

The police surgeon, being near the door, succeeded in delaying the exit of his expert colleague. Dr. Summers rather impatiently returned to the centre of the room.

"Yes?" he inquired. "You wished to know something else?"

"I understand," said the Chief Constable, "that there was a wound on the head of the deceased. Can you give any opinion about this?"

"Oh yes," answered Dr. Summers, thawing slightly by the recurrence of something that interested him. "I believe your conventional head wounds are generally described as the result of a blow with a thick, blunt instrument. In this case we have an exception. It was caused by a thin, moderately sharp instrument. There was an abrasion, or cut, about three inches long, on the top of the skull. When I say it seems to have been made by something sharp, I do not imply an instrument as sharp as a razor or axe blade, but a thin, slightly blunted edge, such as the unsharpened back of a sword, for instance. You take my meaning, I hope?"

"Yes, that seems perfectly clear," agreed the Chief Constable.

"Then," concluded Dr. Summers, "is there anything else you want to ask about this wound before I take my leave once more?"

He gave the Chief Constable a searching look, as though challenging him with having forgotten something important. The latter thought quickly. There certainly seemed to be something he ought to have remembered to ask. He looked quickly for inspiration at his subordinates, both of whom were characteristically occupied. The Inspector was massaging his chin, and the Superintendent was leaning back in his chair with half-closed eyes, which then opened, together with his mouth:

"Could you tell us, sir, whether this wound was inflicted before or after death?"

"Quite so," echoed the Chief Constable untruthfully. "Just what I was going to ask!"

Dr. Summers gave the Superintendent a look of approval, favoured the Chief Constable with a disbelieving glance, and replied: "That is difficult to say with absolute certainty, since it was certainly not done many hours after death; but from the nature of the bruises and absence of much bleeding, I should give it as my opinion that the injury was inflicted a short time after death. I cannot tell you any more certainly than that. I fear it is rather a difficult point, therefore an interesting one."

Dr. Summers thereupon made a second move towards the door, and this time he was allowed to depart without further recall. When the door had closed behind the professor of anatomical studies, the Chief Constable looked across at his immediate subordinate and said:

"Well, Beecham, what do you make of it?"

The Superintendent blinked his eyes and replied shortly:

"Murder, sir."

"That's what I think too," agreed his chief. "I don't see how it can be anything else. No innocent person would move a suicide to a fresh place and fake a fresh hanging. It doesn't make sense."

"There might be one sensible explanation," suggested Beecham. "If the body was found in an awkward place, somebody might undertake to move it."

"I don't quite follow you," said the Chief Constable.

"Well, sir. Suppose a man was inconsiderate enough to hang himself outside your doorstep, you might move the body in order to prevent yourself being interrogated about the matter, especially if you were in any way to blame for the man taking his own life. Now it appears in this case that some of the students had been giving this young fellow a bad time on account of his having let them down over some football match. The Tutor tried to tell me there was nothing in it, but I'm not so sure. He would naturally want to shield his students from any possible scandal."

"There's something in that," agreed the Chief Constable.

"On the other hand, sir, the actual place where the body was found seems the ideal place for the real hanging to have taken place, if it were a suicide. It was secluded, had the required apparatus all handy, and was near the deceased's rooms. And, as you know, there was no known way for him to enter or leave the college after ten, except by the front gate, which he didn't do; so it's difficult to see where else he could have hanged himself except in his own rooms, and, if he had done this, there could be no point in anyone wishing to move the body to a more obvious place. Therefore the only explanation seems to be that he was lured elsewhere and met his death by foul play."

"In some other set of rooms, you mean?"

"No, sir. That wouldn't do. If we believe he must have dropped several feet, it seems he must have been in some open spot, such as the top of a roof. But it's very hard to see where. A college is a large place, and at the same time it's a very public place. Students can walk in the courts from one room to another at any time of the day or night, and some of them keep late hours, especially on Saturday nights. It would be a risky business to climb roofs unnoticed, even after midnight."

"You seem to have a pretty sound knowledge of varsity manners and customs, Superintendent," observed the Chief Constable.

"Yes, sir," replied Beecham. "One never knows when the knowledge will come in handy. When in Rome, sir, one must study the customs of the Romans."

The Chief Constable was pondering this last piece of wisdom, which he was right in supposing to be another of the Superintendent's "figures of speech", when they were interrupted by a constable, who entered to say that a Mr. Gale was waiting outside. The Superintendent became alert again.

"Ah! I'd like you to see this Mr. Gale, sir. He's one of the college fellows and seems to have collected a few bits of useful information. In fact, Inspector Norman tells me he described himself as an amateur investigator of crime."

"Oh, lord!" muttered the Chief Constable, "another amateur expert!" He cast an eye hurriedly over that portion of the report which dealt with reference to Mr. Gale, and then he looked more interested.

"Well, I think we'd better see what he has to say. Ask him to come in, Constable, will you?"

With his smart suit and monocle Gale made a leisurely and somewhat impressive entry, gave them a collective good afternoon, and sank gently into a chair. The Chief Constable acknowledged his greeting and then looked doubtfully down at the dossier. Gale was there described as the Dean of College. It was curious, thought the Chief Constable, that a dean should not be in clerical clothes, especially on a Sunday in Cambridge. Still, these advanced churchmen did unusual things these days. The fellow didn't look any sort of a parson either, with a monocle. Perhaps he modelled himself on Hutchinson's character, the Reverend Mr. Boom Bagshawe. The Chief Constable set himself to put the visitor at his ease.

"Good afternoon, Mr. Gale," he began. "It's very good of you to come down here. And I'm afraid we've possibly chosen the busiest day of your week."

"Busiest?" queried Gale. "Well, as a matter of fact I've nothing much to do on Sundays; in fact nothing at all. It's the best day you could have chosen as far as I'm concerned."

"Oh! Is that so?" said the Chief Constable in surprise. "I was afraid you might have a busy day taking services and preaching sermons and—er—so on."

"I'm not in orders, sir. My main interests, outside the university, are political."

"Oh! ... I beg you pardon. ... I thought ..."

Here the Chief Constable took another quick glance at the dossier in which his Superintendent had clearly defined Gale as Dean of St.

Chad's. After which he directed a scowl of interrogation at that officer, who sighed gently and observed:

"There's deans and deans, as you might say, sir. Mr. Gale here is a Dean of College, and deans of college don't have to be deans of the Church. I've often wondered why, but there it is, sir. Now, if Mr. Gale had been a Dean of Chapel——"

"Well, never mind that now," interrupted the Chief Constable sharply, being irritated by this exposure of his ignorance on university technicalities. "As I was saying, Mr. Gale, I'm very glad you were able to come here today. The fact is, there are some very peculiar features about this case, and it appears that you have already come across certain points which might be of help. By the way, I should introduce myself. Colonel Waterman; and this is Superintendent Beecham. I think you have already met Inspector Norman."

Gale bowed slightly towards the two officers and replied easily: "I quite agree with you, Colonel. There are several very peculiar features about the case, as far as I have been able to judge as an unofficial onlooker. I have made a slight study of such things in an amateur way, and I confess I am most interested in this case."

The three members of the police force received this statement with singular lack of enthusiasm. Intelligent civilians who kept their eyes open and answered useful questions were all very well, but the amateur detective of fiction was, in their opinion, a person who should not materialize in the realms of fact. The Chief Constable returned to the matter in hand.

"My Superintendent has gone over the facts very carefully, and I should be glad if you will let him put certain questions to you in the first place. Then we can discuss any further facts or theories later on."

Gale inclined his head politely towards the Superintendent, who wheezed slightly over the effort of producing and extending a button with its attendant fragment of cloth.

"I understand, sir, that you found this button on the landing outside your door first thing this morning, immediately before you came into the court and discovered the tragedy; also that you believe the button was not lying there on the night previous, and also that the deceased gentleman, Mr. Starbright, had not visited your rooms for a matter of three or four weeks?"

Gale replied that such was the case, and that he could throw no further light on the matter.

"It certainly seems to be the button missing from the deceased's coat," continued Beecham. "It's a lucky chance you happened to see it and pick it up."

Here the Superintendent paused significantly. It occurred to him that Gale had produced the button after the manner of a dog bringing a stick to be thrown. It looked almost like a deliberately planted clue. Possibly Gale read his thoughts, for he remarked:

"I suppose I am naturally observant, and also I have a habit of picking up useful little trifles, such as pins. But it was certainly lucky I noticed the actual coat, otherwise I should have thought nothing more about the button. Of course, it struck me as odd that Starbright should have been wearing a raincoat inside the college after closing hours, especially as there was no rain at the time."

The Superintendent let this pass without comment. He knew enough about varsity conditions to appreciate the point for himself. He went on to inquire into another point needing the knowledge of a man on the spot.

"You say, Mr. Gale, that the button was outside your door. Now I believe a staircase in a college such as yours serves about six other sets of rooms. So I suppose it might point to the fact that there were other places which the deceased might have been visiting when he lost his button?"

"In a number of courts in most colleges," answered Gale, "we should be faced with a choice of six rooms to each staircase. But, fortunately or unfortunately, my rooms are in an old court with only two floors, and it happens that the bottom floor, below my rooms, is occupied by the college museum. This building is carefully locked except when the custodian is present, and all its windows are barred. The staircase itself leads up to two rooms only. There is my own set, and that of an undergraduate immediately opposite."

"So that the button might be said to be equally outside your door and his, in a manner of speaking," said Beecham ponderously. "I should like to hear the name of this undergraduate, sir."

Gale paused for a moment, and cleared his throat to gain time. He was continuing a line of thought which he had been pursuing ever since he had received his summons to the station. He was wondering how far, if at all, he should suggest to the police his own suspicions that Trevor had been mixed up in some way with the suicide of Starbright, if indeed it had been suicide. Gale had not missed the hurried asides between the Inspector and the police surgeon, and he was aware that there was more in the case than met the eye. The last thing he wanted was to direct any unjust suspicion against the captain of football; at the same time he could hardly impede the course of justice by withholding actual facts or going out of his way to shield a young man who, he considered, had displayed a singular lack of frankness in discussing the whole affair. He resolved to go carefully, to state facts but not theories, and, so to speak, to lead the police to Trevor's doorstep and leave them on the threshold to pursue their own further inquiries.

"The rooms belong to a third-year man called Trevor," he said. "He is a very decent fellow with an excellent record both in work and games. I have a certain personal knowledge of him, besides the fact that my disciplinary duties in college bring me into contact with him and the rest of the undergraduates."

Gale paused for a moment, uncertain whether to add what was also in his mind to say. He had, with a certain purpose, refrained from mentioning that Trevor was captain of rugby football. As Beecham was glancing at his notes, Gale decided to take the plunge and added: "As it happens, I took the opportunity of putting a few questions to Trevor this morning, partly with a view to ascertaining whether Starbright had called upon him last night. I did not of course mention the button."

At this the Superintendent pursed his lips doubtfully, whilst the Chief Constable, less tolerant of outside interference, broke in sharply:

"You know, you shouldn't do that sort of thing, Mr. Gale. You should have left it to the proper authorities. In case this young man has any guilty knowledge you merely put him on his guard."

The Dean made no immediate reply, much less an apology. He polished his monocle and replaced it in his eye. The Superintendent ended an awkward silence by suggesting to his chief that they might as well hear what the questions and answers had been.

"Certainly," replied Gale amiably. "But I should like to say first that, as Dean of College, I am mostly responsible for order and discipline there, and thus it seems to me that I have a right, as well as the police, to make certain inquiries of those under my charge. Also, my point was this. When I went to see Trevor, it was immediately after the discovery, and he was still in bed. Thus, if he were innocent of any connection with the tragedy, he would know nothing of it whatever, and would thus be free from any prejudice or nervousness in giving his answers. I do not for a moment wish to criticize the procedure of Inspector Norman, who had a great deal to do in a short time; but since he had left the college without realizing that the button might point to Trevor as well as to myself, I thought it best to observe Trevor's reactions before he had time to learn of the tragedy from other sources."

The Superintendent blinked at Gale with renewed interest. This don, he reflected, might be a dabbler and an interferer, but he was certainly not a fool by any means. He spoke encouragingly to the Dean.

"You speak as though you thought this man Trevor might have some inner knowledge of the tragedy, and might thus need time to concoct plausible answers. May I ask just what you had in mind, apart from the button? Were you thinking of suicide or foul play?"

Again the Dean paused, wondering if he had already said too much. He thought for a moment before answering:

"As a matter of fact, Superintendent, what I had in mind was this. You will probably know, from statements made by the Tutor, that a possible cause for Starbright's suicide lay in the fact that he had quarrelled with the other members of the football team, of which he was a member. There had been talk of some ragging and possible physical violence against Starbright. Now Trevor is captain of rugby football and was likely to know the truth or otherwise of such rumours. Personally I'm extremely unwilling to think that this football quarrel had anything to do with it, but it so happened that I had previously asked Trevor whether any further persecution of Starbright might be expected. He gave me to understand that little of the sort had taken place and that he believed the matter was closed. That was what he told me as lately as yesterday morning, and I believe he meant it. In any case, Starbright was not the sort to be scared by threats of ragging."

"That's quite interesting, sir," agreed the Superintendent; "and what happened at your talk early this morning?"

"This morning, when I called on Trevor soon after eight, he was just getting up, apparently. I broke the news rather sharply to him, to see how he would take it. I judged that he showed just the right amount of astonishment and horror to indicate a genuine surprise. He then told me he knew nothing whatever of any fresh outburst against Starbright. He added that, not being well, he had retired to bed at nine the previous night, after which he had seen nobody and heard nothing."

"In fact," prompted the Chief Constable, "he gave you to understand that he knew nothing about the nature and cause of the tragedy, and it appeared to you that he was speaking the truth?"

"Precisely, Colonel," agreed the Dean, and fell silent. He had decided to say nothing further in the matter of Trevor. The fact that he did not believe Trevor to have been in bed in his rooms from nine o'clock onwards was not one which he intended to state, at present, anyway.

The Superintendent turned to a fresh line of inquiry.

"In your position as Dean, Mr. Gale, you no doubt keep an eye on what goes on in the college. We have heard a certain amount about the unpopularity of Mr. Starbright over this football business. Now you know, and I know, the sort of thing it leads to when some of these lads make a set against one of their own number—ducking him in a bath and that kind of thing. Do you know of any actual incidents which might have caused Mr. Starbright to get depressed and take his own life, or alternately which might have caused others to use violence against him?"

"I cannot tell you anything for certain," replied Gale after a moment's consideration. "According to Trevor, there had been some unspecified incidents last Thursday night, the day the trouble started, but Starbright did not appear to have suffered any injury or ill-treatment. After that, it was stated by Trevor that the incident was closed as far as the bulk of the other footballers was concerned. As regards Starbright himself, I should say, without speaking ill of the dead, that he was a tough, truculent fellow who would have been least likely to have been depressed or frightened into taking his own life. As regards his being the victim of foul play, that, of course, seems a most surprising theory in view of the straightforward appearance of his death. But doubtless you know better than I whether there are any grounds for seriously considering such a possiblity."

Gale paused and eyed the Superintendent narrowly, as much as to say: if you want my opinion on the possibility of murder, you must let me into the secret of what you have found out to suggest such a theory. The Superintendent parried this thrust by starting on a fresh line.

"There is the curious circumstance, which you already know, of the dead man being in possession of a loaded and unfired revolver at the time of death. That seems to suggest that he was going about in fear of some very serious attack. It might further suggest that he was surprised and overpowered without having time to use the weapon. But what can't be explained is why a man with a loaded revolver should go to the difficulty of hanging himself."

"He might have wished to avoid the immediate discovery consequent on the noise of the shot," suggested the Dean. "By the way, might I ask if you have established his ownership of the weapon?"

"More or less conclusively," the Superintendent told him. "There were some spare rounds of the same type in his rooms. Of course he was not in possession of a licence taken out here."

The Chief Constable, who had been fidgeting for some moments, now thought that Gale's sphere of utility was at an end, since he now seemed keener on asking questions than answering them.

"Well, if you've nothing more to ask, Beecham, I don't think we need keep Mr. Gale any longer. We're much obliged to you for coming, of course."

Quite aware of what the Chief Constable was thinking, and feeling averse to being frozen out of an interesting inquiry so abruptly, the Dean hastily decided to add something on which he had at first resolved to say nothing. With a disarmingly casual air he observed: "By the way, Colonel, I understand that in these advanced times it is possible to tell microscopically whether a certain bullet has been fired from any particular gun?"

The Chief Constable admitted guardedly that such was the case: whereupon Gale dipped slowly into his waistcoat pocket and between ringer and thumb produced a bullet which all three police could at once see bore a marked resemblance to the Starbright exhibits. Inspector Norman, bending forward, displayed animation for the first time, the Chief Constable looked startled, and the Superintendent blinked placidly without change of expression. The bullet was passed round and compared with some unfired cartridges.

"It seems to be the same!" grunted the Chief Constable, as though somewhat annoyed by this apparently lucky circumstance. "Er ... may I ask, Mr. Gale, how this came into your possession?"

"I picked it up, or, rather, dug it up, from the middle of the grass plot in Craven Court—that is, the court in which are the rooms of Trevor, Starbright, and myself."

He then gave a very short account of the Thursday night incident; the sound of an explosion, the arrival on the scene of the Tutor and himself, the apparent flight of some undergraduates, the presence and statements of Trevor and Sullivan, and his own suspicions that a revolver had been fired from an upper window, believed to be Starbright's.

"This is rather an important matter, it seems to me," commented the Chief Constable. "It throws a serious light on the possible ill-feeling between Starbright and other students. Did you get nothing of this at your interview with the Tutor this morning, Norman?"

Norman said no, at the same time giving Gale a sour look. Just like these amateurs to stir up trouble for somebody!

"I don't think you can blame either the Tutor or the Inspector for that, Colonel," said Gale, who was now beginning to enjoy himself once more. "Our Tutor is of a very trustful disposition. He was told by the undergraduate Sullivan, you remember, that the noise was that of a firework. He immediately became convinced that such was the case, and it would have been a waste of my time to have suggested otherwise. Such being the case, no doubt he dismissed it from his mind and was unlikely to connect it in any way with Starbright's death."

Inspector Norman looked at Gale with returning affability not unmixed with respect, the Superintendent stayed bovine, and the Chief Constable, wishing to score a point against this over-clever visitor, remarked:

"But if you thought it was a shot fired from Starbright's rooms, why did you not go up and investigate?"

The Dean made another pause before answering. He wished to administer a slight snub without appearing to be unnecessarily rude.

"I think," he said at length, "you are rather confusing the duties of a Dean with those of a policeman. If the former thinks he has heard a shot, or, for that matter, a firework in a public place, it is his duty to make all possible investigations and compile a record of his findings under the assumption that somebody has committed a breach of the peace. In my case, if I believe a shot has been fired, I have sufficient belief in the integrity of those under my charge to consider that any serious damage or mishap would be dealt with by those immediately concerned. Should no damage or mishap have occurred, it would be a waste of time to prosecute tardy inquiries.

"In this instance I had been listening for several minutes to the explanations of Trevor and Sullivan before I made up my mind that a pistol or gun had been fired, probably from Starbright's rooms. By that time, or even sooner, it would have been so much waste of time to have walked upstairs and expected him to own up to what had happened. As regards searching his rooms, one can hardly treat undergraduates like small schoolboys whose lockers one might search at will for hidden cigarettes. Even the police force is restricted in its right of entry and search. I trust I make myself clear."

The Chief Constable said rather shortly that he supposed so, and asked the Superintendent if there was anything else. The latter thought not.

"We shall have to have a word with this Mr. Trevor," added the Chief Constable. "I suppose he will be in his rooms if he is wanted?"

"That's rather difficult to say," answered Gale. "I should think he is certain to be in immediately before and after Hall tonight. That is at eight o'clock on Sundays. If you like, I could make an appointment for you, and then you would not have to wait for him."

"I think, sir," said Beecham to the Chief Constable, "that if it's me who has to interview the gentleman, I'd rather he wasn't warned of my coming. It might alarm him without cause."

"Quite," agreed the Chief Constable, "and I'd be obliged, Mr. Gale, if meantime you'd be good enough to say nothing to him about the matter, and also refrain from putting any more questions to him on your own account. Well ... thanks very much, Mr. Gale. Good afternoon."

As Gale gave him a return word of parting, he could not resist adding: "And if there are any further points I can help you over, I shall be only too pleased to give you my assistance. I shall be most interested to hear of any developments."

The Chief Constable grunted and frowned as Gale left the room. He felt, however, that Gale had been helpful, even if irritating at times. He forced himself to review the case as a whole.

"Now, Beecham," he resumed briskly, "what do you make of it, and what immediate steps do you consider we must take?"

"I make murder of it, sir. Murderer unknown, but likely an inside job. There's been bad feeling and possibly violence already between the deceased and others in the college. The Tutor and the Dean want to make as little as possible of it, naturally. Odd points that crop up are: whether any connection between the death and the robbery, which we've got nothing on up to now; possible places in college where the genuine hanging might have been done; query as to the blow on the head and the presence of the revolver; possible motives from statement of the nearest relative, the uncle we can't get hold of yet. Question young Trevor. Pity we didn't have first go at him. That's your fault, Norman. You should know there's more than one set of rooms to one door-mat in colleges. Then there's that Mr. Gale. Queer customer, Mr. Gale!"

The Superintendent wheezed and blinked with the effort of such a long speech. Thinking, and not talking, was his strong point.

"What do you make of Gale?" asked the Chief Constable bluntly.

"Well, sir, if this were a detective story and not a bit of real life, I'd reckon we had an easy job. He'd be the murderer, who stands by to watch the investigation of his own crime, and hands out a manufactured clue every now and then just to keep the thing going. But being real life I'd say he's just a fairly brainy fellow who likes dabbling in detection. Trouble with him is, he knows he's a bit brainy and that makes him cocksure and swollen-headed. Still, sir, he has his uses."

"They say even in real life the murderer haunts the scene of his crime," mused the Chief Constable. "Still, I can't see a fellow like Gale murdering an undergraduate."

"He lives twenty yards from the scene of the hanging," Beecham reminded him, "and we haven't asked him what he was doing that night!"

"No, more we have! But, then, there are a hundred or so others also with rooms all round. That's the worst of a college. No, I can't see Mr. Gale in the part. He's just a nosy and rather damned aggravating fellow, eh, Beecham?"

"All the same, sir, he's given us our only two solid clues up to now. Maybe he'll walk in with the third, the one we most want."

"What's that, Beecham?"

"The original rope, sir."

CHAPTER XI

At two o'clock that same Sunday afternoon Tom Tanner sat alone in his rooms. He did more solitary thinking than most young men of his age and occupation, and today he felt more solitary and was thinking much harder than usual. He was perplexed, worried, and vaguely irritated. This last state of mind was due to Martin Trevor. Since the coming of Jane Brent he had resigned himself to lose the hourly company and confidence of his friend over those matters connected with the lady in question, but he had expected some explanation of Trevor's behaviour that morning. That Trevor had not been in his rooms at one o'clock that morning had not surprised him, nor had the fact of Trevor's prompting him to support an alibi in the hearing of the Dean; but for some hours to have elapsed without Trevor coming to offer any word of thanks or explanation seemed unusual and unkind.

Certainly the Sunday lunch hour was one during which he was often deprived of Trevor's company. It is a surviving custom amongst all classes in the British Isles to lunch hotly and heavily on the Sabbath, though their weekday fare may be a cold snack. By virtue of his athletic prowess Trevor had been elected to the Hawks Club. Its kitchens and cellars may not offer a vast variety, but there are few places in the world where the roast beef or the steak-and-kidney pie taste better than at the Hawks, though perhaps we all say that because we fed there in the days when we were young, happy, and healthy. Be that as it may, Trevor generally took Sunday lunch there at a table full of rugger players. At rare intervals Tanner was his guest, but the latter refused too frequently to appear as a guest in a club of which he could never hope to become a member. Even so, Trevor generally hurried back to join his friend in an afternoon walk. For this function he was now due, but Tanner reasoned that he might now have other plans.

It was not only the loss of a walking companion that was worrying Tanner. He felt that some very important and urgent matters needed to be discussed between them, but that the broaching of these matters lay with Trevor and not with himself. He decided to wait patiently till half past two, and then, if Trevor was not in college, he would take his exercise in solitary state. This thought prompted him to look out at the weather, and it gave him an added sense of grievance to see that, for Cambridge in November, it was an unusually fine afternoon.

The sun was actually shining. They might have had an unusually enjoyable walk; perhaps stayed out for tea in Granchester or Trumpington. His survey, however, enabled him to observe Trevor appear from the direction of the main gate and make his way towards his own rooms in Craven Court. For a moment Tanner was minded to take no notice of his friend's reappearance in college, but better counsels prevailed, and a few minutes later he made his way in the same direction.

He found Trevor engaged in that laudable Sunday pursuit which the best sons do not abandon at the close of their schooldays, namely the weekly letter home. But the eventful week seemed to produce a singular lack of news suitable for inclusion in that epistle, and he was glad to abandon his labours for the time being.

"Hullo, old thing!" said Trevor cheerfully enough. "I say, I'm sorry about this afternoon, but I've a date for tea at four, so I shan't have time for a walk. Tell you the truth, I hardly liked to come and break the news. I feel a bit of a worm, buzzing off like this all the time, but ... well ..."

"That's all right, old man. You must strike while the iron's hot and all that sort of thing, you know. Pretty fierce competition for girls in these parts."

Tanner infused as much banter as possible into these remarks. It was not easy, and he hoped it sounded convincing. Apparently it did, for Trevor laughed with an air of relief. Then he began to touch on the matter which was on Tanner's mind.

"By the way, it was good of you catch on this morning about my being supposed to be in bed. I didn't know but what you mightn't have come into my bedroom and said I was out without thinking. As it happens, I promised solemnly not to tell a soul where I was. Of course, I didn't kind of think of excluding you from that, but there it is. I expect you quite understand."

"Absolutely, old man. Don't say any more about it."

"But what I don't understand is why Gale should be nosing round so soon after that awful Starbright affair. Why should he come straight to me? Damn it, surely he doesn't think I drove the poor fellow to it! He asked me about it yesterday as well. I can't make it out."

"Well, I suppose it's because you're captain of football, and he thinks you would have had the chief say in going for Starbright."

"Thank God I hadn't; and, anyway, I more or less made it up with him. I say, old man, what do you reckon is the truth of it all? You were in college all last evening, I suppose. I suppose you don't know anything?"

"I'm fairly certain there was no more ragging of Starbright," interrupted Tanner. "I think you can put it right out of your mind that the footballers were in any way responsible for it. What the real reason was God knows. Of course, it might have been hatred or fear of some individual ... one doesn't like to mention names."

"You mean Davies?" queried Trevor, who had less scruples. "Well, I'm pretty certain Davies couldn't have had much to do with anything of the sort last night. I know ..."

He broke off, as if conscious of having said too much. There was an awkward silence.

"There's something going on I don't quite understand," went on Trevor. "Gale was trying to pump me about Starbright letting that gun off the other night, but fortunately I was able to say truthfully I knew nothing about it, as I wasn't there. Anyway, I thought the chaps had passed it off as a firework."

"Gale's a clever fellow," Tanner reminded him. "I don't suppose he was ever taken in over that firework yarn. And, seriously, old man, I think he's got hold of some theory which neither of us quite understands, something which connects you with the tragedy. I really feel you ought to go very carefully."

"But, damn it all, I know nothing at all about it! Of all people, I said or did less unkind things to Starbright than most others, seeing I was captain of rugger. I've an absolutely clear conscience, and so I told Gale."

"I know, I know. But I'm only telling you to be careful about ... well, other things, seeing that Gale seems to be watching you."

"So it seems, but I can't see why. By the way, have you seen the diary anywhere? It was on the table last night, but I can't find it anywhere this morning. Not that it matters much."

"As a matter of fact, Martin, I put it in my pocket when Gale was in here this morning, and afterwards I burned it."

"Burned it! What the deuce for? There's nothing in it that matters, is there?"

"Well, not exactly, except perhaps Starbright's name. Anyway, with Gale taking such an interest in things, I thought it was best out of the way."

Trevor gazed at his friend in perplexity and with a shade of annoyance. "I don't follow you at all," he said at length. "There seems to be a lot of funny business going on that I don't understand. You say you were about late last night and came up here to get a book."

"That's quite true," agreed Tanner. "I did come up here to get a book I'd left; round about one o'clock it was."

"You seem very windy about things in general. I take it you don't know anything about the Starbright business?"

It was Tanner's turn to pause before answering. Trevor noted the pause and felt suddenly uncomfortable and apprehensive. Then his friend replied with conviction:

"If you ask me why poor Starbright committed suicide, I could tell you I have a certain idea, but it has nothing whatever to do with the rugger business. I'm sorry, but I can't tell you any more, so please don't ask. As regards Gale, I honestly can't make out what has made him take this sudden interest in you. All I suggest is that he is doing so, and therefore you should ... well, watch your step for a bit."

"H'm ... I see," said Trevor, not seeing at all. His eye travelled reflectively towards a tall cupboard in one corner of the room and, jerking his head in the same direction, he added:

"You think perhaps we ought to get rid of ... that?"

"Good lord, no!" exclaimed Tanner. "It's safer left where it is. It would never do to be seen with it at a time like this."

"No, I suppose it would look bad, if one were seen. I hadn't thought of it in that connection. All the same, it couldn't possibly have any bearing on the case, could it?"

"Of course not," agreed Tanner hastily. "Only, if anyone saw you with it, it would attract particular attention at a time like this."

"Oh, quite! I see what you mean. And perhaps you're right in thinking we'd better lay off it for a time."

A few minutes later Tanner tactfully withdrew, leaving his friend plenty of time to reach a rendezvous for his four o'clock tea, and strolled thoughtfully back to his own rooms. He was still rather worried, for the interview had closed on an awkward note, and it was clear that each was aware that the other had something to keep back. Still, he felt easier in his mind about things, and was now of the opinion, unhappily an erroneous one, that everything would work out all right.

The fact that things did not reach this desired consummation was due in a certain measure to the irregular and dilatory proceedings of a certain Mrs. Gunter, who was Trevor's bedmaker.

The genus of Cambridge bedmakers deserves more than a passing word. There are twenty or thirty to each college, according to size, and they conform, more or less, to a rigid or sealed pattern in age, appearance, dress, habits, and manner of conversation. If one were to say that one's bedmaker was an ample proportioned old lady not less than sixty or more than eighty, dressed in rusty black with an old-fashioned poke-bonnet, heralding her arrival by the squeak of elastic-sided boots and the rattling of dustpans, and with a fund of conversation dealing mainly with the merits or otherwise of her poor husband (*obiit* MCMV), the idiosyncrasies of other gentlemen she has served, and her various bodily ailments, then one would be giving a fair general description of eighty per cent of her tribe.

It is something of a puzzle to reflect how a moderately populated town like Cambridge can maintain the supply of some hundreds of the genuine article without ever seeming to fall short, despite frequent replacements due to age. Yet Cambridge still gives us the genuine article. Daily they come from those grey, dingy, obscure streets beyond Parker's Piece and the Mill Road, uncharted regions of which the undergraduate is but dimly aware, save that he touches the fringe of that zone in the depressing drive to and from that platform or halt where trains of both the L.N.E.R. and the L.M.S. stop to set down or take up passengers.

What special qualifications or what preparation through their fifty odd years of previous life serve finally to secure these old ladies their appointment as bedmakers I do not know. Their past is often a closed book, and in many respects they present a problem of a nature inverse to that of the genus of beautiful tobacconists' daughters, of whom mention has already been made. In the case of the "bedders" we say to ourselves, can these prim, plain, bonneted old things ever have been skittish, comely, and short-skirted? Whence are they, and what manner of girls can they have been? Of the tobacconist's daughter, or her fair cousin the barmaid, one may well ask, what of the days when their bloom, natural or otherwise, has faded, and the gold (or henna) is streaked with grey? Maybe one becomes a countess in some stately home of England or a queen of the underworld, but for the rest ... But such thoughts present gloomy possibilities. Can it be, after all, that by some strange metamorphosis the siren who sells tobacco today will become the bedmaker of the day after tomorrow? Perhaps that is the most comfortable solution.

When I tell you that Trevor's Mrs. Gunter entered his unoccupied rooms at four o'clock on a Sunday afternoon for the purpose of "straightening up", I am aware that the critic of strict accuracy on Cambridge manners and customs will sit up and take notice. That is all wrong, he will say. Mrs. Gunter would have "finished off" long before, some time in the morning in fact, and would have returned to her obscure home for a "quiet Sunday afternoon". In the ordinary way she would have done so, but this had been a most unusual occasion. In the excitement of the Starbright tragedy the prompt and regular execution of work on beds had gone by the board. An extraordinary general meeting of the bedmakers' social union had been called to meet at the ladies' bar of the "Suffolk Arms" at the earliest moment of opening, and there Mrs. Radpole, who had first seen the advent of the police and had obtained a partial view of the proceedings from an upper window, Mrs. Jenner, who had cross-examined Sergeant Stumpy, and Mrs. Fitch, the bedmaker actually in the service of the dead man, had all been detailed to present full reports.

Only the call of time—I suppose they say "Time, ladies, please!"— had served to bring the meeting to an end, and Mrs. Gunter, a conscientious "finisher off", had returned to Craven Court. She continued some odd jobs until Trevor's departure, since a number of double gins had given her a violent desire for "a nice 'ot cup o' tea", a beverage she was accustomed to consume at the expense of her "gentlemen". Being somewhat of a connoisseur of tea, she had come to the conclusion that the produce of Trevor's caddy was the best available, and she accordingly used it when possible and necessary.

After enjoying a cup of Trevor's tea she decided, being conscientious, to repay the unconscious donor by leaving everything extra tidy, and this prompted her to sweep underneath the sofa, from which she at once unearthed a soft hat of that type, just then becoming fashionable in Cambridge, known as the pork-pie shape. Mrs. Gunter eyed it with approval. It was a jaunty, distinctive hat, of a pleasant green colour and decorated with a multi-coloured feather. She liked her gentlemen to be well turned out, and Trevor had certainly needed a new hat, though they were not often worn by undergraduates. She dusted the hat carefully, and then hung it up on the door on a peg, next to Trevor's old grey homburg. She then took a drop of Trevor's whisky, to settle the tea, and went home.

At half past seven a police car drew quietly up some distance short of St. Chad's front gate, and its solitary passenger climbed slowly and heavily out. Superintendent Beecham did not wish to herald his arrival with a flourish of trumpets, and had furthermore taken the precaution of changing into plain clothes. As he moved slowly under the ornate arch of St. Chad's gateway he might have been anybody or nobody in particular. He stopped at the lodge door for a word with Meadows, whom he knew slightly.

"Good evening, Superintendent."

"Good evening to you, Mr. Meadows. I'm sorry to be intruding officially, but there it is: robbery and then suicide. Got to look into things."

The Head Porter said he supposed so. Beecham, who had decided to see the useful but annoying Mr. Gale before tackling Trevor, inquired about the Dean's movements.

"At the moment the Dean is in Chapel, Mr. Beecham, but he should be out by the quarter to eight. Then you can catch him before Hall, at eight."

"Thanks, that'll do nicely. There's an undergraduate I wanted a word with too: a Mr. Trevor. Nothing serious, I ought to tell you. Just routine. I wonder if he's in college just now?"

"Yes. He came in half an hour ago and I don't think he's gone out since. I reckon you would find him in his rooms."

"I'll wait here and see Mr. Gale first, if I may," said the Superintendent. He also had ideas on the omniscience of head porters. "Tell me, Mr. Meadows, have you any opinions about this Mr. Starbright? Was he the sort of young fellow to do away with himself? Nervy, you know?"

"I should say not. A rough, quarrelsome fellow, but no nerves at all, I should say. Not that he was ever in trouble with the college. Just noisy and took a bit of drink sometimes, but, bless you, we've lots like that. By the way, fill your pipe. I'm sorry I can't offer you a drop, but in here——"

"Quite so, Mr. Meadows; thanks for the thought, all the same. You were saying this man Starbright was quarrelsome. You know a great deal about all the students in college. Would you say he had had some special trouble that might have preyed on his mind?"

"No, Mr. Beecham, I wouldn't go so far as to say that. There was a bit of bother over Mr. Starbright failing to turn up for a match. That caused trouble with the other footballers, but I fancy that had all blown over. No, I can't understand the poor gentleman committing suicide. Now if I'd found him having a stand-up fight with one of the others, I shouldn't have been surprised; but suicide, no; I can't understand it."

"I heard something about some little trouble the other night: a firework being let off, or something. Did you happen to see or hear anything of that, Mr. Meadows?"

"I heard it, and I came out to see what it was about; but the Tutor was already on the spot, so I left things to him."

"Between the two of us, Mr. Meadows, did you really think it was a firework?"

"Between the two of us, Superintendent, no. But the least said the soonest mended, and what was good enough for the Tutor was good enough for me. You can call it a firework if you like, but not what folks generally mean by fireworks, if you get me."

"I heard," continued the Superintendent casually, "that, when you came up, there was a student standing shall we say in the possible line of the firework, but he said he had only just then come into college. I believe it was that Mr. Trevor I was speaking of. Did you happen to notice him?"

"That's quite right," assented the Head Porter; "he told the Tutor he arrived after the explosion and wondered what it could have been."

"I wonder if he really had just come on the scene, as he said?" cogitated the Superintendent, as though the idea had occurred to him for the first time.

"Why, yes," said Meadows. "Now I come to think of it, he passed through the gateway just a few seconds before the noise happened. I shouldn't think he could have had time to reach the other court before the shot ... er ... the firework went off. No doubt he was speaking the truth. A very nice and reliable gentleman, Mr. Trevor."

At that moment a shaft of light fell across the court, and the low sound of an organ could be heard as the chapel doors opened and the white-surpliced congregation began to disperse. The Superintendent, refusing with thanks the escort of the Head Porter, hurried to catch Gale, and the latter, on seeing him, greeted him without surprise and led him towards Craven Court.

"I have just over a quarter of an hour till Hall, Superintendent, and am at your service for that time."

"Thank you," answered the Superintendent. "I really came to have a word with Mr. Trevor, but I thought perhaps it would be as well if you, as an official of the college, were present at the interview. I don't for a moment suppose that anything of importance will result; at the same time it seemed to me that I ought to inform an official of the college, so that he could attend if he wished."

"Quite so," agreed the Dean, "very right and proper."

He felt pleased at being admitted to the further confidences of the police. Beecham, he told himself, was a distinct improvement on his Chief Constable both in manners and sagacity. The Superintendent, for his part, had little expectation of gleaning anything from the visit. Certain suspicions which he had entertained of Trevor had been somewhat dispelled by the statements of Meadows. It now seemed certain that Trevor had not been the target of a bullet fired by Starbright, and there seemed no other reason to suppose that he had stated anything but the truth in disowning any hostile intention towards the dead undergraduate. The Superintendent was a little uncertain what line of inquiry to pursue. Had it been feasible to admit the likelihood of murder, it would have been easier to put direct questions, but with the necessity of keeping up the fiction of obvious suicide it more difficult to gain information.

Trevor was at home and, on hearing the identity of the unknown visitor, displayed signs of surprise and confusion. This did not impress the Superintendent unfavourably, for he had learned by experience that the most law-abiding persons are usually the most discomposed when confronted unexpectedly with the forces of the law. In his view, people who treated him with a show of indifference were often those who were not unused to police interrogation and who generally had something discreditable to conceal. The Dean, in fact, more nearly resembled his idea of a suspicious character. He set himself to allay any nervousness on the part of the young man.

"You are possibly a bit taken aback at receiving a visit from me on this unpleasant suicide case, Mr. Trevor," he began. "It's just routine, really. We are anxious to fill up a few gaps in the case to satisfy the coroner and his jury, more especially to get at the motive, if possible. Thus we want to try and trace the deceased gentleman's movements prior to the tragedy. Now the fact is, late last night, a witness believed he saw Mr. Starbright wandering in the direction of this staircase. We don't know, of course, that he actually entered it. Still, I have just to establish whether or not you saw anything of him last night, and whether, in short, you can throw any light on the matter."

The Superintendent wheezed heavily with the effort of uttering the fabrication concerning the witnessing of Starbright's approach to the staircase. He noted, however, that Trevor seemed relieved and not upset by this supposed revelation. Thereupon he proceeded with his routine questions, jotting down a short digest of the information thus gleaned. His notes, when completed, ran as follows:

M. H. Trevor. Out of college 6 p.m. to 9 p.m. approx. In rooms and straight to bed unwell. 9 p.m. Saw or heard nothing till 9 a.m. approx. when getting up. First learned, of tragedy from Dean. Suggestions re cause of suicide— nil. Admits unpopularity of deceased owing to football trouble and attempt to rag him on Thurs. night, but denies being present or approving (confirmed, Meadows). Later interview with deceased on Thurs. night and parted on good terms. No further speech with dec. Believes no further hostile behaviour by anyone against dec. Can give no further explanation.

As he was noting the answer to his final question, he heard the bell begin to ring for Hall, and rose with a word of thanks to Trevor and Gale. Everything seemed straightforward enough, he considered, except for the malady which had caused Trevor to withdraw from the society of his fellows at such an unusually early hour on a Saturday night. That looked fishy, as also did the very recent black eye owned by the captain of football. It did not seem worth putting a falsely casual question about that. One seldom hears the real truth about black eyes.

As Gale and the Superintendent turned to the door and Trevor stooped to pick up his gown for Hall, there was a knock and Tanner entered. Seeing the visitors he stopped short and gave them a look of quick suspicion and apprehension which was not lost on Beecham. Being assured, however, that the two visitors were about to pass the door in the opposite direction, he stood aside to let them out. Gale reflected that this was the second occasion on which Tanner had appeared at the closure of his talk with Trevor, and that on the previous occasion his last glance had shown him the mysterious disappearance of the diary. Perhaps it was this thought which put his mind on the alert. As he stepped to the door he took a quick look round, his roving eye came to a halt, his mind worked feverishly and suddenly told him what he wanted, and he barely restrained himself from stopping short and exclaiming in astonishment. Instead he preceded the Superintendent to the landing, and, with a gesture of silence, opened his own door and pulled that somewhat astonished officer inside.

It is probable that Gale would never have made his latest and, as it proved, most momentous discovery but for his study of dress, and hats in particular. As he left Trevor's room he had noted, hanging on the door, a good specimen of the latest fashion pork-pie brand, a type on which he confessed himself unable to make up his mind to approve or condemn. He had never noticed Trevor wearing it, in fact there were very few in college, as yet. Still, he had seen one yesterday afternoon, just exactly like that one, with a silly feather stuck in it. Trevor wasn't wearing it though; perhaps the owner had left it in Trevor's rooms that afternoon, for he hadn't seen it there that morning. Now, who was it whom he had seen wearing that very hat? Why ... Goodness! The owner could not have left it there that afternoon. He closed the door of his room and composed himself to speak to the Superintendent. As he searched for words, he heard the running footsteps of Trevor and Tanner as the last notes of the Hall bell sounded. He forced himself to speak calmly to Beecham, who, in rather an aggrieved way, was massaging his arm where Gale had gripped it more tightly than he had intended.

"Er ... Superintendent. I think I shall miss my dinner after all. I think I have just seen something rather surprising. I will ask you to come back to the rooms opposite; then perhaps we can see if my suspicions are correct. There is nobody there now."

The Superintendent silently and patiently followed the Dean back to the other room. The Dean began his explanation *en route.*

"I wonder if you noticed that hanging on the door there were two hats, an old grey one and a new green one, a pork-pie, if you know the kind I mean."

The Superintendent said yes, and what about it.

"I want you," said the Dean, opening Trevor's door and ushering in the Superintendent, "to take a good look at that green pork-pie hat." Beecham gazed blankly at the reverse side of the door, whilst Gale squeezed by his bulky companion to renew his own contemplation of the exhibit. For the moment, however, the Superintendent's bulk was completely blocking his view.

"Excuse me, sir. What sort of a hat did you say?"

"The green pork-pie!" cried the Dean. "Why, man, surely you can tell the one I mean!"

The Superintendent answered never a word. Slowly and sadly he stood aside, giving pride of place to the Dean. The latter stepped forward, stopped, started back, and cried:

"It's gone!"

He gazed wildly round the room, whilst the Superintendent turned a sleepy, bovine eye in the same direction. There was no sign of a green pork-pie hat.

"I tell you," said the Dean vehemently, "the hat was on that peg a moment ago."

"Well, suppose you tell me what is important about the hat," said the Superintendent placidly, "then we'll see if it's worth looking for; and if it's worth looking for no doubt I'll find it."

Now that he was about to make his revelation, the Dean recovered his poise as an amateur investigator.

"I have seen only one hat like that in college. This morning, when I came into this room, I'm certain the hat was not visible. Yesterday afternoon I saw that hat, or its exact counterpart, being worn in the court, and not by Mr. Trevor."

He paused impressively, and Beecham said wearily:

"Then, if you recognized the wearer, perhaps you will say who it was."

"Superintendent, it was Mr. Starbright."

"Ah!" murmured the Superintendent very profoundly. "Yes. I see your point, Mr. Gale. Very interesting. In that case we must find the hat."

"But those two must have made off with it just now," objected Gale. "They are in Hall by now."

"You think Mr. Trevor took it?" hazarded Beecham.

"No, I suspect Tanner," snapped Gale irritably. "It's not the first time he's tried to conceal evidence in this case."

"Is that so?" inquired the Superintendent. "I don't recollect your mentioning Mr. Tanner's name before. What particular piece of evidence did he conceal, may I ask?"

Gale, realizing that he had said more than he had intended, hesitated awkwardly before answering:

"Well, as a matter of fact it was just a matter of college discipline. I don't think it has any bearing on the present case."

"That's as may be," murmured the Superintendent. "Still, sir, possibly you know best. But sometimes odd things connect up, without seeming to at first."

As the Dean made no response to this further invitation to unburden himself, the Superintendent fell silent, and began to gaze round the room. Gale returned to the main question of the moment.

"You say you can get the hat back again, Superintendent. Won't that be a little difficult, if these young men have taken it away with them?"

"I should very much doubt if they have taken it far," said Beecham. "You say they were going straight in to dinner. They would hardly take it in with them. It would be a little difficult to conceal, and if, as you say, it was a distinctive hat belonging to Mr. Starbright, they would not wish it to be seen by the other undergraduates. Now, I wonder, Mr. Gale. You are an official of the college. What exactly is your position as regards the right to search the rooms of students under your charge? One can hardly call them enclosed premises."

"I hardly know," confessed Gale. "But if you think the hat is hidden here, let us go ahead by all means. They won't know, anyway, and we have a good half hour before us."

Without answering, Beecham lumbered across the room, looked into the bedroom and gyp-room, or pantry, and then returned to his starting point.

"It's not visible so far," he remarked. "I wonder, sir, if you would mind taking a look in that corner cupboard. In case of anything being said in evidence, it might be better for you rather than me to be the one to make the discovery."

His detective instincts being aroused, Gale needed no further prompting. Poking his head into the cupboard, which had no lock, he at once gave a cry of triumph and emerged brandishing a hat.

"Got it first shot!" he exclaimed. "You were quite right, Superintendent."

Beecham took the hat and eyed it sleepily. It appeared to be a fairly new hat, and bore no owner's name or other mark of identification.

"How can we be certain it was the property of the deceased gentleman?" he inquired. "There are several hats like this about just now, you know. Could you identify it positively, sir?"

"Well ... that's difficult on oath, of course. But I haven't seen another like it in college."

The Superintendent crossed to the door and, taking down the older grey hat, made a comparison between the two types of headgear.

"This other hat, sir. Would you say for certain that this was the property of Mr. Trevor?"

"Yes, I think I can say that for certain. It is an elderly hat which has well-nigh reached the age for discarding, and I was thinking only the other day, when I saw Trevor going out with it on his head, that it was time he got a new one."

"In that case," said the Superintendent, comparing the hats once more, "I should say the green one certainly belongs to somebody else, for it is a size and a half larger." Moreover he observed that the size of the green hat was such that its owner had apparently put some padding in the lining to ensure a closer fit. Dipping a finger therein he disclosed some folded paper, which proved to be a folded page from an exercise-book bearing the name and writing of Starbright. He showed it silently to Gale, and then stowed it away in an inner pocket.

"Well, that seems to be all for the present, sir, and it makes one think, I must say. I wonder, though, if that cupboard has anything else of interest for us."

"One can hardly suppose it can have that," demurred the Dean; "still, having trespassed once, one might as well make a job of it. ... H'm ... Nothing much. Overcoats, football boots, empty suitcases ... What's this in a dark corner? Funny thing rather. What should he want with a coil of rope?"

A fleeting flash of animation crossed the face of the Superintendent. For a moment he looked almost startled.

"Did you say a coil of rope, sir?" he asked softly.

"Yes, that's right," assented Gale, puzzled alike by the rope and by the interest expressed by Beecham. "Though what it's for I don't quite follow."

"I should like to see this coil of rope," said the Superintendent, and without waiting for an answer he crossed to the cupboard, stooped painfully down, and dragged it out into the middle of the room. It was of moderate thickness and, as far as Gale could judge without extending the coils, about twenty feet in length. Beecham examined his find, paying special attention to the two extremities. Gale noticed that two or three feet from one end the rope was distinctly frayed and chafed. After a few moments the Superintendent suspended his examination and took another look round the room. His eye rested first on the double windows overlooking Craven Court, and then travelled to the smaller, barred window on the opposite side of the room. He crossed to the window and gazed out into the darkness. "I notice a kind of garden below here," he observed. "Is that part of the college, may I ask?"

The Dean told him it was the fellows' garden, and added that the sole entrance was by a locked gate at the end of the passage leading to the college museum, immediately below the room in which they were then standing. He was once more aware that the police were following some line of investigation of which he was in complete ignorance. He made another effort to sound the Superintendent.

"I'm afraid I cannot follow your train of thought," he said, "and I cannot see what bearing this rope has on the case you are supposed to be investigating. If I did, I might be able to give you more useful assistance than is at present in my power."

The Superintendent stood looking out of the window, his heavy forehead creased in a frown. He appeared to be debating some knotty problem in his slow but logical way. In a similar situation his colleague, Inspector Norman, would doubtless have been stroking his chin. At length he reached a decision and, turning to the Dean, said slowly: "You'll realize, sir, that in the ordinary way we police, when we're investigating a case of this kind, like to keep our progress to ourselves. At the same time, if it happens that we're getting help from outside, it sometimes pays us to give away something in order to get a bit of help in return. But that's a risky business, as you can see for yourself. Supposing a crime has been committed, it may mean information leaking out to the guilty party and that party having the warning to cover his tracks or make himself scarce, whereas there's nothing like getting a suspected person in a state of false security, so he'll give himself away through getting careless. Now I'll not deny you've been considerably useful to us, Mr. Gale, and you may be a sight more use yet. So I reckon it's worth my taking the risk of telling you a thing or two.

"But I warn you, sir, that if you pass on this information in certain quarters you may be doing a great deal of harm to justice and a great deal of good to a possible criminal, besides putting me in a hole, so I'll have to ask you to treat what I'm going to tell you as strictly on the Q.T. Silence is golden, as they say, sir. Added to which you, as an official of the college, can make things easier for me when it comes to anything a bit difficult, like searching a gentleman's cupboard, for instance."

"I quite see your point, Superintendent, and I'm quite agreeable to the conditions you impose. Of course I have already gathered from the attitude of the police, as well as from certain observations of my own, that you think there is more in this case than meets the eye. It even appears to me that you suspect foul play rather than suicide, but on what grounds I cannot fathom. As things are, I am more than willing to give you any help I can, and in return to keep my mouth shut until such time as it may be expedient for me to open it. I trust your Chief Constable will see eye to eye with you in this arrangement."

Beecham said nothing to this last pious hope. It had already occurred to him that his superior officer might have other views over his confiding in this meddlesome layman. However, one must take risks to get results.

"You cannot," he said, half to himself, "make an omelette without breaking eggs."

Gale did not quite see the application of this platitude, so he said nothing, and waited for whatever revelations the Superintendent was about to unfold. The latter cleared his throat and began: "In short, sir, the position is this. Mr. Starbright was found hanged in a certain place and manner, pointing to straightforward suicide; but expert medical evidence showed that he must have met his death by being hanged in a different place and with a rope thicker than the cord actually found."

Even the cultivated indifference of the Dean was shattered by this blunt exposition.

"But ... but, this is amazing! It alters the whole aspect of the case. One can hardly grasp it all at once. ... Well, I agree with you, I think, that it certainly looks like murder."

"Exactly, sir. On the face of it, there's no other logical explanation. And I think it will not take you long to follow our line of reasoning from that point. I need hardly suggest it to you, especially as our time here is limited, and there are other things to be done."

"It certainly looks ugly for Trevor, yet ... yet, I can't believe he would be capable of such a terrible thing. Besides, Starbright was a powerful fellow and armed into the bargain. There must have been an accomplice, or else the poor fellow was taken unawares. I confess I'm completely at sea."

"Every trail seems to lead to this room," the Superintendent reminded him. "The button, the hat, and the rope. The question is, though, where he could have been hanged. The evidence insisted on a long drop. There's no place inside the room that meets the case."

The Superintendent was eyeing the back window with a questioning expression. He seemed attracted by the single iron bar which ran up the interior of the window and was cemented at either extremity. He bent forward and looked closer, then seized the bar and gave it a sharp tug. The whole of its upper part came loose in his hand, leaving two or three inches in the lower socket. A downward tug disengaged the larger section from its loose seating in the top of the window and Beecham drew it clear. Gale gazed open-mouthed at this sudden demonstration, and his monocle dropped sharply to the limit of its retaining cord. Bending down for a closer view he observed that the bar had apparently been neatly filed through and loosened at the top. Dust and loose plaster suggested that the fracture had been concealed by plugging the resulting cracks with some disguising substance. At first glance the Dean could not connect this discovery with the tragedy they were investigating, but meanwhile the Superintendent had opened the window and, craning out, was making some further investigations of his own which the Dean was unable to follow closely.

Outside the window was a ledge with sharp stone edges, and in the middle of this ledge, in line with the window bar, Beecham found what he expected. Here the stone was rubbed to a lighter colour and slightly worn away in a little smear of an inch or two in breadth, as though from the chafing of a rope. Leaning out still further with such wheezing and puffing that Gale feared he would fall out altogether, the Superintendent ran his torch along the under edge of the stone projection until the light stopped at a small discoloured patch to which adhered a few fragments like hairs.

The Superintendent paused for a moment to consider how best to tackle a difficult job. Finally he took from his pocket a clean envelope and a penknife, at the same time returning the torch to his pocket. Then, leaning out again with a final and prodigious stretch, he held the envelope, gaping open, under the marked stop, and scraped carefully with his knife. Some dirt, particles of stone, and, as he hoped, some other more important fragments fell into the envelope.

"They're coming out of Hall," said Gale, trying to peer over Beecham's shoulder.

"Right, sir! Just finished in time, I think. May we go back to your room till the coast's clear for me to make my getaway? Then I must be off. This has given me something to think about!"

"You could do with a smoke or a drink, I dare say," offered Gale when they had crossed the passage and entered his own room. "Upon my word, this is most amazing. I take it you believe that poor Starbright was hanged from the window, and that his murderer, or murderers, then carried him down to the archway. But, good heavens, I've just thought of something!"

The Superintendent displayed renewed interest. He was bound to admit that, up to now, Gale's brainwaves had been singularly illuminating. He invited the Dean to proceed.

"Last night, or, rather, early this morning, I was sitting in this very chair reading an interesting novel, and at half past one—I remember the clock striking just beforehand—I distinctly heard the footsteps of two people going downstairs from the room opposite. It struck me they were walking slowly and unsteadily. I remember thinking at the time that they might have been ... well ... having one or two."

"That's very interesting, sir. Very interesting indeed. Would you say that their walk suggested that they might have been carrying a heavy load between them?"

"Well, now you come to suggest it, yes. Possibly."

"Of course, you didn't see who these persons actually were."

"No, most unfortunately not. I almost had the curiosity to look out of my window, but I was comfortably settled, and I felt perhaps that, especially on a Saturday night, it was more charitable to turn a blind eye, or no eye at all, on possible signs of jollification on the part of two of our young hopefuls."

"Quite so, sir."

"I'm sorry not to have mentioned the matter before, but of course I had no idea it would have any possible bearing on the case. Undergraduates frequently keep late hours and can walk about the courts at will."

"Naturally you couldn't know, sir. It just shows I did well to let you into the know. Bread upon the waters."

"Bread ...? Oh, I see! Quite so. Well, I'm afraid this looks very serious for poor Trevor. I've always liked the boy. I can't believe that he ... Still, it looks bad. Do you think, Superintendent, that it will be a question of possible ... er, arrest?"

"Well, now you're asking, sir. That's a difficult point, and the decision will lie with the Chief Constable. There's a few threads to be sorted out yet; then we shall see our way better. By the way, sir, did you hear anyone return upstairs after the two went down?"

"No, I don't think so. Is that important?"

"Why, yes, sir. You see, if one of the two were Trevor, then he must have come back later to turn in for the night."

"Oh yes! Of course. But I'm afraid I went to bed myself not more than ten minutes after hearing the two go downstairs, so there's no knowing whether one of them came back later or not."

"That's a pity," commented the Superintendent; "still, we've got something to go on with. What steps will be taken I cannot tell you."

"It's most upsetting to think that Trevor may be mixed up in this," complained Gale. "I've always liked that young man. Tell me, do you really think there will be a question of his arrest?"

"I should think it highly probable, sir. There is one thing, though. It's fairly easy to keep an eye on him here in the college. He's not likely to ask leave to go out of Cambridge, I suppose. And if he did, it's open to you to refuse it. Let's see: you call it an exeat, don't you? Then, again, he can't get out after closing time at nights."

"No, I don't think he can," assented the Dean with a shade of doubt in his voice. "Look here, Superintendent, I feel somehow responsible for bringing suspicion on this man Trevor. I should like to help him in any way possible."

"You mustn't repeat any of this to him, sir," replied Beecham in tones of concern. "You promised that, you know."

"Oh, I wasn't thinking of doing that! Only, if he's actually arrested he should have somebody to help him in case he does not know of any handy solicitor. I have read law to a certain extent, and could help him until he was properly represented. I wish you would do something for me."

"I'll do anything I can within the bounds of my duty, sir. What did you want exactly?"

"Well, if Trevor is actually arrested and charged, I wish you would let me know at the earliest possible moment. Ring me up, that is to say."

"That would be a slightly irregular thing to say over the 'phone, sir.

But I tell you what I'll do. If you get a message from me asking you to come to the station and see me urgently, you will know it means the young man is either arrested or in difficulties. Then, if he is agreeable, you will be allowed to see him as soon as possible. By the way, have you a 'phone in these rooms? I should like to ring up the station as soon as possible."

"I'm afraid there isn't one nearer than the porter's lodge," was Gale's reply to this. "We're rather primitive in some ways."

"That will do nicely," said the Superintendent, gazing thoughtfully at the coil of rope on the floor. "There's one other thing, sir. I shall have to get this rope down to the station, and I don't want to be seen carrying it through the college. I wonder if you would give me the loan of a bag or suitcase to put it in. I have a car outside the college, and I would send the bag straight back from the station."

"Certainly," replied Gale. "In fact I will do better than that, and save you carrying even a bag. If you will ask Meadows on your way out kindly to send over one of the servants, I will instruct the servant to deliver the bag to your car. Meantime, I hope you will do what you can to make things as reasonable for Trevor as possible."

"I'll certainly do that, sir. Things look black, I admit, but as regards arresting suspects, we don't go acting all hasty, like in some of those murder novels you read. There's too much back-chat in the press, or even in Parliament these days, for us to risk making bloomers over wrongful arrests. Still, I can't say. Though I will tell you this much, which is more than I ought. I think there's more than one man mixed up in this case, and from certain things I've noted I should say that Mr. Trevor might be an accomplice who is partly unconscious of the fact. But I don't know. Personally, I shouldn't take the risk myself of charging him with anything at the moment. That's the best I can say. Well, good night, sir, and many thanks. But, mind, if you please, not a word. I'll give the Head Porter your message."

Whilst Meadows was dispatching the under-porter to the Dean's rooms, the Superintendent was speaking on the telephone to Inspector Norman.

"That you, Norman? Did you get those groups from the photographers? Good! Two of Trevor ... Look here. You have a freshman's group of two years ago. Is it handy? ... Well, look through it quickly and see if you can spot a T. Tanner. Dark fellow in glasses ... He's there? Good. ... Now then. Get hold of Baker, show him the photos, and tell him to memorize the faces of Trevor and Tanner. Then tell him to come up here, to St. Chad's, as quick as he can, and report to me in the car which I shall keep just round the corner, in Gold Street. I'll wait ten minutes from now, then begin to drive back to the station via Downing Street, and pick him up on the way. Got that? ... Right; step on it ... And—wait a second—I want a word with the constable on that night beat before he goes on. Hold him if I'm not back before he goes on. That's the lot."

A few minutes later the Superintendent lumbered slowly out of college carrying a large suitcase, and disappeared inconspicuously round the street corner; after which nothing happened to show that any untoward events were disturbing the Sunday night placidity of St. Chad's. Yet just outside the college a keen observer might have noted the presence of a somewhat shabby and nondescript loafer, who spent some hours strolling up and down, scrutinizing the drains with an expert eye, and sheltering under cover of shop doorways. One might have thought that such conduct would have brought him into suspicion and disfavour with the constable who passed by from time to time. Yet the two passed each other without a glance or sign of recognition.

CHAPTER XII

As the clocks of Cambridge, with their many and various chimes, were striking the notes of nine o'clock on Monday morning, the Superintendent sat alone at his table taking a last look at the reports he had prepared for the perusal of his Chief. The latter had unfortunately been away from his home on the previous night, so the Superintendent had been unable to prepare the ground by telling him the startling developments of the night before. He was due to arrive any time after nine, so no purpose could be served by ringing up that morning.

The Superintendent looked round for Inspector Norman, and then remembered with annoyance that the latter was out on another case, whilst his colleague, Inspector Taylor, was also otherwise employed. In the conventional murder story, as soon as the book murder has been committed and discovered, the whole body of local police is available to give it their full and undivided attention. Should a super criminal begin some species of gang warfare, every squad car, every policeman, and every firearm is instantly available to rush out at a second's notice. In the real life of a police force such, unfortunately, or fortunately for the criminal, is not the case. Besides the daily routine jobs which have to be done, there is an unfortunate tendency for minor crime to rear its head and interfere with the conduct of the big case. In fact, as Superintendent Beecham had wisely observed on the previous day, it never rains but it pours.

He was thinking once more on these lines when the Chief Constable entered breezily and, somewhat to Beecham's annoyance, plunged straight into a monologue of his own, without waiting to hear if any developments had taken place. Beecham resigned himself to hearing him out before breaking his own news.

"'Morning, Beecham. Nippy out this morning. Now we've got to decide a few things pretty quick about this Starbright case. First of all, there's the inquest tomorrow. We must decide what line we want the coroner to take and instruct him accordingly. As I see it, we can do one of three things: either take formal evidence and get an adjournment; we can put all our cards on the table and go for a murder verdict right away; or we can camouflage the thing by simply having the evidence that deceased met his death by hanging, which is true as far as it goes, and get a suicide verdict. Though I don't think the last is quite justifiable in view of what might come out later if we solve the case and make an arrest."

The Superintendent started to say something, but the Chief Constable forestalled him and continued:

"Then there's the question of calling in the Yard. You know I'd rather give you fellows, and myself for that matter, the credit of working the thing out on our own. At the same time, if there's a tricky case and we get no results, there is criticism later if we don't call in the London fellows. And then if we don't have them in reasonably quick, they grumble that it's too late and that the scent is cold, which is a reasonable enough grouse in a way. So, if we still assume it's murder, we must make the decision quick, and ring 'em up pretty soon this morning if they're to do much good. By the way, have you anything to report since yesterday afternoon?"

"Yes, sir, a considerable amount. I'm hoping we may not have to bother our friends at the Yard. I've found what I believe to be the original rope, and the place where it was used. I'm only waiting for the medical report to be quite certain on these points."

"Good lord!" exclaimed the Chief Constable. "Why the devil couldn't you tell me this before? It looks like clearing up the whole thing. And have you any idea of the person responsible? Tell me exactly what's happened."

The Superintendent was at pains to answer this spate of questions. He therefore took them in order, picking his words with care. "I found these things out between eight and nine o'clock last night, sir, and rang up your private address as soon as I had got back here. I was informed that you were not expected home till late, and as you were due here first thing this morning I judged it best to wait and make a personal report. Since you entered the room I have not had the opportunity of speaking until this moment."

"Quite, quite. But get on with it, man! What's happened, and who did it?"

With maddening deliberation the Superintendent opened and consulted a fat notebook, after which he began a careful account of his interviews with Meadows, Trevor, and the Dean. At the outset, however, they were interrupted by the entry of a constable with a message classed as urgent.

"Beg pardon, sir, but you asked to be informed at once of any report on the five-pound note which we sent out about yesterday. A telephone message has just come through about it."

In the excitement of the Starbright case the minor matter of the college robbery had almost been forgotten. Considering, however, that the two matters might well be connected, the Chief Constable asked eagerly for details. He learned that the note had been paid in the previous evening over the bar of the "Golden Lion" saloon lounge.

"Well, that's Norman's pigeon, isn't it?" commented the Chief Constable. "Where is he, anyway? He should get on to that at once."

"He's out at Mr. Montgomery's place near Granchester, sir. In connection with a servant stealing some silver plate, or so they believe."

"A nuisance," grumbled the Chief Constable, "at a time like this. Couldn't you have sent a sergeant?"

"Well, sir, Mr. Montgomery's a J.P. and a town councillor. I considered he would expect an inspector at least. You know what it is, sir."

"H'm ... yes, I see your point."

"Constable, tell Inspector Norman I want him as soon as he gets back; and if he's not back in half an hour send Sergeant Perrin in."

"Very good, sir."

As it happened, the Inspector was back in ten minutes, having more or less completed his case, and was promptly sent off to renew his connection with the St. Chad's robbery. The Superintendent went slowly and methodically through the remainder of his report without any interruption on the part of his superior officer.

"Those are the bare facts of the case, sir. Perhaps I might add certain conclusions I have drawn. Of course, things will be much clearer when the police surgeon's report comes in. I have asked for a comparison of the rope with the marks on the body, and an analysis of the fragments I collected in the envelope, which I believe to contain some hair and dried blood from the body."

"I think I can follow your case pretty clearly," affirmed the Chief Constable, "but go ahead and say exactly what conclusions you have drawn."

"Well, sir. We have the button and the hat to show pretty conclusively that the deceased visited Trevor's rooms shortly before his death. By the way, the hat fits the deceased perfectly, allowing for the paper stuffing. My opinion is that the deceased must have been overpowered and then hanged by being pushed out of the back window with a rope round his neck. The rope shows two sets of frayed marks, one to indicate its being tied round the broken bit of iron bar in the window, and the other where it rubbed against the sharp corner of the window-ledge. I also picked up a few tiny strands of rope off the sill. These would have been rubbed off when the rope was tied or untied to the bar. There was about three inches of this bar, firmly cemented into the window-sill. The remainder, as I explained, had been filed through and loosened at the top to pull out; then replaced and the joint concealed to avoid discovery. The whole thing seems to have been carefully planned in advance."

"And what is your explanation about the fragments of hair and blood?"

"When the corpse had fallen to the end of its drop and life was extinct, the murderer, or two murderers as I think, began to haul it up again through the window. In so doing they allowed the head to strike against the lower corner of the window-ledge, leaving a long, narrow cut on the head and some blood and hair on the stonework.

You will remember, sir, the expert saying he thought the injury was inflicted a short time after death. That fits exactly. Then we have Mr. Gale's evidence of two people, possibly staggering under a burden, who left the room shortly after we assume death to have taken place. The whole thing seems complete except for the identity of the person or persons responsible."

"Well, surely," exclaimed the Chief Constable, "if all these things took place in Trevor's private rooms, and there is evidence that it took long and careful preparation, it's obvious he must have been one of the people responsible. Yet he's still running round at liberty. You haven't even detained him. Isn't that rather risky. If he finds the loss of the rope and hat, which he's bound to, I should think he'll cut and run."

"He's been under observation, sir, and Baker, posing as a dun calling about a bill, learned from his bedmaker that half an hour ago he was still asleep in bed. Of course, sir, I could have detained him on suspicion last night, or got a warrant from a magistrate, but I thought it best to wait for your opinion. And I couldn't get that till this morning. Also, I thought it best to make sure of the medical report about the rope. It might not be the one after all, and then our case would look a bit silly."

"It looks a clear thing to me," insisted the Chief Constable, "and as regards an accomplice, I have my ideas about that. I expect you have, too."

"You mean his friend Tanner, sir."

"Exactly. He seems to have been there at the moment when the hat vanished. He must have known something about that. Have you examined him yet?"

"No, sir. I thought it best to bide my time. In my opinion he looks more guilty than Trevor. I can't make up my mind about Trevor. There's a catch in it somewhere. He suggests to me that he knows little or nothing about the whole thing."

"But, dash it all, if a man was found hanging from a home-made gallows in my drawing-room at a time when I was in the house, would you believe me if I said I knew nothing whatever about it? It's not reasonable. I suggest that Trevor should be charged and Tanner questioned under the usual warning and detained if necessary."

"It's for you to say, sir. But we're dealing with the varsity, and they've a big graft in Cambridge. If things went wrong with the case, we should hear about it afterwards."

"I can't see what doubts you have about Trevor," complained the Chief Constable. "Suppose you tell us your own theories about it."

"Well, sir. The case against Trevor is this. It seems certain that the hanging took place from his window, and it must have been done from inside the room. The rope is still in his room, and presumably he must have known that, because he or Tanner opened the cupboard to put Starbright's hat inside, which in itself is a pretty damning thing to do. Trevor has stated all along, according to the Dean, that he was asleep in his room from nine o'clock that night. The bedroom leads off the sitting-room through an ordinary, thinnish door. It seems impossible to suppose that any other two people could have induced Starbright to enter the room, overpowered him, forced him out of the window, hanged him, and dragged his body up again if the innocent owner of the room was asleep next door.

"Then, again, the filing of the window-bar was a long job. I don't see how or why that can have been done without the owner's knowledge, though I grant these sets of rooms are seldom locked, as far as I can make out, and the students walk in and out of other people's rooms pretty freely."

"Is that so?" said the Chief Constable. At Sandhurst they had been rather more accustomed to lock their rooms when absent.

"Thus, I admit, sir, it looks pretty bad against Trevor. They say truth is stranger than fiction, but it would have to be mighty strange for him not to know what was going on in his own rooms."

"That's just what I'm saying," said the Chief Constable. "If we were to call in the Yard now and tell them the facts, they'd want to know why the deuce we didn't get on with it and arrest Trevor. What are your reasons for thinking we ought to wait, Beecham?"

"I've a feeling, sir, that if Trevor were really guilty, or if he knew the real facts, he couldn't have done and said some of the things he has. He's acted like a perfect fool over the whole thing, and this murder wasn't done by a perfect fool. It must have been the result of some clever planning."

"How do you mean, he's acted like a perfect fool?"

"In the first place, we believe there was ill-feeling against Starbright over his conduct at football, and that in the course of being baited or assaulted by some of the footballers he fired a shot from a revolver. This man Trevor is found on the spot apparently bewildered and saying he knew nothing about it. The prosecution would say, on the other hand, that it was proof of ill-feeling between the two men, and that the murder was Trevor's revenge."

"Why shouldn't that be the case? It seems most likely that the shot was fired at Trevor."

"I don't agree, sir. The shooting happened on Thursday night and the murder on Saturday. That's a very short time in which to make a plan which apparently needed an accomplice, prepare the bar of the window, and smuggle a big rope into college. Besides, the porter states that Trevor came into college through the front gate only a few seconds before the shot was heard, just as he said he had done, so the odds are he was speaking the truth when he stated he'd just arrived on the scene and had no idea what was going on. If he had been making any hostile plans against Starbright, he would have either kept out of the way altogether, or cleared off quick before being seen and questioned."

"There's something in that, but not a lot," commented the Chief Constable doubtfully.

"That's only the weakest point, sir. Now, supposing he had done this hanging, or knew who had, his chief aim would be to make us believe he was elsewhere late Saturday night and early Sunday morning. It's no offence for undergraduates in college to remain in each other's rooms to whatever hour they please. If Tanner had been his accomplice, the two of them could perfectly easily have given each other an alibi by saying they were together in Tanner's rooms. The worst thing, from Trevor's point of view, was to admit being alone in his own rooms, yet that is the story he has stuck to all along."

"Yes, that's certainly curious. What do you suppose the truth of it was? Do you think he was in his rooms from nine o'clock, or not?"

"I should say not, sir. These going-to-bed-early-with a-headache stories always make me think, especially with a young, healthy chap like that. But why say he was there when he wasn't, which is the one way to incriminate himself, is more than I can tell. The only explanation seems to be that he had no idea Starbright met his death out of that particular window.

"Then there's the matter of the hat. Mr. Gale swears the hat was not hanging up on the door when he was in Trevor's rooms yesterday morning. Yet it was there for everyone to see when we both called in the evening. Now, if Trevor knew what a damaging piece of evidence it was, why did he let it hang there? It looks as though he didn't even recognize it as Starbright's hat."

"Yet he seems to have hidden it the moment you went out."

"I think it was Tanner, and not Trevor, who recognized the hat and put it in the cupboard. We don't even know if Trevor saw him do it."

The Chief Constable considered this for a moment, and then drew in his breath sharply, as though struck by a sudden idea.

"I can't quite fathom this Mr. Gale of yours, Beecham. He seems too clever to be true. All the clues and ideas we have up to now seem to have been produced by this fellow Gale."

"That's true, sir. He's proved uncommonly useful for an amateur. Out of the mouths of babes and sucklings——"

"Don't start that business again, Beecham. Look here. What I'm driving at is this: how do you know the hat ever was on the peg?"

"How did ...? I beg your pardon, sir. I don't quite get you."

"I say how do you know it was on the peg. You didn't see it yourself. Gale told you it had been. When you came to look for it, it wasn't there. You've only Gale's word for it that it ever was. He might have planted it in the cupboard himself, together with the rope, for that matter."

The Superintendent's eyes opened a little wider than usual, and he gave his superior officer a look almost of admiration. Really, he was thinking, the old man was getting quite bright.

"You mean, if there were two people in the job, one of them might have been the Dean and neither of them Trevor?"

"Why not?" asked the Chief Constable triumphantly. "His rooms are quite close and everything would have been easy for him."

The Superintendent shook his head slowly and sadly.

"I can't accept that, sir. Gale has given us nearly every lead away from the arch towards Trevor's rooms; the button in particular. I'll grant it may be a loose screw on the part of some murderers to plant clues or even reveal true ones. But seeing the murderer made such elaborate efforts to lead us away from the real place and method of the murder, it doesn't make sense for Gale, as the murderer, to undo all his own plans, and show us the way back. No, sir, Gale's all right, and not all that clever either. He had a bit of luck at first, and the fact of living on the spot and knowing all the people and the layout has given him a bit of a pull over the rest of us. Of course, you might argue he planted the stuff to incriminate this Trevor falsely, but that's a bit far-fetched; and it happens he's gone out of his way to find reasons for thinking Trevor innocent. In fact, he wants to help him in case of arrest."

"Did you tell him Trevor might be arrested?" inquired the Chief Constable sternly. "You seem to have discussed rather a lot of things with this man Gale. I trust he'll keep his mouth shut."

"If I hadn't told him a certain amount, sir," was Beecham's reply, "I shouldn't have got where I have. One has to give away some information in order to get something in return."

"Oh, all right, Beecham. No doubt you've been as discreet as the occasion required."

At this moment they were interrupted once more by the reappearance of Inspector Norman with news of the five-pound note. In the hopes that the question of the robbery might be bound up in that of the death of Starbright, they suspended their discussion of the latter case in order to hear and judge whether news of this minor problem might throw any light on the more serious crime. The Inspector was therefore invited to make an immediate report.

On reaching the premises of the Golden Lion Hotel, the Inspector had sought an audience with the manager, who had passed him on to a blonde but matronly barmaid who had just arrived to set her house in order for the morning opening hour. Here he was not detained long. The barmaid remembered perfectly the circumstances surrounding the presentation of the note. It had come from the pocket of a regular and respected customer, Mr. Joshua Wrench.

Mr. Joshua Wrench was an acquaintance of the Inspector's, as it happened, and lived only a few doors down Sidney Street, where he presided, with considerable profit to himself, over a shop selling wines, spirits, and cigars to those undergraduates whose parents were still able or willing to foot bills for such things and to a steady clientele of other customers, mostly fellow tradespeople who found the varsity an equally good market for their wares.

Entering the Wrench wine-store which, owing to the early hour of the morning, was free from customers, the Inspector sought and obtained an interview with the owner in the back parlour. Mr. Joshua Wrench looked a good advertisement for wines and spirits in general. He was a plump, genial man in the fifties, with a rich complexion which might just be classed as healthy, but not bloated. He strove to conceal a slight apprehension caused by such an early visit from the police, albeit an officer of police.

"Good morning to you, Inspector. You're an early visitor, which makes me think you must have come on business. But that won't prevent you taking a drop of something, I'm sure. Now I've a nice packet of dark sherry just in the right condition. Like velvet, I assure you. Or anything you'd fancy."

"It's early, as you say," agreed the Inspector, "but I wouldn't say no to a plain Scotch and soda. I've had a tiring morning already, and as for my business, that won't take long and is nothing very serious."

"I'm glad to hear that," laughed Mr. Wrench. "Though I haven't a guilty conscience. Say when, Mr. Norman ... right. By the way, I'm sorry to hear of that trouble at St. Chad's. Shocking thing, young fellow making away with himself like that. Still, I must not start bothering you with questions. Got to answer 'em myself, what? Now, what can I do for you?"

"Just a small inquiry, Mr. Wrench. I believe that yesterday, at the 'Golden Lion', you ordered some drinks and paid for them with a five-pound note. That would be shortly after one o'clock."

"That's right, Mr. Norman. So I did, but I don't recall its number. It passed through my hands quick, so to speak. By gum, though. Don't tell me it was a wrong 'un."

"No, quite in order. But you say you only had it a short time. Would you mind telling me how it first came into your hands, for the shop's not open on Sundays, is it?"

"No, it isn't. I can tell you soon enough about that note. It was handed to me a few seconds earlier by a Mr. Julian Parker."

"Julian Parker," ruminated the Inspector. "I don't seem to know that name. I wonder if you'd mind telling me what you know about him, and how he came to give you the note. I don't want to pry into your affairs, you know, but we're anxious to trace the movements of that particular note. I take it Mr. Parker is an undergraduate. You don't know if he's a Chad's man by any chance, do you?"

"Chad's, eh?" said Mr. Wrench knowingly. "Ha, I get you! ... No, to the best of my knowledge Mr. Parker isn't an undergraduate, nor never has been, I should say. Not even of Oxford. Now, as regards how he came to give me the note, well, that's rather asking, as you might say. The fact is, I'm not quite clear how I stand over that, so to speak. It's a question of how far what I say goes, in a manner of speaking. Now you're a gentleman, Mr. Norman, that wouldn't go for to make trouble where it wasn't needed, so I reckon I'll take the risk. But, as I was saying, I don't quite rightly know where I stand."

The wine merchant took a sip of his fine old brown sherry, whilst the Inspector, not wishing to make rash promises, patiently waited for him to proceed.

"I'll tell you all I know, Mr. Norman, because you're a friend, and I'd like to help you with your job. This Mr. Parker is a very considerable customer of mine. Very considerable. I've sent him some big orders regularly, and he's been a pretty good payer in the end, but slow, very slow at times, and especially lately. Well, as you know, yesterday I slipped round to the old 'Lion', as I do regular on Sunday mornings after church, and in the bar I sees Mr. Parker. He takes me aside and asks, can I send a biggish order down to his place before six o'clock that evening?

"Well, as you know, the shop isn't open on Sundays and I've never been asked to send an order on a Sunday before, and between you and me I didn't know, and I don't know now, whether I should be within the law by delivering out of hours on a Sunday. That's the rub, Mr. Norman. I don't want this to go any further."

"That will be all right, I think, Mr. Wrench. I needn't put it in the report. It isn't really what we want to know. The point is, who is this Mr. Parker, where does he live, and what does he do?"

"Ah! That I can tell you, and willingly enough. Twenty-three Cedars Avenue is the address. That's one of those three-storeyed semi-detached old houses down near Parker's Piece. Ten rooms or so. As for what he is or what he does, I can't tell you, but I should say, as one friend to another, that it's something a bit funny."

"How do you make that out?" inquired the Inspector with a show of interest. "Anyway, could you describe this Parker?"

"Forty-five or so. Dark hair and moustache. Curved nose. Looks a bit of a sheeny. Dresses a bit flash. Checks or sometimes dark city clothes, jewelled tiepin and rings. I've only met him here in the shop or odd times in the 'Lion'."

"And what makes you think his business is odd?"

"Well, two things. First, the amount of drink I've sent to his house, which has only himself and his two nieces, so I'm told; and second, the fact he always pays bills in cash, largish ones too, five or ten pounds. And he doesn't look a soaker himself. What's more, he don't do much treating in bars."

"H'm ... that's a bit odd, as you say. How much drink would you reckon to send down there in a week, say?"

"Well, it varies. Say a dozen of whisky and half a dozen of gin once a fortnight. Lots of syphons, and a varying amount of cheap wine and cocktail stuff, and perhaps a dozen of champagne in a couple of months."

"And how long has this Mr. Parker been dealing with you, may I ask?"

"Not more than three months. I could tell from the books, if you want to know."

"No, that's near enough to go on with. And what about these nieces? Have you seen them, Mr. Wrench."

"Surely I have, and I should say nieces is all my eye. Rather flashy bits. West End type, you know. Fashionable clothes, silk ankles, scent. All the doings, you know."

"Ah!" said the Inspector enlightened; "so you think it might be ... er, that sort of a house, eh?"

"Well, no," answered Mr. Wrench. "If you ask me, I don't quite think it is. Leastways the two girls didn't give me that impression. Many's the young undergrad I've seen give 'em the glad coming in or going out of the shop. But there wasn't nothing doing. Quite upstage, those girls. Of course, they might be working on the quiet. Have their own connection, so to speak, but somehow I don't think that's Mr. Parker's lay. Though what it is, you can search me.

"Well, as I was saying, he begs me to send him the stuff down urgent. I thought it over, and then I reminds him he's been owing fifteen quid or so for a month or more, and my terms are cash with discount. I puts that to him and he says he'll pay seven-ten down there and then if I'll send the order, so I closes with that. But the funny thing was this. About half past five, just as I was getting ready to send the stuff off, having given my van-boy a special call, he rings up to say he doesn't want the stuff after all, but he'll send a fresh order in a day or two. Funny business somewhere."

"It seems to be," commented the Inspector. "Now, changing the subject, I wonder if you can tell me when the news of this Chad's suicide first got round Cambridge. I suppose it was spoken of late yesterday, before it came out in the papers today."

"Yes, it was that," assented Mr. Wrench. "I had it at seven, when I went back to the 'Lion'. Tom Wright heard it at teatime, but he has a nephew in the ambulance. By the way, another spot, Mr. Norman?"

"No, thanks all the same, Mr. Wrench; this is my busy morning. I must hop it. Keep that to yourself, about Parker, won't you? Likewise I won't say anything I can help that you'd rather not have said. You follow me?"

"Sure thing, boy," said Mr. Wrench, rendered some what skittish by a second glass of old sherry, coupled with the removal of any fears raised by a police visitation. "Well, I'll be seeing yer."

After covering the half mile between Sidney Street and 23 Cedars Avenue the Inspector met with his first check. The blinds of 23 were drawn and front and back doors locked. Having considered the situation for a few moments, the Inspector was attracted by sounds of activity in the back regions of the house next door, Tracking the sounds to their source, he was soon in conversation with a housemaid who, thrilled by the silver buttons and peaked cap of this super-policeman, proved a willing and useful conversationalist.

Yes, the next door folks had pushed off about six the previous evening; the gentleman, two girls, and the butler-manservant, all in one taxi, with lots of luggage. No, there weren't any other servants. Funny crowd. Kept themselves to themselves. But fast, she would say. Late parties all the time. People coming and going late. But not noisy, she wouldn't say that. Creepy rather. Taxis? No, but people went slinking away late. No, not only men, but girls as well. Music? No, just a bit of wireless and gramophone, but no worse than the folks the other side. No, it didn't seem respectable, somehow. She reckoned they were no better than they should be. Agent's boards? Oh yes. The house had been empty up to three months ago. There had been a board up then. Pitcher & Waldron. Yes, that was it.

The Inspector thanked her courteously, refused the offer of a cup of tea together with an introduction to the cook, and made his way back to the station, considering that Messrs. Pitcher & Waldron could be approached later, by 'phone if necessary. His subsequent report was a bald and businesslike affair shorn of much of the picturesque detail which had given him a moderately amusing morning.

"Well," said the Chief Constable profoundly, "that doesn't seem to get us much further. In fact it rather confuses things. What do you suggest, Beecham?"

"I fancy, sir, that Mr. Parker has flown to London, and that he may not be unknown there. I suggest I ring up Browning at the Yard and see if they can place him. The only thing is, if we apply to them over part of the case, we shall have to let them in on the whole thing."

The Chief Constable considered the matter and then gave his opinion. "It seems to me we shall know in a few hours whether we can wind up the case on our own. If not, we might to call them in anyway. Could you explain this to your friend Browning, and say we shall put the whole thing up to them officially in a few hours unless we decide to make an arrest meantime? Who is he, by the way?"

"Records office, sir. I've dealt with him before, and he'll do what he can without them wanting to know the whole case at once. Of course, the man may be quite unknown to them, but he may be some kind of city twister who runs ramps in the provinces and then skips back to town."

"What do you reckon his line is?" asked the Chief Constable.

"I can't say, sir. But I reckon he's touched some of the stolen money and knows it. Whether the Starbright case is connected with it, we don't know, but it looks to me as though it is. Because the theft is not known outside college, as far as we know, and the murder, or suicide, was being talked of in the town as early as three o'clock yesterday."

"It certainly doesn't throw any light on the murder," agreed the Chief Constable. "Norman, you'd better slip round to the house agents and see what you can pick up there."

The Inspector went out and looked in again almost at once to say that the police surgeon wished to see the senior members present. He was instructed to show the doctor in. The doctor's report was brief and to the point. The rope, taken specially to the acute Dr. Summers, was pronounced as exactly matching the original marks on the neck of the deceased, whilst an analysis had shown that the contents of the envelope included samples of hair and blood from the dead undergraduate. Having been duly thanked, the police surgeon took his departure.

When he had gone, the Chief Constable turned to his Superintendent and gazed at him in silence, as though seeking to read his thoughts. The Superintendent gazed back with placid, bovine eyes which seemed to betray nothing. At length the Chief Constable gave it up and said abruptly:

"Well, what now? What do you advise?"

"I think, sir, we should warn Trevor and question him once more about his movements last night; also his friend Tanner."

"I quite agree, but if Trevor sticks to his story, what then?"

"That's up to you, sir."

"Yes, I know," grunted the Chief Constable. "Don't try to misunderstand me, Beecham; it's irritating. You know quite well what I mean. Should we arrest Trevor, or not? Personally, I think we should. I'm asking you whether you agree."

"I agree we've got sufficient grounds, sir. In fact it might seem funny to some people, the Yard for example, if we didn't. At the same time I'm not satisfied he's our man."

"I can't see your point of view, Beecham. Granted he may not be the principal, I cannot see how he avoids being an accessory; and as such we have every right to charge him with the crime. It's the only way to arrive at the truth, as I see it."

"Maybe, sir. But it would look better if we held our hand, and got the right fellow in the end."

"I can't help that," said the Chief Constable obstinately. "You agree the fellow must have lied to you about being in his rooms all night, don't you?"

"Yes," the Superintendent allowed. "That seems clear enough."

"Well then, if Trevor is lying about that, he may have told a pack of other lies. If the truth's known, he was probably at the back of persecuting this poor fellow, Starbright. In any case, he must be shielding somebody."

"Yes," agreed the Superintendent slowly. "It does look as if he might be shielding somebody; though I don't feel sure even of that."

"Damn it, man! We must assume some things, or we'll get nowhere. I say, we must put Trevor through it. Give him a chance of coming clean, as our American friends would say. Besides, I don't like the idea of his running round loose. We may lose him altogether. I wonder what he's doing just now."

"There may be a report from Baker," was Beecham's reply. "He was told to report periodically, but the office has instructions not to worry us unless anything important comes through."

"Not to worry us!" repeated the Chief Constable. "I should have thought it was important."

"Well, sir, I reckoned you would not want to be interrupted in talking over the main points of the case," explained the Superintendent diplomatically. "Now that we have time to consider it, I'll see if anything's come through."

In response to the bell on the office table a constable entered, and presently returned with a typed slip which, he said, had come in five minutes before. At a nod from his Chief, the Superintendent gave a digest of the contents.

"'Phoned by Baker from a call-box in Trinity Street at eleven-ten. Trevor came out of lecture in King's at eleven, and went into Matthews' Café, being joined at the door by Tanner and two other students. Not yet seen to come out."

"Well, that seems normal," the Chief Constable allowed. "Now we must get those two down here with as little fuss as possible. Will you see to that?"

The Superintendent's first move in this process was to inquire if the busy Inspector Norman had returned. The latter, who had delayed announcing that fact in order to snatch a cup of tea in the back premises, then appeared, looking as far as possible as though he were eager for the next job of work. His report on 23 Cedars Avenue contained little of note. The house had been taken furnished by a Mr. Parker on the short lease of one year. No references had been given, but an advance of a quarter's rent had been accepted instead. This was much as the Superintendent had anticipated. The latter then gave the Inspector some specific instructions, resulting in his departure in one of the station cars, and then left a message to be given to Detective-Sergeant Baker on the next occasion when he communicated with the station. He then produced some routine correspondence for the purpose of occupying the mind of the Chief Constable, and profited by this respite to lean back in his chair, close his eyes, and go through the motions of having a short nap.

CHAPTER XIII

THE main court of St. Chad's was enjoying one of its most peaceful hours of the day as a neighbouring clock chimed the half hour after eleven on that Monday morning in November. The little crowd of outside students who had attended the Bursar's lecture on political economy, given twice weekly from ten to eleven in the college hall, had long since dispersed. Various members of college, whose lectures in that same hour had also terminated, had returned to the seclusion of their rooms, presumably to immerse themselves in private study, but possibly to drink a morning glass of ale and select a winner for some afternoon race of horses. Some bedmakers were moving sedately between staircases, and there was an American party of sightseers of whom the senior member, or paterfamilias, was reading aloud from a guidebook a description of the hall and pointing simultaneously at the exterior of the chapel.

At the door of his lodge, under the arch by the main gateway, Meadows stood awaiting the delivery of letters due at that hour. A figure in blue presently came slowly up the steps into college, but the uniform was not that of the post-office. Meadows frowned slightly. Things had happened and were still happening which had no place in the daily round of a well-ordered college. In his thirty years of varied service at St. Chad's, Meadows could not remember the like. It was all very worrying.

Would he mind the Inspector waiting in the lodge for a short time? No, not in the least. A pleasure, in fact. Let the Inspector fill his pipe and make himself comfortable. The Inspector would excuse him if he carried on with his own job. There were letters to be sorted. He forced himself to banish the frown and look pleasant.

Inspector Norman thanked the Head Porter, but refused a pipe and a seat. Instead, he stood in the doorway and gazed absently out in the direction of the street. He seemed fidgety and ill at ease. After a few moments a nondescript man loafed by along the pavement, glanced through the main gate, blew his nose on a red spotted handkerchief, and shambled out of sight. Had Meadows been in a position to see the individual he would have been surprised to recognize an acquaintance at his bowls club, namely, Detective-Sergeant Baker.

Inspector Norman gave Meadows a word of farewell and strolled to the gateway, where he stood looking up and down the street. He

164

observed two undergraduates, with gowns and notebooks, walking towards him and talking in low and serious tones.

Tom Tanner had hesitated all the previous evening and during the morning coffee session to make any reference to the events immediately preceding Hall, when he had interrupted the visit of the Dean and the Inspector. He had given much furious thought to the matter between then and now, but there seemed no point in reopening the matter. It was Trevor himself who made the first reference to the question as they were strolling back to college.

"By the way," he said, "I meant to ask you. Why did you suddenly pick up that hat and bung it in my cupboard last night? Come to think of it, I don't know what it was doing there. Did you leave it, by any chance? It looked a bit, dashing for you. I hadn't noticed it before."

Tanner eyed his friend curiously.

"You mean to say you didn't know whose hat it was?" he inquired at length.

"No; haven't I just said so?" Trevor answered with a trace of irritation. "I couldn't make out what you were playing at. Anyway, whose is it, and why did you want to hide it?"

"I hid it because I believe it belonged to Starbright. That seemed a good enough reason."

"It belonged to ...? But, good heavens! How do you suppose it got into my rooms? I've never seen it before. What is all this business?"

"I should think it means to say," answered Tanner slowly, "that Starbright must have called in your rooms sometime when you ... you were in bed asleep."

"Good lord, yes! It's more than likely he did! You know he ..."

But what Tanner knew, or Trevor knew, was not to be made common to the two friends, for Tanner suddenly gave Trevor a slight nudge with his elbow. They had reached the steps of St. Chad's, and on the steps stood Inspector Norman, as though enjoying a first view of Cambridge by day. As they mounted the steps to pass him, he gave them a casual look which changed to one of recognition in the case of Trevor.

"Good morning, Mr. Trevor. Nice morning. As a matter of fact, sir, I was hoping to get a word with you. They told me you would be finishing your lectures at eleven and were expected soon, so I thought I'd wait on the chance of catching you."

Trevor returned the Inspector's greeting with a singular lack of enthusiasm, and Tanner eyed him with scarcely veiled suspicion. The Inspector felt pleased with the bit about expecting them soon after eleven. He had made it appear a casual detail picked up in college, whereas it was actually gleaned from the painstaking Sergeant Baker.

"I wanted to find you, sir, because the Chief Constable is at the station, and he is anxious to ask you one or two more questions about that unfortunate business we were discussing last night. He would be very glad if you would come down to the station as soon as possible. As it happens, I have a car round the corner, so we can run you down and bring you back quick enough."

"I'm sure I don't know what all this is about," said Trevor in puzzled tones. "I told you all I knew last night, and that was little enough, goodness knows."

"Quite so, sir. But orders are orders. I waited here and kept the car round the corner so as to attract as little attention as possible. It's just a matter of routine, and probably nobody will notice anything. By the way, there's another undergraduate I've been told to bring along, a Mr. Tanner." (Turning to Tanner.) "Are you Mr. Tanner by any chance?"

Tanner admitted the fact in a non-committal voice. He appeared quietly alert and on his guard.

"Well, that's a bit of luck!" exclaimed the Inspector, trying to register cheerful surprise in order to conceal the fact that he had recognized Tanner twenty yards away. "Well, gentlemen, if you don't mind, we'll be getting along right away."

"We don't want to lug these gowns and books with us," objected Tanner. "Do you mind if we dump them in my rooms? They're the nearer of the two."

Inspector Norman suspected, and Tanner knew he suspected, that this request was mainly dictated by a desire to have a few words alone with Trevor before starting for their interview with the police, as indeed it was. The Inspector hesitated, uncertain how to counter this manœuvre without appearing peremptory. He was unexpectedly relieved of this problem by the obtuseness of Trevor.

"We needn't bother to do that," he remarked obligingly. "We can just bung 'em in the lodge for the time being. Here, give me yours, old man."

Whereupon he took Tanner's books and gown, ran up the steps, and was back in a few seconds, saying lightly:

"Now we can get on with it, and the sooner it's over, the better."

Arrived at the car, the two undergraduates were allowed to share the back seat, whilst Inspector Norman sat in front with the police driver. This arrangement might facilitate some undesirable communication between the two suspects, so the Inspector feared. At the same time he had sharp ears, whilst the interior mirror was arranged to give him a good view of the back seat. The short journey was completed without incident and in unbroken silence.

At the station arrangements had been made for the reception and allocation of the two arrivals. Tanner was to be shown straight to the presence of the Chief Constable, whilst Trevor was to wait in a small room where his mind was to be lulled by the loan of a daily paper. This programme was duly carried out, to the surprise of Trevor. In Tanner's case the proceeding was not unexpected. Entering the private office at the request of the Inspector, he was welcomed politely by an awakened Superintendent and introduced to the Chief Constable, who bade him to be seated.

"You are Mr. T. Tanner, of St. Chad's College, I believe. May I ask your exact age?"

Tanner confessed to being twenty-one years and four months old. The Chief Constable continued amiably:

"We think you may be able to answer a few questions which might help us in investigating the death of Mr. Starbright, of your college. No doubt you are aware of the bare facts, at any rate. Superintendent Beecham, who is in charge of the case, will put these questions."

Tanner inclined his head without speaking. The Superintendent hoisted himself a little more upright in his chair, blinked doubtfully at Tanner for a moment, gave a side-glance at a clerk who had entered silently and was seated at a side table ready to take shorthand notes, and then began to speak in his lazy voice:

"Before I put any questions to you, it is my duty to tell you that you are not obliged to answer anything which you would rather not answer without first having legal advice; also that anything you now say may be taken down and used in evidence, if necessary."

Tom Tanner had resolved to take the whole thing calmly. He was determined not to be rattled. But he was well aware of the significance of this warning, and he could barely restrain a start of nervous surprise. He was clearly under suspicion of being concerned in some crime. He schooled his emotions and replied shortly:

"I quite understand."

"Good," said the Superintendent more briskly. "Well, then, starting at the beginning of things, you will admit that the deceased was unpopular with many members of your college over a football incident which occurred less than a week ago: last Thursday, to be precise."

"Yes," said Tanner at once, "that is so."

"Apart from, or previous to, this incident, would you say that the deceased was unpopular or had any particular enemies in the college?"

Tanner took time to frame his answer to this.

"Starbright was apt to be uncertain in temper, and so it could be said he was unpopular at times; but most of us got on with him all right. We visited his rooms for coffee and that sort of thing from time to time. Sometimes he was argumentative, but there was never any serious row."

"Never?" asked the Superintendent slowly.

"Well, there was one evening quite recently, last Monday to be exact, when Starbright grumbled about his position in the field at football. A number of us were present, and Starbright was rather offensive. As a matter of fact it was that which led up to his not turning out on Thursday, and that was what all the trouble was about."

"Whose rooms was it that this argument took place in?"

"A freshman named Colley, but he's got nothing to do with it."

"Er ... nothing to do with what?" asked Beecham innocently.

"I mean," explained Tanner, annoyed at this attempt to trip him up, "Colley isn't a rugby footballer and so didn't join in the discussion.

Also, as a fresher, he wouldn't say much when the rest of us were third-year men."

The Superintendent considered this dreamily, and appeared to drift away into a side-issue.

"He ought not to have grumbled about his position in the field. He should play where his captain tells him, shouldn't he?"

Tanner said he certainly should have done.

"Let me see," Beecham rambled on, "who is your football captain?"

"Martin Trevor," answered Tanner rather sharply, realizing that the questions were by no means at random. "He's here at the moment, if you want him."

"Yes, quite so, Mr. Tanner," the Chief Constable interrupted unexpectedly. "Kindly confine yourself to answering what's asked, and don't tell us what we know already."

After which he glared distastefully at the Superintendent, whom he considered to be unduly prolix and tedious in his questions. The latter gave him back a glance of sad reproach and went quietly on with his next question.

"I suppose Mr. Trevor was present in Mr. Colley's rooms on Monday when this unpleasant argument took place?"

"That's right."

"Naturally he was annoyed at his captaincy being ... er ... criticized by one of his team?"

"Yes, a bit. But not nearly as much as he might have been. In fact, not so much as the rest of us."

"You say others were annoyed. Would you say that any particular person displayed special annoyance against the deceased then or later?"

Tanner paused again, thinking of Davies. He decided, however, that he had no real grounds for singling out the fiery little Welshman even if he had wished to help the police, which he did not. He therefore said no, he knew of no such person. The Superintendent, noting the pause, wondered if he were telling the truth, and rather thought not.

"Leaving that for the moment, did you have any conversation with the deceased between that time on Monday night and the evening of Thursday?"

"Thursday?" repeated Tanner, at a loss to account for a reference to this day. "No. I didn't see him on Thursday either, except in Hall or possibly in the court at a distance. I can't remember quite."

"I believe some of your friends interviewed the deceased after Hall on Thursday night. You say you were not present on that occasion."

"No, I was working in my rooms at the time."

"Then you know the time and the incident I am referring to?"

"Yes, I heard about it afterwards."

"Er ... what did you hear, Mr. Tanner?"

"You told me I need only answer what I think fit. I don't want to repeat hearsay gossip. I might say something incorrect without meaning to. So I claim my right not to answer that question."

At this the Chief Constable began to blow out his cheeks and show signs of indignant interruption, but in this he was forestalled by Beecham, who went quietly on:

"There is something in what you say, Mr. Tanner. I won't press that question. Now, between Thursday night and the time of the tragedy, had you any knowledge of, or connection with, any further attempt to rag or molest the deceased?"

"I did not know of any attempt. I have reason to think that no attempt was made, or even intended,"

"When was the last occasion on which you saw the deceased?"

Here Tanner hesitated again, and said at length:

"I suppose you mean, when did I last see him alive. The answer to that is, in the distance in Hall on Saturday night."

The Superintendent, momentarily puzzled by the qualification to his question, then asked:

"You mean you saw him after he was dead? How did that happen?"

"I saw him on Sunday morning, after the discovery of the tragedy, when I came to try and get into the baths."

"Oh, I see!" said Beecham. "Yes, of course. I wasn't thinking of that. Now, as regards your own movements on Saturday night."

"After Hall on Saturday night I settled down to a long night's work. I worked in my rooms till about one-thirty in the morning."

"You didn't see anyone during that time?"

"I was quite alone. Nobody came and disturbed me at all."

"You are a friend of Mr. Trevor, are you not?"

"Yes."

"In fact, you might be described as a great or close friend of Mr. Trevor's, and you spend a great deal of time in his company."

"Yes, that's right."

"When did you last see him on Saturday?"

"About six in the evening. We had tea together in my rooms. I believe he dined out."

"And you didn't see him again till after breakfast on Sunday?"

"No, I didn't."

"It seems curious, when you spent so much time together, that you saw nothing of him on Saturday night. It's the sort of time you gentlemen meet socially, I believe—especially Saturdays. But perhaps he was out late that night."

"No, I think not. He wasn't very well, and went to bed early, about nine o'clock."

"How do you know that, Mr. Tanner, if you didn't see him later than six?"

"Well ... he told me so. He's my best friend. Naturally, I should believe what he tells me."

"Quite, Mr. Tanner. Quite. Still, as evidence, it's only hearsay, you'll admit."

"I suppose so."

"I shan't keep you much longer, sir. A few final questions. You say you were working in your rooms on Saturday night. Did you leave your rooms during that time?"

"Yes. I found I had left a book I wanted in Trevor's rooms. I went across to look for it."

"What time was that?"

"I can't say exactly. I didn't notice. Round about one o'clock is the nearest I can say."

"And did you find the book?"

"No."

"How long were you in the room?"

"Ten minutes or so."

"H'm ... You had a good look for it. And you did not see Mr. Trevor?"

"No. I've already answered that question."

"No offence, Mr. Tanner. I meant, you did not look into his bedroom and see him asleep."

"No."

"So you don't really know whether he was there or not."

"He told me afterwards he was. That's good enough for me."

"Whilst you were in Mr. Trevor's rooms round about one o'clock, did you do anything except look for your book, or did you see any other person there?"

Tanner paused for a few seconds only, and then said very firmly and distinctly:

"I shall not answer that question."

For a second there was a silence fit for the dropping of the proverbial pin. It was broken by a kind of strangled snort from the Chief Constable. The Superintendent sat with a face devoid of any marked expression.

"You realize," said the Chief Constable, "that, by refusing to answer this question, you place yourself in a very grave position? We cannot compel you to answer, at this stage at any rate. But by your action you are liable to be charged with a most serious offence. Yon would be well advised to make a clean breast of things, and tell us what you know."

"I wasn't aware, sir, that any crime had been committed, except that of suicide," said Tanner stubbornly, "and I don't see how you can bring a charge against me because of that."

The Chief Constable took a quick look at the impassive face of his Superintendent and, finding no inspiration therein decided to put their combined cards on the table.

"Suppose I suggest to you that we are dealing with a case not of suicide, but of murder. What then, young man? Come! This is a very serious business indeed. If you don't realize that, you are either a bigger fool than I take you for, or else I'm forced to the conclusion that you are hiding something very disgraceful. Now will you answer the Superintendent's question?"

The Superintendent leaned painfully across and said in a low voice to his chief:

"If the witness declines to answer, we cannot bring pressure on him."

The Chief Constable nodded curtly, whilst Beecham turned once more to Tanner.

"Two more questions only, Mr. Tanner. Though I fancy you may not wish to answer the first, at any rate."

"'Oh, well!' replied Tanner wearily, "go ahead, anyway."

"Are you in possession of certain facts concerning the death of Mr. Starbright which you have not communicated to any police officer?"

"I shan't answer that. And the next?"

"Did you, at about eight o'clock last night, see a certain hat in the rooms of Mr. Trevor, and did you, or did you not, move it to a place of concealment?"

"I'll answer that," said Tanner after a short pause. "I saw the hat, and I was solely responsible for moving it."

"In that case perhaps you will tell us why you hid the hat."

"Certainly. I recognized the hat as belonging to Mr. Starbright. I considered that Trevor, had he known to whom it belonged, would not have wished the hat to be in his rooms. So I moved it."

"You imply that Mr. Trevor was not aware of the ownership of the hat."

"I am sure he did not know."

"And do you know how the hat came to be in Mr. Trevor's rooms?"

"No, not for certain."

"But you have a pretty good idea, can we say?"

"I refuse to answer that."

"Very well," said the Superintendent wearily. "There are several more questions I should like to put to you, but I think I should only be wasting my breath. ... I've nothing more to ask the witness, sir."

"Very good," said the Chief Constable in a tone which suggested that, in actual fact, it was very bad for somebody. "I must ask you to wait outside for a few moments, Mr. Tanner."

He pressed a bell, and a moment later Tanner was conducted outside by a stolid-looking constable. He wiped a bead of sweat from his forehead. It had been a trying experience, but he had the doubtful consolation of feeling that at any rate he had spoken nothing but the truth, subject to certain possible reservations.

Meanwhile the Chief Constable sat tapping his front teeth with a pencil, his customary gesture when perplexed.

"It looks very bad to me, Beecham," he said at length. "That young fellow is keeping a lot back. I feel certain he is either an active accessory of murder, or else he is shielding Trevor. Don't you agree?"

"It certainly looks bad, sir. On the other hand, his answers were straightforward up to a point, and I think he was mostly speaking the truth. I think he is shielding some other person, or persons, but I don't fancy he is guilty himself. If he had been, he would have simply denied all knowledge of the matter."

"Well, if he's shielding anyone, who else can it be than his best friend Trevor?"

"If Trevor is his best friend," the Superintendent objected, "Tanner would tell a number of lies to try and clear him altogether if he believed him guilty. I'm not at all convinced of Trevor's guilt. On the other hand, Tanner, when asked if he knew any other enemy of Starbright's, made a distinct pause. He had someone in mind, but decided not to tell us."

"I can't see it," persisted the Chief Constable. "I've a good mind to detain both of them. After all, they're close friends, and the crime showed signs of long and careful preparation. How could any third person have made these preparations without Trevor's knowledge or consent? After all, it was his private room, and as for his not being guilty himself, nobody is going to lend their rooms for someone else to commit murder in."

"That's so," agreed the Superintendent thoughtfully. "Suppose we see what Trevor has to say for himself. Perhaps he will now admit being out of his rooms at the time, and produce evidence of where he really was. If so, that lets him out, and brings us back to Tanner. But if he sticks to the story of being there in bed all the time, which I don't believe——"

"If he does," interrupted the Chief Constable impatiently, "then you must execute the warrant. I've had enough of this."

The Superintendent said nothing for a moment. His brow was furrowed and he looked very thoughtful.

"Very good, sir," he said at last. "As you say."

A moment later they were confronted by a puzzled and mildly indignant young man who confirmed the suggestion that he was Martin Trevor, aged twenty-one and two months, an undergraduate of St. Chad's College. He had some additional remarks to make on his own account.

"And I say, you know, I've been kept waiting nearly half an hour. I had a date for twelve o'clock, and it's past that already. I don't know what on earth I can tell you beyond what I've said already, anyway."

"Mr. Trevor," said the Chief Constable in his best orderly room manner, "let me remind you that this is an extremely serious matter, and you would be very well advised to treat it as such and not waste our time. I refer, of course, to the death of Mr. Starbright of your college."

"So I supposed, but I can't tell you a thing about it. From the fuss that's being made, one might think he'd been murdered."

Beecham's eyes opened wider at this, and he interrupted his superior officer to ask softly:

"And why should you suppose it to be a case of murder, Mr. Trevor?"

Trevor looked a little startled, and flushed uncomfortably. It occurred to him that, in the heat of the moment, he had spoken inadvisedly. For the first time he felt a sense of fear, and resolved to think carefully before making any further utterance.

"Oh, well!" he muttered. "I don't really think so, of course. It's only that I've had police and the Dean round ever since asking funny questions I don't understand."

"Quite so," said the Chief Constable. "It's just a matter of checking up a few points on the case, and I should be glad to hear them for myself. So I should be obliged if you would answer a few short questions which Superintendent Beecham will put to you."

"Oh, all right, sir," assented Trevor more politely. "Though I've told him all I know already, and that was little enough."

At this the Superintendent gave him the necessary warning about not being compelled to answer the questions, coupled with the possibility of his statements being used in evidence. This warning conveyed nothing sinister to Trevor's mind; in fact he thought it rather considerate of the Superintendent. He awaited the opening question with mild curiosity. Presumably it would be only a stale repetition of yesterday's line of inquiry.

Such proved to be the case at the outset. Trevor gave a rapid confirmation of his absence from the Thursday night expedition to Starbright's rooms, his later interview with Starbright ending on a peaceful note, and a denial that he had ever come into contact with the dead man or spoken to him again after that.

"So you had no ill-feeling at any time against the deceased except for this matter of the Thursday afternoon match, and you contend that this ill-feeling terminated, as far as you were concerned, after your interview that night?"

"Yes, certainly," replied Trevor. "I felt a bit fed up with him, naturally, but I was content to let the matter drop."

"And you had no other quarrel with Starbright on any other occasion?"

"No. Of course, sometimes he was a bit quarrelsome and argumentative, especially if he'd had one or two ... er ... that is to say ..."

"That's all right, Mr. Trevor, I follow you exactly. You say you had no other quarrel. Now, were you present with the deceased in the rooms of a Mr. Colley a week ago today?"

"Yes ... Ah! I see what you're getting at. Yes, there was a bit of a breeze with Starbright that night. It was the beginning of the big row, actually."

"How was that?" inquired the Superintendent, as though hearing some news for the first time.

"Well, we were talking about Thursday's big match, and Starbright started grousing and said he ought to play in the centre, and I said he should stay on the wing, and there was some backchat from some of the others. Then Starbright got peeved and said he'd play in the middle or not at all, and then he pushed off. Of course, we didn't take him seriously, and I wasn't going to be messed about like that, so I posted him to play on the wing as usual and he never turned up after all."

The Chief Constable grew gloomy and impatient with the unfolding of this tale. In the first place he could not follow the technicalities of Trevor's explanation, and he also considered that Beecham was again wasting time. The Superintendent, noting the signs, went on quickly:

"Then you, sir, as captain of football, were contradicted and criticized by one of your team in front of other footballers?"

"Yes, it amounted to that."

"And you were naturally very annoyed?"

"Well, so-so. Though, as a matter of fact, the others were more peeved than I was. I didn't think much of it, knowing Starbright. Of course, I thought it was all bluff."

"Be careful, Mr. Trevor. You are telling me that, although you had been publicly insulted by the deceased on Monday, you bore him no particular resentment at the time, and were not a party to attempting violence against him on Thursday night?"

Again Trevor flushed uncomfortably. He now realized the trend of these questions.

"I've told you already I never meant poor Starbright any harm, and I never did him any harm at any time; and I wasn't present at the Thursday night business. I didn't even know it was on."

"Perhaps you could tell me some of the gentlemen who went to Mr. Starbright's rooms on that occasion, or any gentleman who, in your opinion, bore the deceased a particular grudge."

"You can hardly expect me to give them away. They might get into trouble over it with the college authorities. And as for anyone persecuting Starbright to the point of driving him to commit suicide, I simply don't know of anyone, and I don't believe it can possibly have happened, not over the football, anyway."

"Quite," said the Superintendent amiably, "I didn't suppose you would wish to give away the names of your friends on Thursday night, and, if you didn't see them yourself, it wouldn't be evidence anyway."

He paused for a moment, at a loss how to proceed. Up to now nothing had happened to strengthen any opinion on Trevor's complicity or guilt; rather the reverse, in fact. He decided to take the final fences.

"There are only one or two other small points, Mr. Trevor," he said in a casual tone. "Yesterday evening, when I called on you, there was a soft green hat hanging up in your room. Was it one of your hats?"

"No," answered Trevor at once. He seemed less disturbed than the Superintendent had expected.

"Do you know whom it belongs to?"

"I have reason to believe it was Starbright's."

"You say you have reason to believe. Do you mean, you have seen the deceased wearing it, or were you informed by somebody else that it was his?"

"I was told so afterwards. I didn't remember to have seen it before."

"Did you move the hat from its position on the peg?"

"No."

"But you saw it moved?"

"Well, yes, I did."

"And did you inquire into the reasons why the mover, as we may call him, moved the hat?"

"No. Not at the time. We ... I was just hurrying into Hall, and didn't think any more about it."

"And later you thought to inquire into the matter. What explanation was given?"

"Just that it had belonged to Starbright, and therefore I might not want it to be seen in my rooms."

"Why shouldn't you want it to be seen in your rooms, Mr. Trevor?"

"Why? Oh, well! I don't quite know. I suppose because it belonged to a fellow who had ... who was dead."

"Did it occur to you that, by hiding the hat or allowing it to be hidden, you might be hindering the course of justice?"

"No. Why should it?"

"That's not for me to say, Mr. Trevor. Now, just two final points, and I want to warn you most particularly of the importance of answering these fully and accurately. I want you to put out of your mind any previous statements you may have made on the same subject. Just speak the plain truth."

"I say, dash it! Are you insinuating that I haven't been speaking the truth?"

"Not necessarily, sir. But forget it for the moment. Tell me. Did you see the deceased in your rooms or elsewhere any time after Hall on Saturday night?"

"No. I've told you that before."

"Have you any knowledge that he came to your rooms at any time that night?"

"No."

"Had you any reason to suppose he might enter your room at any time that night?"

"Er ... Well ... er ... no. Oh no!"

Trevor stammered and swallowed. He felt the eyes of the Chief Constable boring into his face. The Superintendent blinked and looked thoughtful. Both the officials observed that Trevor's face was scarlet. Obviously they had, so to speak, struck oil.

"Lastly," continued the dispassionate voice, "do you stick to your statement that you went to bed in your rooms at nine o'clock on Saturday night and went to sleep all night without seeing anybody or speaking to anybody? This is very important, I warn you."

There was a short, very oppressive silence. Trevor shuffled his feet, shifted his gaze to a point on the wall in front of him some three feet above and to the right of the two official faces, and said rather huskily:

"That's quite correct. I was in bed all that time and saw nobody. And I don't understand what all this is about."

The Chief Constable breathed heavily, and began once more to tap his teeth with a pencil, whilst the Superintendent sighed gently, and then leaning over conferred in low tones with his superior.

"There's just one question more, after all," he said gently. Rising to his feet he lumbered over to a cupboard and, stooping down, dragged forth a length of stout rope. Trevor, following his movements with apprehension, gave an audible gasp of dismay when the exhibit lay revealed on the floor. If one were to allow oneself a piece of literary exaggeration, one would say his jaw dropped several inches.

"Have you ever seen this rope before?" asked Beecham.

But Trevor was not beaten yet. Regaining a measure of self-control he affected to regard the rope with surprise.

"Well ... I can't say, quite. It's a very ordinary-looking rope. I've seen ropes like it, of course, but whether that special piece it's hard to say."

"Have you recently had a piece just like that in your possession?"

"Y ... Yes, something like that."

"Oh! What do you use it for, might I ask?"

"Er ... nothing. It's just there, in a cupboard. That's all."

"What was your purpose in getting the rope in the first place, and how long have you had it?"

"I never did get it," explained Trevor, brightening visibly. "It was in the cupboard when I took the rooms over. I've only been in them since the beginning of term."

"Did you see or touch your rope any time on Saturday night or the early hours of Sunday morning?"

This question seemed to produce an unexpected *coup de grâce* to Trevor's powers of verbal resistance. He swallowed and stammered for a moment before muttering:

"Oh! No, I ... Oh! Hell! I won't answer any more questions. I don't know what you're driving at."

"I think that's enough, Superintendent," said the Chief Constable with ominous calm. "Mr. Trevor, I've reason to think you are not telling the truth. I will now tell you something which may give you a last chance to answer properly. You seem to suppose that we are dealing with a case of suicide. Let me tell you that actually it is practically certain that Mr. Starbright was murdered. Now then, what about it?"

"M ... murdered?" gasped Trevor, and his face went from red to white. "But ... but, how can that possibly be?"

That is what we are asking you," observed the Chief Constable unkindly. "All right, carry on, Superintendent. Wait, though. Have you anything to add or alter to what you have told us, Mr. Trevor? This is your last chance. ... Very well, Superintendent."

Slowly and sadly the Superintendent intoned words which brought horror and bewilderment to Trevor, even though the last few minutes had prepared him for shocks.

"Martin Trevor, it is my duty to charge you with being concerned in the murder of John Starbright on the night of Saturday-Sunday, the sixteenth-seventeenth November, and to warn you again that anything you say may be taken down and used in evidence."

"But ... but I know nothing whatever about it!" gasped Trevor. "There must be some mistake."

"You've heard the Superintendent," interposed the Chief Constable. "You will have to remain here, of course, and we shall notify the college of our decision. Of course, arrangements will be made for you to be legally represented, and you will come up before the magistrates tomorrow morning for a formal hearing. No doubt you will be remanded at once. I'm sorry, but you've brought it on yourself by refusing to tell the truth. Will you tell Inspector Norman to see to Mr. Trevor, Beecham?"

Trevor made no further utterance, and was forthwith conducted elsewhere by the unimaginative-looking constable.

"Now, what about Tanner?" asked the Chief Constable when he and the Superintendent were once more left alone. "It seems to me he's in the same boat. We should detain him as well."

"Begging your pardon, sir," was Beecham's reply, "but I think he'd be more use to us running loose. I think he knows something about it, and to be quite honest, sir, I'm not satisfied we've got the right man in Trevor."

"I can't see your point of view at all," objected the Chief Constable stubbornly. "Anyway, since we've made our decision and taken Trevor, why not Tanner as well? He seems equally guilty, if not more so."

"I've an idea there may be a third person in the case, sir. I'm thinking that, if we let Tanner loose and watch him, he may give us a lead we've missed. Locked up, he's no good for that."

"There's something in that," agreed the Chief Constable. "But how do you propose to keep an eye on him, if he's loose about the place?"

"My idea is to plant Baker in the college as a workman. He's not known there and won't be noticed. There are men working near the arch as it is. I don't fancy he can give us the slip, and we might learn something from his movements. I'm not satisfied with the case as far as it goes, I tell you, sir, frankly."

"Very well then. Let's have him in again. It's getting on for lunch time, and I had breakfast devilish early."

Half a minute later Tanner stood once more before the official table, looking at the two policemen with a mixture of suspicion and dislike. With his shock of black hair more disordered than usual and his dark eyes glinting watchfully behind his steel-rimmed spectacles, he struck the Chief Constable as a distinctly ugly customer.

"Mr. Tanner," said the Chief Constable sternly, "you must realize that your unwillingness to answer the questions put to you has made your position a very grave one. We should be quite justified in detaining you on suspicion. As it is, you are free to go for the present. Please understand, however, that for the present you are not to go outside the boundaries of Cambridge without leave from this station. Should you do so, you will be at once arrested. If, on the other hand, you decide to make a proper statement at any time, I shall be glad to hear what you have to say. That's all. You had better return to your college at once."

"I'd rather wait for Trevor," was the reply. "I was supposed to be taken back with him in the car."

"Mr. Trevor won't be ready just yet," answered the Chief Constable shortly.

"I can wait," said Tanner stubbornly.

"I repeat, it's no good your waiting. Mr. Trevor will not be ready for some time. You had better get back to your lunch, as Mr. Trevor will be lunching here. In fact, we don't want you hanging about here any longer. Good morning, Mr. Tanner."

Tanner turned and left the station without a word. Fifteen minutes later, with a heavy heart, he was passing once more through the gates of St. Chad's. So preoccupied was he that he almost bumped into a good-looking girl who was standing uncertainly on the steps, apparently suffering from loss of way. She was looking into the main court and biting her lip with a mixture of uncertainty and annoyance. At the sight of Tom Tanner her face cleared for a moment into a look of recognition.

"Excuse me," said the good-looking girl, "but are you Mr. Tanner, by any chance?"

"Eh! What?" replied the gentleman thus addressed, coming suddenly out of a daydream. "Oh! I beg your pardon. ... Yes, that's my name. Can I do anything for you?"

He observed that the girl was good to look at, but, like most girls, she was regarding him with a singular lack of appreciation or interest. She seemed worried and slightly annoyed.

"Oh! Then perhaps you could tell me ... You're a friend of Mr. Trevor's, I know. He's spoken about you and pointed you out in the distance."

"That's right," agreed Tanner, and regarded the girl with renewed interest. His friend seemed to have made a good choice from the beauty point of view, but there was a hint of petulance about the red mouth which he didn't quite like.

"I'm Miss Brent, Jane Brent, of Newnham. I don't know if Martin— Mr. Trevor, has spoken of me. He was to meet me here about twenty past twelve, when I'd finished my lecture and come down here. I've waited an awful time, and the porter doesn't think he's in college. I wondered if you knew where he was. It's too bad of him!"

"Yes, Miss Brent, I do know where he is, as it happens. It's not his fault exactly. He was called away unexpectedly, and wouldn't have had time to have let you know, I'm afraid."

"I should have thought he might have managed it," said Miss Brent rather shortly.

"I'm sure he would have done, if he could have managed it," was Tanner's reply to this.

"What's he doing, anyway?" she inquired with typical female curiosity.

"Well," explained Tanner, searching for words, "as a matter of fact he was dragged off to an unexpected interview at a moment's notice. I wonder, Miss Brent, if I could have a few words with you alone. It's rather important. We could go to my rooms, just inside the court, or to a café, if you'd prefer."

"It seems very mysterious," observed Miss Brent rather coldly. "Still, your rooms will suit me all right. Lead on, Mr. Tanner."

Having led the way into the court and upstairs, swept a pile of books off the best arm-chair, apologized for the absence of all drinks save beer and whisky, furnished cigarettes, and taken a chair opposite his guest, Tanner once more set himself to say what was in his mind.

"I wanted to speak to you about Trevor because I think he's in a bit of a jam, that is to say a difficulty, and I thought you may be able to help him out."

Miss Brent made no comment on this and Tanner was forced to make a fresh effort.

"The fact is, he's got into a bit of trouble—I'm not quite clear what—and I thought if you knew you might he able to do something about it."

"I don't understand you at all," said Jane Brent. "I can't think of any trouble he's in on my account. He was quite O.K. yesterday. Suppose you stop being mysterious and tell me what's up. For a start, where has he gone just now, and why didn't he meet me as he promised?"

"At the moment he's at the police-station."

"The police-station! But ... do you mean, he's been arrested? What on earth has he been up to, and why should you suppose I should know anything about it?"

"I don't know if he's actually been arrested, but he's certainly been what they call detained."

"Whatever has the poor boy been up to?"

"To be quite truthful, I don't really know. In fact I don't think he's been up to anything. But the police seem to think so. I rather believe they think he's murdered somebody."

The effect of this remark was scarcely what Tanner had anticipated. Miss Brent laughed heartily.

"But how priceless! Why, poor Trevor wouldn't hurt a lamb, I'm sure."

Tanner felt a sudden sense of annoyance, coupled with an urge to give Miss Brent a few smart smacks with the back of a hairbrush.

"I don't think it's anything to laugh at," he observed coldly. "It isn't very pleasant to be grilled by the police and be told you're suspected of killing somebody. As it happens, I've been on the mat there myself this morning. I assure you it isn't funny."

It was Jane Brent's turn to undergo a quick change of feeling. She flushed with annoyance, as much with herself as with Tanner, and then she said stiffly:

"I'm sorry. I didn't quite realize you were serious. But please tell me about this. I had no idea anything of the sort had taken place. I heard about poor Mr. Starbright, of course, but I thought that was suicide. Has some other tragedy happened?"

"No, it's the Starbright business, I'm afraid. The police have got hold of some idea that Martin was in some way responsible for his death."

"But how awful for him! Why, he couldn't possibly ... he ..."

"He ... What were you going to say, Miss Brent?"

The girl bit her lip, as though she had said more than she had intended; then, to cover the incident, she continued:

"What happened, and what do the police suspect?"

"I don't quite know. But something took place quite near to his rooms that night, so they think he had something to do with Starbright's death. You see, he says he was alone in his rooms from nine o'clock onwards."

Miss Brent said nothing. She was looking at Tanner with a curiously watchful expression.

"Now I don't believe he was in his rooms at all until late that night or early next morning. If he could prove he was elsewhere at the time, everything would be quite all right."

Tanner paused once more, but the girl did not help him out.

"So," he said, "I thought, in a serious case like this, with a possible charge of murder hanging over him, you might be able or willing to help."

"But how on earth can I help poor Martin? I know nothing whatever about it."

Tanner looked at her for a moment without speaking. The blue eyes no longer met his, and the face seemed to have sharpened and lost much of its pristine charm.

"I thought you might know where he was last Saturday night," said Tanner at length.

"I know where he was, Mr. Tanner? I ... I don't follow you."

"I think you do follow me, Miss Brent. I suggest he was in your company up to midnight at least."

"Really, Mr. Tanner! Of all the cheek! How dare you?"

"I dare because Martin is my best friend. I'm not asking you to go straight to the police and say he was with you. That would probably mean a row at Newnham and your getting sent down. But surely you can get hold of someone who recognized him, and get them to give him an alibi with the police. If you care for him at all, you could do that for him, I should think."

"If Trevor's not guilty, I don't see he's got anything to be afraid of," said Miss Brent ingeniously. "It's just a silly mistake that will all come right."

"I think you're trying to dodge the point," persisted Tanner doggedly. "I'm asking you straight out, were you out with Trevor on Saturday night, and if so, do you mean to do anything to help him?"

"I think you're abominable," cried Miss Brent, "and I'm not going to stay here and be insulted. Good-bye."

"If I'm wrong about that," said Tanner, "no doubt plenty of your Newnham friends can give you an alibi for the time. I'll ask some of them when I see them. Then perhaps I shall owe you an apology, or perhaps I shan't. May I see you to the gate?"

Up to the point of departure Miss Brent had sustained the role of an outraged Victorian maiden. Finally, however, the strain was too great, and, reverting to twentieth-century repartee, she so far forgot herself as to say, or, rather, snarl, in passing out of the door: "Go to hell!"

At which Tom Tanner, who had maintained the courtesies to the best of his ability, was moved to a similar lapse, and replied sweetly: "Any message?"

The door banged, a dislodged fixture-card fluttered from the mantelpiece, and Tanner was once more alone with his thoughts.

Finding the solitude oppressive he strolled downstairs and out towards the main gate. The Dean, in a new check overcoat, was just entering the college and Meadows was hurrying out of the lodge to intercept him. Tanner could not help overhearing what was said.

"I beg your pardon, sir," said Meadows to the Dean, "but a telephone message came through for you about ten minutes ago from Cambridge police-station. Superintendent Beecham's compliments, sir, and he thinks it would be a good thing if you called at the station as soon as convenient. He said he might not be able to see you himself before two o'clock, but it would be all right for you to go earlier if you wished."

Gale thanked the Head Porter and stood wrapped in thought. That meant that Trevor had been charged with murder, or at any rate detained on suspicion. Well, he had better go down at once, he supposed, though there was little he could do. Still, the poor fellow might be glad to see a friend in his gloomy surroundings. Not that he had been much of a friend, the Dean reflected. But for his efforts Trevor would presumably never have come under the eye of the police. Without the button and the hat nothing would have pointed towards his room. Gale almost regretted the hobby which had led him into such a surprising state of affairs. Somehow he did not consider Trevor capable of any disgraceful crime.

Amid these gloomy reflections Gale became aware that he was observed by an undergraduate who seemed anxious but too nervous to approach him. He noticed, with a slight feeling of aversion, that it was Tanner, whose evasion and trickery had given him such food for thought on the previous day. The undergraduate seemed to make up his mind, for he came near and addressed the Dean.

"I beg your pardon, sir, but I could not help overhearing your message. I wondered whether you could do anything about Trevor, if you are going to the station. They seem to suspect him of having something to do with Starbright's death."

"Does that surprise you?" inquired the Dean. "You know, Tanner, I think you know rather more about that than you have been willing to say."

Tanner made no reply. He seemed to be making up his mind to some big decision.

"I'm sure," prompted the Dean, "things have reached a stage when I feel you would do far better to say what you know. I, for one, don't believe that either you or Trevor murdered Starbright. Why not make a clean breast of things before it is too late? Tomorrow Trevor will stand in the dock very probably, and you may be put in the witness-box. You will have to speak out then, or else he guilty of perjury."

"The trouble is, sir, that, if I tell everything I know, it might do harm to several people. They would probably be sent down, myself and Trevor included. So I couldn't very well speak out. Now, of course, if it's a case of Trevor being tried for murder, I don't know what to do for the best. If it were only a question of myself being sent down, I shouldn't hesitate. But there's Trevor, and one or two others."

The Dean considered this for a moment.

"When you say some of you might be sent down, do you imply that you have committed some crime against the civil law, or merely that you have broken some university regulation?"

"Oh, I meant a college rule, sir, in the case of all of us except myself. I fancy I have broken the law as well, but I really don't know whether I have or not."

'Well, in that case," commented Gale in tones of relief, "it can't be anything very terrible. Now, as regards breaking college rules, I cannot, in my position, make rash promises. But from my own point of view I should be more than willing to turn a blind eye to that sort of thing if it were to lead to the clearing up of these mysteries and the release of an innocent member of the college. And I should think the Master and the Tutor would be of much the same opinion, in order to avoid the scandal of a murder trial connected with the college. Come, my boy, why not take the risk? It's the best way."

Tanner considered the matter for a few seconds, then raised his head suddenly.

"Very well, sir. I'll feel easier in my mind anyway."

"Good!" cried Gale. "Let's go along to my rooms. There's no time to be lost."

After mounting the familiar staircase and being placed at ease with a cigarette, Tanner unburdened himself for the space of ten minutes. The Dean listened with rapt attention, but with never an interruption, and it was only at the finish that he put a few questions.

"What a truly remarkable story!" was his sole comment. "Now I think our best plan is to get that down on paper and for you to sign it. Then I can take it to the station. After that, as far as I am concerned, it can be consigned to the flames. I think it is almost all we shall need, though there's one point I should like to clear up."

Tanner looked at the Dean in a questioning way, but the latter turned the conversation by saying:

"I believe I'm right in thinking that the most active opponent of Starbright over the rugger business was Davies. Would you say that's correct?"

"Yes, I think so, sir. But I don't think he did anything after his failure on Thursday night. He talked a lot about it, but nothing came of it."

"He was seen going to Starbright's rooms on the next evening, Friday, whilst the rest of the college was in Hall. I suppose you don't happen to know why he went there?"

"No, I'm afraid I don't," said Tanner in a puzzled voice. He did not see what this had to do with the matter in hand.

"I wonder," murmured the Dean, and then he glanced at his watch. "There's no time to be lost. It's half past one. Wait here, Tanner. If Davies is in, I want to have a word with him, but first I shall ring up the station and ask them to hold up any further action against Trevor until I get there."

"That's very good of you, sir," murmured Tanner.

"Not at all. I got him into this mess, and now it's up to me to get him out again."

So saying, the Dean hurried first to the lodge, where he was quickly on the telephone to the police-station. Superintendent Beecham was engaged, said a voice, and so was the Chief Constable. The Dean took a high tone.

"Very well," he said. "It doesn't matter. But give one or both of them this message. And give it at once, or they may be sorry and so may you ... Eh? Yes, you'll understand when you hear it. Tell them that within half an hour I shall bring definite proof of Mr. Trevor's innocence in the Starbright case. Got that? And tell them to hold up notifying the college or the press about Mr. Trevor. It's all a mistake. ... Will I hold on and speak to the Superintendent? No, I won't. You should have got him in the first place. Just you give him the message. I'm busy, but I'll be along soon."

Leaving the porter's lodge after first ascertaining the location of Davies's rooms, the Dean betook himself in the required direction. He knew little of Davies save that he was a good athlete and noisy at such festivities as bump suppers or rugger dinners; also that he read for the mechanical science tripos and was keen on making amateur gadgets and pieces of machinery. He was fortunate in finding the Welshman at home.

Davies was surprised to receive a visit from a don he scarcely knew. He was just finishing a frugal lunch consisting of bread and cheese and beer, a very usual college meal at that time of day. The Dean reflected that he himself could very easily have put away a similar repast. As it was, he didn't look like getting any lunch. He reflected sadly on the sterner aspects of crime investigation, when a stem chase left little time for eating and sleeping. Truth to tell, the Dean was growing a little weary of sleuthing. As he accepted his host's offer of a chair and a cigarette he observed evidences of Davies's pet hobby. In one corner of the room was a working bench fitted with a lathe and other appliances.

"I've come on rather a delicate errand," he began. "I thought it possible that you might be able to give me a little information on a very important matter, though you may be a trifle surprised or even alarmed when you hear what it's all about."

Davies murmured something about being glad to be of service.

"It's about this unfortunate business of Starbright," explained Gale, at which Davies stiffened somewhat. "Now don't get alarmed, Davies. I know you were no friend of his and that you threatened to do him a mischief, but that's got nothing to do with it, as far as I'm concerned. The point is, and I tell you this in strict confidence, that the police have got hold of some idea that Starbright met with foul play, whereas I'm convinced it was plain suicide. Now you may or may not know that a fully loaded revolver was found on Starbright's body, and the main point the police make is, why should a man hang himself when it would be simpler to shoot himself, and that takes some answering."

"And why do you come to me, sir?" asked Davies suspiciously.

"I may be entirely wrong, but I fancied you might know something about it. I know that the revolver was fired in your presence, and that it was your aim to get your own back on Starbright if possible. I also know that you visited Starbright's rooms in his absence on Friday night."

But Davies only gave him an obstinate scowl.

"I had nothing to do with Starbright's death," he persisted. "I'll admit I didn't like him, but I did him no harm. I hadn't the chance."

"Nobody is accusing you of doing him any harm," explained the Dean patiently. "In fact there is no suggestion that any words or deeds of yours had anything to do with it. What I'm trying to tell you is that an innocent person has been accused of being connected with his death, and a friend of yours, moreover."

"Who is it?" asked Davies, with a flash of interest.

"If I tell you that, you must keep it to yourself. I'm hoping we may settle the matter without a scandal. As a matter of fact, it's Trevor."

"Trevor!" exclaimed the Welshman. "Why, surely he wouldn't do Starbright any harm. He was all against ragging him in the first place."

"So I've been given to understand," agreed the Dean, "but there it is. I assure you, Trevor's in a very nasty position with the police."

"I still don't see how I can help him," said Davies, "though I would if I could. He's a good chap."

"You see," explained the Dean, "the point is to establish why on earth Starbright didn't use the revolver to kill himself. That's partly why the police suspect murder. I'm asking you to tell me any reason why he shouldn't, for the gun is in working order. I have a kind of idea you know something about it."

Davies gave the Dean a searching look. Like Tanner, he had a difficulty in making up his mind.

"It happens I do know something about that," he admitted at length, "but I don't quite see how it helps. Still, if you really think it might get Trevor out of a hole, I suppose I'd better tell you. All the same, I hadn't meant to say anything about it. I might find myself in a bit of a mess."

"I think I can promise you there will be no mess, as far as the college is concerned," the Dean told him. "I believe I know what you are going to tell me anyway, and I shall do my best to see you don't get into trouble over it."

Davies heaved a sigh of relief.

"Very well, sir," he said. "Here goes."

Five minutes later the Dean was cheerfully thanking him. "That's splendid, Davies!" he exclaimed. "Just what I wanted to complete my case! I'm extremely obliged to you. Also, I'm delighted to think my little brain-wave turned out a winner. By Jove! It's two o'clock. Will you be a good fellow and run to the lodge and ask Meadows to get me a taxi at once, whilst I go across and fetch ... er ... go across to my rooms? Thanks. Well, good-bye, Davies."

CHAPTER XIV

"WELL, that's that," grunted the Chief Constable when Tanner had taken his reluctant departure. "There seems nothing more to be done for the present. I think I'll go out to lunch now, and look in again about two."

"We shall have to notify the college about detaining Trevor," the Superintendent reminded him. "Also, there are some more reports for your signature, sir."

"Blast it, yes," said the Chief Constable, "and we can't very well ring up St. Chad's or send a constable about a thing like this. I suppose you or I ought to go and explain it personally to the Master. I'll go up myself, I think, after I've had some lunch. Also, we must tell him that Tanner is under observation and should not be given leave out of Cambridge. I don't much relish the job. ... Meantime I'll polish off these reports. What's the first?"

The reports proved more tiresome, or possibly the Chief Constable more obtuse, than even the Superintendent had anticipated. They were still at work when the clock struck half past one. The Chief Constable flung down the pen with which he had just recorded his signature and said with an air of finality:

"That's quite enough for one morning. I'm off, Beecham."

At that moment a constable entered.

"I beg pardon, sir," he said to the Superintendent, "but a gentleman rang up just now and asked for you or the Chief Constable. Knowing you were both busy, I told the gentleman to state his business and said I would give you the message; but when I heard what he had to say, I reckoned you'd like to speak to him personal and asked him to hang on. However, the gentleman said he couldn't wait, and asked me to repeat his message exact, which I told him I would do."

"Who was it who spoke?" demanded the Chief Constable. "And what did he say?"

"The name was Gale, of St. Chad's College," said the constable.

"That ... that meddlesome busybody!" exclaimed the Chief Constable. "Shall we never get rid of the fellow? What did he want?"

The constable marshalled his facts, and having taken a deep breath recited the details of the message:

"He stated that in half an hour he would call and bring evidence re the Starbright case to show that the accused, Mr. Trevor, was definitely

186

not guilty; and to tell you not to communicate with the college or the press meantime re Mr. Trevor."

"What confounded cheek!" spluttered the Chief Constable. "Telling us our business! What do you think of that, Beecham?"

"It looks as though he'd got hold of something, sir. Maybe we'd best wait and see what he has to say."

"But, confound it, are we to be taught our business by some professor or other? I've made my decision and arrested this fellow Trevor. I mean to go ahead, and notify the proper authorities of what has taken place."

"You know, sir, it's my opinion, and so I told you, that there's great doubt whether Trevor is in any way responsible. It might be wiser to hear what Mr. Gale has to say. After all, he's been mainly responsible for giving us our case up to now. He's no fool, sir. Depend upon it, he's got something up his sleeve."

"I don't like it, I tell you," grumbled the Chief Constable. "Being practically ordered about by an outsider! Still, I'll give him a chance to have his say. I want my lunch, and I'm going to have it right away. I'll put off going round to St. Chad's till I've been back here. If this fellow Gale comes in the meantime, see what he has to say, and I'll consider the matter when I get back. Where's my hat? Oh, thanks."

"Very good, sir," said the Superintendent patiently. "I'll remain here until you return, and take Mr. Gale's statement, if he calls in your absence."

As the Chief Constable struggled into his overcoat and swept towards the door, he narrowly avoided a collision with the constable on duty, who at that moment again knocked and entered.

"There's a gentleman outside who insists on seeing the senior officer present," he announced. "He refused to state his business to the sergeant at the desk, saying he must see you, if you were present."

"Well, I'm seeing nobody just now," answered the Chief Constable irritably. "Tell him to state his business, and, if it's important, he can see the Superintendent. What's his name? Gale, I suppose."

"No, sir," replied the constable. "He says his name is Starbright; Major Starbright."

"Eh? ... Oh! Well, that's different," said the Chief Constable thoughtfully. "I think I'll wait, after all. Send him in, will you?"

The lean, grizzled man of some sixty odd years who was at once shown into the room displayed in his face and bearing the results of many years of hard life and service at home and abroad. In the pre-war struggle of existing on his pay and very little besides, Major Starbright had economized by serving as much as possible in India and West Africa. Wounded at the outset, passed over for a staff job, and finishing in command of a battalion of recruits, he had gained little save premature unfitness from his participation in the Great War. Nor had his private life been very happy or successful. A childless widower at thirty, he had subsequently taken charge of his brother's son John, after the former had fallen on the Somme. John Starbright had served only to add to his worries. His school career had been chiefly remarkable for bad reports and threats of removal, and his entry to Cambridge had been, from every point of view, a narrow shave. It had been a matter of secret surprise to the Major that his nephew had weathered two-thirds of his varsity career with nothing worse than a growing pile of debts. Experience had taught Major Starbright to face the trials of life with indifference and resignation, and of this he gave proof in addressing the two police officers.

"You are Colonel Waterman, the Chief Constable? Good afternoon, sir. I'm sorry not to have been on the spot before. I got back from Scotland only this morning, and came down by train as soon as I had heard the news."

"Thanks, Major," answered the Chief Constable, "and may I offer you my sympathy over this regrettable business? I'm afraid it may have come as a shock to you."

"Not altogether," confessed the Major. "I'm afraid my nephew has always been rather a trouble, poor chap. One never quite knew what to expect next. All the same, I never expected anything quite as bad as this."

"Quite so," agreed the Chief Constable. "I take it your nephew was of a quarrelsome disposition, and made enemies?"

Major Starbright looked as though he did not quite follow this observation.

"I don't know that he made enemies," he replied slowly. "But I'm surprised he should have come to such a finish. With all his faults he was a brave fellow. He never lacked guts. I had hopes he might have made good in the Army. Then he might have died honourably by an enemy bullet; but to have shot himself! I don't understand it. It's not like John to take such a way out. Perhaps I had better know the exact circumstances."

As the Major spoke his thoughts aloud, both the Chief Constable and the Superintendent began to exhibit signs of growing bewilderment. The former broke an awkward silence.

"I don't quite follow you, Major Starbright. Why should you suppose your nephew shot himself? As it happens, he had a loaded revolver in his possession, but he didn't use it at all. He was found hanged."

"Hanged!" exclaimed the Major, astonished in his turn, "Why, that's worse still! The death of a criminal! Poor John! But there's something strange here. If he had a gun and meant to use it, why hang himself?"

"We have every reason to believe that he did not hang himself," said the Chief Constable. "I must tell you we have just detained a student from the same college on the very serious charge of murdering your nephew, or being an accessory after the fact."

"But that's absurd!" remonstrated the Major. "I don't believe it."

"Pardon me, sir," interrupted the Superintendent, "but you seem to be possessed of some knowledge about this affair which differs from the facts as we have them. May I ask what reasons you have for believing that your nephew shot himself?"

"Why! Didn't you know?" replied Major Starbright in tones of surprise. "He fully intended to shoot himself. This morning I found a letter from him which had just arrived by the first post. I supposed you might have had some similar message."

"We know nothing of this," said the Chief Constable blankly. "You have the letter with you, I take it?"

"Fortunately, yes, and very depressing reading it makes. I was tempted to conceal it, in view of the added disgrace it brings on my nephew. But, if complications have occurred and some innocent person is likely to be involved, I must do my duty and explain the whole thing. With your permission I will read you both what he says."

The Major produced a crumpled sheet of paper from his pocket and bending his tired blue eyes, under their shaggy grey brows, upon the writing he began to read in a steady voice, prefacing the contents with a word of explanation.

"This is written on St. Chad's crested notepaper, dated last Saturday, and timed seven p.m. He says:

"*My dear Uncle,*

I am writing this beforehand, in case it may be my last letter. I think this is very likely. I have got into a really bad mess at last and I cannot see my way out. I'm afraid I owe a lot more all round the place than I told you last month, when you said you would help me out for the last time, I have been trying to make a bit by going at nights to a gambling place in the town, cards and roulette, but again I have been very unlucky and owe a lot there as well, so that the man threatens to report me to the college. I don't know if he dare, but if so, I shall be sent down for certain. For that reason I was tempted to do a rotten thing. Last night I took a lot of college money I knew was lying loose. I just had to walk into a room and take it out of a drawer. It was too easy. Tonight I shall try my luck for the last time. If I am lucky I shall pay off this fellow and the rest, and later, I hope, return the college money as well. Then I can make a fresh start. But if not, I am taking my revolver with me, and I shall post this and then put an end to things. It seems the best way for all concerned. I shall do it in the fellows' garden. That's quiet. Of course, things may turn out right, but I don't think they will. If not, please see none of the other fellows are blamed for this. I had a row with some of them lately, but they're quite decent chaps really. Thanks for all you've done for me, and I'm sorry to have been such a trouble.

     Good-bye,

        from your nephew,

          John.

As the Major approached the end of his reading his voice had grown a trifle husky. When he had finished, he cleared his throat and gave the others a quick look, as though afraid of being caught out in a spasm of grief or emotion. The Superintendent broke silence by asking to see the letter and also the envelope.

"I suppose you have no doubt at all, sir, that your nephew actually wrote this himself?" he inquired.

"No doubt at all," was the reply. "He wrote to me at intervals, in fact whenever he was short of money, which was frequently."

"And the postmark," continued the Superintendent, addressing the Chief Constable, "is for the Sunday afternoon collection in Cambridge. That's just as it should be, if the letter was posted after eleven on Saturday night. It certainly seems genuine enough."

"I'm quite at a loss to understand the position," interrupted Major Starbright. "It all seems straightforward to me, yet you say you think my nephew was murdered. He says himself he had no ill-feeling against anyone in the college, and, in any case, young fellows like that don't go killing one another."

"I think it would be better if I gave you an outline of the case up to the present," observed the Chief Constable, "or, rather, I will ask the Superintendent to do so. He has all the particulars tabulated. Just run through the main points as shortly as possible, Beecham, will you?"

Major Starbright listened with a grim, expressionless face as the Superintendent methodically ran through the facts in the short but clear manner of an expert witness in the box, giving due prominence to times and dates. When he had finished, the Major frowned thoughtfully.

"As you say," was his comment, "it's a strange case. All the same, I cannot help thinking that my nephew must have taken his own life, though for some reason I can't fathom he changed his method at the last moment."

"I should like to think so," said the Superintendent, "but there are several difficulties to be explained. The presence of the rope and the filed bar of the window suggest lengthy and careful preparations. I cannot see how your nephew could have made these preparations without the knowledge of Mr. Trevor, the owner of the room. And one can hardly suppose that Trevor would aid and abet your nephew to commit suicide. Then the matter of the revolver takes so much explaining. Why your nephew should not have used the easiest method at his disposal is very hard to understand. Added to which, these two men, Trevor and Tanner, both made extremely unsatisfactory statements. It was quite clear to me that they both had something to conceal, and that neither was speaking the truth."

"As regards the revolver," suggested the Major. "I suppose you are quite certain it was in working order? The simplest thing to imagine is that in some way it failed my nephew at the last moment. He understood firearms, I know, so there could be no question of his having been unable to fire it."

"You may see that for yourself," said the Chief Constable. "No doubt you yourself are familiar with firearms. ... Thanks, Beecham. See, here is the revolver itself, these are six unfired cartridges from the chamber, and here is a broken packet containing another ten rounds of exactly the same type, found in your nephew's room. Then here is a bullet of the same type again which we believe to have been fired from the same revolver only three days ago. We have not yet had time to get an expert ruling on that, it's true, but I'm convinced that is the case."

The Major examined the revolver, broke it open, closed the breech, cocked it, and pulled the trigger a few times.

"I agree with you it seems in perfect order," he observed.

"As regards the previous firing," added the Superintendent, "our first examination showed that a live round had very recently been fired from it. The barrel had been almost untouched, in fact not cleaned at all."

At the end of this explanation he paused to find that the same constable had made a silent entry and laid a telegram on his desk. Having run his eye over it he passed it without speaking to the Chief Constable.

"Ha!" exclaimed the latter, having run his eye over it. "This confirms one part of the case, anyway. I'll read it to you, Major Starbright. It concerns the man who passed the five-pound note which was part of the money stated to have been stolen by your nephew. This man left Cambridge in a hurry yesterday, and we asked Scotland Yard for any particulars they might have about him. It appears they know him. It says:

"Parker, alias Phillips, etc., convicted gambling racecourses and trains, later running gambling houses London and provinces. Noted arrival Liverpool Street last evening. Questioned today. Admits Starbright present at Cambridge house Saturday night and paid note. Detained. ...

"Well, that would seem to clear up one aspect of the case. Good lord! It's after two o'clock. Shall I never get any lunch today? There's nothing more to be done at the moment, Major. I take it you will be staying in Cambridge for the moment. The inquest is tomorrow, and we shall ask for an adjournment. Now, if you'll excuse me, I'll be off and get a bite of something to eat."

"Certainly," answered Major Starbright. "It seems there's nothing more to be done just now, as you say. There's one point, though. This affair of my nephew's is rather a disgraceful thing in itself. I wonder, would it be possible for the added crime of his theft to remain unrevealed? I shall, of course, insist on refunding the money out of my own pocket, though I'm not quite clear what the nature of the fund was, or the amount, for that matter."

The Chief Constable gave Major Starbright a glance of sympathy, for he could well understand the feelings of a fellow-officer; but at the same time he pursed his lips, and glanced doubtfully at the Superintendent.

"I'm afraid that will be rather difficult, sir," said Beecham, interpreting the glance as an invitation to give a ruling on this knotty point. "I don't suppose the matter will come up in the formal evidence tomorrow, but it's difficult to say what will happen later on. If it were a plain case of suicide, we might easily suppress the reading of the complete letter and state a general condition of debt as being the cause. But we have a person charged with the murder of your nephew, and in a murder trial every important detail will have to be followed up and probably quoted. It all depends on how the case goes, The sum involved, by the way, is a matter of seventy-five pounds odd. I should have to get a check from Inspector Norman as to the precise amount."

"Seventy-five," repeated Major Starbright in a gloomy voice. "Well, it's fortunate I can find that amount. Luckily, I've some motor shares that have done uncommonly well. I'd like to give you a cheque right away, and get that off my mind. Of course, if it must be made public, it must. But you can understand my anxiety in the matter."

"Absolutely," said the Chief Constable with sincerity. "And I'll do what I can about the publicity, though you quite see I can't hold out any promises, or even much hope. I myself am convinced that your nephew was murdered."

"I confess I don't understand it," said the Major wearily, "and, talking about going to lunch, that reminds me I've had none myself. To tell the truth, it's been such I a worrying morning that I had hardly noticed the fact."

The Chief Constable paused for a moment, debating whether to carry out his immediate intentions or to vary his programme by doing a kind and hospitable action. The latter and more charitable instinct prevailed.

"Perhaps you would care to join me in a chop or something, if you are alone in a strange town?" he said affably.

The rugged face of Major Starbright softened into his first smile that morning.

"That's a very kind thought, Colonel Waterman," he answered. "I shall be very pleased to join you."

"Good!" said the Chief Constable briskly. "Then let us make a move. I think this is about the third attempt I've made to get clear away to lunch, and I've been stopped each time. Nothing's going to keep me this time, though."

As though in instant refutation of these rash words, the door was once more knocked upon and opened. The same constable entered and this time addressed the Chief Constable.

"I beg your pardon, sir, but a gentleman wishes to speak to you at once."

TROUBLE IN COLLEGE   193

"To me?" demanded the Chief Constable fiercely.

"Yes, sir. At first he asked for the Superintendent. Then, when he heard you were here, he said he had better see you direct."

"Did he?" said the Chief Constable. "Well, I'm not seeing anyone— anyone, you understand—till I've had I my lunch. Who is it, anyway?"

"A Mr. Gale, sir."

"Gale! That ... that meddler! I'm sick of hearing about him, let alone seeing him. No, I won't see him. In fact we don't want him here at all. He had better make an appointment and come back when we are less busy. Send him away, Constable."

"I beg your pardon, sir," came the slow, patient voice of the Superintendent. "I fancy he wishes to represent Trevor. If he desires to see the accused, pending the appointment of a proper legal representative, and Trevor desires to see him, we cannot refuse him access; added to which he's an official of St. Chad's, and responsible for Trevor as an undergraduate."

"H'm ... yes," grunted the Chief Constable. "He'll have to see Trevor, if he demands to do so, I suppose."

"I should suggest, sir, that you hear what he has to say before you report the arrest to St. Chad's," added the Superintendent, and waited for the indignant outburst which was trembling on the lips of his superior officer, an outburst which was, however, unexpectedly checked by a diversion on the part of Major Starbright.

"Gale?" inquired the Major. "Isn't he the Dean of St. Chad's? I've heard my nephew speak of him. I suppose he has come in connection with this case, and that he may be able to throw some light on it. If I may be allowed, I should certainly like to stop and hear anything he has to say. It would interest me much more than lunch."

"Yes, sir," affirmed the Superintendent, backing him up. "Mr. Gale has already been very helpful, and he claims to have made some important discovery."

"Oh, very well, very well!" grumbled the Chief Constable. "I suppose I'd better wait and see what it's all about. Yes, stay by all means, Major. All right! Have him in, Beecham, have him in."

Major Starbright gazed with interest and a measure of surprise at the well-dressed and monocled figure of the Dean, who made a dignified and impressive entry. Gale was not at all his idea of the conventional don. The Chief Constable greeted him rather curtly and presented Major Starbright.

"How do you do?" said Gale. "May I offer you my sympathy and regrets over this unfortunate affair? As Dean of the college I feel a certain responsibility in the matter. Fortunately we are now in a position to clear up certain mysterious features in connection with it."

"I'm glad to hear that," answered the Major. "It seems there's some idea that my nephew met with foul play, whereas he wrote me a letter clearly stating that he meant to take his own life. Perhaps you would care to see it."

"I certainly should," said Gale, taking the letter and adding as he did so, "and you are quite correct. Your poor nephew did take his own life."

He ran a quick eye over the letter.

"Ah! This is really the final link we need to complete the case."

"Will you kindly explain," interrupted the Chief Constable, who had been trying to have his say for some seconds, "what all this is about? My time is very short, and I cannot give you very long. I understand you have some new information or theory about the case. I shall be glad if you would explain yourself as briefly as possible."

Gale looked coolly at the Chief Constable, and paused to polish and replace his monocle.

"Very good, Colonel Waterman," he replied. "In brief, the facts are these. There is no question of murder, and Trevor should be released at once. I am not asserting that he did not give serious grounds for suspicion, and in a certain measure he has only himself to blame. At the same time the truth is that John Starbright committed suicide, so there is no case against anyone."

"Then I should be extremely interested to hear your reasons for that statement," said the Chief Constable heavily. "I confess I find it very hard to believe."

"Before I put the whole thing before you," proceeded Gale, "there is one slight difficulty in which I find myself. I have with difficulty obtained two voluntary statements from undergraduates of my college who have been persuaded to speak in order to save their friend Trevor from an unjust charge. In making these statements they have been obliged to admit certain serious breaches of college discipline of which I, as Dean of College, ought properly to take official notice. Under the circumstances I have gone so far as to tell them that I shall do my best to see that no action is taken in the matter; in short, I have condoned their offences. I am therefore anxious that my part and their part in these irregularities shall be, let us say, kept dark. It occurs to me that since you will shortly be shown to have made a wrongful arrest, you will also be glad if the details of this meeting are not made public. I trust I make myself clear."

"Yes, I see what you mean," admitted the Chief Constable. "For my part I don't care two hoots about your college rules. I'm merely concerned with the law of the land. As regards wrongful arrest, we'll talk about that when you've shown me that such is the case, which I don't yet see."

"As regards the case against Trevor," the Dean continued, "I think I can destroy that at the outset by an alibi. Of course Trevor was out of his rooms till long after midnight on Saturday night. I think that has been clear to most of us. It is also obvious that, except in the greatest necessity, he would not admit being outside the college, since that is a serious breach of college discipline, whilst he could not ask any other member of the college to admit being out with him for a similar reason. As a matter of fact, I happen to have observed that Trevor has lately formed an attachment with a member of one of the ladies' colleges, so I fancy I know why he was out late, and why he absolutely refused to admit the fact. An infatuated young man is the soul of chivalry, you know."

"That's all very well," objected the Chief Constable, "but it's not an alibi. In a court of law it wouldn't stand as evidence."

"No, there's more to it than that. Suppose I tell you that I can produce a witness, if necessary, who saw Starbright dead at a few minutes after one o'clock, and another witness who saw Trevor a mile away, driving a car slowly towards the college, at exactly the same time?"

"Then produce the witnesses," said the Chief Constable shortly. At the same time the Superintendent stirred in his chair and wheezed.

"I shall produce them if necessary," asserted Gale, "but I don't think it will be necessary. Also, I think the Superintendent is about to make an objection. He wishes to point out that the alibi is not watertight. Trevor might have committed the murder shortly before one o'clock, then driven rapidly away from Cambridge, and then turned back just after one. I admit that, and that's why I don't bother to press the alibi for the present.

"Now, I'll go on to the next point. I'll ask you, Superintendent, since you've handled most of the case. What was the first and main fact which suggested murder and not suicide, apart from Trevor's connection?"

The Superintendent considered this for a moment and then replied: "The deceased being hanged when he had a perfectly good loaded revolver."

"Exactly," murmured the Dean. "I see you have the full exhibits on the table. I wonder if I might look at them just once more. These are the six original cartridges, I suppose, and the remainder in the package."

He paid particular attention to the six rounds which had been taken from the breach, and then, in an absent manner, loaded the revolver with six other rounds. Then he gazed absently round the room until his eye lighted on an ancient recruiting-poster stuck up above the mantelpiece and depicting a group of assorted troops in obsolete full-dress uniforms.

"I used to be quite handy with a revolver in the war," he remarked conversationally. "What'll you bet me I couldn't pick off that Highlander in the picture? He's hopelessly out of date, you know. Only bandsmen have those gay uniforms now."

The Superintendent looked highly scandalized, and glanced nervously at the Chief Constable. The latter was boiling with impatience and annoyance.

"Will you kindly say what you have to say, and not waste our time talking about nothing! Come to the point, sir, or I must request you to leave the station."

Very deliberately Gale cocked the revolver and took aim at the poster. As his eye squinted along the sights and his finger tightened on the trigger the Chief Constable's tone turned to one of alarm.

"Here, I say, sir! Look out! That's loaded! ... Stop, I say!"

The Superintendent lumbered to his feet and took half a step forward, as though he contemplated throwing himself between Gale and his target; then, seeming to realize the folly of such a proceeding, he relapsed feebly into his seat. Then the hammer of the revolver fell with a click. At the same moment there was a faint pop, and that was all. Gale pulled the trigger twice more in quick succession. The result was exactly the same.

The silence, where all had expected a deafening explosion, was all the more intense. It was broken by the Chief Constable, in rather a foolish voice, treating the company to a glimpse of the obvious.

"It ... it never went off!" he ejaculated feebly.

"Quite so," agreed Gale cheerfully, "and that removes one of your chief objections to my suicide theory. Starbright tried to shoot himself, but the gun, as they say, didn't go off. To be more accurate, it was the bullet that didn't go off, Starbright tried three times, and then gave it up in disgust."

"How do you know that, sir?" interrupted the Superintendent, his curiosity triumphing over his sense of discipline.

"I should have spotted it the first time I saw the gun and cartridges," said Gale. "As it was, I only noticed it just now. If you look at these six bullets which were in the breach when Starbright died, you will notice in three of them, if you look carefully, that the cartridge caps are distinctly dented, showing that they have been struck and presumably exploded by the falling hammer of the revolver. In other words, three of the cartridges have been fired, yet the bullets have not been discharged. Actually the gunpowder has been removed and the bullet replaced in the empty case.

"I had given considerable thought to this problem, and had come to the conclusion early on that something of the sort must have taken place. I was guided to suspecting an undergraduate, and my suspicions proved correct. If necessary he will make a statement to that effect, but as the bullets have been in the possession of the police all along, and since you can verify their condition for yourselves, you will probably not require him to appear."

"I should like to hear how you made this discovery," said the Chief Constable. His tone was now changed to one of grudging respect.

"It was due to a chain of facts and inferences. On Thursday night a body of undergraduates set out to rag Starbright in his rooms. Out of deference to you, Major, and with all due respect to the dead, I must add that they had justification. The ringleader was a fiery Welshman named Davies. During this affray I believed that Starbright fired a shot from this revolver out of the window, and I subsequently found the bullet. It occurred to me that he was not shooting with intent to hit any of the raiders, but with the purpose of creating a diversion and saving himself by raising an alarm which would reach the ears of the authorities.

"Subsequently the ill-feeling mostly died down, but Davies stated his intention of getting even with Starbright. To do this, it would seem necessary for him to deprive Starbright of his revolver. But Starbright, missing his revolver, might plan other means of defence. Thus Davies's best plan, if possible, would be by some means to make the revolver harmless and silent without Starbright's knowledge, thus rendering him suddenly defenceless at a critical moment. I remembered that Davies has considerable skill as an engineer and metal worker, and that his room contained working tools, including a lathe and vice. Moreover, he was seen entering Starbright's rooms in their owner's absence. Thus the one man who had the motive, means, and opportunity of tampering with the gun or the bullets was Davies. When I put it to him, half an hour ago, that his testimony might be the means of saving his friend Trevor from an unjust accusation, he very sportingly offered to confirm my suspicions on oath, if required."

"That seems good enough," admitted the Chief Constable, "but it doesn't explain the hanging and the moving of the body."

"No, I'm coming to that," said Gale, and he added, turning to Major Starbright, "I'm sorry to show up Davies as having intended mischief against your nephew. At the same time he might unwittingly have been the means of saving the poor fellow's life by depriving him of his intended weapon of suicide. But fate decided otherwise.

"I'll now get on to my main point as quickly as I can. I'm going to read you a signed statement by an undergraduate who is at the moment outside and will confirm it in person, or answer any more questions you like to put. I thought it quickest and simplest to get it on paper in the first place. It is the statement of one T. Tanner, an undergraduate of St. Chad's."

At the mention of his *bête noir* the Chief Constable showed signs of renewed restiveness, and even the Superintendent looked gloomy.

"Well, all I can say is, I hope we shall hear the truth for a change," said the former.

"I don't fancy he told you any lies this morning," observed Gale. "*Suppressio veri,* possibly. However, listen to this. I have confined it to the essential points, the details I am prepared to fill in. By the way, I had no time to obtain the confirmatory evidence of the other gentleman mentioned. That can be obtained later, as a matter of form."

The Dean took out a sheet of foolscap and read as follows:

"Statement by T. Tanner, St. Chad's College, Monday, Nov. 18.

"On Saturday, November 16, I worked alone in my rooms from the end of Hall till shortly after 1 a.m. Sunday morning. During that period I saw nobody. Shortly after 1 a.m. I required a book which I had left in the rooms of Mr. Trevor. I at once went to his rooms,

seeing nobody on the way. On reaching his rooms I observed that his
bedroom door was open and that Trevor was not in bed. The sitting-
room was empty. I noticed that the back window was open, the top
portion of the window bar removed, and a rope tied round the bottom
of the bar with its end hanging out of the window. Going near the
window I heard a slight noise outside. I looked out of the window
and saw first the body of Starbright hanging on the rope by his neck
with his feet not more than two feet from the ground, and also an
undergraduate named Baxter-Smith standing immediately under the
window in the fellows' garden. Baxter-Smith was much distressed
and frightened. He was unable to gain entry to the college, since the
only other way in from the fellows' garden was through the locked
door of the museum.

"Finally I persuaded him to climb up the rope by grasping the hanging
body of Starbright and using it as a means to grasp the rope. This he
did with difficulty and joined me in Trevor's sitting-room. He was
most upset, and wished to go at once to his own rooms. However, by
force and persuasion I made him stop and help me move the body of
Starbright to some other place. We accordingly hauled up the body,
striking the head against the ledge of the window in so doing. Baxter-
Smith then helped me to carry the body to a place of concealment. I
decided that the archway near the baths was the nearest suitable
place. On arrival there it occurred to me that the dead body would
show clear signs of having been hanged, and as there were suitable
materials at hand, I decided to hang the body once more in this new
position. Baxter-Smith was unwilling to assist, and seemed likely to
break down, but again I forced him to help me. We hanged the body
with cord which was near at hand, and I placed a barrel beside it. I
then swore Baxter-Smith to silence, and went to bed.

"Since then I have told nobody of the events of that night. On the
following day I took and burnt a diary from the room of Trevor and hid
a hat which I knew to be Starbright's. I remembered it had been
stuffed in his mackintosh pocket when we pulled the body into the
room and I supposed it had dropped out and rolled out of sight. I am
ready to swear on oath that this is a full and true statement. ..."

"Is that all?" inquired the Chief Constable after a pause.

"That's all," answered the Dean.

"Well, but ... but I don't see it clears Trevor, or proves that there
was no murder," objected the Chief Constable. "Also this man Baxter-
Smith seems seriously incriminated. He was found standing by the
body."

"I think not," Gale contradicted him mildly. "Consider. If Baxter-
Smith helped to hang Starbright, he must have been up in Trevor's
room. In order to reach the fellows' garden he must then have climbed
down the rope and over the body to a spot from which he could only
return by the same route. And I assure you, he couldn't have got back

any other way. All the ground-floor museum windows are heavily barred, and none of those bars are loose, I know."

"All the same, I don't see that Trevor is cleared. You must bring me something better than that, Mr. Gale."

"When you hear the full explanation, I think you will be convinced," replied the Dean. "So far, you have only heard a bare statement of fact by Tanner. I think the Superintendent has already guessed the explanation."

Beecham's face had assumed an expression of unusual interest, coupled with a look of dawning comprehension. His knowledge of university manners and customs had once more given him a lead over his superior officer.

"Yes, sir," he acknowledged. "I think I understand now. But I should be glad to hear your own version, Mr. Gale."

"And what's all this about a diary?" asked the Chief Constable querulously. "I hadn't heard anything about that."

"Quite so," admitted the Dean. "It was only after hearing Tanner's story that I was able to confirm the fact that it had anything to do with the case. But let me explain."

He described noticing the absence of the diary, following the trail to Tanner's rooms, and recovering the page containing the obliterated names of Trevor, Starbright, and two others.

"The book and the entries suggested something familar that I could not place. It is only now that I realize I was thinking of the book in which undergraduates sign their names when wishing to absent themselves from evening dinner. The book is spaced off into days, and generally the names of a few members of college appear one under the other in their respective handwriting. In this case we had four names, of which we could identify two. We know that Trevor and Starbright were both out of college after closing time, that is to say after midnight, and so were two other undergraduates, namely Davies and Baxter-Smith. One of the illegible names was unusually long, suggesting Baxter-Smith, so the whole thing suggested that the book was one which contained the names of undergraduates who intended to stay out late and re-enter the college by some unlawful and secret route. When we then find that Trevor's room contains a back window with a loose bar, giving on to a deserted garden separated by a scalable wall from a back street, it becomes clear that this was one of those hidden exits and entries which exist in most colleges unknown to the authorities, and the reason why Trevor kept a length of stout rope about which he was unwilling to give any account becomes quite obvious.

"Tanner was good enough to give me a full and clear account of the whole business. It appears that this secret avenue has been in use for a matter of years amongst a small circle of undergraduates. When Trevor came into these rooms this year, he inherited the rope and the diary. The procedure was that any of the dozen or so students who wished to stay out late entered their names in the book previously. Trevor or one of the others would then put out the rope after dark ready for the returning wanderers. Each man, on his return, ticked off his name, so that the last one of all would know that the others were in, and accordingly wind in the rope and restore it to the cupboard. There are no other windows overlooking the garden except those of the museum and my own gyp-room, that's a pantry and deserted at night, so the rope was not likely to be seen, and the way in, seeing that all other likely windows are barred and overlooked, was a singularly good one.

"What really happened on Saturday night was this. Of the four truants Starbright was the first to reach the fellows' garden. He had made his last throw, posted his farewell letter, and intended to shoot himself in the fellows' garden. When his revolver failed, there was nothing for him to do except to climb back into college. In so doing it occurred to him that here was a ready method of carrying out his terrible plan. That he would be landing the others in an awkward fix apparently did not occur to him. He put a noose round his neck and dropped to instantaneous death. This must have been any time up to one o'clock or a few minutes after. The next arrival in the garden was Baxter-Smith. He is a feeble fellow, rather under the thumb of Starbright, and given to card-playing. I suspect that he had been with Starbright to the gambling house. I trust, however, that we may arrange to ignore the matter, and that he will never know that Tanner has given him away. That would be the best thing for everyone concerned.

"Then came Tanner, to fetch his book, shortly after one o'clock. We have it from Davies that he and Trevor met on the road a mile away just about that time, so those two must have been the last to return. Incidentally Davies confessed that he engaged Trevor in a fight on that occasion, and you will recollect that the latter still shows signs of a black eye, which you can take it from me he did not possess earlier in the day. Why they fought I cannot imagine, and I did not press for information.

"Thus you will see what a terrible predicament Tanner found himself in. If he left the body hanging, it would be a tremendous shock to Davies and Trevor on their return. Worse still, when the tragedy was discovered in the morning, Trevor would find himself in a hopeless position. If he claimed to have been in his rooms at midnight and after, he would be accused of complicity in the tragedy. If he admitted being out of college, he would be confessing to a serious offence for which he would probably be sent down. In any case the secret of the rope and the broken bar would be revealed.

"Of course, Tanner might have saved the situation by swearing Trevor was with him in his rooms at the fatal time. But Tanner has a weakness for the truth. I fancy, if you go over his previous statements carefully, you will find he never told you a lie. He therefore determined to save his friend by a tremendous personal effort and risk, carried out practically single-handed, for Baxter-Smith must have been a wretched accomplice. And he never even told Trevor what he had done on his behalf. Trevor's apparent ignorance and stupidity about the whole matter was perfectly genuine. He knew nothing about it, and I respectfully suggest you send him back to college in the same state of blissful ignorance. As for Tanner, I don't think I have ever heard of a finer piece of work for the sake of a friend in need. So far as I can see, he cannot be charged with any legal offence. Well, that's the case, Colonel Waterman; are you satisfied now?"

The Chief Constable sat gazing into space. His brows had met in a heavy frown and his pencil was beating a regular tattoo on his front teeth.

"Yes, Mr. Gale, I'm bound to confess I am. But ... but I cannot see how the matter can end here. We have made a mistake over Trevor, I admit, but there is the matter of the inquest. We cannot suppress evidence, you know. This man Tanner's conduct has been most irregular. I really don't know that we can avoid charging him instead."

"What with?" asked Gale bluntly.

The Chief Constable considered this for a moment, and then gazed once more at the Superintendent. The latter lifted a sleepy head and answered the S O S.

"If I may say so, sir," he suggested, "we should do best to let well alone. Send these two young gentlemen packing, and let it go as plain suicide. From what Mr. Gale tells us about the rules they've broken, they'll be glad enough to hold their tongues."

"M'yes," said the Chief Constable doubtfully. "But how about the inquest?"

"Everything straightforward, sir. Dr. Purvis, and if necessary Dr. Summers, will state he died by hanging, and Major Starbright will testify he wrote stating intention to commit suicide owing to pressure of debt. That's all we need, sir."

"In that case," interrupted Major Starbright hopefully, "you might be able to suppress the theft of the money after all. I'd be more than grateful if you could. Mr. Gale, you are an official of the college. If I now write you a cheque for the amount stolen, do you think you could arrange for the college to take it without further publicity?"

"I'm sure I could," answered Gale. "There's nobody who wants to avoid publicity more than myself."

"That's all very well," rumbled the Chief Constable, "but it's all very irregular. You know we can't——"

"Look here, Colonel," interrupted Gale, "we're all in the same boat really. It suits all of us best for this wretched affair to be dead and buried. The only man who has a right to demand a full exposure is Major Starbright. He doesn't want it. He wishes to keep his family name free from the disgrace of theft. I'm Dean of a college, and I'm conniving at overlooking several most serious breaches of college discipline. If there's a showdown, I shall probably have to resign. As for you, sir, you owe me a little for having saved you from a most serious blunder. You have made a wrongful arrest, and mistaken suicide for murder. Publicity will do you no good."

Whilst the Chief Constable was gradually weakening, the Superintendent had rung for Inspector Norman, who at once appeared.

"Give me the exact amount of the Chad's robbery, will you?"

"Seventy-six pounds fifteen shillings, sir," said Norman, "and as regards the search of the adjacent rooms——"

"Never mind that," interrupted the Superintendent. "Forget it."

"Pardon, sir?" said the Inspector, very taken aback.

"That case is over. Napoo. Fini. Now you can get on with the Trumpington job."

When the Inspector had beaten a crestfallen retreat, the Superintendent turned to Major Starbright and repeated:

"Seventy-six pounds fifteen shillings, sir. And I shouldn't wonder if you don't get it back, sir."

"Get it back?" echoed the Major, looking up from the cheque book which he had already taken from his pocket. "How's that?"

"Well, sir, this man Parker was running an illegal gambling joint, and he handled stolen money. He may be charged, or we may give him a fright. In either case you may get the money back. I can't promise, but I'll do my best."

As the Major stammered some words of thanks, the Chief Constable took a deep breath and spoke decisively.

"Gentlemen," he said. "I have decided to close this case on the lines suggested by Superintendent Beecham. I need hardly add that I shall expect you two gentlemen to refrain from further discussion of certain points which have just cropped up. Superintendent, send for Mr. Trevor."

It was a rather woebegone Trevor who soon stood before the meeting. A solitary couple of hours in a species of cell had reduced his perplexity and resentment to a state of uncertain fear and misery. His eye brightened a trifle at the sight of the Dean.

"Mr. Trevor," said the Chief Constable, "I am very glad to be able to tell you that we are now in possession of information to show that Mr. Starbright's death was due to suicide, and that therefore the charge against you is withdrawn absolutely. I should apologize perhaps for the charge having being brought, but at the same time I must say that, had you answered certain questions in a more straightforward and truthful manner, it is probable that you would not have come under the suspicion you did. As it is, you are free to go, and I should suggest that you put the matter out of your mind. In short, you would do best to forget all about it."

At the start of this little speech Trevor had gradually shown unmistakable joy and relief, but the closing words brought a frown back to his face.

"Thanks awfully, sir. It's a great relief. But ... but, all the same I think it's rather rot my having been shut up like this. I knew nothing whatever about the wretched business and I——"

"Mr. Trevor," interrupted the Dean with an assumption of severity, "I think you would do better to leave well alone. Should you cause any further trouble about your case, it might lead to certain fresh inquiries, such as whether you really were in your rooms all night on Saturday. Do I make myself clear?"

Trevor's change of countenance was almost comical. It was evident that Gale had made himself painfully clear.

"Very well, my boy," he added affably. "Then go home, and forget absolutely all about it."

The last act of a busy morning and afternoon was a similar interview with Tanner.

"Mr. Tanner," said the Chief Constable, "you will be glad to hear that Mr. Starbright's death has been definitely established as a case of suicide. I suggest to you, and your Dean of College agrees with me, that it will be better for all concerned if you put the matter out of your mind and refrain from any discussion or surmise about it, particularly with reference to anything which may have passed here today. I regret that you have been put to certain inconvenience and loss of time over it today, though I suggest that you have only yourself to blame. And, speaking unofficially, Mr. Tanner, I think in many ways you are rather a stout fellow. Good afternoon."

"Thank you, sir," said Tanner, with a faint smile. "May I ask if Trevor is still here? I thought, if you were finishing with him soon, we could walk back to college."

"He's just gone," answered the Chief Constable. "I dare say you'll catch him up."

"I think," interposed Gale, "it might be better if you left him alone for a short time. It might be better for him to think things over for himself."

Tanner considered this, and then smiled again.

"Yes, sir," he acknowledged. "I think you're right."

Five minutes later Gale followed the example of the two undergraduates and left the station. It was after three o'clock and once more he took a taxi, wishing to reach his bank before closing time. Leaving the bank with an envelope stuffed with a large number of treasury notes, he once more entered the cab and was driven back to St. Chad's. He sauntered through the court and made his way to the rooms of Mr. Waddington, the Bursar. The owner was at home, and in addition there was present the Tutor, whose aspect was glum and moustaches drooping by reason of the worries which had befallen his college. The Bursar seemed as cheerful as usual, and with a slightly doubtful glance at the Tutor offered Gale a drink, saying he looked tired.

"Yes, I am tired," admitted the Dean. "I think, though, it's a very unsuitable hour, I might do well to have a whisky-and-soda. Just a spot."

This necessitated a move to the dining-room sideboard, where the Bursar's decanter was situated. The remains of a cold lunch were still in evidence.

"Slack fellow, my gyp," grumbled Mr. Waddington. "That should have been cleared hours ago."

As he sipped his whisky Gale experienced a sensation of slight dizziness. He eyed the uncleared table.

"What an appetizing pie!" he remarked. "Veal and ham, I think. I wonder, my dear fellow——"

"Why ... my dear chap, certainly. But ... haven't you had any lunch?"

"No, as a matter of fact, I've not."

"Good gracious! I see. Then help yourself, for goodness' sake. You must be famished. Let me get a clean plate. Why haven't you had any lunch?"

"As a matter of fact I had to go to the police-station, and things took longer than I thought."

"The police-station!" exclaimed the Tutor. "What was the matter? Has anything more cropped up about poor Starbright? Meadows tells me that police have been hanging round the college last night and again this morning. I don't like it. I cannot understand what is going on. I think they are trying to blame these footballers for the tragedy. I'm extremely worried."

"It's absolutely all right," explained the Dean. "I met the uncle, Major Starbright, at the station. He had received a farewell letter from the nephew confessing he had run very badly into debt and saying he meant to take his life in consequence. A shocking affair, but it clears things up entirely, and nobody in the college can feel in the slightest to blame."

"I'm very relieved to hear that," said the Tutor; "most relieved. But I wonder Major Starbright hasn't been to see me."

"He's only been in Cambridge an hour or so," explained Gale. "No doubt he'll be along shortly. By the way, the Master ought to be told, though I expect he'll hear later from the station. I'd go myself, but I feel so confoundedly hungry——"

"My dear fellow, try some of that fruit salad ... or some cheese."

"Thanks. I think I'll have another piece of this excellent pie. Then perhaps some cheese."

"I'll go and have a word with the Master myself," said the Tutor; "it will ease his mind, I'm sure."

And he hurried out of the room.

"More likely he's forgotten all about it," commented the Bursar. "Still, I'm glad it's all settled. Meantime I wish the police would get a line on my Amal. money. That's what's on my mind. I suppose your own detective labours have borne no fruit in that direction?"

The Dean prepared the way for another big moment.

"Let me see, what was the exact amount of your loss?" he inquired artlessly.

This question could not be answered immediately. Mr. Waddington had to turn it up in his books.

"Seventy-six pounds fifteen," he said at length, "and I should think I shall have to whistle for it."

"Then whistle," answered Gale, and drawing the big envelope from his pocket he put down a great number of notes and two half-crowns. "I think you will find this correct."

"But ... good heavens! What is this? Is it my money?"

"I cannot say they are the exact notes you lost, but they are the equivalent, which I hand to you as recovered."

"By heavens, Holmes, this is marvellous! But seriously, old man, what does it mean? Who stole the money, and how did you get it back?"

"Listen to me carefully, Waddington. You have your money back. Be thankful, and don't ask too many questions. I will tell you what you must do. You will call an Amal. meeting and say that the money has been recovered. You can add that no member of the college is in any way to blame for its loss. That is no more and no less than the truth."

"You mean it wasn't stolen by any member of the college? Then who on earth could have stolen it?"

"I didn't say that. There might have been a member of the college who stole it, but there isn't now. Think that over."

The Bursar thought it over.

"Ah! I get you," he said at length. "Yes, de mortuis. ... So that was it? Well, that's a good suggestion of yours for covering it up. And I suppose it was the police and not you who really found it out, you old swanker."

"I think I gave them a certain amount of help," admitted the Dean.

"Well, I'll say you're not such a bad detective after all. These last few days must have interested you very much."

"As a matter of fact," said Gale, cutting himself a slice of cheese, "I've got a bit tired of detective work. It seems a jolly sight too strenuous. I've been on the job for hours today. And, as a matter of fact, most of it is routine work which is waste of a good brain. Just work for the professional policeman. There are other things of greater importance. I've something else in mind just now."

"What's that?" exclaimed the Bursar, scenting one of Gale's new crazes. This would be a bit of exciting news for the Dean of Chapel.

"The future of this country of ours," said the Dean, "lies in the air. We must become air-minded. All of us should set the example to those below us. I am taking the matter up very seriously. In fact, when I take my seat in the House, I shall aim to become Under-Secretary for Air."

"What are you going to do about it meantime?" asked the Bursar curiously.

"Next vacation," said the Dean solemnly, "I shall endeavour to qualify for a pilot's certificate."

"Oh lord!" exclaimed Mr. Waddington. "Then I wonder who on earth will be the next Dean."

CHAPTER XV

Just after eleven o'clock on the following morning, Tom Tanner came slowly down Trinity Street after finishing his usual lecture. Outside Matthews' Café he halted uncertainly. It was a Tuesday, he recollected, and just a week since Colley had come to his table with the news that Martin Trevor would not be present. Under these circumstances, thought Tanner, it would be depressing to drink solitary coffee amid scenes of a pleasant companionship which on these occasions would seem to be a thing of the past. He strolled in rather sadly, however, and took his usual seat. There was really nothing much to do.

"One coffee, please," he said to the waitress, without looking up.

"Make it two, old man," came a voice, and Trevor slid into a seat at his side.

"Why, hullo, old man! I ... I wasn't expecting you."

"Not got a date with anyone else, I hope?" laughed Trevor, and when Tanner had reassured him on this point there was an awkward silence. "I've hardly seen anything of you since that awful show yesterday morning," resumed Trevor at length, "what with that Amal. meeting last night. I tell you it put the wind up me, being bunged in that cell. And I tell you, I simply can't make head or tail of that business."

"I shouldn't bother about it. It's all over now."

"Yes, that's the best part of it. By the way, how did you come to be dragged into it? What did they ask you?"

"Oh! It was just that Gale had noticed me about the court when I came over to fetch that book late on Saturday night. They thought I might have seen something. But I hadn't anything to tell them."

"Oh, I see. By the way, it's a bit of a facer that rope disappearing. Did you take it?"

"No, old man. But I fancy Gale suspects something. We'd best drop that business for a bit."

"Yes, I agree with you. And what's more, Winterton's got the wind up about the Crime Club. He thought the Amal. money show was a stunt of some member's, but the money's back and nobody's lodged a claim, so what with that and the place being stiff with 'Roberts' over the Starbright case, he thinks we'd better disband *pro tem.* It suits me all right after what I went through yesterday, though I didn't tell him so. I'm keeping my mouth shut."

"You're wise."

There was another long pause, after which Trevor remarked inconsequently:

"Women are queer, don't you think?"

"I don't know," replied Tanner, rather surprised. "I suppose so."

"The fact is, old man, this Jane Brent business ... well, it's definitely off."

"Oh! ... er, yes?"

"It's a funny thing. A week or so ago I thought she was wonderful. A day or two ago I wasn't so certain. Then, yesterday, I had to cut a date with her over that blasted police business. Well, how could I help it? I couldn't tell her the full facts for various reasons, and that seemed to feed her up. Then today she wanted me to take her to the pictures this afternoon. I'd agreed to ref. the second team match. After all, it's up to me to take some interest in the second. I haven't seen much of them for some time. Anyway, I'd promised to do it. She then says it's not so bad my playing in the first myself, but if I think a mouldy second match is worth more than her company ... Well, anyway, that finished it."

"Perhaps it's all for the best. I ... I think she wasn't quite your sort."

"Oh? I didn't know you knew her."

"Well, I don't and yet I do. I've met her once, as it happens. Frankly, she's not good enough for you."

"Anyway, I felt a bit of a ... well, I've sort of left you in the lurch lately. I'm looking forward to our old times together."

"As it happens, so am I, old man."

With that dislike of anything approaching sentiment common to most of their age and class, both the undergraduates sought to change the subject.

"It looks as though things were going to be a bit quiet now," said Trevor, "what with no more breaking in late and so on. That reminds me. I can tell you now what really happened on Saturday night. I told the Brent girl I wouldn't breathe a word, but she's a back number, and I shan't tell anyone but you. I hired a car and took her dancing in Bedford. That was all right. A pleasant time was had by all, and I saw her safe back through a window in Newnham. Then I started home round by the backs to escape notice, and stopped for a fellow who appeared to have had a bike smash. Then I'm damned if the fellow didn't pull a gun and stick me up! He was masked and spoke all huskily, so I couldn't place him at all. Well, I reckoned the gun was a bluff, and I went for him. He was a scrapper and gave me a lovely eye. Then, when I shouted something, he suddenly packed up and, would you believe it, it was Davies, trying to do the crime he'd boasted about. We had a good laugh over it, and he decided to chuck up the idea. That was the end of adventure for that night. I stabled the car and got quietly back into college without any hitch."

"Well, that's interesting," said Tanner. "I wondered very much where you picked up that eye. Well, if the Crime Club closes down, we shan't have any more excitement of that kind."

"And you never did your crime," Trevor reminded him. "You know, I don't think you are quite cut out for that sort of thing. You're a clever fellow, but I think, if you tried to mix yourself up in a crime, you'd make an awful mess of it and get found out by everyone."

"Yes," replied Tanner. "Very likely you're right."

THE END

Lightning Source UK Ltd.
Milton Keynes UK
UKOW040714220312

189381UK00002B/10/P